MAFIA MADMAN

THE KINGS OF ITALY
BOOK 3

MILA FINELLI

Copyright © 2022 by Mila Finelli

All rights reserved.

No part of this book may be reproduced in any form or by any electronic or mechanical means, including information storage and retrieval systems, without written permission from the author, except for the use of brief quotations in a book review.

This is a work of fiction. Any names or characters, businesses or places, events or incidents, are fictitious. Any resemblance to actual persons, living or dead, or actual events is purely coincidental.

Cover: Letitia Hasser, RBA Designs

Editing: Jennifer Prokop

"The best weapon against an enemy is another enemy."

— FRIEDRICH NIETZSCHE

CHAPTER ONE

Four Years Ago

Enzo

The memories haunted me.

Though I had been rescued from Fausto Ravazzani's dungeon three weeks ago, there were moments when it felt as if I was still there, a broken shell of a man, weak and delirious on the stone floor. Now I couldn't close my eyes without remembering. Sleep became impossible, the dreams too agonizing to bear.

My body would recover. Each day that I remained on this yacht, healing, I grew stronger, the bruises fading. My mind was another story.

I was no stranger to bloodshed. Raised in a violent world by a violent man, I was taught to hide the cruelty under a smile and a designer suit. I had balanced this easily, never losing my grip on reality while committing even the most heinous of acts.

What happened in Ravazzani's dungeon changed that.

I was no longer the same. My brothers asked me to explain what happened and provide them with details, but I couldn't voice the words. The horrors were too fresh, my humiliation too great. I couldn't stand to be touched. They had to restrain me the first time the nurse changed my bandages because I kept thrashing to escape.

The gentle rocking of the yacht lulled me toward oblivion, but I fought it. I didn't want to relive the horrors of the dungeon in my dreams. When I heard my brothers whispering in the next room I spoke as loudly as I could manage. "*Che cosa?*"

Vito and Massimo appeared at my bedside. "Did we wake you?" Vito said. Closest in age to me, he was my second-in-command and consigliere. "You should sleep."

Impossible. I'd rather learn why they were gossiping like a pair of *nonne*. "*Dimmi.*"

My youngest brother, Massimo, cleared his throat. "I was telling Vito that Fausto Ravazzani has been released from the hospital."

Che cazzo? This soon?

"Surprising, no?" Vito said. "All reports said he was near death."

Getting out of the public hospital was a wise move. Far safer for Ravazzani inside the castello, protected by his soldiers. This was what made him such a difficult target to eliminate.

I had nearly succeeded, though.

Hiding for me was more difficult. Right now I was on a yacht in the middle of the Mediterranean with my brothers. My wife and children, as well as my younger sister, had been secreted out of Italy, far away from me and anything connected with the D'Agostino family, in case Ravazzani's men found me.

Licking my dry lips, I forced out, "When?"

"Yesterday."

This meant I didn't have much time. He would be looking for me, using every resource available to seek retribution. I had to be smarter.

"Water," I said, and Massimo helped me take a long drink. My hand was still bandaged from where Fausto cut off the end of my index finger, and my shoulders throbbed from being strung up by my hands for days. When I finished I pushed a button to elevate the bed. My brothers built an impressive state-of-the-art hospital room on the yacht, complete with three nurses and two doctors. Thank God, because I've never been closer to death.

And for what? Because I dared to grab more power? Because I dreamt of a better empire for my children?

I would not feel guilty for wanting those things. Yes, I had listened to the wrong advice, but my desires had not changed. I was alive and recovering, safe in the middle of the ocean, and soon I will make him suffer.

One thought kept me sane. *An eye for an eye is not enough*.

"Open your phone," I told Massimo. "Find background noise. A city, preferably in Italia."

Vito rubbed his jaw. "You think he'll call you."

I knew it deep in my bones. "Fausto likes to taunt his enemies. He will also try to learn where I am. Tell the captain to cut the engine."

My prediction proved correct an hour later.

As a nurse fed me soup, my phone rang with a blocked number. I looked at Vito and nodded. The nurse was ushered from the room and Massimo began playing background sounds. Vito hit accept and held the phone to my face.

"Pronto," I said as strongly as I could manage.

"Enzo, *come stai?*" Fausto's voice was tight and too loud, a performance if I'd ever heard one. "How are you feeling?"

My stomach burned with fury and frustration. I gripped the sheet in my fist, but kept my tone even. "Never better, Fausto. But enough about me. I hear you've been unwell."

"I'm fine. Stronger than a bull. It's too bad you couldn't stay longer."

Pezzo di merda. I hated his smug arrogance. "Yes, well. Thank you for your generous hospitality. I will have to see how I can repay you."

"There's no need for that," he said. "It was truly my pleasure."

No doubt this was true. Il Diavolo's thirst for blood was legendary in the 'Ndrangheta. But I wouldn't let him get the better of me ever again. "Perhaps you may visit me next time. Your wife seemed to enjoy the beach house."

There was a pause and I knew I'd hit my mark. My lips curled with satisfaction.

He finally said, "Last I heard your beach house was destroyed."

I made a noise like this was nothing. "Everything can be rebuilt, not to worry. Congratulations on your marriage, by the way." He wasn't the only one who remained well informed.

"Grazie. No need to send a gift. You already left one behind."

I stared at my bandaged hand, anger clogging my throat. *Madre di Dio*, he was a *coglione*. He'd maimed me. I would never forgive that.

Before I could respond, Ravazzani said, "Speaking of gifts, did you receive the one I sent you? It should have arrived this morning."

I looked at Vito, who shook his head and began typing on his phone. "No," I said. "I haven't seen it yet."

"A special token, just for you. I hope you enjoy it."

What had Ravazzani delivered? I couldn't begin to guess, but I was certain I wouldn't like it. "I'm sure I will. I'll be sure to send you something in return."

"If I were you, I would focus on my business and family instead." His voice was low and hard, a clear threat.

Except I didn't take threats from this man. I didn't take threats from anyone.

I smiled. "Then it is fortunate you are not me, no?"

"How are your wife and children?" Ravazzani asked. "Your younger sister? They must have been happy to see you upon your return."

More taunts. I wanted to wrap my hands around his neck and squeeze until his eyes bulged from his head. Until blood vessels popped and his skin turned purple. He'd taken my wife and children from their beds, held them at gunpoint. It was inexcusable in our world, where wives and children have always been off-limits.

Ravazzani must've tired himself out, because he said, "I must go, Enzo, but I hope you take care."

"Yes, you take care, as well, Fausto. Please give your beautiful wife a kiss for me, eh?"

I could hear his heavy angry exhales, and I relished knowing I'd rattled him. As if we were friends, he said, "Please do the same with Mariella. Oh, wait. She left, didn't she? A shame. I know how attached you were to your *mantenuta*."

Had he mentioned Mariella instead of my wife to fuck with my head?

The line went dead and I snatched the water glass by the side of the bed with my good hand and threw it across the room. Pain ripped through my shoulder as the glass shattered against the oak paneling. I shouted, "*Brutto figlio di puttana bastardo!*"

"Calm yourself," Vito snapped. "You'll tear open your stitches."

"Angela, the kids—they are safe, no?" I asked.

"Sì, *certo*. Do not worry," Vito said, already texting on his phone. "Ravazzani will not find them in England."

I prayed not. Though our marriage had been arranged, I cared for Angela. She was a good wife and a great mother to my son and daughter. Seeing the three of them held at gunpoint had been the worst moment of my life. After I was captured, Vito sent my family to a friend in England to keep them out of Ravazzani's reach.

"The package," I said. "What was it?"

My brother checked his phone. "They found the box. It was down by the road, dumped by a passing car."

"What was inside?" Massimo prodded.

"Remember Ravazzani's computer expert, the one that we blackmailed to help us kill Ravazzani? Vic, I think." Vito's gaze met mine. "It was his head."

Cristo. "The rest of him?"

"No idea."

I felt no remorse. Vic had been a means to an end, the right tool for the job in the moment. That tool had failed, so it was of no use to me now.

Massimo looked between me and Vito, his expression eager. "What now? Do we send a message back or do we go kill him?" Massimo cracked his knuckles one by one, an annoying habit left over from childhood.

"We are not strong enough," Vito said. "Enzo needs to recover, and we need to undo the damage from the kidnapping."

My brother was not wrong. Being Ravazzani's prisoner had weakened my position in the 'Ndrangheta. Many of our allies had deserted us, and our enemies were using the opportunity to encroach on our businesses. Thankfully the computer fraud enterprise, worth billions of Euros, hadn't been affected. We were still making money hand over fist, which meant I could rebuild everything else.

Ravazzani had tortured me to get that fraud business, doing unspeakable things to force me to sign it over. I never broke, though. He was not the first to hurt me, to make me bleed. My late father, the former Don D'Agostino, head of the Napoli 'ndrina, taught me pain. Taught me to endure agony.

"Do not flinch or I will hurt you more," my father said. *"You must be strong, Lorenzo. Stronger than everyone else."*

But this had been different. Ravazzani had maimed and humiliated me. Treated me worse than a dog. Left me chained and naked for days, and now I lost my family and my freedom because of him. It twisted my mind and fueled my rage.

I had changed. The civilized man from before no longer existed. Now I was inhuman, a creature filled with hate and revenge, and Ravazzani would pay.

Looking at my brothers, I said, "He'll be searching for me on land, so we stay on the water. We stay safe and we stay smart. Stronger together."

"Stronger together," my brothers repeated the D'Agostino family motto.

"Purchase a new boat," I told Vito. "Make sure no one knows it's mine. We'll sail west and hide out on the French Riviera."

My brothers left me alone and I closed my eyes, exhausted. Fuck Fausto Ravazzani. This had always been my game to play, not his, and I needed time more than anything else.

In the end, I would destroy everything he cared about until nothing remained.

CHAPTER TWO

Gia

Present Day
Milan, Italy

A woman was screaming in my face in Italian, but I couldn't understand her. Why was she so fucking angry? I'd arrived on time this morning for work, pastry and cappuccino in hand, ready to tackle the day.

It took a lot to rattle me, so I just sipped my coffee as Valentina continued to rant, her olive skin flushing to almost purple. She was an assistant to Domenico, the owner and head designer of the fashion house where I was currently interning, and she didn't seem to like me much.

But I wasn't here to make friends. I wanted to learn how to take my designs and build a brand, a sustainable avant-garde brand like Domenico's. He'd established one of the world's most exclusive labels before the age of twenty-five.

"*Non capisco*," I said when Valentina took a breath. "*Lentamente.*" I'd been telling people to speak slower ever since I arrived three weeks ago.

Valentina's lip curled. "You," she switched to English, "did not confirm the models yesterday and now we are one short."

"Yes, I did. They all said they would be here."

"Then why are we one model short, *scema?*"

The back of my neck grew hot. I didn't like being called an idiot. People normally kissed my ass, considering my father was one of Toronto's most dangerous men. I was also related by marriage to Fausto Ravazzani, the most dangerous man in Italy.

Except no one here knew my real name. When my father finally relented and allowed me to pursue an internship overseas, I applied under the name Gia Roberts. Domenico liked my designs and offered me a position for one year. I decided to keep up the deception while here, so I told everyone my security guards were because my father was a Canadian politician. It was heaven, being someone else for a little while. I wanted to succeed on my own terms, not because of my connections.

"*Basta*, Valentina." Chiara, Domenico's other assistant, joined us. "I checked Gia's list. All the models confirmed. This isn't her fault."

Valentina walked away, muttering to herself in Italian. I caught the word *troia*, which I knew meant "whore." Nice. Were we back in high school? Valentina reminded me of all the mean girls who'd called me names because I hooked up with lots of guys.

Guess what? I like dick. Sue me.

"Grazie," I said to Chiara, otherwise known as my favorite person here. She was in her late twenties and one of the few who'd made me feel welcome.

"*Prego*, but I'm afraid I have bad news for you."

Sensing I needed caffeine, I took another sip of my cappuccino. "Oh?"

"Domenico wants you to take her place."

My eyes went huge. "Who, Valentina?"

"I wish," Chiara said. "No, the missing model."

The fuck? "You have to be joking."

"I am not joking." Chiara took my arm and began dragging me toward the door. "You are beautiful and the dress will fit you."

Dress? Domenico's designs were more like bondage streetwear. Straps and buckles and very little fabric. The pieces were amazing, but I didn't want to be a model. I wanted to design clothes *for* the models.

I couldn't forget how modeling ruined my mother's life. It led her to my father, a dangerous and controlling man, and she gave up her dreams to hide behind him in Toronto, disappearing into obscurity. That would never be me.

I was destined for greatness, not marriage.

While Chiara pushed the button for the elevator, I took a step back. "Tell him thank you, but I'd rather not."

"There is no refusing, Gia. Domenico is the boss. Unless you want to quit, you are doing it." She glanced over her shoulder at me. "And relax. It is a private show for his most important investor. No one else will be there."

Heat washed over me, a familiar rebellion that always lurked beneath my skin. I had this problem where I didn't like being told what to do. I wasn't a rule follower or even very nice. I was loud and opinionated and stubborn. Basically I'm exactly like my father—which explained why I was his least favorite daughter.

The elevator arrived but I didn't move. "I really don't want to do this."

"*Dai andiamo.*" She grabbed my arm again and led me inside. "Two hours of hair and makeup, then thirty minutes in heels. Considering your day is usually getting drinks and running errands, this should be a nice change of pace, no?"

"Actually, it sucks. I'm not here to model. I'm here to learn about designing clothes."

"Don't let anyone hear you say it, *carissima*. Literally everyone here would kill to wear one of Domenico's new designs, even for a few minutes."

Right, which would only make my new co-workers resent me. Great.

The elevator doors opened and we were greeted with pure chaos. People were everywhere, while racks of clothing and stations for makeup and hair stretched out across the floor. Music blared from overhead speakers, which meant you had to shout to be heard.

I loved it.

Someday this was going to be me, overseeing my collection before it headed off down the runway. Approving hairstyles and makeup palettes, choosing shoes and accessories. I would be the boss, ordering around a team of minions.

"There you are, *bella*." A small group parted to reveal Domenico, and he came straight toward the elevator, his hands moving rapidly. "*Vai, vai.* There is not much time."

Chiara gave me a gentle shove and it became a blur after that. Hands grabbed me and began working me over from head to toe. My hair took forever because I'd worn it in a messy bun today, so they had to start from scratch to get Domenico's straight and stiff style. The makeup was more dramatic than even I would attempt to go clubbing. Finally one of the pieces from the new collection was wrapped around me.

Domenico circled me as they guided my feet into the heeled leather boots. "*Dio santo!*" Then he turned me toward a full-length mirror. "*Sei perfetta.*"

Shit. I looked good. Really good. A complex network of black straps and netting fell just below my crotch, which was covered in black panties, while the top half cut across my small boobs like dental floss. The whole effect was sexy and glam and edgy, somewhere between a dominatrix and a rock star.

Domenico fussed a bit with my hair. "You will steal the show." He started to move away. "We begin in moments."

"It's just for your investor, right?"

"Sì, sì," he said over his shoulder. "A very powerful man. One we must impress, *capisce?*"

I nodded. It was probably some old Russian oligarch. "I'll do my best, signore."

"Call me Domenico," he called and moved onto another model.

The stylist working on me whistled. "He must like you. No one calls him Domenico until they've been here for *years.*"

I didn't know how to respond to that, so I snapped a few selfies and fired them off to Emma, my twin sister. She was at university in Toronto, studying to become a doctor.

TWINSIE: Damn you look HOT

ME: ikr

ME: I'm filling in for a model

TWINSIE: Can you keep the dress

ME: I don't think so

ME: I miss you

This was the longest we'd ever been apart. It was strange not having her around to keep me grounded. And who was making sure Emma didn't bury herself in textbooks?

TWINSIE: Sucks about the dress — and I miss you too

ME: I'll call you later. Don't study too hard!

TWINSIE: I have an OC exam tomorrow

In Emma-speak that meant organic chemistry. She was such a lovable nerd.

TWINSIE: Let's talk after that ok?

ME: Fine but I will fly home and beat your ass if you don't call me after your exam

She sent two laughing face emojis.

TWINSIE: Have fun in Milan!

I sent her the middle finger emoji and put my phone away. Part of me still couldn't believe Papa let Emma and me go off to university, let alone that he'd allowed me an internship in Milan. This was probably Frankie's doing. Ever since my oldest sister married Fausto, my father had given me and Emma more independence. There weren't any discussions about marriages or betrothals, thank fuck, and he seemed willing to let us live like normal young women our age.

When I asked Frankie about it, she said Fausto had leverage against our father and wasn't afraid to use it on our behalf.

Was my older sister the shit or what?

There was no time for anything else because we were herded up and led to the floor below. The other models looked similar to me, same height and build, also with dramatic hair and makeup. The clothes varied in sexiness, but my outfit was the most revealing. Before I had time to dwell on that, the elevator doors opened and we were told to quietly gather backstage. Hair and makeup artists finalized our looks while Chiara and Valentina put us in order.

When we were ready, the opening beats to Britney Spears' *I'm a Slave 4 U* started playing. I had to smother a smile. My sisters and I loved this song growing up, and Britney was a fucking queen.

Valentina hissed at me when I snapped my fingers to the beat. Chiara pointed at her face, reminding me to stay in character. I nodded and adopted the "I don't give a crap" expression I'd been schooled on earlier.

The line began moving as models started walking. When I drew closer I could see lights and smoke synched with the music, and my heart began beating faster. Excitement bubbled in my chest as I climbed the steps and waited for my cue.

I was going to slay this fucking runway.

Enzo

One lesson I learned early in life: trust no one.

This included those who took your money and made promises. This meant I oversaw my investments carefully. Otherwise, what was to prevent someone from stealing from me?

Domenico was one of the few designers I invested in. Fashion was a good way to launder my money and I always loved clothes, and so far Domenico had proven a wise choice. His name was now all over the globe, with designs worn by every celebrity.

Which meant Domenico answered to me and was available at a moment's notice to cater to my every whim. Today that resulted in a private showing of his upcoming collection to see the fruits of my investment. I waited, alone, at the front of the runway, disguised by a pair of sunglasses and a baseball hat.

"Signore." Domenico appeared and lowered himself in the seat next to mine. "I think you will be pleased by what you see."

Doubtful, but I was in Milan for other business so this was an easy way to check up on him. I was still in hiding so I had to be careful, never staying in one place for very long.

Even after four years my feud with Ravazzani continued to burn bright. He wanted me dead, but I wouldn't give him the chance. Instead, I would lay low and plot my revenge. He would never see me coming.

I suffered far more than Ravazzani, losing almost everything—including my wife. She died in a car accident. We weren't close, except to raise our children, but she deserved better than bleeding out on a tiny country road in England.

My children had lost their mother. That tore at me every day. They attended an English boarding school using assumed names, and I saw them for a few weeks each summer when we sailed far from Europe together. Anything more was too dangerous for them. I couldn't risk my enemy finding me and hurting my children.

A poisonous hatred twisted in my gut, vines of rage and darkness that spread to clog my throat and strangle me. This was *his* doing. And Ravazzani would pay.

Domenico signaled to someone in the wings and music filled the room. The cacophony hurt my head as a parade of beautiful women started down the small runway. I struggled to appear interested.

Before my time in captivity, I would chat with Domenico during the show, then eye-fuck two or three of the models. Hours later those same models would somehow arrive at my hotel room and we'd spend the night trading orgasms.

Today I watched silently, stoically, eager for this errand to end.

Domenico shifted. "The inspiration for the collection—"

I held up a hand to cut him off.

I didn't give a shit about his inspiration or the sustainability of the clothing. I didn't care about anything at the moment but proving to him that I was alive and still formidable enough not to cross. I used him to launder money, nothing more.

A woman stepped onto the runway and air whooshed out of my lungs.

That face. I knew it. A memory tugged at my mind, something I should remember. She was beautiful. Maybe I had fucked her.

No, I hadn't. I wouldn't forget having those long legs wrapped around my waist or her—

The fog in my brain cleared and recognition hit me in the chest like a hammer. It was impossible. How had this happened?

She drew closer and the truth settled into my bones. Even through my sunglasses I could tell it was Gia Mancini—and she was here on Domenico's runway. *Che cazzo?*

I hadn't forgotten her from Ravazzani's dungeon as she peered at my broken and bloody body on the ground, regarding me like an animal in the zoo. An amusement for her. That fucking *stronza*.

My shock diminished after a few beats, and I studied her as my mind raced. I hated to admit it, but she was gorgeous. Domenico's design left her almost naked, and I could trace her curves behind the straps she wore. The tall black boots made her legs look even longer as she strode toward me, and her small waist flared out into generous hips. No tits to speak of, but I could see the hint of her nipples from behind flimsy fabric.

Bold and unafraid, she held my eye as she neared the end of the runway. Did she recognize me? I waited to see some sign, some flash in her flat expression, but there was none. Her face remained blank.

She turned and walked away, her ass shifting with every step. I kept my gaze on those two firm globes until she disappeared.

Was this a ploy by Ravazzani? A scheme to draw me out of hiding?

Anger lashed at my insides like a whip. Did he think me so desperate, so *pathetic* as to chase after his nearly naked, sexy as fuck sister-in-law?

Women meant nothing to a man who was dead inside.

At some point, the music had cut off. Domenico was shifting in his seat, watching me closely. I could see beads of sweat building on his brow.

Va bene. If he feared me, he would obey me.

"Bring her back," I snapped.

"Her?"

"The model in the straps and boots."

"I don't think—"

"I want her here. Right now."

Jumping slightly, Domenico began texting on his phone, his thumbs moving feverishly. I sat perfectly still. I tried to see this from every angle, as I did with all problems I encountered. Why her? Why here? It made no sense.

My involvement in Domenico's business was a well-guarded secret. "Would anyone on your staff have told her my name?"

"No, signore," he quickly said. "Only my accountant knows and he has been sworn to secrecy."

This didn't mean much. People could be made to talk. My hope was that I had instilled enough fear in Domenico that he would keep quiet.

"The girl, she's one of your regular models?"

"She is no model, signore. We were short today so she filled in. She is an intern, a nobody. No one you should concern yourself with."

Gia Mancini, an intern? For a clothing designer where I happened to be an investor? *Cazzata*.

I didn't believe in coincidences. Something was off and I would have answers.

"Her name?"

"Gia Roberts."

A version of her father's first name, Roberto. Cute. Did this mean no one here knew of her father or her brother-in-law? If so, this little lamb had waded into a den of lions without the slightest protection.

Unfortunately for her, I was the most dangerous lion.

But things that sounded too good to be true usually were.

We waited a few seconds and then she appeared. Still wearing the revealing dress, she strode toward me with those long legs, and I couldn't help but drag my gaze over her bare skin. She moved with confidence, a woman used to drawing attention wherever she went— and with a body like hers she probably did.

But this was different. This was Francesca Ravazzani's sister, the enemy. Gianna had seen me at my worst—a broken and bloody man on the dirt floor of Fausto's dungeon. Had probably laughed about it with her sisters after.

"Leave," I said with quiet authority.

Domenico stood and hurried from the large room, then I slowly removed my sunglasses, revealing my face, keeping my gaze locked on

Gia the entire time. A storm, wild and fierce, raged inside me, madness brought on by thoughts of my shame, my *humiliation* in that dungeon. I shoved it all down for the moment and stared directly into Gia Mancini's curious eyes. I waited. Silence often revealed what words could not.

She didn't flinch or fidget. Instead she let her eyes drift over me, examining. I braced myself for some recognition, some sign she knew me, but there was nothing except a flicker of feminine interest in her dark brown eyes.

Remarkable.

After a long moment she cocked her head. "Well?"

"What is your name, bella?"

"Gia."

"Your last name, Gia?" I let her name trail off my tongue, a caress of the syllables and vowels.

"Roberts," she said without a twitch. A very good liar, obviously.

"And what are you doing here in Milan?"

She blew out a breath and gave a small shake of her head. "Listen, I get it. A room full of women, guy like you? You're probably used to having your pick. But you're better off choosing someone else. Trust me on this."

"What if I don't want to choose someone else?"

"I would still tell you no."

So mouthy and bold. I wasn't used to being spoken to in such a manner, especially by a woman, but I had bigger concerns. If she was here to trap me, then why turn me down? It didn't add up.

Was it possible? Had she really no idea who I was?

Anticipation tightened my muscles, so I forced myself to relax and appear non-threatening. I couldn't scare her away. "You are American?"

"Canadian." Her lips flattened, like she regretted giving me the truth. "From Montreal."

Another lie. "Ah. *Je peux t'offrir un verre?*"

She blinked at my French, clearly not understanding. Would she admit her lie? "Oh, I was homeschooled and never learned French," she said.

She was clever and stubborn. Deceitful. All qualities I admired. "I asked if I may buy you a drink."

"My answer is no. Are we done here? I really need to get out of these shoes."

Best to let her think she was safe—for now. "Arrivederci, Gia Roberts."

She opened her mouth, as if to say something more, then closed it. Spinning, she walked away and this time I let myself enjoy the view. Her ass was perfection, high and tight, begging to be slapped and fucked.

I smothered the thought. I had to *use* her, not fuck her.

She disappeared and a plan took shape in my mind, the pieces slotting into place like a puzzle. It was perfect. Exactly what I needed to get vengeance on Fausto Ravazzani.

Everything he did to me? I would now do the same to his precious sister-in-law. I would take her and imprison her. Then I'd inflict all the horrors from the dungeon on Gia without a sliver of remorse.

And Ravazzani could only blame himself.

Vito appeared at my side. "Want me to bring her to the yacht?"

"No." I rose and put my sunglasses back on. "I want her followed until my meeting concludes this afternoon. Then I'll deal with her."

"It's good to see you take an interest in a woman again, but are you sure it's wise?"

"That is no woman. That is the enemy."

And I was going to enjoy breaking her.

CHAPTER THREE

Gia

"Who was that guy?" I asked Chiara backstage as I put my regular clothes back on.

Domenico's secret investor had been incredibly handsome, probably in his mid- to late-thirties. He had dark eyes that sucked you in and a chiseled jaw that belonged on movie posters. I'd been around enough powerful men in my life to recognize one, so I knew he was *someone,* but he'd dressed in jeans and an expensive-looking shirt, hardly serious business attire. At least he wasn't in the mafia. No self-respecting mobster would be seen in anything less than a suit in public.

I bet he was an actor or film producer. A famous chef.

"I don't know," Chiara answered. "Domenico keeps the names of his investors very private. You must've made an impression, though. I don't recall any model being called back for a personal interview before."

"It wasn't an interview. He asked my name and if he could buy me a drink." In French. Sexy and could speak multiple languages fluently? I could've orgasmed on the spot.

"And what was your answer?"

"I said no, of course. Like I'd really go off with a random stranger in a foreign country and drink alcohol." Hadn't Chiara ever watched a true crime documentary, for God's sake?

Chiara grimaced. "Sometimes these men, they like a challenge."

"Well, that's too bad. I'm not getting involved with anyone here."

"Why not?" Chiara handed over my black cigarette pants. "Italian men are fun, if you get one who's not too attached to his mamma."

I shoved my legs into the pants. "Isn't that a stereotype?"

"No, definitely not," she said with a chuckle. "They are generally good in bed, and most are very tied to their mothers."

I didn't bother explaining why I wasn't interested. I was still smarting from being cheated on by my last boyfriend, Grayson, who I met at university. After dating him for five months, I caught him sexting with another girl, one he'd been seeing behind my back. Thank God we'd always used condoms.

Cheating was an absolute dealbreaker for me. Growing up I was surrounded by men who had no regard for their vows or a wife's feelings. They all had women on the side, pretty young things who catered to their fragile egos. This included my father. I would never be that sort of girlfriend or wife. I would never look the other way or share a man, the way my mother had.

"Hurry up." Valentina poked her head around the curtain, her frown aimed in my direction. "I have a package that needs to be delivered across town."

"Okay," I grumbled, shoving my feet back into my flats. "Give me a second."

Chiara shifted to see the other assistant better. "Val, that investor, do you know who he is?"

"Yes."

When she didn't continue, Chiara waved her hand. "And?"

She answered in Italian and it was much too fast for me to translate. "What did she say?" I asked Chiara when Val left.

"That she is sworn to secrecy and won't risk her job by telling me. But she said the man is harmless, something to do with finance."

Ah, that made sense. He was probably some playboy venture capitalist. Still, I wasn't interested.

"You need to learn more Italian," Chiara said as we started toward the offices.

"I know, I know. But everyone here speaks English, too. I haven't really felt at a disadvantage."

"People can fuck with you, though. Insult you or lie to you. It's for your own protection." She pushed the button for the elevator. "This is why you need an Italian lover. He can whisper Italian in your ear while you're in bed."

That did sound nice, but so did listening to a language app in my pajamas while eating gelato. Vibrators were a lot less work than men. Guys usually wanted to talk about my father or my upbringing. People outside the mafia were obsessed with it, treating it more like a sideshow than a misogynistic criminal enterprise.

"Here." Valentina was waiting on the office floor with a package in her hand. "Deliver this and try not to get lost again."

I swallowed an angry retort. When I first arrived I'd gotten lost once and Valentina never let me forget it. "I won't." I hurried to my desk and grabbed my purse. A quick glance at my email showed nothing super important, so I took Valentina's package and left.

It was almost one o'clock, the time when Italians took a ninety-minute break for lunch. This was one of my favorite things about working in Italy; they took their rest and their food very seriously.

After checking directions, I slipped in my earbuds and started walking toward the Metro station. Christian, one of the two men my father hired to guard me, followed at a discreet distance. I tried to ignore the guards as much as possible. They worked for my father, which meant I couldn't fire them or convince them they were unnecessary. God knew I'd tried.

Strange, because my father made no secret of his disdain for me. Even when I was younger, it was clear Frankie was the responsible one, the daughter he leaned on to take care of everything around the house. And Emma was Papa's favorite, the quiet studious daughter, the one who never caused trouble. That left me, the rebellious one, always fighting for his attention. But the worse I acted the more he ignored me.

Not once had he said he loved me, that he was proud of me. His words were cold and flat, disapproval in every syllable. Frankie told me it was my age, not to worry about it, but how could a child not seek a father's approval?

By the time I was in my early teens, I no longer cared what he thought. Papa didn't watch me like he watched my sisters, which made it easier to get away with stuff. That suited me just fine.

When I was fifteen one of Papa's guards had taken my virginity. Tony was incredibly handsome and terrified we'd get caught. We hadn't, though, and the two of us spent one glorious summer fucking and sucking before he was moved elsewhere in the organization.

From then on there hadn't been any guards under the age of forty at the estate. I always wondered if Papa found out about Tony and me, but I suspect it was having three teenage daughters that prompted the change, not any concern over my virtue.

Most of the guards hadn't liked me any more than my father had. *"Stay away from that one,"* a soldier had whispered to another one about me a few years later. *"She's trouble. A cock-hungry slut with daddy issues a mile long."*

Fuck that misogynistic pig.

I turned the corner and passed a row of trattorias, their outdoor seats starting to fill up for lunch. In the glass I noticed the reflection of a man across the street staring at me as he walked. Our footsteps matched, like he was keeping pace with me. The hairs on the back of my neck stood up, a chill cascading down my spine. Weird. I peeked over my shoulder at Christian, but he was dodging a set of parents trying to reason with a crying child.

A tram crawled by at that moment, blocking my view of the opposite street. When it finally rumbled out of sight, the man was gone. I blew out a long exhale.

I was being paranoid. Why the hell would someone follow me? Gia Roberts was no one here, just a lowly intern. I needed to get a grip.

After I rode the Metro across town to drop off Valentina's package, I was starving. I stopped for lunch and downloaded a few language apps to try. Chiara was right. Not being fluent in Italian was a disadvantage. I could usually keep up when people spoke slowly, but that wasn't ideal.

After I finished a delicious mushroom risotto, I returned to the office and went straight to my floor. A few people were crowded around my desk. Has something happened? What were they looking at?

"Ciao—" I closed my mouth when I saw a massive flower bouquet on top of my desk. These were fancy flowers, the kinds with names I couldn't pronounce. Like something you would see in a hotel or magazine. Were these for *me?*

Chiara arrived and ordered everyone back to work. "These are very expensive," she told me. "You have an admirer."

"I don't, though. These can't be for me."

"Check the card. They are definitely for you, carissima."

Sure enough, the name Gia Roberts was written on the envelope. I slipped the card out.

I promise to buy you that drink, Gia Roberts.

Shit. These were from Domenico's investor, the man from the show earlier. My heart skipped in my chest as I fingered a pale petal. This was ridiculous. I told him I wasn't interested. Still, I was flattered. No man had ever sent me anything this expensive and beautiful before.

"Are you going to tell me?"

"No." I slipped the card into my pocket. I didn't want anyone at work to know that Domenico's investor was sending me flowers.

"It was the man, no? The investor from the show this morning."

I looked around, making sure we weren't overheard. "Shh. Don't tell anyone, especially not Domenico. I don't want people to gossip about me."

Chiara put her hand on her heart. "I swear, I won't say anything." Then she looked at the flower arrangement again. "*Questi sono molto belli*. He is very serious about you."

I shoved my purse in my desk drawer and tried to move the flower arrangement out of my way. "Then he's wasting his time. I'm fresh out of a relationship where my boyfriend cheated on me. I'm taking a break from all men."

Chiara grimaced, her brown eyes sympathetic. "That may be true, but Italian men . . . they can be very persuasive. I wish you luck."

Her words stayed with me for the rest of the day.

Enzo

I didn't bother knocking.

I kicked the wood with my foot and the heavy door slammed open, bouncing against the wall. The tiny apartment was a mess, with food containers and soda cans littered all over, while the smell of body odor hung like stale perfume. Three screens surrounded a large desk, the chair empty. Where was he?

The sound of a window sliding had me hurrying into the other room. A man was trying to escape into the alley. Massimo stepped forward but I beat him there. I was eager to handle this stronzo myself.

When I caught the man, I grabbed hold of his hair and pulled like I was closing a window shade. Screaming, he grabbed his head and fell back, landing at my feet. A chunk of hair remained in my fist, so I dropped it and gave him a swift kick to the ribs. "Stefano. How nice to see you."

He wheezed, holding his side. "Vi prego, Don D'Agostino. Please don't hurt me."

"Get him up," I told Massimo. "In the chair."

My younger brother lifted Stefano like he weighed nothing and threw him into the desk chair. I pulled zip ties out of my pocket and secured Stefano's arms and legs where I wanted them. Stefano continued to plead with me, but I ignored him.

"Now," I said, dragging a chair from the tiny kitchen area to settle across from Stefano. "Tell me why you've stopped taking my calls."

"You called? I hadn't—"

My fist cracked against his jaw, snapping his head back and rocking the chair. "Do not lie to me, coglione. It will be worse for you if you lie." I gave Stefano a few seconds to catch his breath. I wanted his full attention. "Again, I ask you. Why have you stopped taking my calls?"

"I-I didn't think I needed to work for you anymore."

Exactly as I thought. "You think your debt to me is repaid?"

"Vi prego, signore. There is this woman—"

I hit him again, this time on his cheek. The skin broke open and blood oozed down his face. I relaxed in the chair, my heart not even beating fast. I could break this man so easily. My mind yearned to cause pain and suffering, to soak it in and absorb another's misery like a sponge.

It wasn't easy to keep everyone in line while I was in hiding. They thought I wasn't watching, that they could take advantage of me. Like Stefano. He would soon learn what it meant to defy me, though.

I leaned in. "Do you think I give a shit about a woman? Your only concern is making me fucking money. Your debt is repaid when I say and not a moment before, capisce?"

A talented hacker, Stefano found software vulnerabilities inside a company's infrastructure that allowed us to harvest their data. I employed more than a dozen geniuses like him for my fraud enterprise and made millions off their abilities. Stefano's pathetic living circumstances aside, they were all well compensated.

None of that mattered. I wasn't letting him go, because he was too valuable. Better to let him believe he still owed me the debt in exchange for his father's life.

"I came out of hiding to see you, Stefano. That means I am already pissed off. I already want to beat your face until your own mother won't recognize you."

"No, vi prego—"

"Then we are in agreement, no? You will continue to work for me until I say otherwise."

Blood dripped onto his shirt. "Of course, Don D'Agostino."

I took the switchblade out of my pocket and went to cut the ties holding him to the chair.

Except I stabbed the blade deep into his thigh instead.

Stefano howled, his screams rattling off the cracked plaster. I turned the knife, causing more agony, before I yanked the blade out and cut him loose. He crumpled to the ground, holding onto his leg. Blood was pooling onto the worn carpet, so I stepped around it and bent to grab his face. He was sobbing, but I held him tight and stared into his eyes. "You answer when I call. You do what I say. Or I will come back and shove my knife up your ass."

"Sì, Don D'Agostino."

Satisfied, I let him go and went to the door, Massimo right behind me. I waited until my brother and I were in the elevator before saying, "Have them find this woman he's attached to. Who knows how much he's told her? I don't like it."

"We'll take care of it," Massimo said. "Did you see that place? It was a shit hole."

"It looked like your cabin on the yacht."

"*Vaffanculo*." Massimo put up his middle finger.

I nearly smiled. I loved my brothers. When I was forced into hiding they both came with me, no questions asked. Starting this computer fraud business a few years ago was the smartest thing I ever did. It allowed us the ability to work outside of Napoli, and the D'Agostinos were now more powerful than even our father in the old days.

Soon we'd step out of the shadows and back into the light.

And Gia Mancini was the key.

"Check in with Vito," I told him. "Make sure he hasn't lost her."

Massimo pulled out his phone and started texting. When we reached the ground I put on my hat and sunglasses.

"He's still with her," Massimo reported. "He thought she spotted him at one point so he pulled back a bit."

"Tell him to keep trailing her."

"She has a guard, he says."

Interesting. Her father's doing, of course, but it was a lazy effort, the one guard. Before his oldest daughter's marriage to Ravazzani, Mancini never would've allowed one of his girls out of Toronto, let alone go overseas alone. He'd grown bold, thinking his connections would offer protection here.

Except he was wrong. The threat of Ravazzani's retribution meant nothing to me, because I would kill him first. I was smarter and not nearly as arrogant. He would make a mistake long before I did.

A mistake like letting his sister-in-law live and work in Milan with only one guard watching her.

"Where are they now? We need to make a stop first, but then I plan on meeting her after work." Just like I promised.

CHAPTER FOUR

Gia

By the time I left the office I was beat. Valentina sent me out on two more errands, then yelled at me for not doing them fast enough. No clue why she was being such a bitch, but I was more than ready to go home, relax and open one of the bottles of Ravazzani wine Frankie sent.

I left the huge flower bouquet at work. Finding a taxi at this time of day was impossible, and I wasn't strong enough to carry the huge arrangement on the Metro. The flowers would never make it across town in one piece.

As I walked down the street, I passed a shiny red Italian sports car. My mouth practically watered at the sleek beauty. We never saw cars like this in Toronto. For a few weeks I dated a guy who owned a Maserati, which was fun to drive. But this car made that one look like a junker.

The driver's door of the sports car opened and long jean-clad legs appeared. I slowed, not wanting to miss my chance at learning who owned such a badass machine.

When he straightened I rolled my eyes. Of course, it was him. Mr.

Investor. Anyone who could afford the flowers he sent today could certainly afford this car. Had he been waiting for me?

If so, was I flattered or creeped out?

Behind his sunglasses, his eyes coasted up and down my body, making me flush hot and cold at the same time. "Gia Roberts," he said in his deep Italian voice. God, the sexy way he rolled the first "R" in Roberts almost made me wish it was my real last name.

I stopped in the middle of the sidewalk, a safe distance away. "Well, well. If it isn't my stalker."

"Stalker?" His brows drew together beneath the bill of his baseball hat. "You think I mean you harm? I am wounded, bella."

"Anyone who can't take no for an answer is sus."

"Sus? What does this mean?"

"Suspicious. In other words, you."

I started to walk past him but he kept pace. He shoved his hands in his pockets. "I promised on the card that I would buy you a drink. What did you think I meant?"

"Look. I know you're not used to being refused, but I'm really not up for kicking you in the junk right now. Just take a hint and get lost."

"So feisty. Did you have a bad day? All the more reason to relax and have a glass of wine with me."

I exhaled and paused to hold up my phone. "Do I need to call the polizia?"

He threw his head back and laughed, and I tried not to watch the strong column of his throat. Why was an Adam's apple so hot? He gave me a smile that could charm the panties off a nun. "The polizia? And what have I done wrong, other than flatter you? Ma dai, let me buy you a drink. In a crowded restaurant. What's the harm?"

I did want a drink. Desperately. Today had been long and annoying, thanks to Valentina. "Because I don't know you and, no offense, you're a little old for me."

"I have known Domenico for almost ten years. And I'm too old to share a drink with?"

This man had an answer for everything. Was he so hard up? He had to be surrounded by women everywhere he went. "Why me?"

"Because you're beautiful." He took a step closer and pursed his lips, his voice a deep rumble. "I have not been able to stop picturing you in that dress from this morning. *Sei irresistibile.*"

Whether it was the promise of wine or his charm, I could feel myself weakening. "I don't even know your name. You could be a murderer for all I know."

"I won't tell you my name until you agree." He gestured to the phone in my hand. "Put it on your social media, if you wish. Tell everyone where you are."

I could do that. I opened up my social media account and posted a selfie of me outside the bar. Then I wrote that I was having a drink and tagged the restaurant. "I'm also texting a friend." I sent a text to Chiara that I was having a drink with Domenico's investor and gave her the location of the restaurant. "There. If they find me dead in a basement somewhere, they'll know it was you."

"Why would I want to kill one so beautiful?" He took my arm and led me inside the restaurant. The hostess gave him a come-hither smile as he requested a table in the back, near the kitchen. Weird. Most flashy men liked a seat near the window. Maybe this man was not what I assumed.

He held out my chair, which seemed unnecessary but a nice touch, then took the seat across from me and removed his sunglasses. He had dark, intense eyes, the kind that held dirty secrets and rough promises that sent good girls running in the other direction.

Unfortunately, I was not a good girl.

The hostess presented menus, but I held up my hand. "We're just having drinks."

Mr. Investor amended with, "For now."

The hostess deposited a wine list on the table and then we were alone. I tapped my fingernails on the tabletop. "Are you going to tell me your name now?"

"Lorenzo."

He looked like a Lorenzo. "And what do you do?"

"Computers."

That made sense. He was probably the Italian Steve Jobs or Mark Zuckerberg. "And how do you know Domenico?"

His lips twisted into an amused smirk, his face so handsome that I swear my toes curled. "This feels like an interrogation."

Before I could comment, the server came by to take our drink orders. I grabbed the wine menu, but Lorenzo put his hand on it. "Have you had an Aperol Spritz yet?"

"No." I pretty much stuck to wine.

"*Due*, per favore," he said to the server, then spoke rapidly in Italian.

"What else did you order?" I asked when we were alone again.

"Fruit and cheese. It compliments the drink."

"What's in an Aperol Spritz?"

"You'll like it, I promise. It has a bit of an edge. Like you."

He wasn't wrong. I was the rebellious sister, always in a hurry to experience as much as possible. Growing up, I grabbed every opportunity to break out of the small gilded cage my father had placed us in. Drinking, drugs, sex . . . Nothing had been off-limits. I went to my first rave at fourteen, got my first tattoo at fifteen. Not even Emma knew of my piercing. I was good at breaking the rules and keeping it a secret.

But I didn't like this stranger trying to see inside my brain. I needed to remain distant and polite during our drink, then go home alone.

I cocked my head. "So. Let's return to how you know Domenico."

He chuckled and leaned back, sprawling a bit in his chair. It drew attention to the expanse of his chest, the strength in his arms. "I like fashion. I also like women. It seemed natural to invest in a few up and coming Italian designers when I first started making money."

"Why did you choose Domenico, though?"

"His designs appealed to me. They're rough and raw. Like sex, no?"

My mouth dried out as heat washed over me. Okay, so he was just putting that out there, blurting it in the middle of a crowded restaurant to a virtual stranger? This guy had balls.

I respected that.

God help me, but I decided to play along. "Maybe I like it soft and sweet." I dragged out the last words, whispering them in a pouty bedroom voice.

His nostrils flared, surprise flashing in his dark eyes. I must've shocked him because he didn't say anything for a long second. Then our drinks arrived and the moment was broken.

Score: Gia, one. Lorenzo, zero.

Don't cause trouble in Italy, Emma had said right before I left. *And come back safely.*

I hated disappointing my twin, so that meant no flirting with strangers. One drink tonight in a public bar and that was it. "Listen, I shouldn't have said that. Ignore me. Sometimes my mouth gets away from me."

That caused his gaze to dart to my mouth and I wished I could take the words back. Again.

Because now we were probably both thinking about my mouth and where it could go. At least, I was.

As if we'd declared a truce, we both sipped our drinks. It was orange and bitter and bubbly. I loved it. "Yum."

"You will like it even more with the fruit and cheese, I promise." He shifted to look over his shoulder, out toward the street.

"Worried about your car?" I asked.

"Why would I be worried?"

"That someone might ding it or try to steal it."

He chuckled, like both of these possibilities were ludicrous. "If that happened, I would buy another, Gia Roberts."

"You know what they say about men who drive cars like that."

"Oh?" He sipped his drink, staring at me over the rim of his glass. "Do I seem like I am compensating for a small penis?"

I liked how nothing fazed this man. "No, actually. You don't."

He didn't answer, just smiled like we shared a secret. Whew, these Italian men were hard to resist. Did the rest of the world know how goddamn charming and pretty they were?

I assumed not, otherwise every single woman in the world would be moving here.

He pushed back from the table. "*Scusa.* I must use the toilet. Try not to miss me."

I rolled my eyes. "Don't worry. I won't."

When he left, I pulled out my phone and checked my texts. Chiara gave me a thumbs up in reply to my earlier message about having a drink with Lorenzo. I was about to reply—when light flashed all around me and a loud sound deafened my ears. I gasped, pain suddenly everywhere in my body.

Then I was on the ground with plaster and debris falling from the ceiling. I couldn't breathe. It felt like someone had kicked me in the chest. Hard.

Then it all went black.

Everything hurt.

My ears were ringing, my head a muddled mess. What the hell happened? And why did it feel like I was moving? The last thing I remembered was being on the ground. Nothing made sense right now.

Oh, shit. The restaurant had exploded. I was in an *explosion.*

What about Lorenzo? Was he okay? He'd gone to the restroom just before all hell broke loose.

I couldn't open my eyes, so I focused on my breathing. In and out. In and out. I tried to flex my fingers and my toes, just to see if anything was broken. Sore, but everything seemed in working order.

The ground tilted and I slid to my right. I was in a car, one that just made a turn. Was it an ambulance? I still couldn't hear, so I struggled to lift my eyelids.

As soon as my vision adjusted, I instantly knew it wasn't an ambulance. Buttery leather seats, a tiny interior—like a sports car. From the backseat, I could see a man behind the wheel. Another man was in the passenger seat. I wish I knew what the fuck was going on.

My head throbbed, worse than any headache I'd ever experienced. It was awful, like my skull would split apart. For a moment I thought I might be sick from the pain.

The man in the passenger seat suddenly turned toward me. Lorenzo! He was alive, after all. That was a relief, but why was I in his car? "Wha—?" I couldn't finish the word. My brain and mouth weren't connected at the moment.

He sneered at me, his face twisting into something monstrous and hateful. He looked like a different person, the complete opposite of the man who'd charmed me in the restaurant. I saw his lips move, but I couldn't hear him. All I could hear was this terrible ringing.

I must've passed out again because the next thing I knew I was being carried. Blue sky filled my vision and I was crushed against a warm chest. The noise in my ears had eased slightly, enough for me to hear the sound of boats, like we were at a marina. "Zo?" I slurred, wanting to know if it was him.

There was no answer. I struggled to stay awake, to force the cobwebs out of my brain. Where was he taking me? The hospital? I wondered if I had a concussion. "Please," I breathed.

"*Stai zitta*, troia!" the man said.

Motherfuck. That was the second time someone had called me *whore* today.

I wanted to yell and scream, but my brain couldn't handle it. The edges of my vision went dark and I slipped into unconsciousness.

I resurfaced from the blackness. I was on a mattress, sheets cool beneath me, and light streamed through the thin curtains. Was it the same day? Or the next morning? Shit, I had no idea how long I'd been asleep.

My head hurt, though not as bad as before. Instantly, I knew this was not the hospital. The room was far too nice, with oak paneling and fancy sconces. No furniture, other than the bed and a side table, which was weird. And was I rocking?

Fuck me. This was a boat. A big one, if I wasn't mistaken. Last summer Frankie gave us a tour of Fausto's mega yacht and this was exactly what it looked and felt like.

No, no, no. I didn't want to be on the water. Anything but water.

I rolled onto my back gently and stretched my sore muscles, trying not to think about the deep watery abyss surrounding this yacht. Instead I considered my body. Jesus, I ached. Before anything else I had to find a bathroom.

Groaning, I pushed to my feet and slowly made my way to the

closed door at the far end of the room. My legs were shaking, my body as weak as a baby lamb, but I thankfully discovered a bathroom when I finally reached the door.

To say my reflection in the mirror was shocking was an understatement. I stared at myself, horrified. My face was covered in dirt, my hair wild, and there was a cut on my cheek that had crusted over with blood. *You survived an explosion. What did you expect?*

I needed a shower, but no way could I manage it at the moment.

After I used the toilet, I pulled open the tiny curtains to look out the window. Nothing but blue ocean as far as I could see. We were moving at a fast clip, too.

I shivered.

I couldn't swim. When I was six years old, I slipped off a boat and into Lake Ontario without floaties. I could still remember the terror of slipping under the surface, of not being able to breathe. The claws of death wrapped around my ankles and pulled, almost comforting, telling me to relax, that everything would be okay if I just gave up. My lungs burned for air, the water too murky to see anything, and I knew I was going to die.

I later learned that our nanny jumped in to save me, but I don't remember any of it. That was the last time I went into anything deeper than a hot tub. I had refused to learn how to swim after that.

Ocean or not, I needed to go investigate. Whoever brought me on this boat owed me an explanation.

As soon as I left the bathroom, I knew I wasn't alone. It was like the air in the small cabin had become charged with electricity, dark and dangerous. I gripped the wall to steady myself—and that was when he stepped forward.

Lorenzo.

He'd changed since the restaurant, now wearing a pair of dark jeans and a white button down shirt. His hair was slicked back, as if he'd just showered. The look on his face was not one of concern or welcome. His stare sent a cold shiver down my spine.

Still, I wouldn't let him intimidate me. I was Gia fucking Mancini. No computer billionaire was going to frighten me.

"What the hell?" I blurted. "I need a hospital, not a Mediterranean cruise."

His mouth twisted as he came closer. "You are not in a position to negotiate with me, Gia Mancini."

My muscles locked into place as my heart raced inside my chest. Mancini? I definitely hadn't shared that information with him. "That's not my name," I lied.

"You are Gianna Mancini, the daughter of Roberto Mancini and sister to Francesca Ravazzani. You grew up in Toronto, attended two years of university there before coming to Milan for an internship with Domenico." He paused and lifted one arrogant brow. "Should I continue?"

No, there was no need for more. He obviously knew too much. My fingernails dug into the wooden door jamb behind me, while my damaged brain struggled to keep up. This was bad. Very bad. "How do you know all that?"

"You really don't have a clue, do you?" He moved to the bed and sat on the mattress, then reclined back on an elbow. I wasn't fooled. It was like a lion relaxing out on the plains—right before it devoured an antelope. "And here I thought you were the smart one."

The hatred in his gaze terrified me, and I wasn't all that thrilled about the way he'd called attention to the bed. I held perfectly still.

Except for my mouth, which wasn't big on self-preservation, apparently.

"Look, it's clear you have some sort of beef with my father. But you should probably let me go before this turns ugly."

"My *beef*," he spat derisively, as if the word offended him, "is not with your father. And I am hoping it turns very, very ugly."

My throat tightened as fear shot through me like a poisoned arrow. "If not my father, then who?"

"Your brother-in-law."

"Fausto?" My sister's husband was one of the leaders of the 'Ndrangheta, the most dangerous mafia in the world. I had no doubt that he'd made many enemies over the years. My sister had even been kidnapped by one before she married Fausto.

Lorenzo's expression darkened, his mouth pressing into an angry white line. "So now you see why I will not let you go."

There was something there, some connection that was just out of reach. I wished my head didn't hurt so much. Then this would all make sense—the kidnapping, Fausto's enemies. Lorenzo's animosity toward me.

Oh, fuck.

My gaze snapped to his, realization dawning. *Lorenzo*. How could I have been so stupid? "No," I whispered, shaking my head. "No, it can't be."

"Ah. You finally understand, no?"

"You're Enzo D'Agostino." I recoiled, even though there was nowhere to go. "You almost killed my sister."

He flicked his fingers in a dismissive Italian gesture. "I hardly touched her. She was in no real danger from me."

I rubbed my forehead. Enzo D'Agostino was Domenico's investor. He'd sought me out and convinced me to have a drink with him, then kidnapped me. "So the explosion in the restaurant—you planned that?"

"It was not easy to get that amount of explosives on such short notice. You should feel flattered."

I wobbled on my feet, my head swimming with all this horrific information. He'd killed people in that restaurant today. I didn't have a death count, but there's no way everyone survived. *And he'd done it just to kidnap me.* "You are a fucking psychopath."

It was like the temperature in the room dropped fifty degrees as his body grew very still. "I would be careful what names you call me. I can make things difficult for you, Gia."

"But you won't, because if you wanted me dead you would've already killed me. So, what do you want from me?"

He slowly rose off the bed and came toward where I was standing, and my dread compounded with his every step. His brows were lowered menacingly as his angry gaze locked on mine. Was he rational? Could he be reasoned with? I had no idea, but I was going to fight like hell if he tried to hurt me. I straightened and braced my feet.

He would not find me an easy target, not any longer.

When he was in reach, I lifted my chin and waited. He didn't stop, either, leaning in like we were lovers. He was so close that I could feel the heat radiating off him and smell the fresh scent of his shampoo or soap. Some combination of tea tree, musk and pure insanity. I held my breath and tried desperately not to move, like he was a wild animal that could attack at any moment.

He put his mouth near my ear and whispered, "What I want, Gia Roberts Mancini, is revenge."

With that, Enzo spun on his heel and crossed the floor toward the door.

But I wasn't done. Not by a long shot.

"People will be looking for me. You won't get away with this."

When he turned, the smile he wore terrified me to my very soul. "No one will be looking for you. They all believe you died in that explosion today. A girl who fits your description will be found in the rubble near your phone and identification. She'll be impossible to identify conclusively, so everyone will assume it's you."

My jaw fell open. "No . . ." It was all I could manage before my breath lodged in my throat.

"Yes," he said. "After all, you posted online about being there and you texted your friend. Everyone will confirm you were in that restaurant."

Yes, because he'd encouraged me to post about my location on social media for my own safety. Now it made sense. "You want everyone to think I'm dead."

He grabbed the door handle. "For a little while, yes. Until I'm ready."

Oh, my God. My family would be devastated. Frankie would somehow blame herself, and I couldn't even imagine what this would do to Emma. I knew how upset I'd be if I ever lost her. It would be like cutting off my own limb.

While I was still grappling with this, Enzo disappeared into the hallway and I heard the lock engage on the door. Too weak to remain standing, I sank to the floor and hugged my knees, barely noticing how my back scraped against the oak paneling.

What was I going to do now?

CHAPTER FIVE

Enzo

When something terrible occurs, two kinds of people emerge. The first kind shriveled up and wept, the mind folding in on itself like a house of cards. This group couldn't see past the hopelessness or the fear to save themselves.

The second type fought. These people became alley cats in the face of life-threatening danger, striking out, clawing and scratching to survive.

Something told me Gia would fall into the second group.

But even fighters could be broken. I remained strong when Ravazzani's men burned my skin and shoved a knife between my ribs. And when they broke my bones and dislocated my shoulders. Yet, as time dragged on, I felt myself weakening with infection and dehydration. Every breath became agony, my body mangled beyond comprehension. I hated lying on that cold stone floor, at the mercy of my enemy.

I came close to giving up—and that filled me with such incredible shame and fury. I would never forgive myself for the thoughts that ran through my head in those last hours of captivity. I should have been stronger.

The noise began just then, an incessant banging that could be heard with two decks between us. My kitten had grown claws, it seemed. Good. It would make the end result even more satisfying.

"She sounds pissed," Vito said from the chair near my desk. We were in the office, which was located on the upper deck behind the pilot house.

"Hardly a surprise." I continued to scroll my email, scanning the reports from around the globe.

I employed the best hackers in Italy and eastern Europe to run my fraud enterprise. They also made certain that my email was secure, absolutely untraceable. This allowed me to live on the yacht and control my empire remotely. I took the occasional trip inland to deal with problems, but otherwise became a ghost four years ago.

It wasn't the way my father would've handled it, but I was different. I'd spent the last decade bringing the 'Ndrangheta into the twenty-first century with a global computer empire. The days of shaking down small local businesses for protection money were over.

I would soon transform drugs, too. Ravazzani could keep his outdated cocaine and heroin trade. I had my people working on new chemical compounds that would replace the old formulas. Designer drugs that didn't cause so many overdoses and ruin repeat customers.

"You should go, no?" my brother suggested. "To calm her down."

"She's a prisoner, not a guest. I don't give a fuck whether she's calm."

"What if she hurts herself?"

I nearly laughed. "Considering I plan to make her suffer, I hardly think it matters." I gestured to the phone. "Find out if the room is ready. I want to move her as soon as possible."

Her current cabin, while sparse, was too cushy. She should be uncomfortable, as I had been in Ravazzani's dungeon. The crew was redecorating one of the lower deck cabins to my specifications. It wasn't exactly the same as what I'd endured, but it would be close enough.

Vito began texting. "They need another hour or two," he finally said.

"Tell them to hurry the fuck up."

My brother relayed the message then put his phone in his pocket. "Are you going to tell me what you're planning to do with her?"

Anticipation crawled over my skin like an army of insects. What was I going to do? I was going to break her, humiliate and ruin her. She'd be a shell of a woman by the time I finished, at which point I'd show her to Fausto and Frankie. They'd give me whatever I wanted in exchange for Gia's return.

But it would be too late. Gia would never be the same.

I glanced down at my hand, where Ravazzani sliced off the end of my finger. Every day it reminded me of my time in his dungeon, chained and beaten. Starved and naked. They treated me no better than an animal, killing off whatever humanity I possessed.

Which was exactly what I intended for Gia.

"You'll see," I told Vito.

"I would not like to see you turn into him."

I knew he was referring to our father, who hadn't thought twice before abusing a woman, including our mother. Not one of his sons had been conceived out of love, and I swore to myself as a boy never to take a woman against her will. I would never break that promise. "You don't need to worry. I will destroy her, but not in that way."

My phone rang then, a number I recognized. I swiped to answer. "*Figlio*, come stai?"

"Papà, they are making me call you."

At twelve years old, Luca was my oldest. He looked like his mother but acted exactly like me, somehow inheriting my recklessness and ambition. It was a dangerous combination, one I knew well. "What's happened?"

"A boy has been picking on Nic."

Nic was Nicola, his younger sister. Luca paused for a moment, the unspoken words hanging between us.

No one fucks with a D'Agostino and gets away with it.

"And?" I prompted.

"I took care of it, but they want me to apologize."

I made a dismissive sound in my throat. "That English school is too soft."

"That's what I said." Hints of a British accent now peppered the

Italian sounds in his voice and it made me sad beyond words. My children had been away from their home country for too long. Luca continued, "He's the son of some snooty aristocrat. The father is threatening to hold the school accountable."

"Good. They should do a better job of protecting their female students. Is she hurt?"

"No, I don't think so."

"I want to talk to her. Tell her to call me. Let me speak to whoever is there from the school."

There was some rustling as Luca passed the phone. "Mr. Peretti," the man said in a posh English accent, addressing me by the fake name Angela and the kids adopted when they fled Italy. "This is Mr. Payne, headmaster of the preparatory school. I do hope we can arrive at a satisfactory resolution—"

"Mr. Payne," I said sharply, cutting him off. "My son will not apologize, ever. And you are lucky I'm not coming there personally to tear you apart for allowing my daughter to suffer while under your care. If I find out that anyone there—adult or child—has fucked with either of my children, I will burn that school to the ground. With you in it."

"B-but, sir," Payne stuttered. "The other boy is in the hospital. He is the son of an earl, so you see my dilemma."

I rose out of my chair as anger swelled inside me. "Are you implying that some inbred aristocrat is more important than my children?"

"Indeed not, but surely you are able to understand this is a delicate situation."

Did he think I was stupid? Just some dumb rich Italian? "There is nothing *delicate* about it. This earl's son picked on my daughter and my son put a stop to it. As far as I'm concerned, that boy should be grateful that a beating is all he received."

Payne sucked in a short surprised breath. "We don't condone violence, Mr. Peretti."

"Yet you condone the bullying of a ten-year-old girl?" When he didn't answer, I hardened my voice. "Take better care of my children, Payne. If I hear you've made Luca apologize or that my daughter has had one more run-in with another student, I'll come up there personally and you will be my first stop. Now give my son his fucking phone back."

Some scuffling followed then I heard Luca's amused voice. "You made him nearly shit himself, Papà," he said in Italian.

Good. "I'm proud of you, Luca," I said. "I know this hasn't been easy on either you or your sister, but it won't be long now."

"You're bringing us home?"

My heart squeezed at hearing the hope in his voice. I wanted to see both of them so badly. "Soon, figlio mio. Very soon."

"Thank Christ. It's not terrible here, but the food is awful. We miss you."

"I miss you both, very much. Ti amo, Luca."

"Ti amo. I'll have Nic call you." The line went dead.

Emotions roiled inside my chest, mostly a howling frustration that my children were so far away. They should be at my side. Instead, some pasty-faced English brat dared to pick on my sweet *principessa*.

I leaned over and pressed my palms flat on the desk, my arms shaking with rage. I burned with the need for retribution, to even the scales and reclaim my life. It was past time.

Then I heard the shouting from two decks below.

My mouth curved and ideas began swirling in my head, each one more depraved than the last. I was going to humiliate Gia Mancini, use her to secure my future, and make her wish she'd never been born.

"What are you planning?" Vito asked, his gaze watching me warily.

Straightening, I pointed to his phone. "Tell them I'm transferring her now, whether the room is ready or not."

"Enzo—"

"Fucking do it!" I shouted, slapping my palm on the desk. "And don't question me ever again. I'm the capo, not you."

He raised his hands in surrender then pulled out his phone. I strode to the door, more than eager to go below deck and deal with my little alley cat.

Gia

My throat was raw from screaming but I wouldn't let up. Not until that psycho came back down here and let me out.

He could not keep me locked up forever. I'd strangle him with my bare hands first. I got that he hated Fausto, but there was no reason to drag me into their mafia wars. I was an innocent bystander. Well, mostly innocent. I went into Fausto's dungeon while Enzo was being kept there, but I hadn't done anything to this man.

The naked prisoner in that dungeon didn't resemble the handsome and charming man who'd taken me for drinks. The prisoner had been bloody and swollen, bruised and dirty, his arms hanging at weird angles, the shoulder joints definitely dislocated. Air had whistled out of his cracked lips, his face unrecognizable. He had suffered, but I felt zero sympathy for him, not after he kidnapped my sister and put a gun in her mouth.

So Enzo D'Agostino could fuck right off. If he thought he could lock me up and I'd quietly obey, he would be sorely disappointed.

I started yelling and pounding again, making as much noise as possible. I broke one of the legs off the nightstand and used it like a drumstick on the wall. And when someone finally came to unlock me, I'd use it like a weapon, too.

"You fucking coward!" I shouted. "Unlock me now!"

Keys rattled in the hall and the door unlocked. I flattened myself against the wall, holding the table leg high above my head. The second anyone came in I was going to bash them in the skull.

Enzo stepped into the room and I didn't hesitate. I swung with all my might, but he dodged the blow and wrapped his hands around the table leg. Before I could try again, he jerked the heavy piece of wood clean out of my hands and threw it across the room. "I see you've been busy, micina," he sneered.

I thought about running, but he was blocking the only exit. Besides, where would I go? We were on a ship in the middle of the ocean. "You can't keep me locked up, Enzo."

"Can't I?" He dragged a fingertip along my cheekbone.

I swatted his hand away. "Don't touch me."

"You are incredibly bold for a woman in your position. Making demands when you have absolutely no leverage whatsoever."

"My leverage is that you do not want to fuck with me. Let me go before you regret it."

He threw his head back and laughed. In my face. That motherfucker.

I curled my fingers into fists. Fuck this. I would not make it easy for him.

While he was still laughing at my expense, I darted through the door and sprinted down the hall. I was in good shape, running most every morning when the weather cooperated. So I thought I had a decent chance of getting away from Enzo, just long enough to find a hiding place on another deck.

As I started up the stairs, a hand wrapped around my ankle and pulled hard. My arms slammed onto the step, pain jolting through my elbows before I was yanked to my feet. Enzo leaned close, his eyes dancing with amusement. "Where did you plan to go on this boat? Or were you going to take your chances with the sharks?"

Please. I'd be long dead from drowning before the sharks ever found me. I pushed those thoughts from my system and struggled in his hold. Except he was too strong. His fingers bit into my flesh. "Let me go," I gritted out through clenched teeth.

"Enough of this. Andiamo."

I dug in my heels but he dragged me like I weighed nothing. We went down the corridor. I thought he was taking me back to my cabin, but instead he walked past it.

"Where are we going?"

He didn't answer. This seemed like a bad sign.

We kept walking toward the end, where a door stood ajar. He pulled it open and tugged me in behind him. I couldn't see much because the room was dark, but there was enough light to see metal bars in the middle of the room. A cage? Oh, fuck no.

"I couldn't create a dungeon on such short notice, so I had to improvise. What do you think?"

I couldn't speak through my horror, so I started fighting. I swung with my fists and my legs, clawing at any part of him I could reach. He was not putting me in a fucking cage. I'd rather die first.

Within seconds he had me subdued with some sort of choke hold they probably taught in mafia school. I couldn't move, his arms trapping my back against his chest. I struggled but he didn't budge. All I could do was pant and stare at the cage.

"We use these cages for fishing in dangerous waters, so I had them weld it together, secure it to the floor, and put a heavy lock on it. I also had them make the surroundings a little more hospitable for a prisoner. Do you like it?"

The paneling and light fixtures had been removed from the walls, leaving them bare. The carpet had also been ripped out, so the floors were plain wood. No doubt I would get an infection from a splinter down here.

Really, Gia? You're worried about splinters?

Then I saw the heavy chains on the wall.

Jesus, this guy was crazy. I swallowed my panic and kept my voice steady as I snapped, "You're fucking sick, not to mention delusional if you think you can keep me caged up."

"I can do whatever I want to you, troia. Haven't you realized this yet?"

"Call me a whore one more time and I'll cut your balls off, D'Agostino."

He pushed me toward the cage. "Get in."

I stumbled forward then spun to glare at him. "This is nuts. I had nothing to do with you being kept prisoner in Fausto's dungeon. How is this fair?"

He reached behind his back, withdrew a pistol out of his waistband, and pointed it at me. "I don't give a fuck about fair. I told you I would have my revenge. Now, get in or I will shoot you."

"You're going to kill me? How does that possibly serve your purpose?"

"I didn't say I would *kill* you, I said I would *shoot* you. Any number of places would hurt and make you suffer."

His eyes were intense and clear, with not the slightest bit of hesitation in his voice. He meant it. Enzo was unhinged enough to follow through on that threat.

But a cage? I couldn't make myself move toward it.

Gun raised, he stalked toward me in measured steps and I began backing up, my hands trying to ward him off. "Think about what you are doing. My father and brother-in-law will never let you get away with this. This is your death sentence, Enzo."

"Wrong, this is your death sentence if you don't do what I say. Get the fuck in that cage, stronza."

Another insult. This shitbag didn't know when to quit.

Staring him down, I lifted my chin and planted my feet. "Make me."

It happened in a flash. He lunged and wrapped his free hand in my long hair, fisting it and forcing me to my tiptoes. Then he tugged me into the cage as I grunted in agony. Every strand of hair felt ready to come out of my scalp. "Let go, stronzo," I snarled, turning his insult back around on him.

Releasing me with a shove, he stepped back and snapped the metal door closed, then locked it. I rubbed my head but didn't speak. I was too furious.

He kept the gun pointed at me. "Give me your clothes."

My jaw fell open, fear clawing its way into my throat. "No fucking way."

"I was naked when you came to the dungeon to gawk at me. It seems appropriate, no? Your clothes, Gia. Right fucking now."

We stared at each other, unblinking. My heart was pounding in my chest like I'd run a marathon. Was he going to rape me? If he tried, I was going to bite his dick off.

I had to try to reason with him. "I was in that dungeon for five minutes and barely even looked at you. How is this possibly the same thing?"

"No one said it had to be exactly the same. And I make the rules. Take your clothes off and hand them to me, or I will shoot you in the left knee. It will hurt terribly, probably get infected, and you'll never walk the same again. Is that what you wish?"

How was this happening? Jesus, this was twisted.

My mind raced, evaluating my limited options. Was my dignity worth getting shot? No doubt Enzo had seen a variety of naked women in his lifetime, and I wasn't ashamed of the way I looked. He was doing this just to humiliate me—and my pride demanded I not let him. I didn't want to give him the satisfaction.

He wanted to ogle my tits and pussy? Fine. I would not weep or beg. And as long as I was locked up in here no one could touch me against my will.

I ripped off my blouse and threw it at the bars.

Those opaque eyes never left my face as I stripped off my pants, then my bra. When I was in just my panties, I slowly shimmied them down my legs like I was being paid to do it . . .and his gaze darted to watch, his nostrils flaring slightly. The tiny reaction emboldened me as I stood there completely naked. I kept my arms at my sides, letting him look his fill.

This is what you can't have, psycho.

Finally, he waved his hand dismissively. "Too bad you are so flat. Not like your sister, Frankie."

"Too bad you are so small." I dipped my head toward his crotch. "You know, I remember more of that dungeon than I thought." I actually had no idea what his dick looked like, but he didn't know that. I hadn't peeked at it in the dungeon. Gawking had seemed too cruel, even for me, a cock-obsessed teenager.

Then I realized my mistake. It was *good* that he wasn't attracted to me. I should be jumping for joy instead of insulting him.

My sister's voice was clear as a bell in my head. *Why can't you ever be quiet, Gia?*

A muscle jumped in Enzo's jaw as he shoved the gun in his waistband. Then he bent to collect my clothes, gathering them in his arms. When he straightened, his lips curled with satisfaction. "You look good behind these bars. A pet just for me. Enjoy your stay, Gianna Mancini."

"Fuck you," I hissed under my breath.

Sorry, I mentally told my twin, who would be horrified that I couldn't stop antagonizing Enzo. *I can't help myself. He's such a dick.*

You have to, I could almost hear Emma saying. *Stay safe. I can't lose you.*

Enzo pursed his lips and shook his head, like I had disappointed him. "We have to work on your manners, pet. Soon you will come when I call and sit at my feet like a good girl."

Yeah, that wasn't happening. Ever.

Walking to the door, he said over his shoulder, "Get comfortable, though I doubt it's possible."

"Don't leave me here, you asshole!" I grabbed the bars and shook them, rattling the metal. Too bad I wasn't strangling his neck instead. "What about food? Or a bathroom?"

Never breaking stride, he disappeared into the corridor, then the lock turned. Jesus Christ, this was unbelievable. Why were the hottest men also the craziest?

CHAPTER SIX

Enzo

I returned to the office and threw Gia's clothes on the sofa. Ignoring my brother's frown, I went to my chair and sat. I needed to get back to work.

My organization required a lot of moving money around. We dealt with many different countries and currencies, banks all over the globe. By the time the funds came back to me they were untraceable, which meant the Guardia di Finanza could go fuck themselves.

Originally, my father let me start the computer fraud scheme as a lark, a way to use the degree he hadn't wanted me to obtain. At university I met guys running low-level phishing scams and quickly saw how I could adapt it on a bigger scale. From there we expanded to hacking and data mining, too. The majority of my employees now worked in nice offices on fancy computers, instead of beating up junkies and shop owners for cash.

Vito cleared his throat. "You took her clothes."

"Yes."

Honestly, I regretted it. Gia was gorgeous with her clothes on. Without clothes? She was a fucking goddess. I'd insulted her lack of breasts as a way to deflect my desire, but anyone with eyes would know it was a lie. Her tall lithe form had curves in all the right places, and her small waist framed a soft belly. She had perfect nipples, and an ass that could start a war between friendly nations.

Best of all, because she was waxed bare, I had an unobscured view of the tiny vertical bar piercing her clit hood.

Mamma mia, that jewelry. I wanted to run my tongue over it, nip it with my teeth and gently pull until she panted beneath me.

She hadn't cowered either. As a man who never cowered, I appreciated that. Gia fought me and cursed, held her ground and kept her dignity. Madonna, was there anything hotter?

I opened my laptop and tried to concentrate on work. There were hundreds of emails and reports to look through, but my mind kept returning to that cabin, to that piercing.

Cazzo. I needed to scratch this itch before I did something stupid.

Looking up at my brother, I asked, "The girls we brought out last time, the ones from Cannes?"

His face revealed an utter lack of surprise. "Want me to have them flown out again?"

"Yes. How soon?"

"Two days, probably."

I nodded. "Arrange it. Let the crew know."

"Is this because of her?"

"Don't be ridiculous," I snapped. "I hate everything about her."

He glanced down at his phone and started scrolling. "That's good. Because Massimo says they're watching her in the security room. Apparently—"

Dio santo! I was up and out of my chair before Vito could finish that sentence. I strode to the security room, which wasn't far from the office, and threw open the door. Sure enough, Massimo and two of the crew members were gathered around the screens, their attention glued to one particular monitor. I didn't have to guess which one.

"Che cazzo!" I barked. "Is no one but me working around here?"

Massimo waved me over. "Ma dai, Enzo. You have to see this. She is doing yoga. Naked."

I clenched my jaw, annoyed with myself and them. "Turn it off. I want no one watching that camera but me."

Massimo whined like a petulant child and kept watching the screen. "No, please. There hasn't been a woman onboard yet who is this hot, and you would not believe how flexible she is. I'm begging you, just a little while—Dio cane! Did you see that?"

In three steps I reached the monitor and shut it off. I pointed in all their faces, my expression unyielding. "I am the only one who will watch her from now on. Anyone caught watching her will be cut into pieces and tossed overboard. Am I understood?"

"Sì, Don D'Agostino," they all mumbled, except for my youngest brother. I didn't like the suspicious glint in his eye, but I ignored him. Everyone on this yacht answered to me, including my brothers.

I started for the door. "Massimo, with me."

When we were out in the hall, I put a hand on his sternum and shoved him against the wall. "What were you thinking, encouraging them?"

He tried to remove my hand, but I was too strong. He scowled at me. "She's hot and naked. You can't tell me you didn't look when you had the chance."

I had, but I was trying to forget it. "I want to humiliate her, not get you off. Don't do it again."

"Fine, but you don't know what you are missing in there. Madre di Dio, she did this thing with her leg . . . ." He whistled. "And did you see her piercing?"

A strange feeling came over me, a dark knot in the pit of my stomach. It was anger at myself, at my brother. Anger at the woman in that cage for not hiding herself away from prying eyes. Worse, it was the possessive urge to keep her just for me, where I was the only one allowed to see her.

Fuck it. I was the boss.

"She's my prisoner—mine, not yours. You're not to go in there or look at her. Are we clear?"

"What's going on?" Vito hurried down the hall, his brows pinched in concern.

Releasing Massimo, I stepped back. "No one goes in her room but me." My brothers exchanged a quick look that set my teeth on edge, so I asked, "Something to say?"

Vito studied me and I could almost see his mind turning. "You're not going to let anyone in there? Not even a crew member?" When I didn't answer, he rolled his eyes. "Zo, she will need to eat, to use the bathroom. To bathe."

I dragged a hand through my hair. When the idea of a cage occurred to me yesterday in Milan, I hadn't considered any of these mundane practicalities. After all, Ravazzani hadn't worried about any of those things with me. I'd been filthy, chained to a wall and left to relieve myself in a bucket. Gia would experience the same—or worse.

An eye for an eye is not enough.

"She's a woman, not a man," Massimo added as if I needed this reminder. "They aren't strong, like us."

I wanted to laugh. If he'd been the one struggling to get Gia in that cage, he would not say she was weak.

"She's strong," I growled. "And I will give her everything she needs."

Though it sounded like a dirty sexual promise, I meant basic necessities. She'd receive nothing except what I provided. I would let her eat from my hand, but only after she begged me to feed her.

Vito frowned. "What if you're busy?"

I leaned in and snarled, "Why are you pushing me on this? Hoping I'll let you be the one to care for her?"

"No, but you're acting very strangely. Like you're jealous."

"Fuck off. I'm trying to exact revenge."

"Are you?"

Balling up my fist, I drove it into the wall. Pain shot up my arm and I welcomed it, using it to fuel my anger. "This is none of your fucking concern. Both of you stop questioning me!"

Vito didn't back down, which was why he was my consigliere. "It is my concern—and Massimo's, too. We will suffer the consequences when Ravazzani learns of what you've done. Cristo santo, Zo. We've lived on this boat with you for four years. We have a right to know your plans."

Insieme siamo più forti.

Stronger together.

As I took a breath and calmed down, I could see they were right, though I didn't want to admit it. "Fine. I'll get Cecilia to look in on her."

Vito stroked his jaw, a tell for when he was about to say something he knew I wouldn't like. "You aren't planning on forcing her, are you?"

I couldn't believe he was asking this *again*. I was the one who remembered my mother's cries, hearing her plead with my father to stop. Except he never did. The next day he would disappear and she would stay in bed, bruised and sore, telling us she was "sick." But I knew the truth.

And my brother knew it, too. I glared at Vito. "Even if the thought of sticking my cock inside her didn't make me nauseous, do you honestly think I would do that?"

"No, but you took her clothes, Zo."

"Because that is what he did to me. I will revisit each of my nightmares on Gia Mancini, and you two had better not try to stop me."

Pushing by them both, I stalked toward the lower decks, which was where the crew members could usually be found. Cecilia, the widow of my father's consigliere, was head housekeeper on the yacht, and she oversaw the two maids and the kitchen staff. She asked for the job when her husband died, saying how much she wanted to sail on the open water. I paid her well and she was extremely loyal to the D'Agostinos, to me in particular, so taking care of Gia wouldn't be a problem. Cecilia would follow my instructions to the letter.

And any attempts on Gia's part to gain Cecilia's sympathy or help would fail miserably.

Gia

I tried to keep active in the cage.

Despite the cameras undoubtedly watching my every move, I did yoga and stretches, then push ups and sit ups. If D'Agostino thought he would weaken me by confining me, I was determined to prove him wrong. I would keep fit and ready. All I needed was one small opportunity for escape and I'd take it.

Even if it meant jumping overboard.

I had nothing to lose. The entire world thought I was dead. If I drowned, it was better than being at Enzo D'Agostino's mercy. God only knew what horrors that psycho had planned for me.

Hours dragged by and I grew thirsty. "*I need water,*" I shouted for the tenth time, waving my hands. I couldn't see the cameras but there was no way they weren't keeping an eye on me. Fausto had an entire room dedicated to security at the castello, and Enzo was surely the same. Paranoid mafia motherfuckers. "Water, Enzo! Hello!"

Soon my bladder joined in the fun, and I was desperate to use the bathroom. My skin flamed with indignation and fury. Was I supposed to pee in the freakin' cage? Ugh.

Just when I thought I would explode, I heard keys outside the door. Enzo strode in, looking refreshed and well hydrated, which made me hate him even more. I leaned against the bars to glare at him. "About time, you stronzo!"

An older lady followed him into the room. Her white hair was pulled into a bun, and she wore a cotton floral print dress, the kind that made every woman look pear shaped, regardless of body type. I didn't know what she was doing mixed up with D'Agostino, but I had bigger problems at the moment.

"I need water and a bathroom *now*."

He slipped his hands into the pockets of his jeans, a small smile curving his lips. "This is not a hotel, Gianna. If you want something, you must ask me nicely."

Oh, this son of a bitch. "Unless you want me to pee in this cage you had better take me to the bathroom."

"Pee your cage, then. No one will clean it up and you will be forced to stay in your own filth. As I was."

"You're a monster."

"So I've been told. This is Cecilia. When you are a good girl, I will let Cecilia take you to the bathroom and feed you. Are you ready to ask me nicely?"

I dragged in a deep breath and held it in until my lungs burned. I didn't want to play this game with him. I wanted him to let me go. But he would absolutely starve me and let me die of dehydration if I didn't.

Exhaling, I tried to make my lips form the words . . .but I couldn't.

The seconds ticked by until Enzo said something to Cecilia in Italian. Then the older lady left, closing the door softly behind her. I rested my forehead on the bars, cursing my own stubbornness.

"I sent her outside to wait," Enzo said as he came closer to the cage. "So that you and I may chat."

I waited, not saying a word. I didn't trust this man.

He propped a shoulder against the bars, close enough that I could grab him. I didn't, of course, because it was pointless. I would fight him, but not until I was out of the cage.

"You can't win in a battle with me, micina. I will be the one to give you what you need, but only after you play nice." He dragged a finger over the back of my hand where it was wrapped around the bars. "You will break, Gianna. *Te lo prometto*. Resisting is a waste of our time."

"Let me out of here."

He pursed his lips and shook his head. "That is not asking nicely."

"Please."

Pushing off from the bars, he started for the door. I sagged in relief. Finally, he would allow Cecilia to take me to the bathroom.

"It is too bad you could not cooperate," he said over his shoulder. "Perhaps another few hours will make you more cooperative."

"What? No! I said please, for fuck's sake!" I rattled the bars, panic twisting in my chest. He could not leave. This was unbearable. "What do you want from me?"

He paused with his hand on the doorknob. "Beg me."

I crossed my legs, the pain in my lower half agonizing. But I still couldn't do it. When the silence stretched, he opened the door and disappeared.

"Goddamn it!" I yelled. Then my practical half, the side in literal pain assumed control over my mouth. "Please, Enzo. I'll beg. I'm begging you! Don't leave!" I hated myself for giving in so easily. Tears stung the backs of my eyes as I stared at the door, waiting for it to reopen.

It stayed closed.

Shit, shit, shit. I sank to the ground and curled into a ball. Time crawled. Each second felt like an hour. The pressure in my bladder consumed my mind, and I panted through the pain. It was terrible, worse than period cramps or when I got the piercing. The tattoo on my ribs had been nothing compared to this.

How long has it been? Hours? I wasn't certain how much longer I could hold out.

Maybe I should just let it go, pee in the cage like an animal. Except my brain rebelled at the idea, and from somewhere far away I heard myself whimpering. The door opened, but I couldn't move. I couldn't even lift my head. Let him kill me. At least I wouldn't have to endure this any longer.

The metal clanged and I could hear the cage door swing open. Hands gently pushed strands of hair off my face. "Are you ready to give me what I want?" he whispered.

I had no more fight in me. Licking my dry lips, I rasped, "Please. I'm begging you."

"Va bene, micina. Va bene."

Strong arms slid under my body and lifted me. I gasped and then moaned, fresh waves of pain rolling through me. "Shh," he said. "It will be better in seconds. Just hold on, stubborn girl."

I heard another door and then his shoes slapped on tile. My bottom met a toilet seat. "Can you support yourself?" he asked, keeping his hands on my shoulders to steady me.

"Get out." My voice cracked, relief so close at hand that I was numb.

He let me go and I heard his shoes retreat. I'd been holding in my urine for so long that it took several seconds to convince my body to actually go. When I finally did the release was like an orgasm. My limbs sagged and my eyes watered. God, I never wanted to go through that again.

My legs shook when I stood to wash my hands. When they were clean I cupped my palms, filled them with tap water and drank. The door opened behind me and Enzo appeared. I met his dark gaze in the mirror and expected to see him smiling smugly over his victory. Instead, he looked thoughtful, like he was trying to see inside my head.

I ignored him and swallowed several more mouthfuls of water.

"There's no need for that," he said. "I have food and water out here for you."

"Laced with drugs, no doubt."

"I don't drug women."

For some reason I believed him. I dried my mouth off with the back of my hand. "You prefer mind games."

He blinked three times. Had I surprised him? "Yes, I do," he answered. "And you will learn that I always win."

Only because he'd never played against me.

I was no inexperienced virgin or shy introvert. I knew men and what they liked, their weaknesses when it came to women. And for all his intelligence and power, Enzo D'Agostino was just a man.

He wanted to play games? Fine. But we would play them *my* way.

"Turn around," he ordered, pulling a length of nylon rope out of his pocket. "Put your hands behind your back."

Silent, I obeyed and watched in the bathroom mirror as he approached. So I didn't miss when he checked out my ass and legs with a slow sweep of his gaze before he began winding the rope around my wrists. Yep. Just a man.

I was going to torment him in ways he'd never expect. He was going to regret kidnapping me—but it would be too late. His shit was so fucked and he didn't even know it yet.

Grasping my bound wrists, he marched me into the other room. A single chair waited, along with a table containing plates and water bottles. Thank God. He was going to let me sit and eat.

When I started to lower myself into the chair, he jerked me back up. "That is not for you." Then he sat and pointed at the floor by his feet. "Kneel."

I barely refrained from rolling my eyes. Clearly, Enzo had a real D/s captivity kink. From the moment I woke up in this nightmare he'd threatened me with sitting at his feet. Guess I was about to make his perverted dreams come true.

But he didn't know this girl could top from the bottom.

Holding his gaze, I slowly lowered to my knees, my chest almost touching his thigh. With my hands tied behind my back, my boobs were front and center, the nipples hard points in the cold air. He sat very still, his expression unreadable. Just when I thought he might not find me attractive, his eyes darted to my breasts and he swallowed hard.

Oh, yes. This was going to be easy.

After placing a napkin on his lap, he busied himself with cutting whatever was on the plate. "Are you hungry?"

I stared at the knife in his hand and wondered how I could steal it. "Sort of. I'm more thirsty."

He took a bite of what appeared to be a pork chop with herbs and diced tomatoes, the muscles in his strong jaw working as he chewed. When he finished, he wiped his mouth like he had all the time in the world. "And how do you ask for what you want?"

"*Posso avere acqua per favore*, signore?" My voice was a husky plea, intimate, the kind I'd use to ask a man to fuck me harder.

Enzo froze. I couldn't tell whether he was surprised by my tone or the fact that I asked in Italian. But I'd dined out often enough while in Milan to know how to ask for things—though I'd never spoken to a waiter quite like *that*.

After a long beat he reached for a bottle of water, uncapped it, and turned toward me, opening his legs to surround me with his thighs. One hand slid under my chin to hold me, while the other brought the bottle to my lips. "Drink," he ordered, his fingers pressing into my skin with authority.

I wanted the water very badly, but would I regret drinking it later? "Are you going to let me use the bathroom again?"

"That depends on you, no? Will you be a good little pet?"

Fuck it. I was too thirsty. My lips parted and cool water filled my mouth. As I drank, I watched him stare at my lips the whole time, and a strange tingling sensation crawled over my skin. I hated this man down to my bones, but the way he was regarding me right now—with a pleased fascination—caused my heart to pound wildly.

I need to get a grip. One day and I already have a serious case of Stockholm Syndrome brewing.

He pulled the bottle away, set it on the table, then retrieved his silverware to cut a piece of pork. The muscles in his forearms shifted beneath a topography of sun-kissed skin and brown hair, his hands delicate yet capable.

When he was ready, he held the fork to my lips. "Open," he rasped, and the position and request were not lost on me. It was highly sexual, just as if he were feeding his dick into my mouth. Was he even aware of it?

Fool.

Bending forward, I parted my lips and presented my tongue, then waited with my eyes closed. He slipped the fork into my mouth and I took the piece of meat off the tines slowly, moaning like it was the best thing I'd ever tasted in my life as I chewed. The performance was award-worthy, calling attention to my tongue and mouth in the most depraved ways.

For the record I gave a damn good blow job when I chose to, so I hoped Enzo was rethinking all of his life choices right now.

Just in case he wasn't, I swallowed the meat and licked my lips. "Yum."

A flush worked its way up his neck, his chest now rising and falling quickly. In a flash he had me on my feet, marching me back to the cage with the plate in his hand. He pushed me inside and I stumbled, my hands still behind my back. "Hey!"

Before I even knew what was happening, he'd placed the plate and two water bottles in the cage with me, then locked me in again. "Give me your hands." He held up a switchblade. When I was close enough to the bars, he reached through and cut the rope, freeing my arms.

Turning, he hurried from the room . . . but not before I caught the erection tenting the front of his trousers.

Ha! I grinned as I lowered myself down to eat. If he was attracted to me, he would let me out of the cage.

And if he let me out of the cage, Enzo D'Agostino was a dead man.

CHAPTER SEVEN

Enzo

While I still longed to humiliate Gianna Mancini, I now also wanted to spank and fuck her. My dick was still hard this morning, the skin pulled taut as blood pulsed along my length.

Madre di Dio. It made no sense.

She was nothing to me, a means to an end. My instrument of revenge, nothing more. But now I wanted her. Badly. Seeing her on her knees, at my mercy, taking food and drink from my hand . . .enjoying it. Cazzo, that sight would haunt me.

Up on deck, I tried to work in the tiny office beside my stateroom. Instead, I found myself pulling up the security feed from Gia's room to watch her.

She's my prisoner. I can do whatever the fuck I want.

She appeared on the screen, sitting cross-legged on the floor of her cage, eating breakfast. This woman, she was not shy. She was no wilting flower, but a fierce lioness. Any other in her position would've cried or broken down by now. Gia had remained strong, only begging when her body's needs overwhelmed her. I respected that.

It made me want to tame her even more.

My cock throbbed behind my zipper as I watched her. I craved relief, especially after refusing to pleasure myself since leaving her room yesterday. She stretched her arms over her head, arching her back, her tight nipples begging for my mouth.

I couldn't stand it any longer. Closing my laptop, I quickly unbuckled my belt and unfastened my pants, then got my dick out. I shut my eyes and pictured a random woman on her knees, taking my cock between her luscious lips. Precum leaked from the tip and I smeared it down the shaft to make it slick. Fuck, yes.

Except the more I stroked, the more the woman in my head looked like Gia. I couldn't stop it, not once she was there, waiting for me so sweetly as I fucked her beautiful face. I was rough, holding her hair tightly, making her gag as I shoved deep in her throat. Her eyes would water, but she would love it, begging for more and I would praise her, telling her what a good little slut she was.

My hand sped up as need clawed in my gut. Fuck, I wasn't going to last.

I thought about coming on Gia's tongue, filling her belly with everything churning in my balls, and my muscles tightened. Gasping, I began shooting all over my hand, thick ropes of come erupting from the tip of my cock. It went on and on, both too much and not enough. When I finished, I sagged in my chair and tried to catch my breath. Had I ever come this fast? Not in years, certainly.

I went to the washroom and cleaned up quickly. Clarity returned, and now I loathed Gianna Mancini even more.

When I reentered my office I heard someone knocking on the door. I unlocked it and found Vito there, eyeing me suspiciously. "Ma cosa vuoi?" I asked as I returned to my desk.

"News of her death went up late last night. I thought you'd like to see." Vito was around the desk before I could stop him, which meant he saw the security feed on my screen when I opened the laptop. "Ah. That explains the locked door."

"Shut your mouth, stronzo" I snapped.

Wisely, he said nothing more as I pulled up a news site. There it was, right on the homepage.

BOMB BLAST IN MILAN KILLS 3, INJURES 13
CANADIAN HEIRESS PRESUMED DEAD

"Presumed?" Vito scoffed. "The girl you placed near the table was a perfect match for Gia."

"Don't worry," I said, scrolling the article. "They are still investigating, so they can't say for sure yet. But they will." I clicked to other news sites, soaking in all the information I could find. Roberto Mancini couldn't be reached for a quote, but there was a photo of Gia's twin, Emma, on the street in Toronto. Domenico gave a statement saying Gia worked there under an assumed name, but they were shocked to lose such a wonderful friend and colleague. Then there were photos from Gia's social media account showing her outside the restaurant.

Nothing from Frankie or Ravazzani. Not surprising, but I wished I could see their reaction, their devastation. Soak in their tears.

Instead I'd have to wait until they learned Gia was alive and here as my prisoner. Dio, I looked forward to that day.

Vito's cell rang. He checked the screen and said, "Pietro." This was our cousin, the one who helped run our organization in Naples. "Pronto," Vito answered after putting the call on speaker.

"You with Don D'Agostino?"

"I'm here," I said, leaning back in my chair.

"The house in Pozzuoli was hit," Pietro said flatly.

I frowned. To check for traitors, we often let it "slip" to various members of the crew where I was staying, except it was always an empty house in the middle of nowhere. This time the information had reached my enemy. "Ravazzani must have been very disappointed."

"Torched the place from what I hear."

Vito folded his arms across his chest. "We can trace the leak back to the man responsible, no?"

"Of course," Pietro said. "I had someone take care of that before I called."

"Who was it?"

"Andrea Di Vittorio."

"Cristo!" Vito hissed.

My hands curled into fists and I pressed them into my eye sockets. Andrea was related to me through my deceased wife, and my father had promoted him over the years to give him more responsibility. Why the fuck had he given Ravazzani my whereabouts? "Are we certain?"

"He was the only one who knew which house. The others just knew the town."

"I want to know the connection to Ravazzani," I said, jabbing my finger on the desk. "And I want to do it myself. I want to look Andrea in the face while he explains why he betrayed me." Dealing with my wife's cousin would distract me from my other prisoner.

Vito muted the phone. "Not only is it risky, we would need to turn around. It would take time. We'd need to push the women off another day. Why not let Pietro handle it?"

"Because I'm the fucking boss. Your dick can wait. Do it, Vito."

Vito pressed a button then asked Pietro, "Where are you keeping him?"

"The butcher's shop next to the church on Via Posillipo."

"Will he keep until tomorrow?"

"I'll make sure he stays alive if you're coming."

"We're coming," I said, leaning closer to the phone. "Don't tell him. I want it to be a surprise."

"Of course, Don D'Agostino. A presto."

Vito hung up and then rubbed his jaw. Cazzo, twice in one day with my brother's tell? "Out with it," I ordered. "Just say your piece."

"You blew up a restaurant in Milan. You've kidnapped Ravazzani's sister-in-law. Do you think it's wise to step foot on Italian soil so soon? I think we're better off staying at sea until things calm down."

"I don't like visitors on the yacht." The fewer people who knew of the yacht, the better. In four years only three of my captains had been aboard and I trusted them implicitly. I could see Vito was about to argue so I held up my hand. "Women are different and you know it, so don't try to use that against me."

"I'm not complaining about the women, believe me. There's only so much jerking off I can do."

"Good. So we're in agreement. A quick trip to deal with Andrea, then we'll sail for France to pick up the women."

Vito began scrolling on his phone. "Any idea of how Andrea knows Ravazzani?"

"None. His father was low-level, never would've had those kinds of connections. And Andrea was promoted only because of my marriage to his cousin."

I walked to the cooler and took out a sparkling water. I took a long sip of water, which reminded me of my little alley cat. What was she doing in her cage? The temptation to check the security camera once again whispered across my skin, but I didn't. Let Cecilia deal with Gia instead.

"Have the boys in Munich look into Andrea," I told Vito, referring to my best hackers. "They will know how to uncover any shit to be found. Tell them as fast as they can. I'll instruct the captain to turn around and go back the way we came."

Vito nodded and reached for his phone. "You won't stop by a certain prisoner's room again, will you?"

"Do as you're told, fratello."

"I saw the way you looked at her, Zo. Before you knew who she was."

"And? You think I'm so weak that I will let her tits and ass fool me into forgetting who she is?"

He sighed heavily. "I don't know. You're not the same man as the one who went into that dungeon."

I squeezed my fist to remind myself of my missing fingertip, a habit I'd developed over the last four years. Not that a single reminder was necessary when I had so many—like the scars littering my body or the lingering pain in my shoulders. Or the nightmares, how I hated to be touched. Every day I lived with the aftermath of what Ravazzani had done to me.

"You don't need to worry," I said. "What happened in that dungeon ensures I will never forget—and I will certainly never forgive, no matter what Gia Mancini tries to do."

"I'm your brother and your consigliere. It's my job to worry."

"It's a waste of your time." I started for the door. "She is a means to an end, nothing more."

Gia

I hadn't seen Enzo in a while.

The older Italian lady, Cecilia, returned every few hours to take me to the restroom and bring me food. She was an enigma. While she looked like someone's nice grandmother, she carried a gun and threatened me like a hardened criminal. She wasn't cruel—but she wasn't kind, either. She made me handcuff myself before she unlocked the cage, and never turned her back on me or lowered the gun for a single second while she directed me to the bathroom.

I watched her carefully, biding my time. Could I take her in a fight? I had to be sure. I wouldn't get a second chance.

"How long have you worked for the D'Agostinos?" I asked her as she placed my food on the bottom of the cage. If I could build a rapport with her, get her to trust me, then I would have a better chance of catching her with her guard down. I didn't want to end up with a gunshot wound from a trigger-happy nonna.

She didn't answer.

I kept trying. "Are you related to them?" Still nothing. She relocked the cage, then motioned for me to turn around so she could unfasten my handcuffs. When I was free I rubbed my wrists. "Do you ever get seasick?"

Her face remained stoic, not a muscle twitching. The woman was like a stone, no emotion whatsoever.

As she started to leave I kept talking. "Hey! Do you think I could get a pillow or a blanket in here? I was freezing last night. I won't even be picky about the thread count!"

She slammed the door and locked it.

Damn. Ice cold, that lady. I really did want something warm to cover myself with. Was he going to make me freeze again all night on the hard floor? I waved my arms and called, "Enzo! I know you're watching, you maniac. I want a pillow or a blanket. Come on! It's bad enough you're keeping me locked up and letting Cruella de Ville look after me. Either let me go or bring me a comforter! Organic cotton, if possible!"

Damn it. I kicked the bars. This was pointless. If he was watching, he wasn't coming back anytime soon.

Sighing, I sat on the floor of the cage. If only I could sketch designs while sitting here doing nothing. What were the odds that Cecilia would give me pencils and paper? I snorted. The woman would rather shoot me, no doubt. She didn't have a sympathetic or caring bone in her body. Where was the female solidarity? As a woman, shouldn't she try to help another woman escape this nightmare?

Keys jangled and I tensed. I fully expected Enzo to come barreling in, cursing and berating me for my request.

Instead, it was a man, the one who'd been following me on the street yesterday. And he carried a duvet. "You," I breathed. "It was you in Milan."

"Ciao, Gianna. I am Vito D'Agostino, one of Enzo's brothers."

That explained the resemblance. They both were tall with dark brown hair, the same stubborn chin. Vito's hair was a bit shorter than his brother's, and his expression was thoughtful where Enzo's was suspicious and bitter. "Is that for me?"

He began feeding the thick cloth through the bars. "Here, take it."

No one needed to tell me twice. I grabbed the edge and pulled toward me. "Why are you doing this?"

"My brother . . ." He paused and shook his head. "Do not judge him too harshly. He has experienced things that have twisted his mind." He pointed to his temple, as if telling me something I didn't know.

"Yeah, that's painfully obvious. But he doesn't need to kidnap me and keep me in a cage, for fuck's sake. I didn't do anything to him." The comforter fell into my arms and I quickly wrapped myself in it. God, that small amount of warmth felt good on my naked skin.

"He does not see it quite the same, but believe it or not, we do not condone violence against women."

"Not sure Enzo got that memo."

"That is not the type of violence I was referring to."

Rape, then. If true, that was a relief. It would be one less horror to worry about during my imprisonment.

Vito continued. "But you should keep in mind one thing. The things your brother-in-law did to my brother? They changed him."

"If I'm expected to feel sorry for Enzo, I don't. He kidnapped my sister and put a gun in her mouth."

He lifted his shoulders in an elegant shrug. "It wasn't loaded. And at the time she was just his mistress. We didn't know of her pregnancy."

"What was that about not condoning violence against women?"

If hearing his words thrown back in his face bothered him, he didn't show it. Instead, he cocked his head. "How much do you know about what your father and brother-in-law do, Miss Mancini?"

I didn't like what this implied, that my father and Fausto would do the same. "They don't kidnap women, Signore D'Agostino."

"Don't they? When Ravazzani took Enzo's wife and children out of their beds, then tied them up and held them at gunpoint? What was that?"

He had? Frankie had neglected to tell me that part of the story. Maybe Vito was lying. "Bullshit. Wives and children are off limits."

"Not for Ravazzani, apparently. This was the last time my brother saw his wife. She later died and the children were sent away. So you see, he has lost far more than Ravazzani."

A knot settled in my stomach. I hadn't known this. No wonder Enzo was focused on revenge—but that revenge didn't need to include *me*. "I have nothing to do with Fausto's business. I'm living in Milan, studying to be a fashion designer."

"You are an opportunity, one we will not waste. Still, I will do my best to keep you safe."

"But your brother is the boss." Which meant Enzo had all the power over everyone on this yacht, including Vito.

"True, but I am the only person he listens to." He shrugged in that elegant Italian way. "I will do my best to protect you. If you do as you're told and stop antagonizing my brother, you may just survive what he has planned."

That sounded ominous. "Do you know what he has planned?"

A flash of something—uneasiness?—crossed Vito's face, and the knot in my stomach tightened. "No, but I wouldn't share it even if I did. Bringing you this"—he gestured to the comforter—"is already going against my brother's wishes."

"So why do it?"

"I should probably lie and tell you it's because I hate seeing you suffer."

"But the truth?"

"Is that my brother watches you on the security camera. Only him, no one else. I don't like the ideas he is getting. Stay covered up, Gianna Mancini."

Oh, so this was my fault? "Listen, I'm not trying to *entice* him. What is this, fucking middle school? Do girls need a dress code so the precious boys won't get boners in gym class?"

Vito's mouth tightened, his posture stiffer, angrier. "No, *you* had better listen. My brother is not a boy and you do not want his attention, not that kind. You would be wise to sit here quietly and do as you are told. Do not cause trouble or make him angry, capisce?"

"I can't help it," I snapped. "I am not capable of being a docile and cooperative captive. It's just not in me."

"For your sake I hope you're wrong." He started for the door, his leather shoes slapping on the wooden floor. "Otherwise, you might not survive your stay on this ship."

CHAPTER EIGHT

Enzo

I knew something was wrong even before I opened Gia's security feed the next morning.

She was quiet last night. Too quiet. Each time I walked near her cabin there was only silence. I ignored the urge to look in on her, either in person or on camera, since feeding her dinner Wednesday night. The tape placed on the door was intact, which meant she hadn't escaped. That was all that mattered.

But I could resist the temptation no longer. When the security feed finally filled my laptop, my muscles locked in surprise. Gia was wrapped in a thick blanket. Cazzo madre di Dio! Who had dared to go against me and give her this?

My chest heaved with hot breaths as I watched her, curled up in a tiny ball on the floor of the cage, sleeping. She did not deserve this comfort, this luxury. In Ravazzani's dungeon I shivered and struggled on the cold stone ground without blankets or pillows. She should endure the same . . .or worse.

An eye for an eye is not enough.

This was not Cecilia's doing. She wouldn't dare, considering the woman was as maternal as an insect that eats its own young. Fucking Vito. He was the only person who would try something so bold, so reckless. So utterly disrespectful.

If he weren't my brother, I would gut him like a fish and throw him overboard.

I would speak with him later, after I paid a visit to my prisoner. She needed to understand that charming my brother would do her absolutely no good. I was the boss, her keeper, and clearly she required a reminder of this fact.

Pushing back from my desk, I stormed out of my office and down the stairs. My skin burned with anger and betrayal. Vito's door opened as I stomped along the corridor toward my makeshift dungeon. "Enzo!" he called after me.

I stopped and slowly turned, not bothering to shield the rage and violence brewing inside me. "If I were you, fratello, I would hide."

He said nothing, merely nodded once and returned to his stateroom. I continued to the last door and unlocked it. "Get up!" I snarled at the prone form in the cell as I entered. Her breathing changed as she came awake, but it was taking too long for me. I kicked the bars of the cage, rattling them. "Get the fuck up, stronza."

She had the audacity to slowly stretch instead of instantly cowering in fear. Che palle, this woman. "What do you want, Enzo?"

No one spoke to me with such blatant disrespect except for her. Did she have a death wish? "I told you to get up. I won't say it again."

Wrapping herself in the comforter, she sat up. Long, messy locks of dark brown hair fell around her shoulders, her eyes half-lidded. Combined with her soft expression and relaxed muscles, she looked freshly fucked. My dick responded, even though I willed it not to. Arousal was not the signal I wanted to send at the moment.

"There. I'm up," she said through a yawn. "Now, say whatever you need to say and get out. I want to go back to sleep."

I stared at her, struggling through the chaos of my mind. How to even put it into words? I wanted to humiliate and hurt her, but I also wanted to fuck her. I wanted to bury my face between her legs for so long that her pussy bore an imprint of my tongue. I wanted to slide my cock between her lips and shoot down her throat until she choked on my come.

But I resented this desire for *her*, a woman who was my enemy. It threatened everything I was planning. I needed to make her scream in pain, not ecstasy.

I unlocked the cage and stepped in, then grabbed the comforter. With one mighty tug I ripped the cloth off her body. She rolled onto the floor, her naked limbs going every which way. "Hey! Give that back, you asshole!"

I ignored her and tossed the heavy blanket outside the cage. When I snarled in her direction, she paused, her eyes growing wary. Was she finally grasping the severity of my anger?

"Stand up," I ordered through clenched teeth.

Slowly, she pushed to her feet. Madonna, she was gorgeous, with long legs and olive skin. That clit hood piercing glinted in the light, tantalizing me with its very presence, and the tattoos on her ribs, several lines of dark script, shifted and rippled as she breathed. Even her fingernails were enticing, their deep violet color nearly black, like the color of my soul.

Then I noticed she was studying me in return. Her bold gaze swept up my legs and crotch, my abs and across my chest, and her nipples beaded into tight little points. Arousal? Her breathing was faster than usual, so it might be fear. But I doubted it. I had a hard time believing anything scared this woman.

Which meant she was attracted to me. It seemed inconceivable, considering how I'd treated her, but maybe Gia Mancini and I were the same kind of fucked up.

I filed the possibility away for later. If it turned out to be true, I could use that information against her.

Stepping forward, I closed the distance between us. She didn't move, not that I expected her to. Her neck craned to hold my stare as I towered over her, so close that our chests almost touched. I could see every eyelash, each fleck of gold in her irises. I could trace the tiny creases between her brows.

Carefully, I placed my hand on her throat, wrapping my fingers around the soft flesh. Her pulse hammered against my palm, and power surged through my veins.

"Who gave you this blanket?" I knew the answer but I wanted to see if she would tell me.

Her lip curled. "I can't believe I ever thought you were charming and handsome enough to have a drink with."

But she had because I'd adopted my old persona, though it had been a struggle, just to get her inside that bar. But I was no longer such a desirable and elegant man, not after days of extreme torture. I was twisted, the darkness bubbling ever nearer the surface, with my mind teetering on the edge of sanity at all times. And I didn't give a fuck. It would only make me more feared, more powerful in my world.

My nostrils flared. "Answer the question. Who gave you the blanket?"

"I'm not saying." Her voice was soft but strong. "I need all the friends I can get around here."

"You have no friends on this yacht, Gia. And anyone who helps you will be punished."

"Really, Enzo? For a comforter?"

I didn't care for her flippant tone, so I tightened my fingers on her throat. Then I leaned down and put my mouth near her ear. "Do you think your brother-in-law gave a fuck about my comfort when I was naked and cold on the stone floor? Was I allowed a pillow or a blanket?"

"If you're going to strangle me, I wish you would just do it and get it over with. All this foreplay is really boring."

Dio, that fucking mouth. Unable to stop myself, I inhaled her hair and skin. Cecilia had let her shower, but Gia still smelled a little like explosives. I liked that scent on her. It made me want to lick the smoke from her skin. "Interesting choice of words. Do you want to fuck me, *micina*?"

She struggled in my hold. "I'd rather fight you."

I didn't doubt it—and hard to say which I'd prefer at the moment. Fucking and fighting both sounded like good ideas.

She continued trying to pull away from me. "And I don't know what *micina* means so stop calling me that."

"It means kitty cat." I paused. "You know, *pussy*." I smirked, hoping to infuriate her. "And fighting would just end with you begging for my cock."

"You're delusional. Are you so hard up out here on the ocean that you need to kidnap women for sex?"

"I am never hard up for women. If I weren't so disgusted by you, I'd have you gagging for it by now."

She made a disbelieving noise in her throat. "Please. So that erection I saw yesterday was from disgust?"

Blood surged to my dick, hardening me still more in my jeans. Cazzo, this she-devil. I wanted to tie her down and gag her, then fuck her until she came so many times that she cried. "Maybe the sight of a woman on her knees, begging, gets me off."

"I wouldn't doubt it. I guess I'd have to feel your dick right now in order to test that theory. Since I'm not on my knees, you won't be hard, right?"

Would she dare?

No one touched me. Since my release from the dungeon, I couldn't tolerate the feel of someone's hands on me, except for a simple hug from my children. Being touched reminded me of being restrained and tortured, humiliated for days. Fearing when they would return and inflict more suffering.

But I was a man and I still needed to fuck. So with women, I bound their wrists during intimacies, leaving me in complete control at all times. This situation hardly qualified as intimate, but Gia was unpredictable enough to actually grab my dick. I couldn't risk it.

I immediately stepped back, and she quickly looked at my crotch. "You're hard," she whispered. "Very hard."

The door suddenly opened and my head shot up. Cecilia paused in the entry. "Mi scusi, signore," she said, backing out and closing the door.

"*Figurati!*" I shouted to the older woman. "*È tutto a posto!*"

I left Gia's cell wide open as I crossed the room. It was my way of telling her she could try to escape, but it would be pointless. When I reached the door, I told Cecilia in Italian, "Don't let her out of your sight when the cage is unlocked."

Cecilia dipped her head. "Of course, Don D'Agostino."

"We have guests coming tomorrow night. Vito told you, no?"

"Sì. I will have everything ready."

"Grazie. Speaking of my brother, have you seen him?"

"Signore Vito is eating up on the spa deck," she said.

Perfect. Dealing with my brother was exactly the outlet I needed at the moment to vent my frustration. He would learn not to disobey my orders, especially when it came to my prisoner.

"Enjoy your stay, pet," I threw to my captive as I walked out.

"Drop dead, you maniac," I heard her call after me, and my lips twitched as I fought a smile.

A baseball hat covered my head as I entered the butcher's shop in Napoli. One man was behind the counter, the rest of the place empty. The point wasn't to actually sell meat. My men used it for all sorts of purposes, but mostly for the bloodiest of work. The drains in the meat locker made for easy cleanup.

Removing my sunglasses, I pushed through to the back, Vito and Massimo right behind me. Pietro met us in the hallway. "Don D'Agostino," he said, with a deferential dip of his chin. "Come stai?"

"I've had better days. Let's get this over with."

We started forward and Pietro glanced over my shoulder at my brothers. "Vito! What's happened to your face? You meet up with a jealous husband?"

Vito was notorious for sleeping with married women, at least back when we lived here. The injuries today were from me, however. Hitting him had reduced my anger somewhat, but I was still pissed at him for giving Gia that comforter.

Vito chuckled, though it sounded hollow. "The husbands, they get lazy and fat, make it easy for men like me to take their wives to bed." A non-answer, Vito's favorite when outside the immediate family. It was what made him the perfect consigliere.

Pietro held open the door to the meat locker and we all went inside. "You think with your dick too much, coglione."

"There's no such thing," Massimo said, elbowing me. "Right, Enzo?"

I didn't answer. Massimo was busting my balls, as he'd been doing since I punched Vito at breakfast. Both of my brothers had accused me of acting jealous over Gia, which was absurd. My cock wanted her, but jealousy? No, I needed her miserable and frightened, unable to sleep at night and exhausted from wondering when I might kill her.

When she was a broken shell of a woman, I would call Fausto and let him see my captive. Then he would give me whatever the fuck I asked for, or I'd slice up his sister-in-law and drop her into the ocean like chum.

But there were other issues at the moment. Like finding out how my dead wife's cousin had betrayed me.

Andrea hung from a meat hook by his bound hands, his head hanging down. The tips of his toes barely brushed the floor, and I knew from experience how much this position hurt when you couldn't support your body weight. Ravazzani had left me in just such a position for days. Even now I couldn't lift my arms over my head without a twinge of pain. But today, I felt absolutely nothing as I drew closer to my prey, ready to slaughter him.

"Cugino," I said, and Andrea jolted in surprise. Excellent.

Snatching his hair, I tilted his head back until he could see my face. "I hear you've been busy," I snarled. "In Pozzuoli."

"I don't know anything," he wheezed.

I didn't believe him. Guilty men begged just as convincingly as the innocent ones when they felt threatened. "How many favors, Andrea?"

A moan escaped his mouth, his eyelids fluttering shut.

I shook his head like a rag doll. "How many favors have I done for you since I married your cousin?" I slapped his face and his eyes opened. "Twenty? Thirty? You ask me to loan you money. I got you the house in Sanremo for you and your mistress. More responsibility in the 'ndrina. A cut of the fraud empire. You leaned on your connection to Angela to get more and more from me."

I held out my hand and someone slipped the handle of a knife into my palm. I clutched it and put the tip of the blade under Andrea's right eye. "And what have you done to repay me, cugino? You told Ravazzani where to find me—"

"No!" He struggled like a fish on a hook, but I didn't let him go. The steel punctured his flesh and blood trickled down his cheek.

"Hold him," I told my brothers. Massimo and Vito held Andrea's shoulders to steady him.

"Please. Madre di Dio," Andrea whimpered.

"Your God won't save you now. Only me. So tell me what you did. How did you get the message to Ravazzani?"

"I swear, it wasn't me!" He almost shouted it, his face white with pain.

I leaned in and moved the tip of the knife to right below his eye. "If you don't tell me everything, I will pop your eye out of your socket and let it fall to the ground. You'll be able to see it with your good eye, your useless eyeball lying in the dirt."

"Please, Don D'Agostino," he whispered.

My patience evaporated and I held his head where I wanted, and I began to dig the tip of the knife into the side of his eye socket.

"Wait," he wailed and I paused. "The son," he said. "I met him in a club."

Stunned, I stepped back. "You met Giulio Ravazzani in a club?"

"He didn't use that name at the time, but yes."

Giulio Ravazzani left the mafia years ago to go live his gay life in Europe. No one had seen or heard of him since. And believe me, I'd tried to locate him. Now Andrea claimed he happened across Giulio in a club and befriended him? "Cazzata. I don't fucking believe you," I snarled, slamming the butt of the knife into his temple. "You're lying, you piece of shit."

Andrea swung on the hook for a bit, his body limp. Had I knocked him out? "Strip him down and pour ice water on him. If I have to cut off his balls to get answers, I will."

When we finally revived Andrea, he was naked and shivering. I ran the knife down his chest, a shallow cut that wasn't life-threatening but would sting like hell. "Now you had better tell the truth, cugino. Or I'm going to feed you your balls one at a time."

"I'm . . .not . . .lying." After several breaths he said, "It was a gay club."

"You're not gay," I snarled. "I've seen you with more pussy than Vito and Massimo combined."

"Hey!" Massimo frowned, offended. I ignored him.

"I like women but . . .sometimes I let men suck me off."

I looked at Vito for confirmation, but my brother just shrugged. I closed in on Andrea again. "Are you saying you fucked Ravazzani's son?"

"No. I take Bianca with me. She likes to watch strangers . . .suck my cock."

"None of this fucking matters," I said, slashing his chest again. "I don't care who you like to fuck. How did you betray me, Andrea? Spit it out before I slice you open."

"Someone took a video of me with a stranger. They were blackmailing me. I-I asked Giulio for help."

"Help with what?"

"The man who was blackmailing me. Giulio killed him."

Using my thumb, I pressed on Andrea's dislocated shoulder and listened to him howl for a few minutes. When he quieted enough, I said, "You didn't think to come to me, your cousin and capo?"

"Mi dispiace," he sobbed. "I didn't want anyone here to find out."

"Where was this?"

"Amsterdam."

Giulio Ravazzani, in Amsterdam? I filed that away for later. "What name was he using?"

"Gabriel Sánchez."

Spanish. Smart. Close enough to Italian to not draw attention.

Andrea continued to cry. "Please, I don't know anything more than that."

I pressed on his shoulder again, harder this time. When the screams died, I snarled in his ear, "I decide when we are done, pezzo di merda. Where did you meet him?"

"A cafe. Someplace near Sarphatipark."

"And in exchange for making your problem go away he asked for my whereabouts?"

"Please, Don D'Agostino. I had no choice—"

I didn't need to hear more. I sliced his throat in one clean motion, severing the arteries and letting him bleed out.

I instructed Pietro to finish with Andrea, then addressed my consigliere as I did the best to wipe my hands. "Get his electronics. I want them sent to Munich. See what the boys can find on them." Giulio would be too smart for that, but it was worth checking. "Then have them start looking for any trace of Gabriel Sánchez in Amsterdam."

"I will," Vito said with a nod. When I started to leave, he asked, "Where are you going?"

"To see the priest."

Vito's face expressed his unhappiness but he knew better than to try to stop me. "Go with him," he said to Massimo.

I strode to the back of the butcher shop and went out the door. It led to an alley where I could gain access to a side door into the church. I slipped inside, greeted by familiar stained glass and gleaming oak hundreds of years old.

The air immediately changed, growing still and stale. It was like time stopped here, the Catholic church so rooted in the past that everything modern had passed it by. I used to find it comforting, a place to quiet my mind. I didn't like religion, per se, but I enjoyed the routine of it, the relief of knowing what was to come. The D'Agostino family had helped build this church and I sent unholy amounts of money here every year even though I was no longer a regular visitor.

My shoes made no sound on the old marble floor. Massimo was loud, though, so no doubt Father Valerio knew of our presence. I hadn't been here in three years. I was past due.

Statues of saints stared down at me as I slipped into the confessional and closed the door, then I knelt, the worn wood digging into my knees. Penitent, I folded my hands and waited. Minutes later, I heard the other door close softly.

"Buongiorno, Lorenzo," Father Valerio greeted after he opened the screen. "It has been a long time."

"How is your arthritis?"

"Bene, grazie. Shall we begin?"

"Sì."

"*In nomine Patris et Filii et Spiritus Sancti,*" he said and we both made the sign of the cross. "Amen."

I bent my head. "Bless me, Father, for I have sinned. It has been three years and four months since my last confession." It had been right after learning of my wife's death. I came in the dead of night and roused Valerio from bed to hear my confession, needing to purge the guilt and sorrow from my heart. It hadn't worked.

"Our loving and merciful God is always ready to hear your sins, my son. Trust in his forgiveness."

"I killed a man twenty minutes ago."

Father Valerio cleared his throat delicately. But this wasn't the first murder I had confessed, nor would it be the last. He asked, "And are you remorseful, my son?"

I nearly laughed. "Let's get this done, Father, and I'll be on my way. And remember, you never saw me. If you tell anyone, your collar won't save you from my retribution."

I walked out a few seconds later, my soul saved.

CHAPTER NINE

Gia

As the afternoon crept on, I knew I had to get off this yacht. Enzo was unhinged. A freaking duvet had sent him over the edge. He wanted to keep me locked up, naked and cold, so he could humiliate and torture me. There was no telling what would happen if I stayed.

The boat had turned yesterday, with the sun appearing on the other side of the yacht. That meant we were headed back toward the Italian coast. Why?

No way had Enzo changed his mind about keeping me captive, so something else must have happened. Whatever the reason, I was grateful. Closer to Italy meant closer to help, closer to my sister and her powerful husband. If I could somehow get back on Italian soil, all I needed to do was whisper Fausto's name and I would gain sanctuary, instantly safe from whatever Enzo planned.

But it meant getting in the water.

I wasn't sure I could do it, but what choice did I have? I couldn't stay here. Maybe I could find a small kayak or raft somewhere onboard.

Chatting up Cecilia had gained me nothing, so I observed instead. I watched her habits and mannerisms, the patterns of her visits, looking for a weakness. Anything I could exploit to get free, even a single hairpin I could steal off her head.

Unfortunately, the woman was brisk and efficient. No loose hair pins or paper clips I could use to try to pick the lock on the cage. She kept a gun on me the entire time I was out of the cage and never left me alone, not even to go to the toilet.

And then I got my lucky break.

Late in the afternoon she took me to the bathroom when a knock sounded at the door. Cecilia glanced over her shoulder. "Stay here," she ordered and then disappeared.

Holy shit. I was alone.

I knew I didn't have long. There wasn't time to search for a weapon or prepare, so I did the only thing I could think of in that instant. I took the toilet paper roll off the wall, pulled the metal tube apart and yanked out the spring. I wasn't sure if I could hide it in my hand without her noticing. When I tried to compress it, the spring slipped from my grip and shot onto the floor.

I went rigid, then lunged for the tiny piece of metal. Panicking, I slipped it into my mouth. As long as she didn't suddenly decide she wanted to have a conversation with me, I should be okay.

My hands were shaking when I put the contraption back together, praying it held together long enough to fool Cecilia. Then I flushed and went to wash my hands.

Cecilia returned and looked me over. The metal spring hurt my gums but I kept quiet. I needed this to escape.

Predictably, Cecilia said nothing as she escorted me back to the cage. Once I was inside she placed a plate and three water bottles on the ground, then secured the lock. As soon as she left the room, I coughed into my hand for the cameras and covertly took the spring from my mouth. I put it under my thigh for the moment, just in case someone was watching me.

I hadn't picked a lock in years. Hoping to discover something scandalous like my father's cash or drugs, I learned how to pick locks as a teen, but I only found boxes of boring paperwork and old furniture. Talk about disappointment.

I finished my dinner and drank all the water. When I escaped I would need my strength. My fear of the ocean and inability to swim meant I had to find a life preserver or floatation device before I could kick to shore. God only knew how long that would take, but I had to be ready.

The minutes crept on. Cecilia returned to remove the empty plastic plate and give me more water. I decided to wait for everyone on board to go to bed.

When all was quiet I hunched over, keeping my back to the camera, and began working on the spring. I needed the metal as straight as possible to work the lock open. Then I broke the metal in half. It was difficult work but I only needed two small two pieces. As casually as I could, I bent one of the pieces to form a 90-degree angle. My fingers were sore and raw by the time I finished, but I did it. I now had a pick and tension tool.

The problem was the camera. Obscuring simple movements using my back was one thing; picking a lock was another. Vito said that only Enzo watched my security camera, but he couldn't watch it all night. The man had to sleep at some point. I would just have to risk it. What other choice was there?

Then I heard the faint sounds of bass. Laughter—*female* laughter. Holy shit. Were the D'Agostino boys having a pussy party up there?

My lips twisted into a grin. This was perfect. Hopefully Enzo had some girl sucking him off and wouldn't notice my escape until it was too late, the idiot.

I waited a little longer. I needed them drunk and distracted. Horny and naked and alone. So I listened and stretched, giving it as much time as I dared. Then I went to work.

The lock on the cage was the kind you might buy in a hardware store, but it was the same one my father had used on his liquor cabinet back in Toronto. It only took me a few minutes to remember how to manipulate the pins. Once I had them in place, I turned the tension tool and the lock popped open. Fuck yes!

I crept out of the cage as quietly as I could manage. I closed my eyes and focused on my breathing. I braced myself to be discovered at any moment, Enzo charging in like a bull and tossing me back in the cage.

No one came in.

As far as I could tell, Cecilia hadn't locked the cabin door when she left. They probably thought the lock on the cage would be enough to hold me. Or maybe this door didn't have a lock on the outside. I didn't know, but I prayed as I turned the knob.

It was open.

Holy shit. *Let's go, motherfuckers.*

Slowly I pushed the wood open, peeking to ensure the hallway was clear. No one was there, thank God.

Naked, I tiptoed down the hall and up the narrow stairs. I needed to find a raft without being seen or heard, and the best place to do that was probably the deck closest to the water. Unfortunately, from the noise, this was exactly where the party was taking place. It was too risky.

I went to the front of the yacht instead. There had to be something I could use to stay afloat, even if it was a life preserver. I skirted the galley, which was dark, and edged toward the bow. The layout of the yacht was not exactly like Fausto's larger craft, though it was every bit as nice. Gleaming wood and cream walls, everything neat and luxurious. Nothing but the best for kidnappers and murderers.

I slipped through a door and ended up in an empty office. Enzo's? There were two desks with computer monitors and a bar against one wall. A man's long-sleeved dress shirt was flung over the back of one of the chairs, so I grabbed it and put it on. The expensive fabric felt heavenly after being naked and cold for so long.

Next was a bedroom. Wow, this was fucking sweet. It had a wall of windows looking out over a deck—

Shit! I crouched down. There were people out on the deck.

Holding perfectly still, I listened, petrified of being discovered as I peeked at them. A young man, probably late twenties, was there, a naked woman on his lap. He bent, snorted white powder—I assumed coke—off her boobs. Classy. Another man was in the hot tub. It was Vito, and he was not alone. There were two women in there with him, one who was clearly riding his dick in the water and another sitting at his side, kissing him.

I didn't see Enzo.

This worried me. Maybe he was in one of the bedrooms, preferring privacy for his sexy times. That didn't really seem his style, but what did I know?

I had to get to the other end of the yacht. If I jumped over the side here, I would panic and drown. Already my heart was racing inside my chest, my breath shallow and fast, like I couldn't get enough air.

Calm down. You can do this.

Retracing my steps, I slipped outside, holding onto the railing with a death grip as I moved along the windows surrounding the empty dining area. Wind whipped through my hair and blew through the thin shirt I wore, and the music grew louder. The water glowed an eerie turquoise around the yacht's lights below the surface. Goosebumps broke out on the back of my neck when I contemplated what lurked in those depths, but I had to take my chances.

I wasn't going back to that cage.

I edged around to the stairs—and drew to a halt. Enzo. Fuck! He was sitting on the small sofa, facing me. Thankfully, his eyes were closed, his head thrown back while a woman was on her knees between his legs, her hands tied behind her back, giving him a blow job. It was the most relaxed I'd ever seen him, his face awash in pleasure. His fingers were fisted in the woman's hair as he guided her movements, showing her what he liked.

Deep and rough, from what I could tell.

Not even the loud music could drown out the woman's moans as she sucked him, really selling the porn-star vibe Enzo no doubt required of his lovers.

Maybe the sight of a woman on her knees, begging, gets me off.

I shouldn't be watching.

Except I couldn't look away.

Heat blasted my veins as I stood there, transfixed. I told myself it was just surprise and embarrassment, but I suspected it was something else. I imagined myself in her place, on my knees between his legs, forced to take his big dick down my throat and suck on him.

Shit. I really needed to get the hell out of here. There was only one thing I could do.

Before I could think better of it, I grabbed a cushion from a nearby chair, climbed over the rail, and dropped into the abyss.

Enzo

A tiny splash cut through the noise in my brain and my eyelids flew open.

I was glad for the interruption. My mind had unwittingly wandered to thoughts of my naked captive below deck during this blow job, wishing I could fuck her face instead.

I pulled Helene off my dick and stood. She didn't say anything or move, merely looked at me with big curious eyes. "*Attendez*," I barked in French as I tucked my cock back in my jeans and walked away.

When I reached the side, I instantly knew what happened. My muscles tightened with fury and surprise, the sight of those long limbs and dark hair in the water like a jolt of electricity to my heart. She was flailing, not really swimming, clinging to a cushion. Did she honestly believe she could reach landfall this way?

Then she lost her grip on the cushion and disappeared beneath the surface. It finally occurred to me.

She couldn't swim.

Cazzo! I didn't stop to think. I climbed up on the side and dove in. The water was cool, my jeans absorbing the moisture like a sponge to weigh me down. I kicked hard to the surface, found her head bobbing in the dim light, and began swimming her way.

When I looked up again, I couldn't find her. Minchia!

No, unacceptable. I wasn't going to let this one go so easily. It was too perfect, and I had come too far. I needed her alive to exact my revenge.

I pushed any other possible reasons far from my mind.

Where the fuck was she?

Then she appeared, her desperate gasp for air rippling across the water and turning my blood cold. I swam furiously, hurrying to reach her before she went under again. When I reached the spot where I last saw her, she had vanished. The saltwater stung my eyes as I swam down and the moonlight was no help. But then my fingertips brushed fine strands of hair.

I grabbed as hard as I could and pulled her toward me.

Once I had my arm around her waist I fought for the surface. We broke through and I sucked in air, Gia doing the same at my side.

She didn't fight as I swam us toward the back of the yacht. Once there, I wrapped her arms around the metal ladder. "Hold this," I shouted, then climbed onto the platform. Turning, I quickly dragged her up next to me, where she collapsed, her eyes squeezed tight. I panted and tried to catch my breath, watching her carefully as she began coughing.

"Why?" she rasped through her coughs. "Why did you save me?"

I slid a hand over my wet face and considered the question. The real answer was . . . murky. I wanted to say it was because she was a bargaining chip, one too valuable to lose. Except the truth probably had more to do with the woman herself and this unhealthy fascination that seemed to grow the more I was in her presence.

But I would never admit that.

"I told you. Revenge." I knelt and picked her up. Tears streamed down her face and she hung limp in my arms. Uncharacteristically, something in my chest turned over, some long-dead piece of me coming back to life in the face of her defeat.

I didn't want her defeated. I wanted her to fight and defy me.

None of this made sense, but I'd long since stopped trying to understand the way my post-dungeon brain worked. That place altered me, like it had rearranged my DNA—and I hadn't been exactly level-headed before that. Now I was a mess of a man.

But as I held a naked and shivering Gia against my chest and carried her up onto the yacht, I knew exactly where I was taking her.

Helene said nothing as I strode by and grabbed a blanket off the sofa. "Stay here," I told her and tucked the blanket around Gia as best I could without putting her down.

When I passed the bridge, a crew member appeared. His gaze

widened when he saw me, dripping wet and carrying Gia. "Don D'Agostino. Are you all right?"

"Have hot tea sent to my stateroom."

He nodded and disappeared. I continued toward the bow and went into my bedroom. Still carrying Gia, I went toward the hot tub out on my deck, where my brothers were partying with their women. "Get the fuck out of here." They stared at me as if they couldn't believe what they were seeing. "Go!" I shouted, not wanting to explain myself. "Go to the other end of the yacht."

Massimo gently moved the girl off his lap, setting her on the deck, then grabbed his booze and coke before leaving. Vito whispered to the women with him in the hot tub and they got out, put on their robes and disappeared. He scratched his jaw thoughtfully, watching me.

I didn't want to hear whatever my brother had to say.

Spinning on my heel, I strode to my bathroom and started the hot water in the shower. Gia shivered against my chest, even under the blanket, and I suspected the scare was the cause, not the cool plunge.

Vito had a towel wrapped around his waist by the time he appeared in the bathroom doorway. "Enzo—"

"I don't fucking want to hear it," I snapped. Gia started, though I doubt she understood the Italian. More like she was reacting to my tone. Softening my voice, I told Vito, "Later."

He sighed and closed the door, and I stepped into the shower fully clothed with Gia still in my arms. I held her in the spray and steam until she whispered, "Please put me down."

Carefully, I set her on her feet but didn't let her go. I held onto her waist, steadying her, while trying not to watch the way the water droplets cascaded over her lithe frame, sliding over the plump mounds of her ass and down her long legs.

"Stop checking out my ass." She leaned against the tile, burying her face in her arms, hiding from me. "God, please. Just leave me alone."

Her shoulders shook and I suspected more tears were the cause. In a flash I stripped off my wet clothes and tossed them on the floor of the bathroom. I grabbed the shampoo and poured a liberal amount on her head, then began working it through the long strands of hair.

"What are you doing?" she asked over her shoulder.

Wasn't it obvious? "Washing your hair."

"I mean why are you being so nice to me?"

I wasn't sure. If I were smart, I would toss her back in that cell, triple lock it, and throw away the key. But I couldn't do that to her, at least not right now.

I massaged her scalp, working the shampoo into a lather, and she moaned. The sound went straight to my dick, making my already full balls even heavier. Instead, I tried to focus on her hair, gently rinsing her under the spray. "Can you swim?"

Suspicious red-rimmed eyes flicked to mine, like she was assessing whether to be truthful or not. "No. I almost drowned when I was eight. After that I never went in again."

"Cristo! What were you thinking, jumping into the water like that?"

A spark lit her gaze, one I was familiar with. "Oh, I don't know. Maybe that I wanted to escape my *cage* by any means necessary, even if it means dying."

Shaking my head, I reached for the conditioner. She stood there, unmoving, letting me tend to her. "You don't mean that."

"Yes, I fucking do!" She shoved at my bare chest. "Get the fuck out of here, Enzo."

I waited for the bile to fill my throat at the contact, but it didn't. Che cazzo?

She turned away from me. "Please, I am begging you. For the love of God, just leave me alone for five minutes."

I studied her back, a strange disappointment settling between my shoulder blades. Should I stay? Something told me not to leave, but I couldn't think straight with her naked and wet, standing just inches away from me.

Unsure, I rinsed off and slipped from the shower, then wrapped a towel around my waist and left the bathroom. I pulled on a pair of athletic shorts, but didn't bother with a shirt. The tea arrived, so I had them set the tray down on the bed. Then I grabbed my phone and texted Vito to discover exactly how my captive had escaped. I wanted answers.

I couldn't put her back in the cage, not until I knew it would hold her.

But was I really keeping her here? With me?

A woman hadn't slept in my bed since Mariella and my wife. What if I had a nightmare? It was too great a risk. No, I would restrain Gia and then sleep in my office downstairs.

I thought about her naked body in my bed, her scent on my sheets, and I could feel myself growing thick again. She was feisty, unpredictable. Taming her would be a challenge, one I would enjoy immensely. She would be an incredible fuck. I was nearly salivating for it.

Snarling, I tugged at my hair. What the fuck was I doing? Ordering her tea? Helping her shower? She'd tried to fucking escape me! I should be spanking her ass raw then chaining her to the wall in her makeshift dungeon. I was pathetic, panting after that girl's pussy.

You must be strong, Lorenzo. Stronger than everyone else.

My father's words still rang in my ears all these years later. He would be furious if he saw me thinking about this girl—my enemy. This had to stop.

I got up and moved the tea tray into the hallway. Then I found a pair of handcuffs and sat on the bed to wait.

CHAPTER TEN

Gia

Tears were a waste of time.

Logically, I knew this. Except the shock of almost drowning combined with Enzo's unexpected tenderness after rescuing me—not to mention losing my best chance at escape—was too much to bear.

My tears mixed with the water as I stood there and wondered what was going to happen now. Would he put me back in the cage? There were chains on the wall in that room, too. Maybe he'd use those this time.

Whatever he decided I knew Enzo would not allow me another opportunity to get free.

I was stuck on this yacht, at his mercy.

Exhaling, I closed my eyes and tried to gather my strength. I let the hot water soak into my muscles as I pushed aside the horror of almost drowning once again. God, why had I jumped in so recklessly?

Emma would be furious with me for almost dying. *Stay safe, Gigi.*

I'm sorry, Em. I'll do better.

Okay, fine. So Enzo would treat me like dirt until I could figure something out.

Maybe I should try seducing him. I'd considered it before, the night he fed me on my knees. It probably wouldn't take much encouragement to actually succeed . . .but at what price? What piece of my soul was I trading away to sleep with my family's enemy?

In the end it didn't matter, because I didn't have another play. Enzo would feel no pity, no remorse over any violence he inflicted on me. I wasn't sure what his endgame was, but it didn't seem like he was interested in getting any kind of ransom, either. He just wanted to make me suffer.

The door to the bathroom bounced open and I started. What the hell?

A shirtless Enzo stormed in, his face like a thundercloud. He opened the shower door and turned off the water. "Get out."

"What are you doing? I wasn't finished—" He grabbed my arm and tugged me out of the shower. I dripped all over the tile floor, my feet slipping. "Hey! Let me go, you neanderthal."

He ignored me.

I tried to dig in my wet heels as he dragged me out of the bathroom, but he was bigger and stronger. We entered the bedroom and he tossed me onto the bed like I weighed nothing at all. His eyes were . . .scary wild. Fear shot through me and instinct had me scrambling to get away, but he was quicker. He clutched my ankle and pulled me back, then arranged me so my head was on the pillow.

What was he planning? The vicious look on his face said it wasn't movies and popcorn in bed. "Let me go. Stop manhandling me!"

"Stop squirming. You are staying here."

Here, with him? Was he serious?

While I grappled with the shock of that statement, something metal closed around one of my wrists and I realized what was happening. He was handcuffing me to his bed, goddamn it! "Quit it!" I struggled, but it was too late. I was restrained.

He laughed as my foot connected with his hip. "Keep scratching, micina. I like it."

"I bet you do, you psychopath." I twisted and turned, but the metal just dug into my flesh, making me wince. Enzo dropped down on the bed, his hands pressing on my thighs so I couldn't move.

He loomed over me, this big Italian mobster, and my eyes dragged over his torso. I hated to admit it, but his body was fucking impressive. Olive skin, scarred and rough, pulled taut over bulging muscles, making him look like some violent warrior of old. The perfect amount of wiry dark hair dotted his chest, and his abdomen was a mountain range of ridges and bumps. Wow.

I didn't know what to make of this confusing man. He'd been so gentle with me, carrying me to the shower and washing my hair. Now he was shackling me to his bed. Did he hate me or want to care for me? And why hadn't he let me drown?

His lips twisted cruelly and his gaze glittered. "I like you like this. Helpless and at my mercy. Maybe I should restrain both of your hands."

"Don't you dare, asshole."

"Hmm. Would you prefer to go back to your cage instead?"

"Yes," I lied as I struggled to catch my breath.

"I don't believe you—and it doesn't matter. I like you here, tied to my bed. My sheets will smell like your pussy." His stare slowly swept over my naked body and goose bumps raced along my skin.

"Is this where you sexually assault me?" God, why had I asked that? Now he would be thinking about it.

"I'm not going to touch you."

"Your crazy eyes and the bulge in your shorts say otherwise." Both were impossible to miss.

"You interrupted my blow job tonight. I was just remembering Helene's mouth and how good it felt wrapped around my cock."

"Liar. You were in the cold water, so this isn't left over from your friend-for-hire up there."

"That *friend-for-hire* is a French actress."

I rolled my eyes. "She must be to make you believe she actually enjoyed slurping on your dick."

A startled sound escaped his throat. "Madre di Dio. Your mouth is nothing but trouble."

If seduction was the only path left, now was my chance. I had to take this opening.

I gave him what I hoped was a naughty smirk. "Well, I've been told my mouth is good for some things."

He froze, brows lowered like he was trying to decipher my flirtatious comment. Wind whipped along the windows as the yacht gently rocked in the water, but neither of us spoke. *Come on. You know you want me, Enzo.* I just needed him to uncuff me. Then I could work my magic on him. Soon he'd be under my spell and I could find some way to escape.

Instead of freeing me, he pushed off the bed and stood. "Don't worry. You will beg for my dick before it is all over, Gianna."

I forced a heavy dose of bravado into my voice and said, "More like you'll be begging, *Lorenzo*."

He leaned down and pressed on my forearms to keep me still as his mouth met the shell of my ear. "Game fucking on, micina."

The seductive words were like a narcotic to my system, causing my muscles to tighten and my blood to sing. My core clenched, and I honestly wondered if I'd just made a grave mistake. Now he would see this as some kind of a challenge.

It shouldn't be difficult to best him. Pretty sure I could retain the upper hand and make him want me more than I wanted him. How hard could it be when his dick reacted like this during our brief interactions. He wanted me so bad.

Poor mobster. I was going to destroy him.

Then he strode away from the bed, toward the door, and I watched his back muscles shift as he moved. Damn, he was ripped. Was there a gym on this yacht?

Focus, Gia.

I drew in a deep breath. I had a battle ahead of me and this was no time for distractions.

―――

Enzo

I woke up alone, in my office.

I kept my distance from her last night. I had desperately wanted to stay with her, which was dangerous, so I had forced myself to leave. This gave me a small amount of peace.

Rolling over, I stared at the ceiling. Cazzo, she was the hottest woman I'd ever met, but it was her feisty attitude that really turned me on. No woman had ever spoken to me the way she did, cursing at me one minute then flirting the next.

I've been told my mouth is good for some things.

Blood surged along my length, hardening me, and I palmed my dick, willing it to stop. I needed to remain in control, get a grip on this raging desire I felt for her. I ached to kiss her, to take her mouth and shove my tongue past her lips. I wanted to taste that stubbornness and backbone, break her down bit by bit until she was pliant in my arms.

It was a nice fantasy. And wouldn't that be the ultimate revenge against Ravazzani, to turn his sister-in-law into my willing fuck toy? I would have her every way possible, convince her to like it, until she was completely and utterly mine.

Then I would show my new pet off to the entire world. Fausto would lose his mind.

The idea of it took root and blossomed in my mind, and I began to plot the moves required to turn my plan into a reality. I didn't think it would be difficult. She eye-fucked me last night when I held her down on the bed, her nipples forming tight points. She obviously wasn't repulsed by my body. I would start there.

The door opened and Vito strolled in, a demitasse cup in his hand. He looked annoyingly refreshed, like he'd fucked away all of his stress last night. I sat up slowly and ran a hand through my hair. "What time is it?"

"Just before seven. Here." He handed me the cup. "I figured you could use it."

My brother knew I hardly slept any more. He encouraged me to use sleeping pills, saying I needed the sleep, but I resisted drugs. My mother had overdosed on pills to escape my father after enduring years of his cruelty. I hadn't blamed her.

No, it was preferable to stay awake until I exhausted myself, then catch one or two hours of fitful sleep. Anything more and my dreams became full of helpless pain and agony.

The result left me exhausted but not tired, a description that only those with chronic insomnia could truly understand. It was a bone-deep weariness, like my mind was dragging through mud. Still, it was better than reliving what happened in Ravazzani's dungeon night after night.

I grunted my thanks as I accepted the cup and downed the burning hot liquid in two swallows. "The girls are gone?"

"Yes, as of two hours ago. Massimo is still passed out below. How is your captive? Alive, I take it."

"Yes, she is alive."

"What happened last night?"

"It is obvious, no?" I set the empty cup on the table. "She jumped."

"And you saved her instead of letting her drown?"

"She is too valuable to lose, not yet."

"Too valuable—or too fuckable?"

"Maybe they are one in the same."

"Have you fucked her yet?"

Leaning back on the sofa, I frowned at him. "Why do you care? Hoping it's your turn?"

He took his time in answering, his lips thin with anger. "Because you're obsessed with her, fratello, and I don't like it."

"You don't have to like it. You only need to do what I say. How did she escape, by the way?"

"She picked the lock. Cecilia must have left her alone in the bathroom because the spring in the toilet paper roll was missing. No doubt that's what she used."

She knew how to pick locks? Clever micina.

"This is not amusing, *testa di cazzo*," Vito snapped, jabbing a finger in my direction.

"I am not amused," I snarled. "And do not push me, stronzo. I will decide Gia Mancini's fate, no one else. Do not try to interfere again." I gestured to his face. "Or I will do worse to you."

Vito ran his hand over his jaw as he stared at the wall. Quietly, he said, "She is changing you. Distracting you."

"Distracting me? From what? A blow job?" I lowered my voice and met his gaze. "I know what I am doing, and my plan will bring Ravazzani to his knees, te lo prometto. Trust me."

Whatever he saw in my eyes caused my brother to nod, his shoulders relaxing. "Fine. Will you tell me what you're planning?"

I normally confided in my consigliere, so I don't know why I suddenly had the urge to keep this from him. Because it was her?

The reason didn't matter. I didn't wish to discuss Gia any longer, so I switched topics. "Any news from Amsterdam? Have they found Giulio Ravazzani?"

"As of last night they were still digging. Gabriel Sánchez is a common name."

I got up and went to my laptop. "I want to send Alessio to Amsterdam."

"You want to put a hit out on Giulio."

"Yes, and Alessio owes me after fucking up on that job in Siderno."

Alessandro Ricci was the best sniper in Europe. Trained by the Italian military, Alessio became an assassin for hire and was used by everyone, including government agencies. I'd paid him to kill Fausto Ravazzani four years ago, a job he failed to complete. Only I knew that he'd been the one to take the shot at Ravazzani, and I planned to use that information to get what I wanted out of Alessio. Which was to kill Giulio Ravazzani.

Vito nodded once. "As soon as we have Giulio's location, I'll have Alessio on a plane."

"Good." I would attack Ravazzani from all sides. His son, his sister-in-law. His drug trade. Anything I could destroy, I would. He would be nothing when I finished with him.

I sent Vito for more caffè then tried working, but I couldn't concentrate on my laptop. Worse, my eyes kept drifting to the security camera application. Only I had access to the cameras in my bedroom, and the temptation to watch her gnawed at me.

Was she asleep?

The idea of her curled up in my bed had me opening the camera feed before I could stop myself. I needed to see what she looked like while she slept, relaxed and unguarded. The image loaded and I could see her, laying on her side with one arm locked above her head, hair spread out over the pillows.

I could go in there and do anything I wanted to her right now. The violent part of my brain told me to wrap my hands around her throat and strangle her. The other part urged me to slide in behind her, lift her leg, and feed my dick into her pussy. Make her moan and scream my name.

Dio, I liked that idea.

But I wouldn't do it. This was about breaking her down, making her beg, willing to do whatever I wanted. I had to remain patient. The end result would be worth it.

Without second guessing my decision, I closed the security feed and my laptop, then left the office. I made my way below and directly into my quarters.

The sight of her in person was so much better than on the computer. Gia's eyes were closed, long lashes resting against her cheeks, with her breathing even and steady, soft and trusting. *Mozzafiato*. Why was she so goddamn beautiful?

I stretched out on the bed beside her but didn't touch her. Then I folded my hands behind my head and waited. Morning light now flooded the room and I doubted she would sleep much longer.

Ever so slowly she moved toward me. First her feet rubbed against my legs, her toes seeking. Cazzo, her skin was so soft. I took deep breaths, waiting for the panic to set in at another's touch, but nothing.

I didn't understand it. Was it because she was asleep? No, because she'd touched me in the shower, as well.

A minute later she shifted back to press against my side, her ass nestled into my hip and blood rushed to my cock. She smelled like my body wash, a hint of thyme and almonds. I couldn't help but roll toward her, let my fat length wedge between those plump cheeks. Cristo santo, her ass was perfection.

She would beg for my cock to fill that tight hole.

I knew the instant she came awake. Her breath changed and her muscles tightened ever so slightly.

"Buongiorno, mia prigioniera." *My prisoner.*

She stiffened. "What are you doing?"

"I was just lying here when you cuddled up against me. Rubbing up on me like a kitty cat."

"Bullshit. I would never."

"Should I show you the security tape to prove it?"

"You are *filming* this?" Her head tilted as she tried to spot the camera.

"There are cameras everywhere on this boat, micina." I dragged my hand over her thigh. "But don't worry. Only I have access to the cameras in my stateroom."

"Were you watching me last night?"

I hadn't been, not last night, but she didn't need to know that. "Yes."

"You're a sick fuck, Enzo."

I knew this to be true. "I bet you like the idea of me watching you. You certainly put on a show for cameras when you were in that cage."

She tried to edge away from me and I let her. She wouldn't go far, not with her wrist still shackled to my headboard.

"I need to use the bathroom."

Reaching into the pocket of my shorts, I withdrew the tiny metal key and unlocked her single cuff. She didn't waste any time, hurrying from the bed like it was on fire. Her bladder, or was she running scared?

Minutes later I heard the shower turn on. I rose from the bed and started for the bathroom. It was time for the games to begin.

She was already in the water when I came in. Her head snapped toward me as I pushed off my shorts. "What are you doing?"

"Showering."

"Not with me. Get out."

I pulled open the glass door and went in. She backed away, careful not to touch me, as I moved toward the spray. Closing my eyes, I let the water rain down on me, slicking my skin, and I could feel her gaze taking it in. I knew I was in good shape. Some nights I worked out for two or three hours in the yacht's gym. My dick was already half hard, hanging thickly between my legs.

Without saying anything, I reached for the soap and squirted some in my hands. I used it on my body, washing my arms and chest, and she didn't even pretend not to watch. Her attention remained riveted on my hands, so I slowed as I cleaned my stomach, dragging the lather over every ridge of muscle, waiting for her to look away. Except she didn't.

"Like what you see?" I asked.

A flush crept over her neck, her chest rising and falling, but she gave me a sneer. "Don't be ridiculous. I don't want you—or that monster."

I was fully hard now, the length pointed directly at her. I gave myself a soapy stroke. "*Non sei curioso?*"

"Curious? About your dick?" She took the body wash and began cleaning her arms and shoulders, moving with unnecessary efficiency. "I know how a dick works, Enzo."

"You aren't a virgin?"

"If you're hoping to ruin me by popping my cherry, you're wasting your time. I haven't been a virgin for a long, long time."

Then she slid her hands to her breasts and I watched the tiny bubbles caress her olive skin and catch on the hard points of her nipples. Mamma mia, I wanted to lick and bite her, clean her with my tongue. Before I even knew it, my hand was back on my cock, squeezing.

When her soapy hand edged between her legs, that piercing winked up at me, taunting me. She cleaned her folds with her fingers, rubbing all over, and I couldn't stand it any longer. I blurted, "I have a proposition for you."

"Let me guess? You want to fuck me. Do you really think I'm that easy?"

No, but I was positive I could seduce her into cooperating. Except I didn't want one time. I wanted her greedy for my dick non-stop, begging for it. "It has nothing to do with fucking. It has to do with whether you go back in your cage or not."

I knew this would entice her. She cocked a brow then shoved past me to rinse in the spray. The water slipped over her skin and my tongue rubbed against the back of my teeth, the need for her strangling my lungs.

"What would I have to do?" she asked.

My voice was husky with desire as I said, "Make yourself come and let me watch."

CHAPTER ELEVEN

Gia

Was he serious? "You want to watch me masturbate?"

"Sì." Now he was stroking his dick, the muscles in his arm flexing as he pumped that giant rod between his legs. God, he had a gorgeous cock and I felt an answering tug in my lower half.

I was already wet—I felt the slick moisture between my legs a few seconds ago—but I hadn't let anyone watch me buff my muffin before. It was intimate, a private time for me and my fantasies, with no real men allowed. Only fake ones. The idea of someone observing it made me feel vulnerable, exposed. Like my layers were stripped away, removing any protection and leaving my most basic, non-bitchy self.

"Why?" I asked, still mesmerized by his jacking off.

"For the same reason you are watching me do this. It is sexy, no?"

I wasn't sure I could do it, but I really didn't want to go back in that cage either. "I need to understand exactly what you're offering. I make myself come with no help whatsoever from you and you won't put me back in the cage? Or chain me to the wall? Or cuff my hands to your bed."

"Sì. Te lo prometto."

There had to be a catch. This was too good to be true. "Where will you put me?"

"In a room with a bed."

"And a bathroom?"

"And a bathroom."

After the past twenty-four hours that sounded like a swanky hotel. And my plan had been to seduce him. I just hadn't expected it to be this easy. I would be leading him around by his dick in no time.

Stupid Italian mafioso. My days of being his prisoner were numbered.

"Okay." Hiding my smirk, I reached for the shower door handle. "Let's go."

"No." He held my arm, keeping me in the shower. "Right here."

The shower was on the small side, his large bulk taking up most of the room. I would feel more comfortable on a bed with Enzo standing far, far away, but I sensed from the wild look in his eyes that idea wouldn't fly. "Switch places with me, then."

We passed one another and I let my ass brush his thigh. I heard him suck in a breath and had to smother a laugh. *Ha, ha.* He had no idea who he was up against, did he?

Enzo said nothing, just moved into the spray as I went to the opposite end of the shower. His jaw was taut as he observed me, his hand now back on his cock, stroking. "Now, micina," he whispered, his sigh like a wisp of steam in the air. "Let me see you work your clit."

"Stop talking." I closed my eyes and tried to shut him out as I slid my hands between my legs. "I need to pretend like you aren't here."

"Cazzata. You like watching me work my cock. Open your eyes."

"No," I said stubbornly.

"Do it, or the deal is off."

My eyelids flew open and I glared at him. "Asshole." I pinned my stare on his junk and tried not to think about who it was attached to.

My pussy was swollen, slick. Primed for sex. I flicked the piercing, teasing myself, and I heard Enzo growl in his throat. I began circling with my fingers, the jewelry digging into the pads of my fingers. My clit throbbed, peeking out from behind its hood, and I rubbed as I watched his fist squeeze the head of his cock. A bead of moisture appeared on the tip and he used his thumb to smear it all over the head. I inadvertently licked my lips, wondering about his taste, and waves of heat rolled through my limbs, settling in my core.

"*Toccati*," he murmured. "*Apri le gambe.*"

"In English, stronzo."

"Touch yourself and open your legs, *troietta*."

Little slut.

God, I wanted to hate him for that, but a blast of heat tore through me. "Jesus," I whispered as I widened my legs slightly. "You're such a dick."

"Hmm. Do you like to be called names, Gianna?" He let go of his cock and placed his hands on either side of the shower, displaying himself for me. "Do you like your hair pulled? Do you like to wear a man's come on your face?"

Shit, when he asked those things in his low Italian-accented voice, it sounded like pure sex. No doubt Enzo fucked like a beast, rough and dirty. I hadn't experienced that yet. The men I had been with treated me politely, like I was made of glass. My five month relationship with Grayson had been the longest, and most of the time I'd finished myself off in the bathroom afterward. I once asked him to spank me and he said he didn't want to degrade me that way.

Something told me Enzo would not have a problem fulfilling that request.

Except I didn't plan to let him have the upper hand. "Is that what you like to do to women in bed, Don D'Agostino?"

Ignoring my question, he stared at my hand between my legs. "I wish you were sitting on my face right now. I would lick you and bite you, suck on your clit until you passed out. I want to pull on your piercing with my teeth until it stings, then make you come so hard you squirt all over me."

Jesus, fuck.

My fingers moved faster, my pleasure climbing, expanding. I stared at his wide cock, which jutted out proudly from his body, bobbing in the steam, with its smooth skin and veins along the side. The head was flushed and round, dripping with pearly liquid. I imagined that thickness drilling inside me, splitting me in half and filling me up, more than I'd ever felt before. My pussy clenched around the emptiness and I moaned.

"Use your fingers inside your pussy," he said. "Imagine it is me."

It was like he could see my thoughts. I screwed two fingers inside my channel, craving that burn as I first stretched, and I pumped until the digits were fully inside. I panted, my eyelids so heavy they were now slits.

"You like that, no?" he purred. "Tell me, micina."

"I like it."

"Do you wish that was my cock?"

I licked my lips as I stared at his erection, too turned on to lie. "Yes."

He grabbed himself again, strong fingers wrapping around the shaft as he pulled. "I would fuck you so good, *sporca puttana*. Deep and hard. I would give you all my come, everything I am saving up in my balls just for you."

"God, don't you ever shut up?" I wheezed as I started stroking my clit again. My legs were shaking, my movements uncoordinated because I was so turned on. So close. So *needy*.

"And you'll take it, no?" he continued, clearly not caring that this was a one-sided conversation. "I have never seen a woman so hungry for it. Didn't those boys in Canada know how to fuck you? I bet they left you unsatisfied."

Get out of my head, mafioso.

I kept going, the orgasm so close I could practically taste it. *Yes, yes, yes.* I knew this was going to be good.

"Stop."

The word cracked off the small enclosure like a whip. Without meaning to, I obeyed him, my hand stilling. Then I realized what I was doing, playing his game. Fuck this. I wanted an orgasm, so I kept rubbing. "No way. I'm too close."

The lines of his face hardened, his muscles swelling, and the look in his eyes was almost maniacal. "Stop or our deal is off."

Somehow I forced my hand onto my thigh. "You're an asshole."

He reached to shut the water off, then kept lazily tugging on his shaft. "Get on your knees."

Shit. I should've known he wouldn't let me get off easily. "Why?"

"Because I fucking said so."

I didn't look away. Was this a humiliation game? This man was unpredictable and evil. I should be trembling in fear.

I was trembling, but it wasn't because I was scared.

What was he going to do? I had no idea.

Which meant I had to find out.

Slowly, I bent my knees and sank to the damp tile, my legs spread obscenely, putting everything on display. My engorged clit pulsed, my pussy no doubt swollen and flushed, and he took it in, mouth going slack as his hand moved faster along his cock. Oh, he liked this. His chest heaved, breath sawing out of his lungs. "Beg me," he said in a low rumble. "Beg me to let you come."

I could play this his way . . .or he could play it mine. Of the two of us, I was certain I could last longer without an orgasm.

Hands resting on my thighs, I began crooning, "Can you see how wet I am, Don D'Agostino? Can you see how turned on I am by watching you jerk that big cock of yours? I bet you have to use lube when you fuck, you're so big. Do the women scream when you're pounding inside them? Do you make them bleed, leave their pussies raw?"

His hand flew, pumping harder, squeezing, his breath stuttering. "Minchia!" he hissed. "That fucking mouth."

"You'd like to fill it, wouldn't you, Don D'Agostino?" He grunted and I knew I'd guessed right. "See my lips stretched wide as you shoved down my throat, so deep it would bring tears to my eyes. Would you make me drink your come, swallow it down until my belly was overflowing—"

"Cazzo!" he shouted to the ceiling as he threw his head back. Thick ropes of come erupted from the tip of his cock, his big body convulsing, shuddering, while his face slackened in pure pleasure. With his expression free of his usual evil cynicism, he was so much more handsome. Without realizing it, I moved my fingers to circle my clit again as I watched this dangerous but fallible man fall apart.

It was beautiful.

When his eyelids shot open he narrowed his dark gaze on me. In two steps he had his hand wrapped around my arm, roughly pulling me to my feet. "Hey!" I said, trying to get away as he tugged me out of the shower. "I played along. Now it's my turn."

"You didn't play along—and now you will suffer for it."

Once again he was towing me, wet, out to the bedroom. Would I ever get a chance to towel dry on this fucking yacht? "Will you stop dragging me around? It's getting old."

"What is also *getting old* is the way you disobey me. You will be punished now."

I didn't care for the idea of Enzo's "punishments." He'd tied Frankie up and shoved a gun in her mouth, after all.

He threw me onto the bed, then followed to pin me down with his body. "Get off me, mafioso! You're too heavy." I couldn't see what he was doing but it was something at the head of the mattress. Strong fingers grabbed my hand and tugged until my arm straightened, then I felt a large strap around my wrist. Shit! "You promised you wouldn't cuff me again."

"I am not cuffing you. I am strapping you down."

"That is the same thing, motherfucker."

I began struggling at that point, trying to fight him with everything I had. I didn't want to be at his mercy. He was supposed to be at mine! I called him every curse word I knew as he reached toward the other side and fished out another strap. Fucking BDSM equipment. In any other circumstance I'd be jumping for joy, ready to play.

Instead, I was fantasizing about strangling him with the strap.

By the time I was bound with my arms stretched out over my head, we were both breathing hard. I continued to struggle, so he pinned my legs down with his torso.

Eyes shining in triumph, he slid open my thighs. "Look at this poor pussy. *Sei bagnata*. So wet." Using his middle finger, he flicked the piercing once. I gasped, the shockwaves reverberating through my clit, my belly, all the way to my toes.

"Goddamn it," I spat, hating him for turning me on. Again.

"Beg me." Another flick. The light touch was like a hot poker in my veins and I moaned.

Then I clenched my teeth, fighting my body's reaction. This was not how it was supposed to go. I should be driving him wild, making him pant for *me*.

"It would feel so good, no? My tongue on your clit, licking you. Those boys you were with, did they know how to eat your pussy? I bet they had no idea."

Jesus, his voice.

Then he began whispering in Italian, which I didn't understand, but the sounds were sexy as fuck. I caught the words for *face* and *mouth*, and I could guess he was talking about eating me out. I didn't want to tell him he was right, that I'd never come from oral before. Grayson had done it a few times when I asked, but he didn't seem all that into it so I stopped asking. Enzo seemed really, really into it, if his expression was anything to go by.

I felt myself slipping under his spell, wanting to beg, if only to experience it just once. I was curious about this so-called cataclysmic orgasm that resulted from getting head that women talked about when men weren't around. My body thrummed with arousal, with every beat of my heart like a drumbeat between my legs. My hips bucked toward his face.

"That's it," he switched to English. "You want it so badly, mia sporca puttana. Say it. 'Ti prego, Don D'Agostino.'"

This was happening all wrong. "Wouldn't you rather let me suck on your cock?" I tried.

Chucking softly, he blew on my clit and my back arched, the hot air a painful caress on my hypersensitive flesh. I stared at the ceiling and tried to breathe. Tried to calm my racing heart. "Here," he said, "I will help you. Repeat it. *Voglio la tua testa fra le gambe.*"

I knew *voglio* was "I want" and *gambe* meant "legs." I could fill in the rest based on our position. "I'd rather die than beg you for anything."

He pushed up off the bed using his arms, then stood there and shook his head. "We will see if you truly mean that, no?"

Turning, he started walking toward the open closet on the other side of the room. I strained unsuccessfully to pull free of the straps as he disappeared inside. "Wait, where are you going? You have to let me go."

He was in tight boxer briefs when he emerged, a pair of jeans in his hands. "I am going to work for a few hours. Do not worry, I'll be back." He stepped into the jeans, his muscles popping and shifting as he dressed.

"Don't you dare leave me here, you asshole." I was a mess, throbbing and wet. The smell of sex—of me—hung heavily in the air. I needed my hands free to find relief.

"Are you ready to beg?"

"No," I shouted. "Did your time in the dungeon make you hard of hearing?"

"Mentioning the dungeon is unwise, Gianna." Scowling, he went into the closet again.

I couldn't resist needling him. "Why? Don't like to be reminded of when you were treated like this?"

"Because it reminds me of how much I want revenge on your brother-in-law—and *you* are that instrument of revenge."

When he returned he'd already pulled on a t-shirt, but it was the expensive kind. With his designer jeans, expensive watch, and wet messy hair, he looked like a cover model. I'd seen enough of them in Milan while working for Domenico. Enzo could grace the cover of any men's magazine.

But it was the confidence in his shoulders, the hard scrape of his jaw, that set him apart as someone dangerous. Someone ruthless. This was no pampered gym rat; this was a cold-blooded murderer.

A murderer that I desperately wanted to fuck me.

God, what was wrong with me?

"I want to go back to the cage," I tried. At least there I would have the use of my hands and I wouldn't smell him all around me.

"No." He walked over and stood on the side of the bed closest to me. One fingertip reached to slowly trace the tight point of my nipple. I tried to twist away, denying myself the pleasure, but only managed to hurt my wrists. He chuckled, the bastard. "I think I will keep you right here, waiting and ready for me. *A presto*, micina."

Was he for real? My body felt like a wire, taut and on the edge. Before I could incinerate him with my eyes, he turned and strode to the door. My jaw fell open. Was he actually going to leave me like this? "Don't you dare go, D'Agostino! I swear to fucking God, I will stab you the first chance I get if you walk out of here!"

"I hope you do," he called over his shoulder. "The sight of blood gets me hard."

CHAPTER TWELVE

Enzo

Drink nestled in my palm, I leaned on the railing and watched as the yacht cut through the blue water. We were headed southwest, away from Cannes and toward open water. I thought about Gia, shackled to my bed, her pussy weeping and swollen, and all I could focus on was shoving my cock in that tight wet hole.

No one would blame me for taking her. Considering my history with Ravazzani, they probably expected it. But I would not rush this. It would be far more satisfying if she were willing.

I needed to break her down, win her over until she would do anything I asked—suck me, fuck me, beg me. I wanted her mind, not her body. She would be my little toy, my little pet. Just thinking of Gianna that willing, that subservient, made my balls ache. Ravazzani would hate watching his sister-in-law debase herself for me, which was what I looked forward to most.

I sipped my drink and tried to clear my mind as the wind whipped through my hair. I didn't like my reaction to her. She should be scared of me, terrified of what I might do to her, yet she fought and cursed me every chance she got. No woman had ever acted this way with me. They knew my job, my reputation. They always did what I said, no questions asked. Yet Gia continued to push me, needle me.

Didn't she realize the danger in winding me up?

Rules and boundaries meant nothing to me, and since escaping the dungeon I wouldn't even know how to obey any. I teetered on the edge of sanity at all times. My only goals were to protect my family and get revenge on Ravazzani by any means necessary. I didn't care about Gia's feelings or her comfort.

Can you see how turned on I am by watching you jerk that big cock of yours?

She had looked so perfect, on her knees at my feet. Exactly where she belonged. I would make her pay for wringing my come from my balls too soon.

The door slid open behind me and my brothers emerged on the deck. Massimo looked disheveled and hungover, like Vito had just dragged him out of bed.

"Drinking already?" Vito asked as they both leaned against the rail next to me.

"Don't let me smell it," Massimo said, turning his head away. "Or I'll puke over the railing."

I glared at my youngest brother. "You need to stop drinking and using so much."

"Says the man having a drink at ten o'clock in the morning."

"I can do whatever the fuck I want," I snapped. "It is not the same for you. Alcoholics and junkies get sloppy. When you get sloppy, you die."

"Ma dai, Enzo. I am allowed to party every now and then. "

"Define now and then. From what I see it's every day."

Massimo shoved off from the railing and turned. "I'm going back to bed before I throw up."

When Vito and I were alone, he said, "Try not to be too hard on him. He's bored and missing his old life."

"I don't give a fuck what he misses. You think I don't miss Luca and Nicola? Our sister? My home? I'm trying to keep us all alive."

Vito held up his hands. "I know that, but he's young. You

remember what you were like at that age. It's all about proving yourself and pussy."

It hadn't been like that for me. I was still under my father's thumb while he forged me into the man he wanted me to be: ruthless and merciless. A remorseless killer. He'd mostly succeeded. It had taken five days in a medieval dungeon to complete the job.

I didn't want to talk about all of this right now. "Was this why you came out here?"

"I just heard from my contact in the Questura di Milano. Ravazzani is trying to get a DNA test on the girl found in the bar explosion."

I paused, my drink halfway to my mouth. "Che cazzo?"

"That was my reaction. He must suspect it's not Gia."

"How?"

"I have no idea."

"Let's go inside and get Ravazzani on the phone. After all, I haven't offered my sympathies yet."

"Are you certain that's wise?"

"He will expect me to call." It was what we did, after all. We took every opportunity to swing at one another. If I didn't poke this wound, he would wonder why and suspect my involvement. "It looks suspicious if I don't."

We went inside and I pulled up city noises on my phone while Vito dialed. He set his phone on the table near me as it rang. Dragging in a deep breath for calm, I waited for the testa di cazzo responsible for all my troubles to pick up.

"Pronto," a familiar deep voice said, one I still heard in my nightmares.

"Ciao, Ravazzani. Come stai?"

"D'Agostino. It has been a long time." There was movement in the background, like he was going somewhere private.

"I hope I haven't caught you at a bad time," I said. "I hear you aren't working as much these days." Rumor was he mostly spent time with his wife and children—something I would also be doing if he hadn't stolen my life from me.

"I always have time for you. How is your vacation?"

Vacation. Bastardo. "I called to offer my sympathies."

He didn't speak for a long second. "For?"

"Your sister-in-law. I heard she was in a terrible accident. Such a shame."

"Sì, very terrible. Curious, also."

I kept my voice light. "Is that so?"

"The camera footage from both the street and the restaurant was deleted remotely. It would take a talented computer hacker to wipe those cameras clean."

Yes, it would—which was why I employed the most talented hackers in Europe. "That is strange. So you suspect foul play?"

"The world we live in, we are always suspicious, no?"

"Sì, certo. Which was why I am looking into the arson of one of my properties. It's in Pozzuoli, outside of Napoli."

Silence from the other end.

"I don't understand," I continued, "because the house wasn't even in my name. Whoever came looking for me must've been very disappointed to find it empty. Enraged, even."

I could almost hear him grinding his teeth before he said, "Maybe they traveled a great distance and thought the least you could do was be there to greet them."

"I suppose, but unexpected visitors are never welcome. I plan to have a word with whoever invited them." In other words, Giulio Ravazzani.

"I understand. I feel the same about whoever is responsible for my sister-in-law's death."

"Surprising that your name didn't protect her in your own country, no? That must sting. Does this mean you are slipping, Fausto?"

"I guess we will see in time. I must hang up now. My wife and children need me. You remember what that was like, no? It must be hard for you, to be separated from your family for so long."

I clenched my fists and imagined ripping the beating heart from his chest. "And how is *la tua bella moglie*? Please give her my love."

He hung up.

Sighing, I closed my eyes. I hated him so very much. "He suspects me."

"Yes, that's clear," Vito agreed. "But he still doesn't know about Angela's accident."

This was a relief. "Which means he doesn't know Luca and Nicola are in England." It was possible he respected my children because of what would happen if he didn't. He now had young children and they would become fair game—a possibility any father would wish to avoid.

Vito reached to turn off the sound on my phone when I didn't move. "I can try to delay the DNA test, if you want."

"Yes, whatever it takes. If the officer won't take a bribe to do it, let's get Stefano or one of the others to delete whatever records necessary to slow it down."

"Of course. Are you coming up to the office?"

I checked my watch. She had been restrained for three hours, naked and horny. Had she suffered enough?

Anticipation buzzed as I thought about her swollen clitoris, pushing against that metal jewelry. Nipples hard in the cool air. My micina would be spitting mad by the time I returned, desperate for relief. I couldn't wait.

It was time to go and play with my pet.

Gia

I woke up trapped and disoriented.

Pillows and soft sheets. Right, Enzo's bed. He left me here and I'd fallen back asleep. I tried to shift, but I couldn't move. Something was weighing me down.

I came fully awake then, my eyes squinting against the bright sunlight streaming through the glass. In the distance there was nothing but blue as far as I could see.

Why couldn't I move?

"Enjoy your nap?"

Oh, that asshole! I bucked and kicked out with my legs, hoping like hell I caught him in the junk. "Get off me!"

He chuckled. "A shame. I liked you sleepy and sweet."

I tried to shove him farther away without the use of my hands. "Release me now, Enzo."

In a flash he was on top of me, all that hard muscle pinning me down to where I couldn't move. Oh, God. I could feel him everywhere, especially his cock, which was thick against my belly. Fighting him only turned both of us on, apparently, and now I was thinking about sex. About that big dick and what it would feel like inside of me.

And I hated him for it.

Hot breath gusted over my cheek as he nuzzled me. "Ah, you like fucking and fighting when you wake up, don't you, *troietta*?" His lips coasted over my jaw and caused me to shiver.

"Get off me." My voice was weak, as if my body wasn't fully on board with that decision.

"Are you ready to beg for it?" He ground his hips into my mound and I nearly whimpered as my piercing dragged against his shaft.

"I will never beg you for anything, mafioso."

He chuckled darkly, then surprised me by rolling off. "Would you like to visit the toilet?"

After being cuffed to the bed for hours, I would think the answer was obvious. But if he thought I would beg for that again, he had another thing coming. I would piss his bed first. "Yes."

Without saying anything, he undid the straps around my wrist.

Eying him suspiciously, I rubbed my wrists and tried to get feeling back into my numb arms. "What's the catch?"

"No catch. I am trusting you to use the toilet and then return to bed."

"And if I don't?"

"Then I will chase you—and you won't like what happens when I capture you."

My heart kicked hard in my chest, the thrill of disobeying him twisting through me, luring me, despite the risk. And it was very risky. My life was in this man's hands. There was nothing to prevent him putting me back into the cage. Hell, he could throw me in the ocean now that he knew my weakness. He could torture me. He could cut off body parts and mail them to my father if he wanted.

And still the desire to rebel pricked at me.

"I'll be good," I said sweetly. Too sweetly, but I really needed to pee and get a moment away from him.

His brows lowered like he didn't trust me. "And don't pleasure yourself in there because I will know and punish you."

"Seriously, how has a woman not murdered you before now? You are the *worst*."

"*Vai avanti*," he said and waved his hand toward the bathroom.

The bathroom door was almost completely shut when he spoke. "Oh, I forgot to mention that I will be checking every orifice when you return to the bed. So, don't think about hiding the spring from the paper roll anywhere."

I froze. So he'd learned how I escaped the cage. I suppose I shouldn't be surprised. "I don't know what you're talking about."

"I guess we will see when you return, no?"

Bastard.

I took my time using the toilet and washing my face. As I brushed my teeth, I eyed Enzo's razor and the sharp blades. I wished I could take one, hide it, and use it to secure my freedom. But he would expect me to smuggle a weapon out of the bathroom. Would he really check my orifices? I clenched my butt muscles, squeezing tight as if to keep him out. He'd better not even try.

After drinking some water from the faucet, I decided to face him. Whatever hell he had planned for me today, I could take it.

I unlocked the door and stepped into the bedroom. He was exactly where I'd left him on the bed, except he seemed anxious, on edge. The lines of his face were stark, his body unnaturally still as he stared out at the water. When he saw me, his gaze narrowed like he was trying to see into my brain. I walked with my head high to my side of the bed and waited. "Well?"

"Lie down."

Instead I gave him a full body turn. "No weapons, as you can see."

"I gave an order, Gia. Get on the bed."

"My orifices are off limits, D'Agostino."

The side of his mouth hitched like he found me amusing. "It will be easier for you if you don't make trouble."

"But I like trouble," I said without thinking, because it was true.

I hadn't thought about how this would come across, though. I was basically challenging him.

His expression went hard, a little scary. "I will give you the count of three. If you are not in bed before then, I will come to get you and there will be consequences."

We stared at one another and I tried not to react as I contemplated this. I had no idea what he would do if I disobeyed him, but if I wanted to get under his skin then I had to play his game. For now.

I lowered myself onto the bed and stretched out. Satisfaction flared in his espresso-colored eyes, then he said, "Arms above your head."

"You don't need to restrain me."

"I'll decide whether it is necessary or not. Arms, now."

Slowly I lifted my arms. He reached over and secured a cuff on one wrist. Then he got up and walked around to restrain my other hand, as well. I stared at him, wondering what he was going to do. I didn't like being so off-balance with anyone, especially a man who had sworn to use me as revenge. "What now?" I couldn't help but ask.

He didn't answer as he strode toward the end of the bed. His strong naked chest was distracting in the sunlight, with a myriad of scars and rough marks criss-crossing his skin like a road map. This was a cruel man, unyielding and unafraid of violence, yet he'd treated me so gently last night after he rescued me. What did that mean?

I pressed my lips together when he produced a set of the same restraints at the foot of the bed. Oh, shit. Did he mean to secure my legs, too?

The question was soon answered when he grabbed my ankle and worked the cuff over my foot.

"You don't need to do this," I rushed out. "I'm not going anywhere." Thanks to the wrist restraints.

The cuff pulled tight on my right leg. Satisfied, he moved to the other side and I started taking deep breaths, fighting the urge to kick and fight. What was he planning? Why did he need me spread-eagle on the bed? With any other man I would assume it was some sex game, but Enzo was more into punishment than pleasure.

When I was tied down, he climbed onto the bed, his muscles shifting as he crawled between my thighs, and my nerves twitched and twisted in my belly. This wasn't good. Why didn't I fight him earlier? Our positions should be reversed right now, so I could crawl all over him and drive him wild.

His palms slid up my thighs and goose bumps broke out all along my skin. He flicked my piercing once, his voice a seductive whisper. "Should I let you come, bambina?"

Little girl.

Heat bloomed in my pussy, those words charged in ways I couldn't begin to unpack. Was he really going to play the daddy card right now? Fuck. It was like he could see into my mind on how best to manipulate me.

"Don't," I pleaded, not even caring that I sounded weak.

He gently traced my entrance with his middle finger. "Just as I thought. Wet." He brought his finger to his mouth and licked my arousal off. "You like that, when I call you little girl."

"No, I don't," I said, my chest heaving with the force of my breath. "You don't need to do this."

"Do you ache inside?" He slipped his finger directly into my channel, pressing deep until he was completely seated. Then he curled his finger, hitting a spot that I'd sworn was an urban myth.

My back bowed off the bed, limbs pulling tight against the restraints, and I bit my lip to stay quiet. I did not want to think about how good any part of him felt inside me, how that finger wasn't nearly enough. "Please," I panted, not sure what I was asking for.

He pumped his hand, the friction both delicious and frustrating. Then he added another finger, going slow until it was in, and I whimpered. The pressure was fucking amazing.

"Look at how beautiful," he said, "sucking in my fingers. So greedy, this pussy. Do not worry, micina. I am going to take very good care of you."

CHAPTER THIRTEEN

Gia

I held my breath.

I didn't know what was about to happen. I only knew it was going to be bad.

If he teased me, it would be awful. Worse than awful. This morning had been frustrating enough. I didn't want to go through that again.

But if he actually pleasured me, if I surrendered to him, it would be humiliating. He would gain the upper hand, and that was what scared me most.

Licking my dry lips, I forced out, "I don't need you to take care of me. Let me take care of you instead."

He pumped his fingers lazily, in and out, in and out, dragging against my sensitive tissues. I inhaled sharply, the pleasure streaking through me like lightning. "Of course you do," he said darkly. "You are *una sporca troietta*, so eager for it. So needy."

My body strained toward the source of that bliss, chasing it and making a liar out of me. "No, I don't. I'm not. God, no. Fuck, yes." Was I babbling? I could barely keep track of the conversation as he fucked me with his fingers.

"Hear how wet your pussy is for me?" The slick sounds filled the bedroom and I wanted to die of shame. He chuckled. "I can smell you from here."

Then his fingers left my pussy and I relaxed slightly, until he slid them into the crack of my ass, searching. Oh, shit. Fuck no. I clenched, hoping to prevent what I suspected was coming. "Relax," he crooned. "Let me in. Let me feel you, check you for any weapons you might be hiding."

Bullshit. He wasn't checking for weapons. "This is ridiculous. You know I'm not hiding anything."

He found the puckered ring of muscle and circled with the tips of his fingers. I pulled against the restraints, trying to edge away from him. Not because I didn't like being touched here. Entirely the opposite.

I liked it too much.

And I didn't want Enzo to use that knowledge against me.

"I'm not hiding anything, I swear. Let me suck your dick." I would give him the best blow job of his life. Whatever it took to prevent this.

"Shh." Bending, he pressed a kiss to my piercing. "I only want to make you feel good."

My body betrayed me, instantly going soft at the words, and he took full advantage. The tip of his finger breached my ass, and the familiar burn lit my stomach, a pinch chased by unbelievable pleasure. I often used anal toys when masturbating, and I always came like a rocket. *God, please don't let this man learn how sensitive I am there.*

He invaded carefully, giving me time to adjust, watching my face the whole time. I tried to keep my expression from revealing anything I was feeling, but when he twisted and pumped, I moaned deep in my throat.

"Cazzo, that's nice, no?" he murmured, then flicked his tongue over my piercing. "You are a dirty girl, aren't you? You like having your ass played with."

"Oh, fuck."

"That is my favorite place to put my dick." Another flick of his tongue as he worked his fingers and I moaned again. "You can take me there, I think."

"No way. You're too big." I panted, shaking my head back and forth on the pillow. "Stop talking and make me come, mafioso."

He grunted and began using his lips and tongue lightly on my piercing, as if investigating the feel of the metal. It clanked against his teeth. The pressure inside me wound tighter, coiled like a spring, and I couldn't catch my breath. Then his thumb slipped into my pussy.

The fullness, oh my God. Before I could stop myself I was rocking my hips, desperate, out of my mind, pushing myself onto his fingers and fucking his hand. I writhed and cursed, so close to an orgasm. I needed this. It was there, barreling toward me and taking up all the space in my lower half, rising up from my toes.

"That's it. Use my fingers to get off," he said. "Madre di Dio, you are the hottest thing I've ever seen."

Then he started eating me out. He licked and sucked like I was a meal and he was starving, his attention focused on my clit, swirling and sucking, and I suddenly knew what I had been missing out on all these years. My God, it was amazing. He mastered my body in seconds, like some sort of pussy wizard, because I was instantly on the verge of coming. My thighs started shaking and my lungs couldn't pull in air.

And he stopped.

"No!" I shouted. Lurching, I tried to bring my mound closer to his face. "Don't stop. Oh, God."

He pressed a kiss to my thigh. "Beg me, Gianna. Beg me to make you come."

"Why are you doing this to me? You fucking psychopath!" I was right there, hovering on the edge, air sawing in and out of my lungs. I wanted to scream, I wanted to cry. I wanted to claw his face with my fingernails. I wanted to crawl into his lap and ride his cock to orgasm.

"Those are not the words. Try again."

He pulled away when I tried to move closer, denying me, his thumb and fingers barely inside me. It was awful, worse than this morning. I was so hot and aroused that the air felt painful on my skin.

Two fingers pinched my nipple. Hard. "Say it and I'll let you come."

My body was uttering the words before my brain could tell it not to. "Please, Enzo. Please make me come."

His mouth returned to my clit and with two swipes of his tongue I was convulsing, my vision going dark as the pleasure dragged me down. The walls of my pussy clamped around his thumb, while the muscles of my backside clenched on his fingers. I heard myself yelling as if from a distance, the high so unbelievably good, better than any drug I'd ever tried.

It seemed to go on for days but was probably only seconds. As I came down, the shame crept in to replace the euphoria. I had begged Enzo D'Agostino, my sister's kidnapper and sworn enemy of the Ravazzani family, to make me come. I enjoyed it, too. He had touched me and I enjoyed it.

Jesus Christ. What was wrong with me? I sagged onto the bed, defeated.

He slowed his movements, then eased his fingers out of me. I winced. The absence of lube was noted. He moved lower and licked my entrance, swirling to collect the additional slickness, then shoved his tongue inside me, spearing me. I gasped, the sensation catching me by surprise, only to be chased by toe-curling pleasure.

He didn't stop, either, fucking me with his tongue, growling as he held my legs open as wide as they would go. "You are so wet," he snarled. "I fucking love it!"

"So good," I muttered, long past the point of coherence. "Yes, God! It's so good."

After a few more thrusts of his tongue, he shifted to my clit, but there was no teasing this time. He licked me ruthlessly, relentlessly, until I began shaking, my hips rocking as I chased a second orgasm.

I nearly levitated off the bed when it finally crested, my body splintering apart into a million pieces, destroyed. I screamed his name and strained against the ties holding me down as it went on and on, wave after wave of white-hot bliss.

Enzo came up on his knees and began furiously jerking his cock. His gaze locked on my swollen pussy until his movements grew uncoordinated, his hips stuttering, and hot jets lashed all over my belly and chest. Like he was marking me.

He squeezed to get every drop of come out of his dick and onto my body, then sat on his haunches, chest heaving. I was covered in him, the liquid cooling on my bare flesh. Pleasured and used by the last man I should ever be attracted to.

Oh, how the mighty had fallen.

"You look good like this." He traced a fat droplet and rubbed it into my skin. "Drenched in my come. Sei una sporca puttana."

"Enjoy it," I panted, "because this is the last time it will happen."

"You liked it." He smeared more of his come, watching his fingers with a strange light in his eyes. "Admit it."

"Temporary insanity brought on by lack of food."

He threw his head back and laughed. "We will see the next time, no? Now that you know how good it is between us, I don't believe you'll fight nearly as much."

Shit. That was exactly what I was afraid of. "There isn't going to be a next time, asshole."

He flicked my piercing and I jerked, sucking in a sharp breath as a jolt of lust arrowed through me. He smiled darkly at me. "There will be many, many times, troietta. And you will love every minute of it."

The promise sent a shiver down my spine and I said nothing more. He rolled off the bed, faced the windows and stretched, letting me secretly look my fill at his big body. Sculpted calves and thick thighs. A hard, muscled ass and a trim waist. His back was a complex series of muscles wrapped in scarred skin. There were what appeared to be gunshot scars, along with stripes—had he been whipped?—and slashes and burns. No wonder he was crazy. No one could endure all that pain and emerge sane.

I had to find a way to resist him. To destroy him. It was what my sister deserved. It was what *I* deserved, too.

And now I was in close enough proximity to bring him down. All I had to do was play whatever games he had in mind, make him believe it was mutual, and get him to lower his guard. Then I could shove a knife directly into his heart.

I could kill Enzo D'Agostino.

It was perfect.

Enzo started for the bathroom and my jaw fell open. Was he actually leaving me here? "Untie me," I barked at his back. "So I can clean your spunk off!"

"I don't think so. I like seeing it there. And it will be a good reminder for you, no?"

He disappeared into the bathroom and I was left alone. In Enzo D'Agostino's bed, covered in his come.

Fuck my life.

Enzo

I strode to the galley where several crew members were working on tonight's dinner. I requested lunch for two in my stateroom, whatever they could plate up quickly, then called the maintenance crew for a long length of chain.

Provisions for the afternoon.

I nearly jerked off in the shower after leaving her, even with my come still drying on her skin. I couldn't stop thinking of how beautiful she looked, how hot her pussy and ass felt on my fingers. How responsive she was to my touch. Cazzo, I wanted to play with her all day, drive her to the brink of orgasm and deny her, if only to see what I could make her do.

I hadn't expected to enjoy eating her out that much. I did it to make a point, to show that I controlled her. To make her beg, then brand myself on her mind and body until she'd do anything I asked.

But the taste of her, the feel of her clit on my tongue . . .and that piercing. Mamma mia, I had nearly lost it. I hadn't been able to stop, coaxing a second orgasm out of her.

I'd never wanted to fuck so badly. It took all of my self-control not to thrust my cock inside her and ride her until I emptied myself.

Soon. Very soon.

No one knew better than me how torture worked. The anticipation was the worst part, the waiting for what came next. It ensured that Gia would be wary, on edge when I returned. She would look forward to my visits because it meant her mind could stop spinning with worry. It was all part of breaking her down.

Deciding work could wait, I returned to my stateroom. Gia was spread-eagle on the bed, her eyes glaring daggers at me. I slipped my hands into my pockets, not bothering to hide my grin. "Did you miss me, mia sporca puttana?"

"Untie me, motherfucker."

"Such a mouth. I'll have to see if I can find a better use for it later."

A knock sounded on the door. "Prego!" I shouted.

Gia's eyes widened, suspicion filling her expression. "Who's here? What are you planning?"

"It's the crew." Hector and two other young men entered, their arms filled with everything I needed for lunch out on the deck. They kept their eyes averted as they walked.

Gia was faced away, her skin a dull red. Then I noticed her rapid breaths and how her nipples had stiffened. Did she like to be watched? I had to find out.

I stretched out on the bed beside her. She tried to move away, but it was no use, thanks to her bindings. I traced my finger over the dried come on her smooth stomach as my crew worked just on the other side of the glass.

She twitched and twisted in an effort to evade my touch. "You are trying to humiliate me."

I leaned down to lick around her nipple, pleased when she shivered. "I think you like it."

"I don't."

"What if I made you come while they watched?" I bit the peak gently. "They could see me eat your pussy and finger your ass. Would you like that?"

"No," she breathed, but there was no certainty behind it. She was arching toward me ever so slightly, though she probably didn't realize it.

All three crew members were purposely avoiding looking in the direction of my bed. Smirking, I returned my mouth to her breast and sucked hard. When I released her, the skin was red and puffy. I put my lips near her ear. "They try not to watch, but can't help themselves," I lied. "Do you think their dicks are hard from seeing your gorgeous body laid out like this?"

She closed her eyes. "Haven't you humiliated me enough for today?"

No, not even close.

"You can always go back to the cage, micina. But I hadn't thought you were so easily beaten." I slid my hand up her thigh slowly, giving her plenty of time to realize what I was doing. "They are still looking, wanting you. Wishing they could be the ones kissing and touching you."

She trembled, her breath hitching, but she said nothing.

My fingers reached her pussy, and the moisture gathered at her entrance told me everything I needed to know. I slipped two fingers inside her and her back bowed. Cazzo, she was beautiful. "Oh, mia sporca puttana. You do like this."

"Fuck off, Enzo."

I continued the fantasy for her. "The men are distracted, working much slower so they can see what I am doing to you." She panted and I pumped my fingers, fucking her with them. I leaned down to whisper, "Should I invite them to join us?"

"Don't you dare," she snarled and struggled against her bindings.

I didn't have any desire to share her, but that didn't mean I couldn't tease her with the possibility. "Are you certain? One could fuck your mouth, another your pussy. Another could suck your tits. Wouldn't you like to have several men worship your body at once?"

The walls of her cunt tightened, more moisture flooding her channel. Yes, she very much liked that.

"Don D'Agostino," Hector called, not glancing at the bed as he hovered near the doorway. "We are finished. Would you like anything else?"

I continued pumping my fingers in and out of Gianna. Though her eyes were closed, she was on edge, her body vibrating with excitement and terror. It was a heady cocktail, one I wanted to savor. "Grazie, Hector. Did you bring the chain?"

"Sì, Don D'Agostino. It is on the table."

I licked Gia's nipple. "Bring it here."

Hector turned to do as I asked and Gia hissed, "I hate you."

If her pussy wasn't clamping down on my fingers like it never wanted me to leave, I might believe her.

Hector covered his eyes and tossed the thin chain in my direction. It landed on the floor, five feet from the bed. I took pity on him. "You can go," I said, pulling my hands free of Gia before rising off the bed to collect the chain.

The crew members disappeared. I unfastened the restraints around Gia's legs, then found a thick leather ankle cuff in my drawer and secured it on her right leg. She said nothing as I released her hands, just lowered her arms and rolled her shoulders.

I began pulling the chain through the metal loop on the ankle cuff. She asked, "What are you doing?"

"Securing you then feeding you lunch."

"Haven't we played this game already?"

"Yes, but I have to be sure you won't jump overboard again."

"You don't need to worry about that. I definitely won't."

"Forgive me if I don't believe you." Bending, I wrapped the other end of the chain around the base of the bed, then locked it with a set of handcuffs. Unless she could lift a bed that was bolted to the floor, she wasn't going anywhere. I motioned with my hand. "Up, pet. Come eat."

CHAPTER FOURTEEN

Gia

This had to be a trap of some kind.

Enzo wasn't seriously going to let me walk around with my hands free, was he? I'd been under the impression he was intelligent, some kind of mafia wunderkind. So why wasn't he worried about my retaliation?

Because he doesn't think I'm capable of it.

Good. Let him underestimate me—and when I shove a knife in his heart I'll have the last laugh.

I rose off the mattress and slowly stood. My body was sore but still aroused, thanks to the mafioso's mouth and fingers. If only he didn't affect me like this, but it was like he reached into my brain and plucked out my darkest thoughts.

Wouldn't you like to have several men worship your body at once?

Duh, yes. I mean, wouldn't every woman? Maybe Enzo wasn't so perceptive after all.

My captor was sitting at the table out on the deck, calmly pouring sparkling water, unconcerned. But there was a noticeable bulge in his jeans. Clearly I hadn't been the only one turned on by what just happened. This was exactly what I wanted. He wasn't immune to me, which meant I had leverage.

Without an ounce of shame, I strode out onto the deck, grateful to feel the sun on my skin. Being naked never bothered me, and spending time around designers and models made me realize I had nothing special. I tilted my face up toward the sky and stretched, letting him get a nice long look at me.

When I finally sat, he shifted in his chair and reached between his legs to adjust himself. Ha. I hoped he was hard and miserable.

I reached for the water. "You aren't going to make me sit at your feet this time?"

"Are you so anxious to eat from my hand, pet?"

He was turning it back around on me, even though he'd been the one to rush from the room the last time. That he didn't want to repeat that experience spoke volumes.

Instead of answering, I concentrated on the food. I took some pasta and vegetables, and dug in. He said nothing for a long moment, just frowned at me. "You're hungry," he commented, like this was some big revelation.

"Yeah, genius. That is generally what happens when people aren't given food for long stretches of time." I cut him a sharp glance. "Didn't they feed you in Ravazzani's dungeon?"

He snorted and stared out at the water. "No."

Jesus. He'd been there for *days*. "Were you starving after you escaped?"

"I could not eat solid food for two months."

A hint of pity settled in my stomach but I pushed it away. He had kidnapped and hurt my sister. Whatever happened to him in that dungeon was deserved.

I stared at his finger, the one with the missing tip. Did it bother him? Fausto had given that piece of Enzo's hand to Frankie as a fucked-up gift. Was Enzo aware of that?

"Admiring your brother-in-law's work?" Enzo sipped his water and flexed his fingers on the hand I was studying.

"Were those the fingers you had inside me?"

He paused, like the question surprised him. "No. I used this hand."

He lifted his other hand off the table and held the fingers up to his nose. "Cristo, I like the way you smell, micina."

"You're an animal." I tilted my chin to the hand with the missing finger, not willing to let it go just yet. "Did it hurt?"

"A bit, but not nearly as much as the surgery to repair it after the infection."

Yikes. I smothered a wince—then I nearly smacked myself. I shouldn't feel sorry for him. I returned my attention to my food, determined not to ask him any more questions.

"It's also numb," he continued. "So if I want to feel the warmth of your pussy or your ass, I must use my other hand."

"We can stop talking about it now."

"But why? You don't wish to hear how I had to relearn how to close my fist and how to type? How sometimes I swear I can feel it itch?"

I finished the bite I was chewing then wiped my mouth with a napkin. "I don't feel any sympathy for you. You knew what you signed up for when you agreed to take over as don, and again when you took on Fausto Ravazzani."

His expression turned so menacing, so angry that the hair on the back of my neck stood up. "You speak of things you do not understand. If you don't learn your place, I'll send you back to the cage."

"And what is my *place*, Enzo? I'm not your guest or your lover, so you don't get my cooperation or my silence. Put me back in the goddamn cage if you don't like it."

"You think I cannot make you cooperate?" He shoved his chair back from the table and stood up. The bulge between his legs was still there, still prominent. Reaching out, he wrapped his hand across the back of my neck and pulled me to my feet. "I see you staring at my dick. Maybe I should shove it down your throat, make you choke on it."

I ignored the way my body reacted in his rough grip. "I will bite it off if you do."

His fingers tightened, his thumbs stroking my skin. "I don't think so. I think you want my cock in your mouth every bit as much as I want to put it there."

I stared up at him. Everything inside me told me to fight, to lash out. Logically, I knew I shouldn't, but I was a big ball of hormones and anger around this man. None of that would get me what I needed though, which was to earn his trust. I had to remain cool, stay in control at all times.

I had to play his game, then beat him at it.

I licked my lips. "Maybe I do, but you haven't earned it yet."

He looked at me like I had two heads. "You think I have to earn a blow job from you?"

"I don't do it for any random guy I meet." I shoved at his chest to put some distance between us and surprisingly he let me go.

His gaze narrowed, studying me, as he retook his seat. I helped myself to another olive before I lowered myself into my chair. I needed to eat as much as possible. Who knew when he'd feed me again?

He sprawled in his chair. "Dai, Gianna. *You* don't like giving blow jobs?"

What did that mean? I heard the judgment in his voice. Did he think just because I liked men that I should like having their dicks in my mouth? "I didn't say that. I said I don't do it for randoms. It has to be someone I actually like."

"Why? I ate your pussy and I hate you."

Every muscle in my lower half clenched at the memory. It had been fucking fantastic. "Fine, but most guys don't."

His jaw fell open and he blinked a few times. "Get the fuck out of here. You are lying."

When I didn't answer, his mouth curled into a knowing, sinister smile. It was then that I realized my mistake.

He instantly jumped on this new piece of information, his body angling toward mine. "Has anyone given you head before me, micina?"

I focused on my plate and mumbled, "Yes, of course. Jesus, get over yourself."

"Now I see why you came so hard—twice—when I licked your pussy. I am very good at it, no?"

I wasn't about to give him the truth, so I went with snark instead. "I couldn't say. I've never had another kidnapper give me head, so I have nothing to compare it to."

"Finish your lunch," he said darkly, his expression inscrutable.

Somehow, I knew he was planning something. It was in the tightness of his shoulders, the rapt attention on my movements. His gaze never wavered, never left my face, and I . . . didn't hate it.

I pretended to ignore him while I continued eating, sliding the fork in my mouth and licking the tines slowly. His soft intake of breath emboldened me, and I sat a bit straighter in my chair.

It was empowering. I felt *powerful*. I was his captive and chained to his bed, but in that moment it seemed as if I held him in the palms of my hands.

I was learning that being around Enzo was like walking a tightrope, thrilling and scary at the same time, so different from the other men I'd encountered. He could hurt me at any time, but something told me he wouldn't, not after saving me in the water last night. There had been plenty of time for him to torture me, yet he hadn't.

And he might coerce me into something sexual, but he wouldn't rape me. Other than degrading and pleasuring me, he hadn't touched me. Nor had he forced me to touch him.

We were playing a game, but I didn't know the rules. Good thing I never bothered following rules anyway.

He didn't rush me, merely sat silently and watched as I ate. When I couldn't stand another bite, I wiped my mouth with the napkin. "I'm done."

"Go use the bathroom and come back."

The dominance in his voice had me rising before I could stop myself. As I walked to the bathroom, I wondered why I'd obeyed so easily. I could pretend it was part of my act . . .but had I been acting?

It was considerate of my kidnapper to allow me just enough chain to reach the bathroom. A far cry from when he locked me in the cage and made me beg. Was I softening him? I used the toilet and washed my hands, then dampened a cloth and wiped the dried jizz off my body.

You are the hottest thing I've ever seen.

I hadn't expected compliments. Taunts and threats, yes. So maybe I was getting under his skin a little.

Good.

When I couldn't delay it any longer I took a deep breath and opened the door. Enzo was stretched out on the bed, naked, staring straight at me. The breakfast table had been removed, the crew long gone. His venti-sized cock was half hard, resting against his thigh. He patted the mattress. "Come and lie down. It's time for your reward."

Enzo

I watched as Gia snuck a glance out at the deck. Looking for someone to rescue her?

I bit back a smile. There was no rescue for her. Not from me. "Now, Gia."

She responded to my command, instantly crawling onto the bed, and I liked how eagerly she moved when I used that tone of voice. Silent, she stretched out on her back and waited, a good little pet.

But I could see inside her mind. She wasn't broken yet, which meant this was an act to earn my trust.

Poor misguided micina.

I had no trust to earn. If Gia thought I would ever let down my guard around her, she was mistaken. She was a means to an end for me.

Still, I could play along, let her believe I was falling under her pussy's spell.

"Arms up," I said, pleased when she obeyed. Rebellion swirled in the brown depths of her gaze but she said nothing, merely watched as I secured her hands to the bed with the cuffs. I left her legs free for now.

When she was cuffed I propped up on my elbow and regarded her. She was so fucking beautiful. Where her older sister resembled a porn star, Gia was more like a Hollywood actress. Classy and refined, with legs for days, but a hint of an edge, sort of like the young Angelina Jolie.

"Spread your legs," I ordered. "Show me your cunt."

A muscle jumped in her jaw but she did as I asked. Her piercing beckoned like a red cape to a bull, but I decided to make her wait. Instead, I took her nipple in my mouth and sucked until she whimpered. Then I switched to the other side and gave it the same attention. "Your tits are gorgeous," I told her before I scraped my teeth across her nipple. "Can you come just from having them sucked?"

"That's not a thing." Her voice was breathy and full of derision. "It's just something porn and romance novels claim to make women feel inadequate."

I shook my head at her naiveté. "I have made many women come this way."

"Sure you have," she muttered.

Cazzo, her mouth. If I didn't have plans for her, I would spend all day sucking on her tits until she orgasmed. I moved between her legs, with my face directly above her pussy. "I'll save that for another time. I'd rather continue our discussion from lunch."

Wrinkles formed on her brow as she frowned at me. "What discussion?"

I nuzzled her slick folds, inhaling the musky scent of her arousal. She was already wet and swollen. This was going to be easy. "About head," I said vaguely before wrapping my tongue around her piercing and playing with her.

She watched me, our eyes locked as I swirled my tongue around that small piece of metal. Her lips parted slightly as her breathing picked up, and I began licking her earnestly, focusing on her clit. She was slippery and delicious, and I could feel her thigh muscles begin to shake on either side of me as her noises grew louder, more desperate.

"Oh fuck. Oh God. Oh fuck."

Yes, almost there.

Her clit tightened against my tongue and I immediately backed off, sliding to kiss her inner thigh. Gia sagged into the mattress. I waited for her to chastise me, but she didn't. Her chest rose and fell as she tried to catch her breath. I crawled up to her tits and began working her nipples, sucking one while twisting the other. When she rocked her hips against my stomach, I returned to her pussy, tonguing her again.

I stopped just before she came.

I did this two more times. By the fourth time, she was panting and moaning, an incoherent mess. "Goddamn it," she whined. "Are you trying to get me to beg for an orgasm?"

I released her nipple with a pop. It was puffy and red, wet from my mouth. "No."

"Then what the fuck? Please, Enzo. I can't take any more teasing."

"Let me fuck your mouth and come down your throat. Then I will let you come."

"You asshole." She writhed, trying to buck me off her. Except I was too big and too determined. I would have this. I crawled toward her pussy again.

"No, please. It's too much."

I pressed soft kisses to her clit, which was engorged. "Tell me you want my cock in your mouth. Tell me you'll swallow my come."

"Enzo!"

"Call me *padrone* and let me fuck your mouth." I flicked her piercing with the tip of my tongue.

"I don't know what that word means, so no."

"It means master." No other woman had ever called me by the name before, but I knew Gia would hate it—which was why I suggested it.

"Fuck off. I'm never calling you that."

I teased her again, shoving my tongue in her entrance, spearing her like a cock. Her back arched as her limbs trembled, and she let loose with a string of creative English curse words. I nearly smiled as I eased off to kiss her stomach.

"Please," she nearly screamed.

"The word, Gianna. *Dimmi*. Then you will open your mouth and swallow my dick."

She squeezed her eyelids shut. "God, I hate you. No, it's more than that. Hate is too tame a word for how much I despise you."

I ignored her and sucked on her clit a few times. She tried not to react, to fool me, but I was paying attention to her body, not her face. Sweat coated her olive skin, every tendon straining as she tried to hold out. She couldn't last much longer. When she was close, I pulled away.

It was then I saw defeat twist her features. She finally realized she could not win.

I pressed a kiss to her stomach. "Say it and I'll let you come after I come."

"Please, padrone," she whispered. "Per favore."

The bolt of pleasure I received from this small victory topped anything I'd ever experienced as Don D'Agostino. Better than the power, the money, all of it. My cock throbbed, and I had never been harder. More desperate.

I straddled her head, my knees on the pillow supporting her, and I aimed my cock at her mouth. "*Mettilo in bocca.*"

Her lips parted and I took full advantage, sliding my erection into that warm haven, and it was even better than I imagined. My eyes nearly rolled back in my head, and I had to take a moment to collect myself so I didn't blow my load too soon. Then her tongue fluttered on the underside of the shaft and my hips flexed, shoving my cock deeper. "Cazzo, Gianna!" I gasped as I bumped the entrance to her throat.

She was gorgeous, so fucking sexy with her lips stretched around my shaft, and I slowly began fucking her mouth, watching as my dick disappeared and reemerged coated with her saliva. "Bellissima," I breathed. "Tu sei perfetta."

There was determination in her gaze as she stared up at me, like she was going to give me the best blow job of my life or die trying. Unable to help myself, I went faster, the feel of her too tight, too good, and sizzles raced along the backs of my thighs. I grunted, using her mouth to get off, holding onto the headboard and thrusting my hips roughly. Her eyes watered but she never broke away, never gagged, just took everything I gave her silently. A perfect pet.

My perfect pet.

Instantly my balls tightened and I was coming down her throat, hot jets exploding into her mouth as I trembled and shook, the orgasm like nothing I'd ever felt. It was incredible, going on and on, like she was turning me inside out, draining me dry. "Minchia!" I shouted to the ceiling. "Drink me down, beautiful girl."

Finally I pulled out of her mouth, and a long strand of my come mixed with her saliva trailed from her tongue to the tip of my cock. It was dirty and visceral, an image I would never forget as long as I lived. Then she licked her lips, breaking that last connection, but didn't say a word. I stroked her hair. "La mia troia," I crooned, then positioned myself between her legs. "I will give you your reward."

Sucking me had made her even wetter. Slickness pooled at her entrance, so I shoved my fingers inside her cunt and tongued her clit quickly. I didn't have to wait long before her muscles contracted and she yelled, "Oh, fuck!" Her thighs pressed to either side of my head as she convulsed, her pussy milking my fingers, and for a brief moment I wished she were coming on my dick.

When she relaxed beneath me I eased up, knowing she would be sensitive and sore. But I was pleased. She'd given me what I wanted. Without removing my fingers, I stretched out on the bed beside her, propped up on one arm. "Do you like me now, micina?"

If her gaze could kill me, I would die on the spot. There was nothing but pure loathing staring at me. "I want to chop off your balls and throw them overboard."

I chuckled. "See? We can hate each other but still have amazing sex."

"If I argue with you, you're just going to edge me until I agree."

"Now you are learning. It will be much easier for you if you don't fight me." I slowly pulled my fingers from her pussy and brought them to her mouth. "Lick."

She stuck out her tongue and let me slide my fingers in her mouth. "Madre di Dio," I whispered, fullness building in my balls again as she cleaned herself off my skin. "Sei molto sporca."

As much as I wanted to keep teasing her, I did need to work. My empire did not run itself. Reluctantly, I drew back and got up off the mattress. She was tousled and flushed, limp and well-used. Dio cane, I liked seeing her like this in my bed, restrained and at my mercy.

I redressed then freed her hands. "Stay out of trouble."

"You're leaving me unrestrained?"

"Even if you manage to pick the lock on the chain, where will you go? Into the water again?" I shook my head. "I don't think so."

"Maybe I'll find a weapon and cut your heart out when you come back."

So bloodthirsty and fierce. No doubt she would try if she found a weapon within reach, but she wouldn't.

What she didn't realize is that I no longer feared death. I had faced it and survived. Now my days were haunted and my nights were full of agony. Whenever my end came I would welcome it.

I pulled on my shirt and headed for the door. "I hope you do, micina. I hope you do."

CHAPTER FIFTEEN

Gia

I tilted my face up to the sun as the breeze kissed my warm skin. We were anchored in the middle of aqua blue water, a brilliant sky shining above. There was nothing around us, and I was alone on the deck, the chain around my ankle allowing me enough movement to even reach the hot tub.

If I could forget whose yacht this was—and the medieval ankle bracelet—I would be in heaven right now.

All day yesterday I looked for something to pick the lock on my cuff. Unfortunately there'd been nothing. Enzo took the toilet paper roll spring away and there wasn't anything else sharp enough to help me escape. I did find his clothes, which allowed me to at least cover myself. I didn't care if it made him mad or not. He'd already humiliated me enough.

It was clear Enzo liked clothes. He had more clothing than almost anyone I knew, a closet full of designer shirts and jeans, suits and shoes. I recognized the labels—all Italian—and the stuff wasn't cheap.

He hadn't come back last night or this morning, which left me with nothing to do but think. Mostly about that blow job . . . .

I wanted to say I hated it, that I felt violated afterward, but it would be a lie. It was powerful, letting him fuck my mouth and seeing the stunned pleasure on his face as I sucked him. He would be thinking about the blow job for a long, long time. It hadn't taken but a minute or two for him to come, either.

Bellissima. Tu sei perfetta.

I didn't want to admit, even to myself, how much I liked it when he praised me. How sad was it that a man who'd kidnapped me was the first to really boost my confidence? It was so fucked up. But Enzo had no reason to lie, no reason to win me over with false compliments. The words were honest, reluctant, as if he couldn't quite believe it either.

My toes curled as I recalled his voice speaking all those sexy words. Jesus, the man could talk dirty in Italian like no one's business. I didn't know why I reacted so strongly to it, but I did.

"Ciao! Permesso?"

It was a male voice, but one I didn't recognize. Turning, I tugged Enzo's t-shirt a little lower over my bare thighs and crossed my legs. "Prego!"

God, I hoped this was food.

A young man, probably in his late twenties, walked through the bedroom and out onto the deck. The dark hair and chin were pure D'Agostino. It was the man I'd seen snorting coke off a pair of boobs the night of my escape.

He held up the tray in his hands. "Ciao, bella. I brought you lunch."

I sat up straighter. "Hello. Thank you."

He set the tray on the table and lowered himself into the empty chair. "I'm Massimo. The fun brother."

I couldn't help but smile. "Then I am very glad to meet you at last."

With a wink, he added, "I am also the handsome brother."

All three D'Agostino men were handsome, but I wasn't about to tell him that. Not even waterboarding would get me to admit it. I studied the tray. "And what did you bring?"

He rubbed his hands together dramatically. "Let's see. I brought us sandwiches, wine, salad . . . ." Then he dug into his pocket and tossed a packet of white powder onto the table. "And a party."

It wasn't my first time seeing cocaine, but I gaped at him. "You know I'm your brother's prisoner, right?"

"Which means you probably need an escape even more than I do."

I reached for a sandwich, delighted to find fresh mozzarella, tomato and basil on a ciabatta roll. "Does he know you snort your lunch?"

A little divot formed between his brows as he frowned. "I thought you were the wild Mancini daughter."

"I am—and I've done coke before. Just not in the daylight."

He slid the packet of powder aside and took the extra sandwich. "Well, another few weeks on this boat and you'll see. You'll be desperate for any kind of entertainment, too."

"How long have you been on the yacht?" I asked and took a bite of the sandwich. Oh, God. I almost moaned. It was the best thing I'd tasted in forever. Italians really knew their food.

"A little more than four years."

That made sense. From what Frankie said, everyone assumed Enzo was hiding out in Italy or Europe. They didn't know Enzo had taken to the water instead. Clever, clever mafioso.

I opened the bottle of wine and filled a glass to the brim. *Drink up, bitches.* "Must get lonely."

Massimo shrugged. "We bring women out every few weeks. It's not terrible."

I remembered the fuck fest the night of my escape, the woman giving Enzo a blow job. Massimo and Vito had been busy, too. "Isn't that risky? One of them might talk."

"They don't know our real names. Besides, we keep moving, never staying in one place for very long."

"Well, you're welcome to hang out with me during the day. I am bored out of my mind."

"I shouldn't stay too long." He helped himself to the wine. "My brother won't like it if I'm here."

"Fuck what Enzo thinks." I took a healthy swallow of white wine. "He's a dick."

"He wasn't always like this," Massimo said. The comment was

similar to what Vito told me back in the cage, that the dungeon had changed Enzo for the worse.

"Forgive me if I don't believe you," I muttered. "I know what he did to my sister."

Massimo shrugged before leaning back in his chair, wineglass in his hand. "For the most part he left her to hang out with Mariella at the beach house."

I didn't want to debate Enzo's concept of hospitality with Massimo. Talk about a losing battle. Since he seemed chatty, I decided to pump him for information instead.

"What was Mariella like?"

He made a noise and tilted his face toward the sun. "A stronza. But she was beautiful and did anything my brother asked of her."

Something about that bothered me. I didn't like thinking about Enzo dominating another woman, getting her to do as he pleased. Wait, another? I meant *any*. I didn't like thinking about him dominating any woman.

Shit, that didn't sound right either.

I sucked down more wine. "What happened to her?"

"She is in Milan, living with some designer. Maybe you know him? Brunello Calli."

I knew of Brunello. He was older and very exacting. The models complained about him all the time. "He seems a little old for her."

"Some women like an older man, no?"

I considered this as I drank more wine. "How old are you and your brothers?"

"I am twenty-eight, Vito is thirty-two. Enzo is thirty-eight."

Shit, he was eighteen years older than me. Almost double my age. Why wasn't I repulsed?

Setting that aside for now, I asked, "There's four years between each of you?"

"Telling, no? I think it is safe to say that none of us were spontaneous."

"Your parents weren't happily married, I take it?"

He snorted. "There was no one happy in our household growing up. My father was a cruel man. Enzo won't like it that I told you, but it's true."

Ouch, that was grim. My father may have ignored me, but my sisters and I had a happy childhood. Mostly because Frankie looked after Emma and me. Who knows what would've happened if not for my oldest sister? "What about Enzo's wife?"

"You are very curious about my brother." He studied me, and I didn't care for the speculation lighting his dark gaze. "If you hope to understand him, you are wasting your time, bella."

That I believed. "Call me Gia. And why do you say it's a waste of time?"

"Because he's one step ahead at all times. There is no outsmarting him."

Maybe, maybe not. Enzo hadn't encountered someone like me before. "Maybe, but I'm curious about a woman who looks the other way while her husband carries on so openly with his mistress."

Massimo appeared confused by my remark. "This is how things are done here. No good Italian wife wants her husband in that way."

Hello, patriarchy. Nice to see you again. "How do you know that? Did you ever ask her?"

"Che cazzo! Ask Enzo's wife if she liked to fuck? *Ma sei pazza?*"

"What does that mean?"

"Are you crazy?"

So, the masculine version of "crazy" was *pazzo*. I had to remember that word. "Women like to fuck, too, Massimo."

"I know that," he mumbled, not meeting my eye. "But not wives. They are chosen for purity, to look out for our homes and raise our children."

This sounded like something he'd heard a hundred times and then memorized. I gestured with my hand, pinching my fingers together and shaking them. "As you Italians say, cazzata!"

He chuckled, the wind ruffling his dark hair. "I like you. You're funny."

Ridiculous that feminism was a novelty here. "Marriage is long and hard. When you choose a spouse you have to find someone who respects you, who is your equal."

"I sort of blanked out after you said long and hard," he said with a smirk.

Laughing, I picked a cherry tomato off the salad and threw it at his head. "You're disgusting."

"And also charming. Admit it."

He was, actually. I had no idea how Massimo and Enzo could possibly be related. "Fine, yes. You have a certain charm, for women who are into cavemen."

"How is this for a caveman? I think we should finish our lunch then take this bottle of wine to the hot tub."

That sounded like an excellent idea, except for one problem. "I don't have a swimsuit."

"Mariella's clothes are probably still on board. I can find you one."

Oh, super. Just what I wanted. Costuming myself to look like Enzo's former mistress.

Still, that hot tub sounded nice. "Okay. Any chance you'll unlock me?" I pointed to the cuff around my ankle.

"If I do, my brother will string me up by my balls, bella."

"Won't he be mad that you're here?"

"He and Vito are busy working. They're usually on calls and email all day."

"So, what do you do?"

"*Boh* . . . watch movies, lay in the sun. Swim. Talk to the crew."

No wonder he was partying and snorting coke. Massimo was eager for responsibility and Enzo gave him nothing to do. "We can entertain each other, then."

"Va bene." He pushed back from the table and stood. "I'll go fetch Mariella's things."

"Can you do me another favor?"

"As long as it doesn't require unlocking you, yes."

"It doesn't. I want paper and pencils to sketch with."

"Like, drawings?"

"Designs. I'm going to become a clothing designer."

He grinned down at me. "I love clothes, but I love the models more."

I rolled my eyes toward the sky. "Of course you do. Guess what? If you let me go, I'll introduce you to some."

"Dai, Gia," he said with a smirk. "With one phone call I can have ten women here to ride my dick. My brothers and I are swimming in beautiful pussy."

A stone settled in the pit of my stomach. I didn't know why that bothered me, but it did. Best to not unpack that now. "How could I forget?"

"Don't worry," Massimo said as he walked away. "If it makes you feel better, I've never seen my brother act this way over a woman before."

I grabbed my wine, wondering what Massimo had seen on my face to make such a ludicrous comment. I wasn't jealous. Enzo could fuck every woman from here to Rome for all I cared. Did these people honestly believe I wanted his attention?

Please, padrone. Per favore.

Hot shame prickled over my skin. I refilled my wine and tried to tell myself there hadn't been a choice. He'd forced me to say those words. Hadn't he? Then I recalled the orgasm I'd experienced shortly after . . . .

Totally worth it.

―――

Enzo

The man on the other end of the conference call droned on and I listened with half an ear. Vito and I were in our office on the upper deck, but I was thinking about my prisoner. Her scent, her skin. The look on her face when I finally let her come. She was too perfect, with a feisty attitude and fucked-up appetites that matched my own.

I wanted to chase her through the woods, then catch her and fuck her on the ground, with her struggling and pretending to fight me. Cazzo, I wanted to bring her to heel. Right the fuck now.

From his seat opposite me, Vito reached to mute the phone. "Are you paying attention? And don't lie, because I already know the answer."

"Then why are you asking the question?" I went to unmute the phone, but he caught my arm.

"We can't afford mistakes, Zo."

I scowled at him. "And what is it exactly that you're worried about, fratello?"

"Your head has been out of it for days and we have serious business to deal with."

I shook off his hand, then unmuted the phone and interrupted our contact in Belgium. In flawless French, I answered every single one of the issues raised, recounting them nearly word for word. My gaze never left my brother's, and I could see his surprise. By the time we disconnected a few minutes later, I had satisfied both sides and saved us a fuck lot of money.

Leaning back in my chair, I raised a brow at him and struggled for calm. "You were saying?"

He put his palms up. "I apologize."

"Do not question me again. I am getting tired of having this conversation with you."

My brother didn't seem convinced. Instead, he stroked his jaw thoughtfully with his fingers. "We should take a video of her and send it to Ravazzani."

"No." The reaction was instant and visceral, based on emotion and not logic, but everything in me rebelled at the idea. Gentling my tone, I said, "Not yet. It's too soon."

"The longer she stays, the greater the chance this backfires on us."

"And how will it backfire?"

We stared at each other, the moment stretching in the stillness. The yacht was anchored, so the engines were quiet, the water calm. I knew what Vito was thinking, and I wondered if he had the balls to say it to my face. I was already on edge. Maybe a fight with my brother was exactly what I needed to take my mind off my little captive.

He threw up his hands. "Fine. I can see you aren't ready to give her up. Will you at least tell me what you are planning?"

"Again, no. You won't like it and I won't be talked out of it."

"You plan to hurt her."

"Not in the way you are thinking. Where are we with the search for Giulio Ravazzani?"

"Gabriel Sánchez left Amsterdam yesterday and boarded a flight to Barcelona. That's all I know."

"He probably heard Andrea Di Vittorio went missing and knew he'd been compromised. No doubt he's using another alias by now."

"Yes, this is what we assume. I have them searching all the Barcelona flight records and airport security footage."

"Have them also check Madrid. It's possible that the ticket to Barcelona is a misdirection."

"If Barcelona is fake, then Giulio could be anywhere in the world."

"True, but misdirection works best if it's close to the truth. He wants us to believe he's in Barcelona so we don't look at the other cities in Spain. Try Madrid, then Málaga."

"I will." Vito began texting on his phone.

An hour later, I was on the phone with a bank manager I worked with in Haiti, moving money around, when Vito got my attention. He held his cell up in front of my face. "Stefano is calling," he mouthed. "Probably about the DNA test."

"Answer it and put it on speaker," I ordered, then told my contact I would call him back.

Vito pressed some buttons and set the cell on the desk. "Pronto."

"Ciao, Vito. I assume Don D'Agostino is with you?"

"I'm here," I said. "Report."

"That database you asked me to alter? It was no problem. I've deleted some of the relevant files and changed the others left behind."

"Va bene," Vito said. "Good work, Stefano. The money will be transferred this afternoon."

"Grazie, Stefano," I added. Then I decided to add another task to his list. It was something that had been weighing on my mind. "I want you to do something else for me."

"Of course, Don D'Agostino." He sounded resigned, but I didn't give a fuck.

"I want you to look into the background of someone. I want to know every detail of their life, no matter how small or insignificant. Capisce?"

"Sì, no problem."

"Every detail, Stefano. Include health records. I will see you well compensated for it."

"I understand. I just need a name and a birth city."

"Gianna Mancini, Toronto."

Vito grew very still across the desk from me, but I ignored him.

"I'll report back as soon as I can," Stefano said. "It shouldn't take more than a day."

"Good. Email me the usual way."

We rang off and I went back to my laptop, leaving Vito to stew in his disapproval. Finally, my brother said, "Do you still deny that you are obsessed with her, fratello?"

I scrolled through my list of unread emails. "The more information I have on her, the more I can use against her."

"Cazzata!"

"Watch your tone with me. And when I want your opinion on my prisoner I will ask for it. Otherwise, keep your mouth shut and let me handle it."

"Just promise to think with your head and not your dick, per favore."

I wasn't certain that was a possibility at this point, so I said nothing.

CHAPTER SIXTEEN

Gia

Things were looking up for this prisoner, even if only a tiny bit.

I now had a friend on the yacht. Massimo returned again today with lunch and wine, and I discovered that we had a lot in common. He was fun to be with and, even better, he was nothing like his oldest brother.

Massimo brought me pencils and paper, which had allowed me to sketch designs last night and this morning. He also showed me where the TV was hidden in Enzo's bedroom and where to find the collection of DVDs.

And best of all, Enzo hadn't returned since the epic blow job I'd given him. He was probably still reeling, trying to tell himself he didn't want a repeat performance. But he'd be back, ready for more of my special skills.

At least, I was pretty sure he hadn't returned. I had a vague memory of a warm body behind me during the middle of the night, holding me tight, soft breaths in my hair. The empty side of the bed had been cold this morning when I finally woke up, so I couldn't be sure.

Massimo and I relaxed in the hot tub after lunch. If it weren't for my ankle chain, I could almost pretend I wasn't a captive. He was showing me funny videos from social media, then a cooking video went by.

"Wait," I said, grabbing his wrist. "I want to see what they are making."

"It's spaghetti carbonara, the way they make it in Roma."

"There are different ways to make it?"

"The true classic way is with pancetta. Americans try to cheat by using bacon."

"Americans," I scoffed, making him laugh. "What do they know about food?"

"Exactly. I will make this sometime for you."

"You can cook?"

He dipped his head, like he was embarrassed. "It's not hard."

There was more to this story. And the number of cooking videos we'd passed on his feed suddenly made sense. "Wait, you can, like, really cook, can't you? You're interested in food."

"I liked cooking. It gives me something to do. But once we're back on land I will take my place as a true D'Agostino. A killer and an enforcer, helping to run the 'ndrina."

"Why can't you do that now?"

"They don't want my help. They treat me like I'm stupid. A kid. Especially Enzo."

I didn't want to defend my captor, but I thought this was selling the mafioso a bit short. "Have you talked to him about it?"

Massimo snorted. "Do you think he is reasonable in his current state?"

"Obviously he wants to keep you hidden and safe right now, but you won't always be stuck on the yacht—"

"*Having a nice afternoon?*"

We both started at the sound of the furious deep voice near the door. Massimo remained silent, but I met Enzo's dark glare with one of my own. "Yes, so feel free to leave before you ruin it."

"I don't think I'll be the one leaving, micina."

Massimo stood up and immediately got out of the hot tub. "Mi dispiace, fratello—"

Enzo put a hand up and strode forward. "I will deal with you later. Go find Vito."

Silent, Massimo grabbed a towel and wrapped it around his waist. He walked away and I heard the door close, my attention still on the angry mafioso standing by the hot tub. "I don't know why you're mad. I'm still shackled."

His fingers began unbuttoning his shirt. "I hadn't realized you were bored, Gianna."

"I'm a captive on some psycho's yacht and have nothing to do. Of course I'm fucking bored."

His shirt hit the deck and I tried not to stare at all the toned olive skin on display.

"So you didn't do a line or two while you and my brother were hanging out?"

Was that what he thought Massimo and I were doing out here? I put a heavy dose of snark into my voice. "It's a bit early in the day for coke and this is hardly a nightclub, but I wouldn't turn down some molly. Do you have any?"

"I'll have some delivered tomorrow," he answered as he unbuttoned his jeans.

It just occurred to me that he was undressing. "What do you think you're doing?"

"My pet needs to be entertained, apparently." He pushed his jeans down his thick thighs and my eyes nearly bulged from my head.

"Do you always go commando?"

Instead of answering, he climbed into the hot tub and sat. "Come here, micina."

"I'm fine where I am."

"Get over here right now, or I'll tie you to my bed and edge you until you cry."

"Why?"

"Because I'm going to punish you and if I have to ask again, I'll edge you *and* take a belt to your ass."

"You wouldn't dare."

His smile was positively devious. "Never doubt my words, Gia. I always say what I mean. Get the fuck over here. Now."

My heart raced as I floated closer. I never knew what he was going to do . . . and it excited me like nothing else. I found myself at his side, body humming with possibility. I started to put my hands on his shoulders, but he snatched my wrists and pulled my arms behind my back. "Climb on top, facing me."

He held my wrists with one hand, while his other palm settled on my hip, helping me straddle his lap. The position arched my body forward and thrust my tits out. My nipples were poking through the bathing suit top, and he wrapped his lips around one and sucked hard.

I whimpered and I could feel his cock thickening, lengthening in the water. There was a dark energy bubbling between us, one that fed off our anger and lust.

He scraped his teeth over my cloth-covered nipple then released it. "Rub your pussy on my cock. Make yourself come like the filthy pet that you are."

A small shiver went through me, but I looked down my nose at him. "Fuck off, Enzo."

He untied the strings of my top and let it float away. The cool breeze brushed over my breasts as he spent long minutes sucking and biting each tit, leaving marks I'd no doubt feel for days. He pinched and pulled on my nipples, almost abusing them, and I couldn't help but moan. Something about his dominance and aggression fired me up. The more he gave me the more I wanted, arching toward him and silently begging to keep going.

"I'm not going to touch your pussy," he whispered, licking my collarbones. "If you want to get off, you need to use me and grind against my dick."

I was so wet, my body already on fire and eager to come. My shoulders ached from being restrained but in a good way, and I longed to roll my hips on his fat cock. My clit was pulsing, and I wasn't sure why I was denying myself. If he wasn't going to pleasure me, I could do it myself.

As if to press his case, he kissed my throat, then sank his teeth into the flesh, and a long groan tumbled from my mouth.

"You don't need to resist." He moved his lips along my jaw and I swayed toward him. "Your pussy must be wet and needy. Think of how good it will feel to come."

"God, you are the worst." Defeated, I eased lower and pressed my sex onto his cock. He was so hard and thick, more than enough to get the job done. Enzo grunted but remained still. I wasn't sure what his game was, but I needed this orgasm.

"Go ahead," he whispered. "Slide your clit all over my dick." He feasted on one of my nipples, applying pressure, and that did it. I began moving, giving a tentative rock of my hips, and the silky friction of my bathing suit bottoms on his shaft was my new favorite thing, like chocolate and cashmere all rolled up into one.

I moved faster.

Soon my hips were churning, the pleasure building, and he leaned back to watch me. I didn't even care. I could take what I needed without any help from him, thank you very much. "Fuck! So good, mafioso. So, so good."

"That's it, bella. That is a good girl." The words sent me higher, my muscles tightening in readiness. He was inside my brain again, but I was too close to stop.

He kept talking. "Feel how hard I am? I want to slide inside your cunt so badly, tear you apart and split you open. Wouldn't you like to be full of my cock?"

My mouth slackened as I continued to work myself on his dick. It was amazing, but feeling him inside me would be a thousand times better. "Yes. God, yes."

"Beg me to fuck you, mia sporca puttana."

I couldn't, so I said nothing. I just needed to come.

"I know you want to," he said. "Your body was built to take my cock. Your pussy is so empty right now."

"Oh, God," I gasped, nearly there. Everything inside me was coiling up like a spring and my thighs trembled.

His lips brushed my ear. "Do you want to struggle, micina? Do you want to fight me? Then I can hold you down and fuck you so hard—"

That did it. "Fuck, yes!" I started convulsing, every molecule in my body awash in pleasure. Bright light flooded the backs of my eyelids and I felt his hands go to my hips, helping me ride out the rest of my climax. "So good," I panted, my fingers threading through his hair.

I leaned my forehead against his as I tried to catch my breath. "Did you enjoy the show, il pazzo?" *Madman.*

He wrapped a large hand around my throat. "Who said it was over?"

I sucked in a surprised breath as Enzo stood with my legs still wrapped around his waist, my ankle still chained. He climbed out of the hot tub like I weighed nothing at all, water sluicing down our bodies.

When he was on the deck, he let me slide along his muscular frame. I wasted no time in putting distance between us—which meant I could see the giant erection he was sporting. Of course I'd felt it moments ago when I was grinding on him, but to see it was . . . *whew.* The thing was fucking impressive. And intimidating.

Unfortunately, I always loved a challenge.

When I was done lusting after his dick, I met his gaze. From his smirk it was clear he knew what I'd been thinking about. He leaned against the edge of the hot tub and folded his arms. Glittering dark eyes traveled the length of my body in return, and pinpricks coasted over my skin. "Let's play a game," he rasped in a deep voice.

"No, thanks."

"That wasn't a question. I am going to fuck you, Gianna. Right now."

I grabbed a nearby towel and wrapped it around my body. "Whoa. That's hardly a game and I am not consenting to it. Do you hear me, Enzo? Not consenting."

His upper lip curled, his expression wicked. "You consented not even five minutes ago when you were riding my dick. Don't you remember?" He bent, reached into his discarded pants on the ground, and withdrew a small key. "Besides, we both know you will like this game."

"No."

"Stop pretending. I know what you like."

Exactly what I was afraid of. I was still turned on, despite the fantastic orgasm moments ago. Something about the way he spoke to me, handled me—rough and rude—was unlike anything I'd experienced and for some reason I got off on it.

She's trouble. A cock-hungry slut with daddy issues a mile long.

While I was still struggling with insecurities both past and present, Enzo reached down to fist his cock, stroking. Muscles popped as he worked his shaft, and I stared, mesmerized. Ugh. Even his balls were sexy, and balls were definitely *not* sexy. Why, why, why was it this man who had this effect on me?

"Here is the game," he said. "I give you a ten second head start to run. Then I will chase you. And when I catch you, I'm going to pin you down and fuck you."

When, not if.

My fingers twisted in the towel as images of him holding me down, thrusting between my legs bombarded my brain. The idea of it was so wrong, yet my pussy clenched as desire squeezed my lungs like a fist.

I tried to keep my voice even. "What makes you think I want this?"

He shook his head. "Because I mentioned it and you came hard on my dick two minutes ago. I think you like the idea."

My breathing picked up, nostrils flaring as I struggled to get enough air. He noticed, of course, his gaze darting to my chest, and he smirked. "Wouldn't it feel good to fight me as hard as you can? To hit and kick me as much as you like before I stick my dick inside you?"

"No," I whispered weakly. I was so wet between my legs and it had nothing to do with the hot tub. My mouth was suddenly dry, so I licked my lips. "You're insane."

"Sì, certo. But you can't hide from me, Gia. I see everything you are thinking. You're panting right now even as you consider it."

Get out of my head, mafioso.

"Your other choice," he continued, still slowly stroking between his legs, "is to get on your hands and knees on my bed and present your ass for me."

"No way. I will never let that thing in my ass."

He actually rolled his eyes. "Don't lie to yourself, micina. I promise you will love it more than you love my fingers there, which is to say a lot."

I let that go for now. I had bigger problems on my hands. "I want option c—none of the above."

"Cazzata. Your pupils are dilated and you're nearly hyperventilating from horniness. Hurry up and decide."

"I could give you another blow job."

The edge of his mouth hitched. "So eager to suck me again. I like this, Gianna." He walked over and I tightened my grip on the towel. What was he going to do?

Panic fluttered in my throat as he bent at my feet. Using the key, he unlocked the cuff on my ankle and it fell to the ground, freeing me. Then he looked up at me, his eyes wild. "We begin now. Ten, nine, eight—"

I dropped the towel and started running.

My heart thumped hard as I sprinted for the bedroom, heading toward the door that led to the rest of the yacht. I flew like lightning through his office and into the main corridor. Every inch of my skin was alive, blood pumping feverishly in my veins. I could do this. I could get away from him, hide, and eventually escape. It was what I wanted, wasn't it?

Don't lie. You want him to catch you. Overwhelm you and fuck you.

I couldn't. It was wrong. Women weren't supposed to want something like this, especially with their kidnapper. *What is wrong with me?*

Then I heard him behind me. Has it been ten seconds already?

Shit, shit, shit. Fear and excitement blended together in my head and I pushed myself to go faster, trying to reach the stairs before he caught me. I could almost feel him chasing me, his lust and aggression a perfume in the air, and my body responded to it despite myself. We were two animals in heat and I was his prey.

Just as I grabbed the railing to the stairs I was lifted off my feet and dragged into a hard naked chest. The confusion in my head meant my fight became real and I struggled, but he pinned my arms to my sides. "Let me go, you fucking asshole!"

Instead of answering, he turned and carried me back the way we came.

I flailed, my legs kicking anywhere I could reach, and he grunted when my heel connected with the side of his knee. I did it again, harder.

"Basta, stronza!" he growled in my ear, his arms tightening around me.

I didn't listen. I kept kicking and writhing, a wildcat determined to hurt him at all costs. His erection, huge and hard, pressed into the crack of my ass. "Don't you dare, Enzo. I swear, I will kill you!"

He chuckled darkly as we entered his office, like this was a big joke. It infuriated me, and I was able to land a kick on the inside of his knee this time—which caused him to stumble. I broke free and started running again, toward the door out to the deck.

This time I wanted him to catch me.

I wanted it with a desperation that should have scared me. I wanted him to need me more than anyone has ever needed me, like he would die if he didn't fuck me. I wanted him to overpower me in the very best ways.

Before I could contemplate where I was going, he tackled me. His big body slammed into my back and took me down to the office carpet, one of his arms bracing our fall.

"Fuck off!" I clawed and scraped as he battled to get me under control, muscles straining from the effort, until he just decided to pin me down using his body weight.

I couldn't move. His legs covered mine, his chest smashed to my back, and his big hands were locked around my wrists, restraining me. I yelled and cursed at him every way I knew how. I tried to ram the back of my head into his face, but I couldn't get enough leverage in my prone position. He kept me there, unmoving, letting me tire myself out.

He shifted to hold me with one big hand, and then blunt fingertips slipped into my bathing suit bottoms to prod at my entrance. "Madonna, just as I thought. Dripping."

Humiliation had me struggling once more, and my nipples scraped against the carpet. "It's fear, not arousal," I gasped under his massive bulk.

His chuckle echoed through my ribs. "Liar."

One thick finger penetrated me and the pressure sent my pulse soaring. I smothered the urge to rock my hips. Fuck, that felt good.

"How many fingers before you give up the fight, micina?"

Goddamn this man. He was drawing this out, always determined to break me down no matter the circumstances. Like everything was a game and he had to win at all costs.

I tried to buck him off once more, but the movement only brought his finger deeper inside me. I sucked in a short breath. "I will never stop fighting you. Even if my body temporarily wants you, my mind never will."

"I guess we will see, no?" A second finger shoved inside, rougher than the last. The slight burn was quickly chased by a rush of need. He gathered my hair, pushed the heavy mass to the side, and licked the nape of my neck. "So hot, so wet. It's like heaven. I can't wait to stick my cock in here."

"Just do it, il pazzo!"

His dick jerked against my ass. "Hmm. I like it when you call me that."

"You would." I both hated and loved that he was winning. I needed to prove that I still had fight left in me. So I stretched and bit his thick bicep, clamping down hard.

"Cazzo!" He let out a choked laugh, his hips ramming forward. "You'll make me come!"

The fucker actually liked it. I let him go and went limp. There was nothing I could do, no injury I could cause, to hurt this man sufficiently. He'd been tortured by the best in the business, after all.

He shifted and removed his fingers. I whimpered, my swollen tissues weeping with need. He untied my bottoms and tossed the flimsy cloth aside. Then the crown of his dick dragged against my entrance, teasing, and I actually tilted my hips, eager for the invasion. He kissed between my shoulder blades. "That's it. You're ready for me, no?"

I was beyond denial, beyond caring. "Yes," I admitted into the carpet.

"Show me. Take me inside, troietta."

This was so dirty. So wrong. Yet my body was humming, almost burning alive with lust. There was an embarrassing amount of wetness between my legs, more than I would've thought possible considering the circumstances.

I should hate this. I'm a failure at feminism.

Emma would be so disappointed in me if she knew. But he was right. I wanted him inside me.

I adjusted my hips, seeking, and the head of his cock slipped inside me. *Fuck, yes.* I didn't stop, continuing to rock my hips, writhing underneath him, to bring him deeper. I was wild for it, desperate to reach the finish, toward the explosive orgasm I knew awaited me.

"Shh," he said in my ear. "I'll give you what you need."

He took over then, but pressed in much slower than I expected. The beginning had been about domination and strength, but now he invaded so carefully, like he wanted me to feel every twitch and tiny movement. This was almost seduction, and it was worse than the chaos of moments ago. But there was no stopping it. I craved this, *needed* it.

With a growl, he gave a final thrust of his hips and filled me completely, and the air left my lungs in a rush. He was hot and hard and so big, his dick impaling me, with the heavy weight of his body preventing me from moving. All I could do was lie there and take it. Which made it a thousand times hotter.

"*Fuck*," he said on a long exhale, then whispered a long string of Italian that sounded both bewildered and excited. Finally, he braced his knees on the carpet and rose up onto his elbows to thrust inside me. He no longer held me down but I wasn't going anywhere, not until we traded orgasms. He owed me that at least.

Ragged breaths gusted against my cheek as he began to move, his hips meeting my ass. "You are mine, Gia Mancini. Until I decide otherwise this pussy belongs to me."

I couldn't respond, because his dick was destroying me in the very best way. I loved the way he felt inside me, like there was no room for anything else. No insecurities or worries, no past or future. Just this, right here. Perspiration coated my skin and he surrounded me, his cock pounding, pounding, pounding into my body. The pleasure built and I closed my eyes, focusing on the orgasm just out of reach.

The sounds of skin slapping and heavy breathing filled the room. He fucked me like it was his purpose in life, completely dedicated to the task and never slowing down for a second. With every savage thrust I slid a little on the carpet, and I was so close to coming, my muscles clenching and straining....

"You belong to me, no? Say it, Gianna."

The words twisted inside me, driving me higher, and the walls of my pussy contracted around his cock.

"Minchia!" he grunted. "Do that again."

I squeezed around him once more, and he groaned. "Tell me. Let me hear you say it." His fingers slid between my body and the carpet, moving lower until he found my clit. He rubbed me in tight circles. "Let me hear you say you belong to me."

The words fell from my mouth on a gasp. "I belong to you."

Everything changed. He rode me even harder, without mercy, his fingers never leaving my clit. "Vieni per me, mia bella troietta."

Come for me, my beautiful little slut.

The combination of the words along with the stimulation became too much. Shocks raced up from my toes as the orgasm rushed over me. My brain went offline, everything going blank for a long moment as the euphoria transported me into space. "God, yes! Oh, fuck," I heard myself shout from far away while I shook uncontrollably.

When my climax finally ebbed, he moved to his knees and lifted my hips to change the angle. It allowed him deeper, and after a few pumps he swelled inside me, his hips stuttering just before hot jets of come filled my pussy. "Dio cane!" he roared, his fingertips sinking into my flesh. No doubt I would be covered in bruises tomorrow.

That should've horrified me, but it didn't.

After a moment, his movements slowed but he kept rocking, his dick still pulsing inside me. "Take it all, micina," he crooned and lowered to kiss my spine. "Take all of my come. You earned it. Sei proprio una brava bambina."

You're such a good girl.

Jesus, I wished he would stop saying things like that. I flushed from head to toe and basked in the praise. He continued peppering my skin with kisses, displaying a tenderness I hadn't expected. I melted like hot candle wax on the floor.

"Sei bellissima," he murmured as he dropped kisses along my spine. "Sei perfetta."

You're so beautiful. You're perfect.

I flushed at the compliments. Was this really happening? Enzo D'Agostino, sweet? Why wasn't I shoving him off me and berating him for being so rough?

Abruptly, he pulled out and fell to the side, his body sprawled on the carpet, not touching me. Cool air rushed over my skin as I angled to see him and tried to catch my breath. He stared at the ceiling, arms wide, chest heaving, while sweat rolled down his temples and into his thick dark hair. We stayed like that for a long time, neither of us speaking. I didn't have a clue as to what to say. I felt destroyed in the very best way.

He dragged a hand down his face. "I haven't been inside a woman since the dungeon, and I always used condoms before."

Oh, right. He'd gone in bare, hadn't he?

I cleared my throat. "I have an IUD, so there's that."

Blood trickled down his inner arm and I realized it was my doing, when I bit him earlier. I almost apologized, but he was my kidnapper. I didn't owe him apologies. So, why did it feel like I did?

"Soak in the hot tub," he said and pushed to his feet. "Otherwise you will be sore tonight."

He didn't help me up or even look in my direction. Instead, he jerked on some clothes and walked out of the office, leaving me on the floor. Naked, filled with his come, and unshackled.

I couldn't move, too tangled up in my own thoughts. There was a lot to unpack here, but two things stood out from the chaos swirling in my brain:

I had allowed Enzo D'Agostino to fuck me, and it was the best sex of my life.

CHAPTER SEVENTEEN

Enzo

I climbed the stairs and strode into the office. Massimo and Vito were both there and they looked up from their phones when I walked inside. I ignored their shocked expressions.

I understood their concern. I wasn't sure what the fuck was happening with me, either. I felt confused and angry and on the edge of my sanity. Sex with Gia had been better than I expected—but that still didn't explain the affection I showed her afterward, foolishly kissing and praising her like a lover.

She was no doubt laughing at me down there, pleased at what an idiot I'd become for her. Thinking her magic pussy made me weak, that she could control me with her tight cunt and little gasps.

The worst part? I wasn't sure she couldn't.

Weak and tired, I had crawled into my bed with her last night, needing to feel her soft skin against me again as I slept. She had cuddled close to me, sighing in her sleep, and the darkness in my head had receded for a short while.

It infuriated me.

Vito was the first to speak. "Are you alright? We heard fighting. And your arm is bleeding."

I didn't answer.

Massimo's gaze was wary as I took the seat behind my desk. "Zo, I swear. I didn't do anything inappropriate."

"No? So it wasn't you who brought her wine and food? Gave her a bikini and sat with her in the hot tub?"

"Yes, but—"

I jabbed a finger into the desktop. "I told you no one sees her but me. I told you to stay away from her."

"Mi dispiace!" He slammed his hands on the armrests and pushed up out of his chair. "But I am fucking bored. We've been on this yacht *forever* and nothing ever happens."

I was around my desk in a flash. My fingers wrapped around my brother's throat and I shoved him into the wall, pinning him. "What *happens* on this yacht, pezzo di merda, is that you stay alive. I keep you here so that we all fucking stay alive! I keep my children in England, away from me, so they stay alive!"

"Easy, both of you." Vito was there, pulling me away. "Everyone is on edge, no? There's no reason to fight."

I stepped back. "Stop acting like a selfish brat, Massimo, and stay away from her."

"I'm not trying to fuck her, I swear," he said. "But you have to admit, she's beautiful to look at."

A red haze coated my brain and I lunged, ready to draw his blood. Suddenly Vito blocked my path. "Calm down," he said. "No one is going to touch her, capisce?"

I pointed in Massimo's face. "*Vattene*! I have calls to make and emails to answer. You know, *boring* things that earn us money and allow us to stay alive."

As I went to my chair I heard Vito tell Massimo, "Get out of here."

Earlier, when I heard Massimo and Gia laughing out on my deck, I had been in the middle of updating a spreadsheet. Instead of opening it again, I checked my email.

I sat up when I saw what awaited. Stefano's report on Gia.

I clicked on it eagerly, desperate to learn all I could about this woman. It started with the basics, her age and family, where she grew up and went to school. I kept scrolling. Next were her friends, where she lived in college and her grades.

And her ex-boyfriend.

Che cazzo?

Stefano had a photo, a social media post, of Gia smiling up at some coglione, his arm around her. Grayson Webber.

Gritting my teeth, I read on.

She caught Grayson texting another woman, Julia Delgado, whom he had been secretly seeing on the side. The relationship ended abruptly.

That testa di cazzo had fucked another woman behind Gia's back?

Che idiota! A woman like Gia in your bed and you cheat on her? She was better off without him.

I kept reading. There were photos from a design exhibition Gia had entered at university, which explained the sketches I'd seen in my room last night. She wanted to be a clothing designer.

"When will we next reach a port?" I asked my brother, who was working at his desk near mine.

Vito checked the time. "We refilled the fuel tank at Cannes, so it won't be for a while. Did you need something? I can have it brought out."

"I want an electronic sketch pad and stylus. Have them put software on it for a clothing designer."

Vito's jaw fell open. "Tell me you are joking."

"Would you rather I put her back in the cage?"

"Of course not. But *gifts*?"

"You are the one who wanted me to treat her kindly, no?" I kept scrolling the report. "And it's not a gift as much as a bargaining chip."

That must've satisfied my brother because he returned to his work and left me alone. Finally I found what I'd been looking for. Gia's health report.

She hadn't lied about the IUD, which was a relief. Also, she had no sexually transmitted diseases as of her last checkup, which had been right before she moved to Milan. And there had been no men since Grayson.

For a woman who liked sex as much as Gia did, she wasn't as active as I would've assumed. Had that boy, the one who cheated on her, broken her heart?

And why did I care if the answer was yes?

Gia

The engines started up again that evening.

I was sitting on the deck, bored and restless, the dark ocean all around us. After Enzo left, I'd soaked in the hot tub, then showered. I dressed in a pair of shorts and a top from the pile of clothes Massimo had brought. At every turn I'd expected my kidnapper to come into the suite and taunt me, then force me to disrobe. To put me on my knees and make me beg.

Except the door remained closed.

At the very least I deserved food. Didn't he know I was starving? I had a small fridge full of bottled water, but that wasn't enough.

Clearly he thought he could fuck me and then ignore me. That I would stay put like a good little pet, even when I wasn't chained. I guess he didn't care if I starved. Cecilia normally brought my food, but there'd been no sign of her after Enzo left this afternoon.

Vieni per me, mia bella troietta.

Wincing, I picked at my chipped nail polish. And why wouldn't he assume that he could treat me like shit? I opened my legs so easily for him, told him everything he wanted to hear. He was probably recounting the entire experience for his brothers, all of them laughing at how desperate I'd been. How slutty, how pathetic.

Fuck that.

I was not desperate or pathetic. He couldn't treat me like this and get away with it. I was always telling Emma to stand up for herself, so why wasn't I following my own advice? In the past, when someone wronged me, I made sure there were consequences.

I was Gia fucking Mancini. I would not let this stronzo control me.

Rising, I went through the bedroom and into the empty office. I purposely didn't look at the carpet as I continued into the main part of the yacht. I had enough reminders of what happened earlier, no need for more.

Laughter echoed ahead, so I followed the sound. Laughter equaled happiness, which meant Enzo was clearly not involved. Good. I could do without seeing his smug face.

I entered what was a dining area and found Massimo and Vito at the table. Their smiles died when they saw me. "Signorina!" Vito said, standing as he studied me from head to toe. "What are you doing?"

"Looking for food." I pointed to the platters on the table. "Do you mind?"

"Not at all." It was Massimo who answered. He rose and held out a chair for me. "Please, join us."

"Thank you." I sat and started filling an empty plate with chicken piccata in a lemon and caper sauce.

Vito poured me a glass of white wine. "He took off your chain. I hadn't expected that."

Neither had I. And it appeared Enzo hadn't filled his brothers in on all the details from the afternoon. "Your brother is full of surprises, I guess."

The two men exchanged a glance I didn't understand, so I turned my attention to the food. Fuck, it was good. Rich and buttery smooth, the chicken melted in my mouth. "God, this is amazing," I mumbled. "Whoever cooks the food on this boat is worth every penny."

Massimo grinned slyly. "I made it."

"Wow, Maz. It's really fucking good."

"Have as much as you like," Vito said. "If I had known he wasn't bringing you dinner, I would've sent some in."

"Speaking of Lucifer, where is he?"

Massimo chuckled until Vito shot him a disapproving look. "He's in the office, working late," Vito said.

"I am sorry if I caused you trouble today, bella," Massimo said, though his sparkling eyes told me he wasn't all that remorseful.

"No worries." I grabbed a piece of bread and dipped it in the piccata sauce. "Your brother's a dick. Nothing you did changes that."

"You would be wise not to anger him, Gia."

This advice was from Vito, who was really starting to piss me off.

"Want me to cover up, Vito? That way I won't entice him with my feminine wiles again."

"Too late for that," Massimo muttered.

"What you both don't understand," I snapped, "is that I don't want to be here. I am not trying to seduce your brother."

Massimo held up his palms in surrender and Vito just sipped his wine. I focused on eating. After a few moments of silence I couldn't take it anymore. "I noticed the engines started back up. So where are we going? I hear there are some nice beaches in Siderno."

"Cute," Massimo said. "You are very funny, bella."

"Fratello," Vito hissed, then spoke a long string of rapid Italian. Massimo rolled his eyes but kept quiet. I wished I understood that exchange. Was Vito pissed that Massimo complimented me?

"You don't like me, do you?" I asked Vito.

He tapped his fingertips on the table as he stared at me for a long moment. "It does not matter whether I like you or not. I do not want a woman—a Mancini, no less—to cause trouble between brothers."

Brothers, plural? Massimo was on his phone, not paying me a bit of attention, so he missed the horrified expression I was surely sporting. Was Vito actually worried I would start sleeping with his younger brother, too? Jesus, as if I would. I wasn't interested in Massimo that way.

A familiar voice shouted, "Vito! *Dove sei?*"

"*Eccomi!*" Vito called back.

I froze, then forced all of my muscles to relax. I wasn't doing anything wrong. If he didn't like me eating dinner out here, that was too damn bad. I reached for more chicken piccata.

Enzo hurried in, a stack of papers in his hand, uttering rapid Italian —and drew to a halt when he saw me sitting at the table. I kept chewing, boldly meeting his surprised stare. *Your pet slipped her leash, mafioso!*

He'd showered and changed since our epic bang fest in his office, but his hair was disheveled, like he'd been running his hands through it in frustration. He didn't look like a man who'd just had the best orgasm of his life.

No, that was just me, I guess.

Whatever. I hoped that the bite mark on his arm hurt like hell.

"Join us," Massimo said, gesturing to the empty chair.

"Or don't," I said. "Seriously, please don't."

"I hadn't realized everyone was eating," he said in a low menacing voice. "I think I will eat, too."

Fuck me.

He lowered himself into the seat at the end, across from me, and poured a glass of wine. Then he reached over and refilled my glass. "Enjoying the food?"

Lifting up another bite, I said, "It's the best thing I've had in my mouth since being kidnapped." *Take that, Enzo.*

The corner of his mouth twitched before he turned to his brothers. "Both of you. Out."

Massimo practically jumped out of his chair and left the room. Vito went more slowly, making sure to share a glance with Enzo before leaving. It was similar to what Emma and I did, a silent communication that Frankie called our twin mind-meld. Were Enzo and Vito so close they could read each other's minds?

When we were alone Enzo reached for a piece of bread. He dipped it into a plate of olive oil and took a bite. I tried not to stare at his mouth or the strong jaw while he chewed.

"What are you doing in here, micina?"

"Eating." I gestured to my plate. "Have you forgotten that prisoners need food?"

Suddenly, with a mighty shove, he pushed all of the platters and plates off the table and onto the floor. I watched, mouth agape, as everything crashed to the ground, all that glorious food now wasted. The stretch of wooden table before him was now clear.

"Come here." He held out his hand, his dark gaze glittering in the overhead light.

"Why?" I didn't trust him not to do something terrible.

"Get up and walk your sexy ass over here, bambina."

"Or?"

"Then it's back to the cage."

I wasn't certain he meant it, but I couldn't take the chance. Besides, he'd already done his worst. He'd fucked me and I loved it. There was no lower than that.

Chin high, I stood and walked over, and when I was within reach he snagged my wrist and scooted back to make room for me between his thighs. Before I could put up a struggle he stood, grasped my hips, and lifted me onto the table. Then he towered above me, surrounding me, as I sat on the table.

He leaned in and dragged his nose along my cheek, his hands going to my waist. The proximity meant I could smell some kind of citrus soap or shampoo. I could see the rough whiskers coating his jaw, the tiny flecks of amber in his eyes. I hated that I couldn't stop noticing these things. Worse, that I found them attractive.

I was so distracted that I didn't realize he was undoing my shorts.

"What are you doing?" I said, my voice breathier than I would've liked. "I'm pretty sore from earlier, D'Agostino."

"I told you. I'm eating." He put a hand on my sternum and pushed my back flat onto the table. Then in one quick motion, he had me naked from the waist down.

Oh, shit. He meant *me*.

I stared at the ceiling and tried to come up with a reason why I should put a stop to this. Except the excitement galloping through my veins was begging me to let it happen. I remembered how good he was at oral, how he knew exactly what buttons to push to make me come so hard, and I wanted to experience it again.

Lowering himself back into his chair, he pressed kisses along my inner thigh, and goose bumps ran up and down my legs. "Nothing to say?"

Predictably, his smug satisfaction brought out my snark. "Do you need pointers?"

He chuckled into my skin, his hands spreading me wide. "I am well acquainted with your pussy by now, so no. But feel free to be as loud as you like. Scream so the entire yacht knows who you belong to."

God, I shouldn't find that so hot. It was wrong, yet I was dripping at the idea of everyone hearing me, of everyone knowing what Enzo was doing to me right now in full view.

Someone could walk by and see us.

I shivered, my pussy clenching. Was I supposed to fight him on this? I was confused, drunk on desire, and way more excited than I wanted to admit.

His tongue met my folds and I sucked in a breath. "Mmm," he growled low in his throat. "You are so wet. Is this for me?"

I let out a gasp when licked up the length of my slit. "It's for the chicken piccata."

The tip of his tongue played with my piercing, moving it around and causing me to squirm. Each swirl and flick sent little sparkles through my core. "Cazzata," he whispered. "This is for me. You like the possibility of someone seeing me eating you out, of everyone hearing you come."

I did. I really, really did.

"Maybe, but all you're doing is talking so I guess—"

He sucked on my clit and that shut me the hell up.

CHAPTER EIGHTEEN

Enzo

After Gia came on my tongue, I pulled her upright then slipped my hands under her ass to lift her. For a second I thought she might fight me, but she just wrapped her arms and legs around me and held on while I carried her toward the stairs. She muttered, "I really hope someone disinfects that table before the next meal."

My lips twitched, laughter sitting in my throat. "I just gave you a fantastic orgasm and you are worried about germs?"

Sighing, she rested her head on her arm, her forehead tucked against my throat. I could feel her sweet breath on my skin, her scent all around me. I held her tighter.

I climbed the steps, exhaustion making every step feel increasingly heavier. Surprisingly, Gia stayed silent. Was she also confused over this insane pull between us?

When I reached my bedroom I pulled down the covers, lowered her onto the bed, and began shedding my clothes. Still naked from the waist down, she pushed up onto her elbows and watched me. "Take off your shirt," I ordered.

She did as I asked, but frowned. "My pussy is out of commission, D'Agostino. I think you've broken her."

I slid into bed and laid down next to her. Then I dragged the covers up over both of us. I was half hard, but I could wait until she'd recovered to fuck her again. "Relax. I just want to sleep."

"Where did you sleep last night?"

"Here, but not for long." I came in around three, desperate for a few hours' rest, and left when the sun came up.

Gia didn't try to touch me, just kept her hands folded on her stomach. I moved in closer, rolling to face her and throwing an arm over her middle.

"No wonder you're so fucked up. You're an insomniac."

"You like my kind of fucked up," I whispered into the softness of her hair.

She didn't deny it, and we stayed there in silence for a long moment, sleep tugging at the edges of my mind. Everything was slowing down, getting hazy, and I welcomed it. I would allow her a few more minutes of freedom before restraining her again for the night.

"What happened to your wife?"

Her question jolted me wide awake. "Why do you want to know?"

"Did you kill her?"

"You think I would murder the mother of my children?" I shook my head. "Dai, Gianna."

"It's not unheard of in the mafia."

This was true. There had been rumors about old Mommo and how his wives kept disappearing. But I didn't want to think of that bastard ever again. I hoped he was burning in Hell right now. "It was a car accident," I said.

"Oh, that's terrible. Were your children in the car with her?"

"No. She was with one of my guards. Neither were wearing their seat belts and they were killed instantly."

"How awful. Do you miss her?"

I frowned. "Our marriage was not like that. It was a partnership, not love."

"I guess I understand that. I think my mother regretted marrying my father as she grew older. At least, that's what Frankie said."

"She died when you were young, no?" Everyone knew of the beautiful Sophia Romano Mancini, a famous model before Roberto married her and took her off to Toronto.

"Yes, when I was eight. What are your kids like?"

"Why so many questions?"

She lifted a shoulder. "I'm curious. If you want me to entertain myself, buy me a phone."

I grunted. The likelihood of that was zero. "Luca is my oldest, he's twelve. Nicola is nine."

"Did you ever spend time with them?"

I leaned back to see if she was serious. "Che cazzo? Of course I did."

"Oh." She nibbled on her bottom lip.

Ah, so Roberto hadn't been a good father. Neither had mine. When Luca was born I vowed not to repeat the mistakes of the past. I never wanted my children to grow up as I had, in terror and hatred. Tortured and tormented. I would protect them from all the violence and ugliness of my world.

And it had worked, until Ravazzani dragged them from their beds.

I settled in next to her once more and closed my eyes. The words began tumbling out before I could stop them. "Luca loved food and was always in the kitchen. I showed him my nonna's recipes, took him to the market. Even at eight years old he was good with knives. He could dice an onion like a restaurant chef."

"That's sweet. What about your daughter?"

An ache twisted in my chest when I thought of my principessa. "I had recently taught her to ride a bicycle," I said, my voice gruff. "She fell and scraped her knee, so I put on a special purple bandage because it's her favorite color."

"You love them."

"Do not sound surprised. I love my children more than anything else in the world."

"Then where are they? Why aren't they on the boat with you?"

My skin turned hot, the muscles in my back tensing. Was she really so clueless? "I have them somewhere safe. My life is under constant threat, so my children are kept in hiding for their own good, far away from me. Some place where Ravazzani will never find them."

"Fausto wouldn't hurt your kids, Enzo."

I snorted at her naiveté. "He held a gun on my son and daughter, threatened them in front of me. There is no limit to what he would do to hurt me or my family, if he felt justified."

"Do you see them often?"

I wasn't certain how much to tell her. "No. Only for very brief periods of time."

"Those few days must be nice."

It was. I couldn't begin to describe how much those visits with my children meant to me. Without them, I wasn't certain that I would have survived the last four years.

She was silent for a long time and I could feel myself slipping toward sleep. Then she said, "I wish my dad had taught me how to ride a bike."

"You can't ride a bike?"

"Of course I can." She stared up at the ceiling, smiling, like she was reliving a good memory. "Frankie taught both Emma and me. The guards laughed at us the whole time, but Frankie made them turn around. It was so funny, all these big scary men facing away from us because she didn't want our feelings hurt."

I watched her beautiful face and my chest swelled. It felt like something missing had suddenly been returned. A sense of déjà vu, almost. I was comfortable with her in ways I wasn't with anyone else, even before the dungeon.

But why was I cuddling her and sharing my intimate thoughts? I hadn't done that with either my wife or Mariella. This woman was my *captive*. She would take whatever information I gave her and use it against me at her first opportunity. It was what anyone would do in her shoes.

Cazzo, I was a fucking fool.

Reaching up, I grabbed one of the restraints affixed to the headboard. "Give me your hand."

She rolled to the other side of the bed and stood up. I leaned up, ready for battle. "Where do you think you are going?"

"To the bathroom. Jesus, calm down. If you're chaining me to the bed, I'd better pee first."

Closing my eyes, I let her go. I'd rest until she returned, then cuff her to the bed again.

CHAPTER NINETEEN

Gia

I stared at myself in the bathroom mirror. I barely recognized the person reflected there.

It was late, well after midnight. My pussy still tingled from the absolutely stellar orgasm he gave me on the dining table.

Everything Enzo did to me was wrong, so fucked up and wrong. I normally didn't trust men, especially after Grayson. Yet I trusted Enzo. He hadn't lied to me. He told me exactly why I was here and what I meant to him. Revenge on Fausto.

So why wasn't I fighting him any longer? Instead, I was collecting orgasms like some women collected designer handbags.

Sei bellissima, sei perfetta.

My stomach fluttered at the memory. I liked when he turned sweet and whispered sexy Italian in my ear. I liked how he praised me during sex. I liked his insane need for me, when he turned almost feral when we fucked. I liked the way he talked about his kids, the way he was sacrificing everything to keep his family safe. I liked how smart he was, how ruthless. How unpredictable.

Shit. I liked him. Like, really liked him.

What the fuck?

Enzo blew up a restaurant, kidnapped me, and locked me in a cage, for fuck's sake. He was capable of unspeakable violence. Yet this didn't repulse me nearly as much as it should have.

Jesus. A little more than a week with him and I was already dick drunk.

I was not supposed to like this man. He was my kidnapper. Plus, he was a mafioso. I could never have feelings for a mafia man like my father. Papa had stolen my mother's future and made her miserable with his cheating and controlling lifestyle. That life might work for my older sister, but it was not what I wanted.

Yet I was swooning after Enzo like a thirteen-year-old girl who just received her first kiss. God, I was screwed up, just like Papa's guards said. Maybe I did have daddy issues. Maybe growing up in the life changed me and made it impossible to escape. Was I fooling myself by hoping for a normal relationship and career?

My eyes turned glassy in the mirror, tears stinging the backs of my eyelids. My plan had been to seduce Enzo, get close to him and then kill him. But I hadn't thought about hurting him in days. I wasn't certain I even could at this point.

I love my children more than anything else in the world.

He'd taught his daughter to ride a bicycle. And put a purple bandage on her knee when she fell! I gripped the counter and hung my head. My whole life I'd wished for that kind of attention from my father. How could I kill Enzo and deprive that little girl of a father who loved her like that?

But I didn't want to be Enzo's pawn, either. This had to stop. I had to do something before it was too late.

Enzo was in the other room, waiting on me, so I needed to pull it together. Otherwise he would know something was up. That man was scary perceptive. I practiced a blank expression in the mirror. When I felt confident in my acting I opened the door and walked into the bedroom.

I sagged in relief.

Enzo was asleep. I watched as his chest rose and fell evenly, his long lashes kissing the tops of his cheeks. The lines of his face had eased and he appeared so much younger than when he was awake. Carefree, without the bitterness and anger that usually etched his expression.

My God, he was a handsome man.

Get a grip, Gia.

I needed to do something. Swimming to safety was out of the question, but there had to be a phone somewhere around here. A laptop, a tablet . . . something I could use to let my family know that I was okay. If Fausto learned I was on a yacht off the coast of wherever, couldn't he launch a rescue mission?

Was Enzo pretending to be asleep? I doubted it. He would be trying to cuff me to the bed instead of playacting. I had to risk it.

Quietly, I put on a t-shirt and shorts, then started creeping toward the door, my toes digging into the carpet silently. The whole time I kept my eyes trained on Enzo's face, bracing myself for him to wake up and tackle me onto the bed. If he discovered me sneaking around, he would lose his shit.

He didn't move, his breathing steady, even when I reached the door. *Here goes nothing.* I slipped out and moved into the office. I didn't dare turn on a light, but I could see well enough. The desk was empty except for some papers and a few pens. The desk had no drawers with locks to pick. Damn.

I hadn't seen Enzo with a cell phone, but Massimo carried one. Was there a common phone for the staff to use? Somewhere on this boat was a way for me to communicate with the outside world and I was going to find it. I kept going.

The galley was dark and so was the dining area. A quick search turned up nothing useful. Below were staterooms, where I had the best chance of running into someone else. That meant I had to climb up to the next deck.

I didn't know what I was going to find, so I went slowly, taking each step without making a sound. At the top of the stairs there was a well-lit room where a man sat behind the controls. I bent quickly, hoping he didn't see me. That must be the pilot house.

Keeping low, I started to explore. A gym. This explained how Enzo kept in such amazing shape. But it held nothing but a faint stench of cleaning solutions and body odor.

The next room was a big office, the one Enzo clearly used.

Bingo.

I slipped in, closed the door softly, and let my eyes adjust to the semi-darkness. Two desks faced each other, and the bigger one had a pair of giant monitors on top. That had to be Enzo's. *Please, please, please let there be something I can use.* I crept over and almost passed out from excitement. A closed laptop!

My hope died a few minutes later when I couldn't guess Enzo's password to unlock the damn thing. Shit.

The desk had four drawers. They were locked, of course, but all I needed were picking tools. I quickly found two paper clips in a little cup on the second desk.

It seemed to take forever, but I opened Enzo's drawers one by one. In the bottom drawer I found what I was looking for. A satellite phone.

Holy shit. *Let's go, motherfuckers!*

It was half charged and not password protected, so I was dialing before I took my next breath. When the phone started ringing I could feel my heart trying to pound its way out of my chest.

"Hello?" my twin whispered.

"Emma, it's me!" Tears sprang to my eyes, relief pouring through me like water. "It's me, it's me, it's me."

"Oh God, Gigi. I knew it! I knew you weren't dead."

"Enzo D'Agostino kidnapped me before the bomb went off."

"So where are you now?"

She sounded off. Strange and too quiet. Like she was hiding. "What's wrong?"

"I'm—Shoot. I think they heard me."

My muscles clenched and I could feel her anxiety through the phone. "Where are you?"

"I'm in Milan. I came to try and find you."

"You *what?*" I screeched. "Why in the world did Papa allow that?"

"He doesn't know. He thinks I'm at school. It's a long story. Can we talk about this later? There are some guys following me and they don't look friendly. At all."

I sucked in a breath. "What the fuck? Who are they? Tell me exactly where you are—"

The line went dead.

"No!" I looked at the phone, stunned. "Goddamn it!"

Emma. She was in trouble. My stomach knotted painfully. Who would possibly want to hurt my sweet sister? I tried to call her back twice but she didn't answer. "Fuck!"

I had to reach Frankie.

Just as I started to dial, light flooded the room. Whirling, I found Enzo standing there, his brow pulled low over furious dark eyes and his muscles bulging.

No! God, not yet.

I backed up, trying to get away from him as I kept dialing. "Stay away from me, D'Agostino!"

"You've been bad, micina." His voice was low and tight, the promise of retribution in every syllable.

"Do not come near me!" I dodged around the desk, but he was quicker. In an instant his long arms caught me and ripped the phone out of my hands. "No!" I screamed at the top of my lungs, fighting him with everything I had. This wasn't about me any longer; Emma was in trouble and I had to help her. It was all my fault.

I clawed and scratched at him. I kicked and punched wherever I could reach, attempting to get the phone out of his hands. I was wild, unhinged. A woman with nothing to lose.

He grunted when my fist connected with his jaw, and his arms instantly immobilized me. "Basta, Gianna!"

"She's in danger, you ape! I have to do something. I have to tell someone who can help her, asshole!"

Suddenly, I was on the floor, a furious mafioso pinning me down. "Calm down. I am serious, Gia. Calm down or I'm taking you to the cage."

I struggled a little more, hoping to break his hold, but when it became apparent that he wasn't going to relent, I sagged into the carpet. The backs of my eyelids began to burn, so I turned my head and tried to catch my breath. Had those men caught her? I couldn't bear the thought of Emma in danger.

"Who the fuck did you call?" Enzo barked.

A tear slid from my eye, along my temple, and into my hairline. "My sister," I whispered. "Emma. She's—" I swallowed a sob. "She's in Milan. She said there are men chasing her. Then the phone cut out." My breath hitched and another tear fell. Shit, I was going to lose it.

"She came to Milan? What the fuck was your father thinking, letting her go there?"

"He doesn't know. He thinks she's at school."

Enzo eased off slightly, keeping a firm grip on me but at least not smothering me. "She came looking for you."

"Yes." I started crying then, not even caring that he was witnessing my pain. "Please, Enzo. I know you hate me and my whole family, but please. You have to let me call Frankie. Fausto can save Emma."

His lips twisted into an ugly sneer. "Fucking Ravazzani. I can do more than him—and much faster."

"But . . . ." I rolled to my side and studied his face as hope sparked in my chest. "Will you help her? Please, Enzo."

His gaze dipped to my mouth. "What will you do for me in exchange?"

I should've known he would try and bargain with me, that he wouldn't help me out of the goodness of his heart.

That's because he has no heart.

I turned it back on him. "What do you want?"

"Your complete obedience in all things."

"Sex, you mean."

"All things, Gianna." His fingertip trailed over my cheek then along my jaw. "I want you to accept your fate, to bow to my wishes. To serve me and please me. To do whatever I fucking want, when I want it."

Did I have a choice? I had no way to contact Frankie, and who knew what was happening to Emma right now? I would let Enzo degrade me for the rest of my life if it meant saving my twin.

"Yes, yes. Now please, go and save her! Whatever you need to do."

His eyes glittered in triumph. "Give me your word. If you break your promise, you will both suffer for it."

There was no hesitation in the way he said it, no hint of hyperbole. I believed he meant every word. "I promise to do whatever you want if you save Emma."

He pushed off the ground with one hand, a feat that would've impressed me if I weren't so worried about my sister. "Let's get to work, micina."

Enzo

With two phone calls I discovered who took Emma Mancini and where they were keeping her.

I glanced at Gia, sitting across from me, and her tear-streaked face tugged at something inside me. She looked at me earnestly, hopefully, like I could solve all the problems in the entire world.

No woman had looked at me in such a way. Angela had been wary, resigned. She knew the man I was, knew exactly what to expect in our marriage. Mariella viewed me as an important man who would buy her nice things, take her nice places, and never make any demands on her other than physical ones.

The way Gia looked at me, like I was her protector? Her savior? Madonna, I could get used to it.

I hung up, rang the pilot house and asked them to return to Milan immediately. Then I explained the situation to Gia. "There is a group of Russians working in some of the bigger cities, preying on young girls at the airports. Girls who seem lost, who travel alone. Emma must have attracted the wrong attention when she arrived in Milan and these men followed her."

Gia swallowed hard, her hands folded in her lap. I'd never seen her so still. "What do they do with the girls?"

"Sell them into brothels or to wealthy foreign buyers." The local 'ndrina usually took a cut of the profits to look the other way, but I didn't mention this.

Her face fell, her eyes going wide with panic. "We can't let that happen to her. We're going to save her, right?"

I liked that she considered us a team, even though we were really on opposite sides. For some reason I wanted to reassure her. "I will get her out."

"Will they hurt her? Are they raping her right now?"

I shook my head. "That isn't how it works. They view her as merchandise. They will want to keep her pure, unharmed. Otherwise, no buyers."

She exhaled and some of the tension left her shoulders. My poor micina, carrying so much worry, but I would make things better for her.

The office door flew open. Vito was there, dressed in jeans and no shirt, his hair tousled. "Did we turn around?"

"Yes," I answered. "We have another errand in Milan."

"Who?"

"Emma Mancini." I nodded at Gia.

Vito blinked as if he'd just noticed her presence, then narrowed his eyes on me. "Che cazzo?"

"She's been kidnapped by the Russians, probably to be sold on the open market."

"And?"

I knew what he was thinking, the worries that were likely rolling through his head. But I owed him no explanations. "And we are taking care of it."

"Speak English," Gia snapped. "What are you talking about?"

My brother rubbed his jaw. "I need to speak to you alone," he continued in Italian.

"No." I started dialing again, this time to Stefano. It paid to have hackers on the payroll.

"Enzo, I'm serious." Vito was in front of my desk now. "We must discuss this. You can't honestly care about your whore's—"

I hung up the phone before I finished dialing. "Mind your tongue, fratello," I snarled.

"Madre di Dio! Is she leading you around by your cock now?"

I was on my feet, advancing on him. "I am the capo, Vito, not you. I make the decisions, not you. That is the way it will be until I'm dead." I kept going until we were just inches apart, then whispered, "If you want to challenge me, then by all means try and take the crown. But I promise it won't be easy."

"I don't want the crown," he spat and retreated a step. "But this is terrible timing. What about Gabriel Sánchez? We are supposed to be finding him, no?"

I lifted a brow at Vito and said in English, "We deal with Emma Mancini first."

"Are you going to bring her aboard?" Vito asked in Italian.

My lips curved into a small smile. Did he honestly think I hadn't figured out how to use this to my advantage? Not only did it give me more leverage with Ravazzani, it gave me leverage over someone else, too. "Sì, certo."

"I see."

"Va bene. Now, get Massimo up and bring him here. We have to meet with some Russians in Milan."

Vito left and I went behind my desk. Scooting back, I patted my lap. "Lock the door and come here."

Wariness crept over her expression and she didn't move. "Why?"

"Because I have to make a call to help your sister and I want to play with your tits while I do it."

She rolled her lips together, like she was holding in a curse or a refusal, but we both knew she would do whatever I wanted. Maybe I would keep her on the yacht indefinitely, until I grew tired of her. I would have both Mancini twins soon, and I could use Emma as leverage with Ravazzani instead. I wasn't ready to let Gia go.

Do you still deny that you are obsessed with her?

I shoved Vito's voice out of my head. This was not obsession—this was power. It was convenience and revenge. I wasn't done debasing Gia in all the ways I knew how. Until then, she was staying with me on the boat.

Silently, she flicked the lock on the office door then made her way over to me. Her obedience got my dick hard. Blood rushed through my body, my heart pounding with satisfaction, as she slid onto my lap. She sat gingerly, like she was afraid to relax, but I knew that wouldn't last. I wrapped my arm around her and arranged her to my liking, with her ass on my crotch and her back to my chest. I moved each of her legs to straddle the outsides of my thighs, leaving her spread open for me.

My lips coasted over her throat, inhaling her womanly scent while I tasted her soft skin. "So beautiful, so compliant," I murmured. "Take this shirt off. Present your tits to me."

She did as I asked, revealing the smooth golden skin of her upper body. Her breasts were small but I could still squeeze them, and I was pleased when her nipples hardened. I pinched one, and she gasped. "Yes, that's it. I like this. Maybe I'll keep you here all day while I work. Would you like that, bambina?"

"I don't think you would be very productive." Her voice was husky, the way it got when she was turned on.

"Are you wet?"

"Enzo, my sister, remember? Focus."

"Oh, I am focused." I sank my teeth into the place where her neck and shoulder met. She moaned and I bit back a smile. "Pick up the satellite phone."

She tried to give the phone to me, but I kept kissing her shoulder and massaging her tit. I said, "Ring this number." For every button she pushed I tugged on her nipple. By the time the call connected she was squirming on my semi-hard cock.

"Give me the phone." With one hand, I grabbed the phone and dipped the other into her shorts. She was warm and wet, and I played with her piercing, loving the feel of it beneath my fingertips.

"Pronto," a voice said on the other end of the phone.

"Stefano, I need something."

"Of course, Don D'Agostino. What is it?"

I began strumming Gia's clit, rubbing her in tight little circles. She melted into me, her body letting me do whatever I wanted. "There is an abandoned house on Via dei Garofani. Number twenty-five. I need to see who goes in and out, how many men are inside. Can you get cameras there?"

"Yes. I can go in the morning—"

"Now, Stefano. Immediately."

Gia sucked in a sharp breath, her limbs vibrating as her hips rocked into my hand. I continued to work her clit, spreading the slickness all over her warm flesh. Then I fed one finger inside her and she moaned.

Stefano cleared his throat. "I'll go now. Then I'll call you when everything is in place."

"Good." I licked Gia's earlobe as I hung up.

"What was that about?" she panted as I pumped my finger.

"I am putting cameras on the house where your sister is being held. I need to know how many men are inside."

"Then what?"

"Then we go in and get her out."

"Will you kill the Russians?"

I pressed the heel of my hand against her clit. "Do you want me to?"

"Fuck, yes," she sighed, and I wasn't sure if we were talking about the Russians or her impending orgasm. With Gia, probably both.

I continued to finger her, loving the way her walls gripped me. I wished it was my cock instead, but she was too sore and I had things to do. Soon, though. "Would you like me to hurt the men who took your sister? Kill them with my bare hands? Coat my skin with their blood?"

She reached above her head and threaded her fingers through my hair. "I shouldn't think that's hot, but God help me, I do."

"Because you are as fucked up as I am. Dirty and twisted, like me."

"No," she groaned, arching her back as I pressed on her g-spot.

"Do not deny it, mia sporca troietta."

When she said nothing, I removed my fingers and patted her thigh. "Up."

"Wait, what's happening?" She got to her feet awkwardly, her shorts unbuttoned to show off her tanned flat belly. Mamma mia, I could spend days exploring her body.

"I must get to work." I rose and grabbed her face in both my hands. "Go back to bed and let me plan how to save your sister."

"When will you sleep?"

Was she worried about me? A knot formed in my chest. No one had cared enough to look out for me in a long time.

Bending, I kissed her hard and deep. Her lips were soft and lush, her tongue eager against mine, and I took my time. I hadn't kissed a woman in forever, but this felt natural. Easy. Gia gave every bit as good as she got, too, her mouth unafraid and bold as her hands threaded through my hair.

When I finished, she was staring at me with a strange expression on her face. "That's the first time you've kissed me."

I wasn't ready to explore why I had decided to kiss her now, so I slapped her ass and stepped back. "Don't worry. I will come down to finish what we started here in a little bit."

She nodded and pulled away from me. I let her go, my arms falling to my sides. As she crossed the floor, I added, "And do not touch your pussy. I will most definitely know and I will take great pleasure in punishing you for it."

Her gaze sparkled with challenge as she said over her shoulder, "It's mine and I'll touch it if I want, mafioso!"

I was smiling when she slammed the door behind her. *Game fucking on, micina.*

CHAPTER TWENTY

Gia

I paced Enzo's bedroom, trying to stay calm. Somehow I managed to sleep a few hours last night, but I'd been wide awake since daybreak, panicking over what was happening to Emma.

I forced a deep breath. There was no doubt in my mind that Enzo would save my twin. I thought of him at his desk, so intense, intimidating other people into doing what he wanted. He got shit done, that was for sure. A small group of Russian sex traffickers were nothing for Don D'Agostino, my unhinged and crafty mafioso.

My? I bit my lip, my chest swelling with a heavy sigh. Yes, I was clearly in deep shit when it came to this man.

Emma's arrival in Italy needed to serve as a reminder of my priorities: protecting my family. As soon as Emma was safely returned to Canada, I could concentrate on getting Enzo to drop his revenge against Fausto. I didn't want Frankie hurt, either.

But this had to wait until after Emma was safe, away from the Russian traffickers. And where was Enzo? I was going out of my mind down here. It was late afternoon and I hadn't seen him all day. He and his brothers had been sequestered up in the office, making plans.

I had to know what was going on. When were we leaving to go rescue Emma?

Leaving the bedroom, I hurried to the stairs. Two men were at the controls in the pilot house and they both stared at me as I walked by, then dipped their chins almost respectfully. Huh. That was weird.

A minute later I was pushing my way into Enzo's office without bothering to knock.

All three D'Agostino brothers were there, with Enzo behind his desk and Vito and Massimo both in chairs. Each of them looked up at me like I had two heads. Did no one ever interrupt them?

"Gianna, we are busy," Enzo said. "Wait below for me."

"I'm not *waiting below* any longer," I snapped. "What is going on with Emma's rescue?"

Enzo's dark gaze narrowed on me and he leaned back in his chair. He spoke a rapid string of Italian to his brothers, and the younger D'Agostino men stood and headed for the door. Massimo winked at me as he passed and Vito pretended as if I didn't exist.

When we were alone, I said, "Please, tell me. What's happening? I'm going bonkers down there."

He steepled his fingers and considered me. "Do you doubt my abilities or my word to free your sister?"

What? Where was this coming from? "No, but I need to know when this is happening. It's been almost twenty-four hours."

"It has been a little over sixteen and I am waiting until nightfall. Any other questions?"

I didn't like his dismissive attitude, like I was some hysterical female. "You know this is my twin we're talking about, right? You're acting as if I'm meddling in your precious mafia business."

"You are meddling. I said I would take care of it, which means you trust me to handle it, Gianna."

"No, that is not how this works. I am not your little mafia wife at home raising your kids. And I'm definitely not your mantenuta, hanging out downstairs, painting my nails until you arrive to gift me with your magic penis. I'm a Mancini and this is my *sister*."

"And I will bring her back here, alive."

I was afraid of this. "No, *we* will bring her back here alive."

He chuckled like this was a big joke. "You will not be going, micina."

"I am going with you, Enzo. This is non-negotiable."

The amusement died on his face. "You think this is a negotiation? With me? You have nothing to bargain with. Whatever you have I will take. We have a deal, remember?"

Oh, he was really too much. I folded my arms across my chest. "Yes, I promised obedience, but that will only happen *after* my sister is rescued. Until then, I will fight you tooth and nail on everything, especially on coming with you to Milan."

"I like fighting with you. And if we do, prepare to get fucked on my office floor."

"God, you are impossible." I shoved my fingers in my hair and dragged in a deep breath. I had to reason with him. "I have to be there, Enzo. She'll be scared, possibly drugged. Probably hurt. Someone needs to hold her hand and make sure she's—"

I couldn't finish it, my throat closing up like a fist. Tears threatened and I struggled to hold them in. I had to be strong for Emma; I couldn't fall apart.

With a handful of steps, he was around his desk and pulling me into his arms. He was strong and solid, so very warm, and he smelled like the shower soap I was secretly addicted to. His heart thumped against my cheek and I sagged against him, letting him hold me up for a moment.

"Allow me to handle this for you," he said quietly. "You will stay here and stay safe."

"Please, no. I know I sound crazy but I need to be there, to touch her as soon as possible. She's my other half. I need to make sure she's okay."

"It is too dangerous, Gia. I can't be worried about you and the Russians at the same time."

He would be worried about me? Before I could prevent it, pleasure wrapped around my heart like vines, burrowing and digging deep. I couldn't handle this man when he was sweet.

I lifted my arms and put them around his shoulders, letting my fingers play with the ends of his soft hair. "I will stay out of the way, I promise. I'll wait outside."

"You are trying to manipulate me."

"Sì, certo," I said in my best Italian before pressing tiny kisses to his jaw. "Per favore, il pazzo. Let me come with you."

"I like hearing you speak my language," he whispered, nuzzling me until his mouth found mine. He kissed me softly, tentatively, like he was surprised by the need, and I met him eagerly, trying to convince him with my lips.

Within seconds, he slanted his head and took over, his hands wrapped around my skull, his tongue now in my mouth. Lost in a sea of sensation, I held on, the room spinning. Our battles fell away and all I could focus on was this kiss, this inexplicable lust that exploded every time we touched.

Finally, he eased back. "I must bring my brothers back in. There are more details to work out before we leave."

"We? Meaning me, too. Right?"

"No, Gianna."

"I'll be so good, padrone," I whispered, clutching him tighter. "I won't cause any trouble. I'll be your perfect bambina."

"You are always trouble, micina. And I will not change my mind. It's not safe."

"I won't do anything to jeopardize my safety, I promise."

He stepped away, putting distance between us, and his expression turned flat and serious. "You will stay here. I'll lock you up if I have to."

This was really pissing me off. He wasn't listening to me. "Fuck that. I'm coming with you."

A devious smile spread over his face, the kind he wore right before he did something evil to me. His fingers gestured to me as he moved in. "Come with me, pet. It's time for your leash."

I edged out of his reach and snapped, "If you put me in that cage again, I will cut off your balls, D'Agostino."

"You are still trying to give me orders. Haven't you learned by now who controls you?"

With a burst of speed, I darted around the desk, putting the heavy wood between us. Unmoving, we stared at each other. I could see his right eye twitching, so I tried once more to appeal to his intellect. "Enzo, please. Be reasonable. I'll go crazy if I have to sit here and wait while you try to rescue her."

"And I will go crazy if I have to worry about your safety in Milan. No, you stay on the yacht. Trust that I will handle this for you."

Trust? Ha! He would ask for the one thing I found it impossible to give, especially with men. "No offense, but I don't trust anyone with my twin's safety except me."

The change came over him immediately. It was like all the air had been sucked out of the room. His expression turned hard, his body a wall of granite. This was the mafia don, the il pazzo that inspired terror throughout Italy. The man who'd gone up against Fausto Ravazzani . . . and lived.

Enzo's gaze glittered as he approached and I didn't dare move. He was terrifying. This wasn't like before, during our games, when I wanted to wind him up to see what happened. This was a dangerous man who'd been pushed to the very edge.

This was a man you didn't fuck with.

He backed me up against the desk, his big frame crowding mine as he wrapped his hand around my throat. "I take orders from no one. I explain myself to no one. I am the boss, Gianna. For good or bad, I am the fucking boss. So when I say you are staying here, you are fucking staying here. And I won't hesitate to chain you, put you in the cage, or tie you down to make it happen. Capisce?"

I stared up at him. I desperately wanted to challenge him but my self-preservation instincts kicked in. "Fine," I forced out from behind gritted teeth. "I'll stay."

He relaxed, his grip on my neck easing slightly. "That is the right answer. Now, do I need to restrain you? Or can I *trust* you to be a good girl while I'm away, rescuing your sister?"

Asshole. "You can trust me on one condition." He lifted an arrogant eyebrow but said nothing. I pointed in his face. "I want to talk to her on the phone the second you have her somewhere safe."

"Va bene. I will have Cecilia bring you the phone to speak with Emma when the time comes."

"I mean it, Enzo. The very second she is safe. I need to hear her voice."

Enzo

As we readied to take the small motorboat onto shore, Gia lingered nearby, watching. I knew she was nervous and would much rather accompany us to Milan, but I couldn't allow it. She would distract the men, distract *me*.

The breeze pushed her hair out of her face and I admired her beauty. Madre di Dio, she was gorgeous. Tonight she looked so young and vulnerable, the usual snark gone from her expression, replaced with worry over her sister. There were times I regretted that we hadn't met under different circumstances, that she wasn't related by marriage to my worst enemy. That I'd met her in a bar or a nightclub and convinced her to come home with me.

She would have made the perfect mantenuta.

I checked my weapons one more time, asking Vito, "Have you been in touch with Stefano? Is it all set?"

"Sì. They obviously have no idea who she is, because there are only ten or so men inside."

I chuckled. "It is their mistake."

"What are you saying?" Gia asked over the wind. "Is my sister okay?"

"She's fine," I said in English. "They have ten men guarding her."

"How many do you have?"

"Five, including me."

"Oh, God." Gia covered her mouth with one hand and grabbed my arm with the other. "You're picking up more men, right? Or they are meeting you there?"

I snorted, my fingers curling around her throat. Her pulse

hammered against my palm. "I don't need more men to take on ten Russians."

She stared at me like I'd said something incredibly stupid. "No, no. You need more. I expected you to have, like, an army waiting. Guys in full tactical gear with machine guns and grenade launchers."

I wanted to laugh but I knew she was not thinking clearly because of her sister. I put my mouth near her ear. "Do not worry, bambina. This is what I do best."

My phone buzzed with the call I had been waiting on, so I released her and answered. It was Stefano with another report on the Russians. He believed they were likely Bratva, based on their tattoos, which meant we needed to make another call.

"We need to reach out to Campione when we finish," I told Vito in Italian once I rang off, referring to the head of the Lombardo 'ndrina. "These are Bratva, so Campione needs to be prepared."

"Cazzo," Vito hissed. "We should've known."

"What's wrong?" Gia asked, her head swiveling between us. "Has something happened?"

I wasn't used to explaining myself to women, but it was natural with her. Maybe it was because she was my prisoner or it could be her personality. Gia was easy to talk to and she was strong. Resilient. Sort of like me. "The Russians are mafiya, Bratva. They are not low-level traffickers, and they could retaliate against the Italian 'ndrina in the area."

Her face paled. "Oh, shit. Bratva? You're getting more men now, right? You're not still thinking about going in there with only five of you, are you?"

Massimo laughed and Vito smiled. I tried not to sound offended. "Woman, do you honestly believe the Bratva are more terrifying than the 'Ndrangheta? That we would be scared of a few tattoos and missing teeth? Ma dai, Gianna."

"This is my sister's life, you asshole. Stop being so blithe and condescending!"

I shook my head. "Just wait and see. Trust me. These Russians are no match for the D'Agostinos."

After giving her a brief kiss, I descended into the small motorboat.

My brothers followed and we were soon flying across the short stretch of water toward dry land. I purposely did not turn to look at Gia, though I could feel her worried eyes on my back.

Once we reached the Genoa docks we piled into large SUVs and drove off. Milan was a two-hour drive north, and I found myself watching the nighttime landscape of my home country through the window hungrily. I fucking missed it. The sights and smells, the ability to eat at a restaurant. To walk down the street without a disguise.

Once I had these things back I would never take them for granted again.

We discussed business on the drive, and before too long we were in Milan. A rush of adrenaline surged in my bloodstream, my mind craving the violence, anticipating the bloodshed. It was the time to focus.

Rico, one of my men, pulled the car to a stop. We were a block away from the house where the Russians were keeping Emma Mancini. We piled out of the two SUVs and rechecked our weapons. An older woman emerged from her house, took one look at us, and promptly returned inside. I heard the locks on her door engage. Smart woman.

Two of my men trailed behind me as I moved toward the rear of the house. Vito and Massimo went to the front. I waited a few seconds then kicked in the back door with my foot, sending the wood crashing open and the Russians scurrying for weapons. I killed two before they could pull their guns out.

A bullet barely missed me, so I ducked and fired in the direction of the shot. My men were behind me, now firing into the kitchen, as well. It was over quickly. Four Russians were dead, and we moved on from the kitchen, going deeper into the house. I could hear my brothers shouting as they fired at Russians in another part of the house, but I preferred not to speak. I didn't want my enemy to know my location until it was too late.

I pointed for my men to check the adjoining rooms, while I headed to the stairs. I crept up the steps slowly, because I knew a Russian must be hiding near the top. I could practically smell his cheap vodka and fear. I caught a subtle shift in the light against the wall and sneered. *Che idiota!*

I lifted my hand above my head and fired three times. A thump followed as the man hit the floor.

Then I moved at a faster clip so I didn't get caught on the stairs. Once at the top I began searching each room. My men were now on the second floor, too. I heard shots fired in a room down the hall, but ignored them. Emma was here somewhere and I needed to find her.

Movement behind me registered a second before a garrote snapped around my neck. Thankfully I got a few fingers under the cord before it went taut, so I dropped my gun and yanked with both hands, trying to prevent the garrote from strangling me. My attacker was strong, though, and I strained to keep a precious inch between that cord and my skin. I didn't have much time.

Using my legs, I shoved backward, ramming the Russian against the wall. He grunted and cursed, so I did it again, hoping to daze him for a split second. Then I reached for the large knife I had strapped to my belt, which I instantly plunged into his thigh.

He screamed and his arms loosened. I spun and this time drove the knife into his belly, yanking up to inflict more damage. Face contorted with pain, he tried to shove me off, but couldn't manage it.

"Where?" I asked in Russian, shoving my knife in deeper. "Where are the girls?"

"There are no girls," he said on a wheeze.

"Bullshit. Tell me where they are or I will spill your intestines all over this floor."

"I-I . . . ."

He hesitated and I twisted the knife, which I happened to know personally was excruciatingly painful. I could feel his blood leaking everywhere, coating my hands and clothes. I almost welcomed it. This was what I had been born to do.

When he stopped screaming, I gave him one more chance. "Tell me right now or I'll slice off your dick first."

"On the other side of that wall." He tipped his head. "There's a fake room."

He was of no more use, so I pulled my knife from his belly and sliced open his throat. Deep red seeped from the wound and some sprayed onto my face. I tried to wipe it off as I let him fall to the floor. "In here!" I called out to my men.

Soon Vito and Rico appeared. "Where?" Vito's head swiveled. "I don't see anything."

I was already feeling the wall, trying to determine how it opened. "Behind this wall somehow."

A voice from inside the wall shouted, "It opens from the other end. A wardrobe in one of the bedrooms."

We went to the bedroom on the other side, and sure enough a cheap wardrobe was against the wall. We pushed it out of the way and found a locked door there. "Get back," I called, then shot off the padlock.

When we got the door open we discovered seven girls inside, most of them dirty and dressed in tattered clothes. The stench coming from inside the room was awful. It was clear some of the girls had been here a long time.

"Cristo santo," Massimo murmured.

Emma Mancini had her arm around one of the younger girls, who couldn't have been more than thirteen or fourteen. "Who are you?" she asked me in Italian, her gaze taking in my bloody appearance.

"I am Enzo D'Agostino. Your sister sent me."

Emma nodded, as if this was what she expected. "Here," she said, guiding the younger girl forward. "Take her out first, please."

"My men will help these other girls. You are coming with me."

Unlike her stubborn sister, Emma didn't argue. She lifted her chin and bravely stepped forward, ready to accept her fate. I took her arm and led her through the house, past the dead bodies.

When we were outside, she asked, "Have you hurt my sister?"

"No."

I didn't let her go, just kept walking her toward the car. Vito and Massimo would stay behind to deal with the aftermath, so Rico got behind the wheel of the SUV. Emma and I slid into the backseat, where I handed her a protein bar and unopened bottle of water. "Here."

"Grazie," she said softly and uncapped the water. She finished it quickly, so I handed her another.

Blood was drying on my clothes and skin, and my body buzzed from the battle. It was a high like nothing else, and I'd missed it during the last four years. Looking at Emma, I said, "It was stupid of you to come to Milan."

"I want to see her."

"Do not worry." The edge of my mouth curled. "I'm taking you right to her."

CHAPTER TWENTY-ONE

Gia

I couldn't stop hugging my sister.

As promised, Enzo had rescued Emma and let me speak to her on the phone as they were driving back from Milan. Two hours later, the small motorboat appeared in the distance and I didn't take my eyes off my twin the entire time.

I grabbed her the second she stepped onto the deck. The lights on the yacht had let me see how badly she was treated by those Russian assholes. I needed to reassure myself that she was here, unharmed and safe. "I thought I'd never see you again."

"Same. I'm so happy to see you."

Tears slid along my cheeks and down my jaw. We stayed like that for a few minutes, and something settled inside me, like I'd reconnected with the other half of my soul.

Finally I pulled back. We both grinned and wiped our faces. Then, at the same time, we realized we had an audience.

Enzo was leaning against the side of the yacht, observing us. I looked him over. He was covered in blood, even his face and hands.

Would you like me to hurt the men who took your sister? Kill them with my bare hands? Coat my skin with their blood?

A shiver raced through me. "Still alive, I see."

His mouth curled in that arrogant way of his and he pushed off from the edge of the boat. "Still alive, micina. And I've done as promised. You know what it means, no?"

Obedience in all things. "Yes."

"Va bene." He looked over my shoulder. "Cecilia, see that Miss Mancini is settled below and given food and water."

"Sì, Don D'Agostino."

He gestured to me. "Come, Gianna. I want you in my stateroom."

"No, Enzo." I grabbed Emma and held on. "She's just arrived. I want to spend time with her."

"Later." He motioned to Cecilia. "Take Miss Mancini, please."

"Enzo—"

He swung toward me, chin lowered in challenge. "Remember our deal? You are mine, Gianna. Whatever I ask, whenever I ask it."

"It's okay, Gigi." Always the peacemaker, Emma gave me a squeeze. "I'm exhausted. I just want to shower and sleep. We can catch up tomorrow."

I kissed her cheek. "I'll see you first thing in the morning."

"Good." She hugged me, whispering in my ear, "Be safe. Be smart."

I nodded, and swallowed the lump in my throat as she was led away from me. At least she was with me here on the yacht, away from those Russian assholes.

A hand grabbed my wrist. "Come." Enzo said nothing more and began towing me below. I followed, knowing what was probably going to happen.

And I wanted it.

I was already breathing hard, anticipation thumping in my veins. I was past the point of denying my need for him. So whatever fucked up path we were taking, I was willingly on it. After all, I had agreed and I was a woman of my word.

When we reached his stateroom, he pulled me close, his hands settling on my hips. Blood dotted his skin, soaked his clothes, and I wasn't sure why I wasn't totally repulsed. He was like a knight returning from battle.

"Do you want to hear how I did it, micina? Do you want the details of how I killed those men?"

God help me, but I did. Between my legs pulsed with every beat of my heart. "Yes."

He smoothed my hair off my face, his voice threaded with pride as he said, "Of course you do, my bloodthirsty bambina. Get in the shower with me and I'll tell you about it while you suck on my dick."

I turned and walked toward the bathroom, and he slapped my ass on the way. As I turned on the water in the shower, he began stripping off his soiled clothes, revealing a body that I was becoming addicted to.

I got naked and stepped into the shower. Water ran down my skin and through my hair. When I opened my eyes, he was there, fully naked and his cock already hard. Madre di Dio, as he liked to say. I moved aside so he could wash off the blood. "Here."

He stepped forward and let the water sluice over his frame. A stream of pink ran down the shower drain as he quickly washed. Turning toward me, he said, "You know what I want."

It was safe to say we were both on board for this. I wasted no time in dropping to my knees on the slick tile. He didn't move, so I shuffled forward until the tip of his erection was within reach. I opened my mouth and sucked on the head, using my tongue on the underside.

His palm swept over my wet hair. "C'è la mia bambina."

There is my little girl.

I pushed my face toward his pelvis, taking more of him. He filled my mouth, so thick and smooth, and I could taste the precum leaking from the tip. I closed my eyes, savoring the sensation, loving the power this gave me over his pleasure.

He rocked his hips, fucking my mouth, and I took it eagerly, relaxing my throat to keep from gagging. I made sure my lips stayed tight on his shaft, and I fluttered my tongue until he grunted.

"Eyes up here."

I looked up at his face, which was taut with lust, his pupils wide. He began speaking then, telling me of kicking in the back door and shooting two men before they could even reach for their weapons. The Russian he'd shot while on the stairs. Then the man who tried to strangle him, the one he'd sliced open with his knife.

By the time he finished, I was panting, more turned on than I could stand. I started to reach between my legs, ready to make myself come, but his fingers twisted in my hair. "Not yet. Put your hands behind your back."

I obeyed and his nostrils flared at my compliance. "Who do you belong to, troietta?"

I knew he wanted an answer, so I started to release him. He shook his head and held me in place. "No, don't pull off. With your mouth full of my dick, tell me who you belong to."

Holding his gaze, I gave a garbled answer around the rigid flesh. "*Mmmu*."

Satisfaction twisted his expression and he pushed deep, making me gag. "That's right. What a good pet you are. I think I'll reward you." Turning off the water, he stepped back and his cock fell out of my mouth. "Up."

After I rose, he pointed behind me. "Go to the bed. Lay down, arms above your head and legs spread."

I didn't bother toweling off as I left the bathroom. Instead, I stretched out on the cool sheets, the water drying on my skin and making me shiver. My clit was swollen and begging for attention.

Enzo strode into the stateroom, his glorious cock bobbing with every step. He was going to shove that monster inside my pussy and I couldn't fucking wait.

Putting one knee on the bed, he reached between my legs. "Dio, you're so wet. Did hearing of my murders tonight turn you on?"

He shoved two fingers inside me and I gasped, my upper half bowing. "God, yes!"

"Is this pussy empty? Do you need me to fill it?" He pumped his hand, giving me a taste of the friction I craved. "Beg me. '*Scopami forte, padrone.*'"

I dug my fingernails into the headboard. "Scopami forte, Lorenzo!"

"Cazzo," he ground out. "I want to edge you for hours but I can't wait." In a flash he was on his knees between my thighs, lining up at my entrance and pushing in.

The pressure was a lot to take. I wasn't sure I was one hundred percent ready. "Oh, shit."

"Shh," he said, smoothing his palms down my legs. "You can take me, bambina."

He watched as his cock spread me open, his hips moving slowly, like he wanted me to feel every centimeter. My eyes nearly rolled back in my head. "So good, mafioso. Jesus, you're killing me."

He dragged a hand up my hip, along my ribs and over a breast, until he reached my throat. "No, I'm not killing you . . . but I easily could, no?" His fingers covered my neck and squeezed, not enough to cut off my air but enough to cause my eyes to pop open. He was smirking down at me. "You're alive at my mercy, Gianna."

As if on cue, a flood of moisture coated his cock just then and he tunneled farther inside, now in almost all the way. He squeezed my throat a little harder. "You like that, no? Being at my mercy."

Was I scared? Was I turned on? What was happening inside me right now?

My lips parted with the force of my breaths, my pulse throbbing beneath his hand. He slid in as deep as he could go, his cock fully seated and taking up all the room inside me. I wriggled my hips, trying to urge him on. I needed to come so badly. "Please, you have to move."

Instead, he held still and stared at me. "I am going to choke you while I fuck you."

Panic filled my chest. I wasn't ready for those kinds of games. That was next level shit. "No, wait. Don't hurt me."

His lips curled into a deviant smile, one I recognized well. "Micina," he crooned, "I will not hurt you. Te lo prometto." He gave a gentle thrust of his hips. "I am going to squeeze the sides of your throat. It will make you lightheaded and your orgasm will be a thousand times more intense."

I knew many people were into breath play and strangulation, but it seemed dangerous to me. I swallowed. "And I'm supposed to trust you?"

"Yes, you are. Do not worry, I know how to do this correctly. You will love it." He stared at his hand on my throat, then withdrew and rammed into my pussy, and the friction sent shockwaves through my limbs. He growled deep in his throat. "Obedience in all things, remember?"

Shit, this was some kind of fucked up test. "Shouldn't we have a contract or a safe word? Or . . . ." My words died when he gave a rough thrust, rocking my body, and I cried out. "Oh, yes! More of that."

"No agreement or safe word. The fear and danger will make it more exciting for you."

"Doubtful. It'll just make it more exciting for *you*."

"Certo." He began stroking in and out, his hand resting on my throat. He wasn't applying any real pressure, just building the tension, making me wonder when he would start, and for some reason the uncertainty made it hotter. Sweat broke out on my forehead, my body already primed to come, so I rocked my hips, trying to hit the right spot to send me over the edge.

"Look at me," he ordered.

I cracked my eyelids and read the intent in his gaze. Fuck, was I ready? I really liked the feel of his hand on my throat, and somehow I knew Enzo wasn't going to kill me like this. Whatever he was planning, it wasn't death by dicking.

And even if I felt a bit stupid, I did trust him in this.

I nodded.

As he started fucking me again, he squeezed the sides of my throat, pressing. I never looked away from him, unsure what I was feeling as the blood flow into my head slowed. He watched my face. "There you go, bambina. It feels so good, no?"

The fear and excitement sent me spiraling. "Oh, God," I said, now lightheaded.

He rode me hard, rocking the headboard into the wall, and my inner muscles tightened around his dick. He growled. "I can feel you. Fuck!"

He released my neck, and what followed was a rush I'd never experienced in all my life. My pussy clamped down as the orgasm slammed into me. My hoarse shout echoed throughout the room, and I dug my fingernails into his arms as the climax went on and on.

When I finally came down, he was watching me with an expression that bordered on awe. "Madre di Dio, you are the sexiest thing I've ever seen."

Before I could speak, he began moving, holding nothing back as he used his whole body to fuck me. Grunting from the effort, he held me down as his hips slammed into mine, a man possessed, and not even ten strokes later he was coming, his back arching. He let out a loud curse, his dick pulsing inside me, and I tried to catch my breath.

He didn't immediately pull out. Instead, he hung his head, closed his eyes, and stirred his hips, like he wanted to prolong our connection. I could feel his come leaking out of me, our combined juices soaking the mattress, and it was insanely hot. I longed to touch him and feel all those sweat-covered muscles.

Finally, he rolled off me and sprawled onto the bed. "Fuck, Gianna."

I knew exactly what he meant. "Why is it so good?"

"I wish I knew. Let's shower and sleep. Then I'll fuck you again in the morning."

The next morning I went to find Emma as soon as I woke up.

Enzo had disappeared at some point, letting me sleep in. I was grateful, though part of me was disappointed that he hadn't made good on his promise from last night. Maybe there was a mafioso emergency that was more important than having sex with me.

My sister was already awake and drinking coffee in her room. Huh. No one brought me coffee today. And her door wasn't locked. I was relieved, though it seemed strange.

"Hey, Em," I said, dropping down on her perfectly made bed. "How are you feeling?"

"Tired. I hardly slept while in Milan, so I feel like I could sleep for days."

"Then you should. There's no need for you to be up and around."

"I wanted to see you. When I asked earlier I was told you were still asleep."

"Yeah." I leaned back on my hands. "I was up pretty late."

"You're having sex with him."

I knew this was coming. My twin would spot a lie a mile away, too. "Yes."

"Willingly?"

"Yes."

"So you're not being held captive here."

I swallowed my guilt. I hadn't felt much like a captive lately, not while Enzo was giving me the best orgasms of my life. "Yes and no."

Emma lifted her eyebrows. "You have a lot of explaining to do."

Not wasting any time, I told Emma of my last day in Milan and the bombing. "I'm a captive, but he's not forcing me to do anything against my will."

My sister's expression grew darker during my story. "What happened once he got you aboard the yacht?"

"He locked me in a cage."

"That jerk! It must have been awful for you. No wonder you aren't fighting him any longer."

I pressed my lips together, trying not to let my thoughts show, but Emma knew me too well. My twin's eyes narrowed. "Wait, why do you look guilty? Like that time you borrowed Frankie's diamond earrings without asking her and lost them."

"Stop. I want to hear what happened to you. Did those men hurt you?"

"This topic is not finished, but fine. The Russians mostly left us alone. We didn't shower or eat very much. And don't get me started on how we went to the bathroom."

"We? How many women were with you?"

"Six others. Really, I can't complain because I was there for only a short time. Some of those girls had been locked up for weeks. One of them was just thirteen years old."

"God, Em. I'm so fucking sorry."

"Don't be sorry. It was my stupidity that got me kidnapped. I should've been more careful. It was actually a blessing that Don D'Agostino kidnapped you, so that he could come and rescue me and the others."

Hardly a blessing, but I didn't argue. "Why didn't you call Frankie?"

"There wasn't time," Emma muttered, staring at her coffee instead of me.

The reason became clear. "She didn't know you were in Italy."

Emma grimaced. "She thought I was delusional with grief. She said you were dead and that I needed to come to terms with it."

God, my poor sisters. Here I was, hot tubbing and fucking while my family thought I was dead. "If there had been a way to contact you sooner I would have."

"I know that. I let it go with her because of her pregnancy. She was so upset at hearing you were dead that Fausto was worried she would lose the baby."

"That makes me feel worse. Jesus Christ." Fucking Enzo. And this was also Fausto's fault, too. All of the stupid Italian mafia men were to blame, dragging their families along in their petty bullshit.

"She's fine. He moved a doctor into the castello, and she's been monitored around the clock."

"That's a relief."

"So back to you and Enzo. I'm worried about you."

I didn't want Emma upset. She needed to relax and recover, not worry about me. I tried to downplay it. "There's nothing to worry about. I like sex and Enzo is spectacular at it."

"You can't be serious. You're really trying to play this off like he's some fling?"

"It's not a big deal. I have it all under control."

"This is a big deal, Gigi. You're sleeping with the man who tried to have Fausto killed, and I'm having a hard time believing it's consensual. I don't want him forcing you to do anything you don't want to. Help this make sense. Has he brainwashed you?"

"No, of course not." I tried to think of a way to explain it. "We have this connection. It's like hate fucking on steroids. Whatever it is, I can't resist it. But don't worry, I'm working on a plan."

Emma pinched the bridge of her nose between her thumb and forefinger. "It's all those enemies-to-lovers romance novels you read growing up. That stuff isn't real! Enzo D'Agostino is a dangerous psychopath. We have to get off this yacht."

"I've been trying, believe me. It's not so easy. We're surrounded by water."

Emma glared at me and folded her arms. It was her *I don't believe your bullshit* stance and it worked like truth serum on me.

A confession poured out of my mouth. "Em, I don't want to like him and I'm terrified by how easily I give in. It's like he knows exactly what to say, exactly what to do to get inside my head. I've never had a connection like this with a man before."

"Oh, shit."

For Emma to curse, I knew the situation was serious. I flopped back down on the bed. "I'm a mess. A cock-hungry slut with daddy issues a mile long."

"Who told you that nonsense?" she snapped. "Was it Enzo? Because I will slap his face."

"One of Papa's guards a long time ago. I mean, maybe I really am the family fuck up, the disappointing Mancini daughter." The one my father liked least and the one the guards thought was a slut. Maybe I deserved to be kept by a dangerous mobster, used as a sex toy for his amusement.

Emma was suddenly on the mattress next to me, her hand grabbing mine tight. "You know that's not true. You are not disappointing or a fuck up."

I wasn't certain I agreed. I held onto her, so grateful to have her here, even if it meant we were both prisoners now. "Just promise to stay away from Enzo."

"Well, I want *you* to promise to stay away from Enzo."

I couldn't. Worse, I wasn't sure I wanted to.

When I said nothing, Emma rested her head against mine. "What am I going to do with you, Gigi?"

"Let's forget about all this and go sit in the hot tub for a while."

"Hot tub?"

"Come on." I sat up and pulled her upright. "This boat has one or two perks. Soak with me and then you can take a nap."

Enzo

My foot bounced on the dining room floor as I waited. Where the fuck was she? The room was empty save for me, our dinner spread out on the table.

I wanted her here. No, I *needed* her here.

My mind was spinning, overrun with thoughts, and I was tired.

After what seemed like forever, she walked in and everything calmed inside me. Domenico's leather dress, the one she'd worn on the runway in Milan, had been delivered earlier today. So I gave it to Cecilia with a note that Gia should wear the dress to dinner.

Cazzo, she was hot. The leather straps hugged her curves and criss-crossed her body. She looked fierce and sexy, and my hands itched to touch her.

She stopped and glanced around. "Where is everyone?"

"It is just us for dinner. Come here, micina."

Gia frowned at me. "I want to see my sister, il pazzo."

No, that was not how this worked. I pushed my chair back from the table and patted my thigh. "Here. Right now."

She glared at me and I could see her mind turning over my order. Weighing the consequences of refusing me. Was she willing to risk sending her sister to the cage or would she obey me?

When she still didn't move, I lifted one brow arrogantly, not caring if I pissed her off even more. I liked when she got feisty. It made fucking her even more explosive.

Then she started toward me, her long toned legs making my mouth water. Waves of dark silky hair spilled over her shoulders and down her back, plump lips set in an unhappy line as she approached.

"Can I sit in the chair instead?" She pointed at the empty seat next to me.

I didn't say a word, just kept my eyes locked on hers. She would not win this battle with me.

With an annoyed huff, she slid onto my lap and shifted sideways, her legs to the side of mine. "You're an asshole," she said under her breath.

My hands clamped around her hip and I hitched her closer. I was getting used to feeling her pressed against me. "Careful. You know what happens to disobedient girls."

"They get orgasms?"

I smoothed my palm over her thigh. "No, they get spankings."

"Where is my sister?"

"In her stateroom." I handed her an Aperol spritz. "Here. Since we never finished ours in Milan."

"Oh, you mean because you blew up the restaurant? Thanks for the concussion, by the way." She sipped her aperitivo. "Mmm. These are so good. Even if they do remind me of almost dying."

"I would not have allowed you to die. Now, finish your drink so we can eat."

We drank in silence until she asked, "Do you ever feel guilty about the things you do?"

My answer was immediate. "No."

She swallowed more of the Aperol spritz, then cradled the glass against her chest and leaned away to see my face. "Seriously? You don't feel guilty about killing a handful of innocent people to kidnap me?"

"It was three people. And being the don means I must do whatever is necessary. I don't make these decisions lightly, but I cannot show weakness. You should know this from your father and your brother-in-law."

"I'm not exactly in the mafia inner circle. Like, for a long time I thought my dad was just a regular businessman."

I tucked a silky strand of her long hair behind her ear. She wore no makeup, no jewelry, and she was still the most gorgeous woman I'd ever seen. "We are all regular businessmen."

Her lips twisted into a smirk. "Sure. Regular businessmen with guns who torture their enemies."

"Eh, we are no different than world leaders and the presidents of big corporations. They are just as dirty and ruthless as the 'Ndrangheta."

"That sounds like rationalizing."

I finished the rest of my drink and set the glass down. "I don't need to rationalize what I do. Especially not when I make more money in a year than nearly anyone else in Europe."

"More than Fausto?"

Hearing my enemy's name on her lips caused my muscles to tense. "Even more than Ravazzani."

"Really?"

I rolled my eyes. "Sì, really. It is why the feud with Ravazzani started in the first place."

Her head whipped toward me. "I thought it was over my sister."

"Dai, Gianna. She is beautiful, but she's not worth starting a war over."

"Then what was it about?"

"Your brother-in-law tried to muscle me into giving him a percentage of my business. Instead of agreeing, I let another talk me into retaliating."

"Huh."

"What does this mean?"

She finished her drink and held up the glass for me to take. "The way I always heard it, you saw my sister on Fausto's yacht and couldn't stop staring at her. Then you kidnapped her."

I snorted and reached for an olive, which I held up to Gia's mouth. "I never wanted to fuck her, if that is what you are thinking."

Parting her lips, she took the olive inside her mouth, making sure to lick my fingers as she did it. Cristo santo, I liked that.

She peeked at me through her lashes. "You said Frankie was more attractive than me."

"I have proven many times this is not the case. She never made my dick hard, not like you."

"You think I'm pretty, don't you, mafioso?"

This conversation was veering into territory more like flirting than humiliation. I had to get the evening back on track. "Would you like something to eat?"

"Yes, if it's allowed, Don Pain-in-My-Ass."

Madonna, the mouth on this girl.

I reached for the food. The bread baked by my chef rivaled the best in Italy, so I dipped it in oil and brought it to Gia's mouth. "Try this."

She reared back and tried to take the bread from me. "I can feed myself."

I moved her hand away, trapping it by her side. "It is my responsibility to feed my gorgeous pet. I want you here on my lap, where I can take care of you."

"You can't be serious."

I dragged my nose over her cheek and inhaled her sweet scent. "Do I ever say anything I do not mean?" I held the bread up once again. "And you know what happens if you refuse."

Slowly, she leaned forward to take a bite of bread from my hand. "Va bene," I told her, kissing her bare shoulder. "See how easy that is?"

Though she might claim otherwise, I suspected Gia secretly liked this. I could see her pulse hammering at the base of her throat and her skin was flushed. I bet if I put my fingers in her pussy right now they would come away dripping with her cream.

We continued like this, talking and eating throughout the rest of the meal. After a while her body relaxed against me, and we even laughed once or twice together. The longer it went on the more turned on I became. I liked her to be helpless and dependent on me. It made me want to tie her to my bed again and lick her pussy until she screamed.

I held a bite of fish to her lips, but she shook her head. "No more. I'm stuffed."

I kissed the spot behind her ear. "Good girl."

"Do I get a reward later?"

"Maybe. What would you like?"

"To stay with my sister tonight."

I chuckled. "Dai, you should know better than to ask that."

"Can she and I watch a movie together after dinner, then?"

I hadn't expected this bargaining. I stroked her soft cheek with the backs of my knuckles. "You spent all day with her."

"Were you watching us today?"

A bit, but I would never admit it. "I know everything that happens on this yacht, micina."

"God, you're such a control freak. So, can I watch a movie with her or not?"

"If I agree, what will you do for me in exchange?"

"Not punch you in the junk for making me sit on your lap during dinner?"

I had to fight a smile. "Do better, beautiful."

"I'll come to your room later."

I stroked her leg and considered it. As long as she did what I wanted I supposed there was no harm. "When we're done here, you and your sister may watch a movie in my stateroom."

The tension left Gia's body. "Thank you, il pazzo."

I pushed her long hair over her shoulder and caressed her jaw. "You were very good during dinner. I like holding you on my lap and feeding you."

"That's because you're fucked up."

I grabbed her wine glass and held it to her mouth. "Sì, certo. But I suspect your pussy is dripping right now, which means you are fucked up, too."

She dutifully swallowed the crisp white wine, then licked her lips. "You're not giving me a choice."

"And you like to be forced," I crooned before kissing the slim column of her throat. "It is why we work so well together."

"As long as it keeps my sister away from you I'll let you believe whatever you want."

Such lies from such a pretty mouth. It was time to see who was right.

I patted her hip. "Up."

She stood quickly, like she was eager for this to be over. But her nipples were hard beneath the leather, her eyes dilated with lust. Her body wanted me, even if her mind wasn't fully cooperative. That worked fine for me.

"Take off your panties," I told her.

"Why?"

"Because you are mine and I am telling you to do it."

She bit her lip and glanced around the dining room. We were alone but anyone could come in at any time. "Didn't we do this already?"

"That doesn't mean I won't ever repeat it. Lift your skirt and get up on the table."

With a heavy sigh, she hitched the dress and started to sit.

"Remove the panties first," I said.

I could see her hands tremble as she pushed the leather panties off her hips. They slithered down her long legs and she kicked them off right before she got up on the table. I took a long second to admire her, contemplating all the depraved things I wanted to do to her. My desire to touch and taste her never abated, while the craving to fuck her twisted in my blood like a virus. I was crazy with it, obsessed.

No woman had infected me like this. Was it because she was Ravazzani's sister-in-law? I had to assume so. Why else would I want Gia Mancini so badly, if not to ruin her?

I pulled my chair closer. "Put your feet up and spread your legs."

She did as I asked, leaning back on her hands, and I could smell her arousal, see it glistening on the swollen lips of her pussy. I inhaled, the scent filling my lungs and making my balls heavy. "Soaking," I murmured. "Just as I thought."

Her chest rose and fell as her breath came quicker. She liked being on display for me. I decided to reward her first. "I have a present for you."

She blinked then narrowed her eyes suspiciously. "If you've tied a bow around your cock, I am literally going to gag."

My lips twitched. How could she make me laugh at the exact same time I wanted to fuck her?

"That surprise comes later," I said, reaching under the table. I presented her with a plain black box.

"I don't understand." She stared at the box like it contained a dozen snakes. "You're giving me a gift?"

"If you don't want it, I'll take it back." I started to take the box out of her hands, but her fingers tightened around the cardboard.

"The fuck you will, mafioso." She pulled it back and quickly tore off the lid. "Oh, my God. You bought me a tablet?"

"And a stylus. You can use this for your designs instead of pencil and paper."

"I-I don't know what to say. This is amazing. Thank you."

"You are welcome. And don't bother checking for internet service. It has been disabled."

"Couldn't resist ruining the moment with a dig that I'm your prisoner, could you?" She hugged the tablet to her chest, a smile splitting her beautiful face. "Still, this is awesome."

I held up the box. "Here. Put your new toy away."

"Why?"

She put the tablet back in the box and I set it on the floor by my chair. "Because I want to play with *my* toy right now."

There was tiramisu for dessert, so I gathered some on my fingertip and held it up to her mouth. She dipped her head and sucked the creamy dessert off my finger, her tongue lapping at my skin greedily, her eyes closing in bliss. A rumble of approval escaped my throat.

I gathered more tiramisu and smeared it on her piercing. She whispered, "Oh, God. What are you doing?"

"Having dessert."

CHAPTER TWENTY-TWO

Enzo

My children were permitted one call a week with me, and I looked forward to those calls more than anything else. They were like air, reassuring and necessary to my very survival. Being apart from Luca and Nic was like a bad dream—something I had to endure but every second tore apart my soul.

Vito and I were in the office, working, but I had the phone by my hand, the ringer switched on. Every few seconds I glanced down to make sure I hadn't missed the call. I was moving money around, using my contacts around the globe to launder the fraud income, distributing it to various smaller businesses. It was complicated and detailed, and it required my complete attention. Unfortunately, I was distracted.

I needed to see her. I switched my screen over to the camera in my bedroom. The screen filled with the image of her spread out on the bed, watching tv with her sister. While Emma and Gia looked similar, there was no mistaking them. Gia was crackling energy and sex, while Emma was quiet and reserved.

My cell rang and I hurried to answer, not even bothering to look at the number. I knew who it was. "Pronto."

"Ciao, Papà!"

My heart squeezed at the sound of my daughter's voice, and I had to close my eyes against a rush of emotion. God, I missed them. "Ciao, Nicola! Come stai, principessa?"

"Good, Papà, good. Is Uncle Vito there, too?"

"Yes, he's here, too. Do you want to talk to him?"

"No," she said. "I didn't want you to be lonely."

I swallowed the knot in my throat. "You're very thoughtful to think of your Papà, but you don't need to worry about me. Tell me about school. How are your studies?"

Nic launched into a long explanation about her classes and I soaked in every word. I loved to hear her voice and she sounded so happy. There were no more issues with the boy who'd picked on her, and she had many friends according to Luca. She'd inherited my intelligence and Angela's thoughtfulness, and I was certain no man would ever be good enough to marry her.

"When will we see you again?" she asked. "We have a break coming up soon."

The words were a dagger in my chest. "The summer, principessa. You know the rules."

"It's still not safe for us?"

My free hand curled into a fist, the missing tip of my finger apparent. "No, it isn't, I'm afraid."

"I don't want you to die, Papà."

"You don't need to worry. What do I always say?"

"That you're smarter than any man in Europe."

"That's right. Is your brother there?"

"Sì. Ti amo, Papà. I hope you have a good week!"

"Ti amo, Nic. Never forget that everything I do is for you and your brother."

"I know. Ciao!"

There was some shuffling, then my son's voice sounded in my ear. "Hello, Papà."

Hello? "Che palle. You've stopped speaking Italian, then?"

He gave a laugh that sounded deeper than usual, like his voice was changing. "No, of course not. I was trying to annoy you."

My boy was trouble, much as I'd been at his age. "Are you certain that's wise, figlio mio?"

"Probably not, but it's too easy with you."

I couldn't argue with that. "Any more problems with Nic and that boy?"

"No, he's leaving her alone."

"Va bene. Let me know if anything else happens."

"I will, Papà." He sounded annoyed, as if I didn't trust him to handle this on his own.

"Tell me what's going on with you. How are your classes?"

"Boring as fuck," he said in English.

"Ma dai, Luca! Watch your mouth." Then I couldn't help but add, "If you're going to curse, do it properly. In Italian."

He chuckled. "I started playing rugby, Papà. I like it better than football."

I frowned. Rugby? That English school was stripping away his heritage and I hated it. But I couldn't complain. My children were alive and that was what mattered. "You like it because it allows you to tackle and hit the other boys."

"Sì, certo. They are hosting a dance next week for the entire school. A girl asked me to take her."

I smiled sadly. I should be there to talk to him about women and make sure he continues playing football. "What did you say?"

"She's two years older than me. I said yes, of course."

A bark of laughter escaped my throat. Porco dio, my boy. "Then be careful and be safe. Do I need to send you condoms?"

Vito swiveled in his chair to face me, his jaw falling open.

"I already have them," Luca told me proudly. "We stole some from the older boys."

"Do you need anything else?"

Luca said no, and we chatted a few minutes more before hanging up. I rubbed my eyes, wrung out and angry. It never got easier, the distance between me and my children. Except for a few weeks every summer, they were living their lives far away from me, experiencing things I had no control over. I could offer no guidance, no advice. This was time I would never get back with them.

But they were safe. Without a proper home with proper security, they would be at risk with me here on a boat. Not to mention they'd have no friends, no teachers. What kind of life was that for a child? At least now, using assumed names, they could behave like normal children, living normal lives. With me, they would be no better than prisoners.

"Luca needs condoms?" Vito asked.

I sighed heavily. "A dance at school. An older girl has asked him to go with her."

"I fucked my first girl at twelve."

I'd also been twelve my first time, but this was not helpful. "They are so far away. I hate it."

"I know, but they are alive."

My foot bounced on the floor, my mind growing agitated, restless. "I'm anxious to finish this. Where are we with the airports in Spain? Have they found Giulio?"

"We don't need Giulio Ravazzani anymore. We have both Mancini girls. Ravazzani will give us whatever we want to get them back."

It wasn't the first time Vito said this. "I want to totally destroy him. His family, his business, his entire life."

My brother scratched his jaw.

"What?" I snapped.

"I think you aren't ready to let her go."

I snarled, baring my teeth at him. "If you are saying she means more to me than my children, I will shove a knife between your ribs, fratello."

"Dai, Enzo. I'm not saying that, but I've seen you with her. I know how you watch her on the cameras, how you obsess over her. You're fucking her all over the boat. It's nothing like Mariella. This is different and you know it."

"*Ma vattene a fanculo!*"

"You can tell me to go fuck myself all you want, but you know I'm right. You have feelings for this girl. But you have to know that it can't go anywhere. She will either end up dead or back with Ravazzani. Are you prepared to do what is necessary?"

"You talk to me as if I am an imbecile. This was part of my plan, to turn her into my pet. To ruin and humiliate her, then use her to blackmail Ravazzani."

"Yes, that's what you said. But is this still what you are planning? You aren't even restraining her any longer. She could kill any one of us at any minute."

"She won't. Didn't you see her at dinner, eating from my hand? And stop treating me like I'm a child. We will find and kill Ravazzani's son, then I will take his entire empire."

Vito held up his palms, placating me. "As long as you're sure."

"You're testing my patience. Perhaps Massimo is ready to become consigliere instead."

Vito snorted, not threatened in the least. "Be my guest. He's downstairs smoking weed. I can't wait to hear what advice he gives you."

"How do you know this?"

My brother pointed to the open window. "I can smell it."

I stood and stretched, ready to put this day behind me. I longed for my bed and the woman currently in it. "I'm going down. Come with me and take Emma Mancini back to her room. I want her locked in tonight."

Vito said nothing and I could hear his disapproval in the silence as we went down the steps. I didn't care what he thought. I was the capo and this would be handled my way. If I wanted to fuck Gia, then I would. That was all I needed from her—her pussy and her ass. That was all I needed from any woman.

The TV was on in my suite, with Gia fast asleep on the bed. Her sister was awake, watching whatever nonsense was on the screen. "You're dismissed," I told Emma. "Vito will take you back to your room."

She nibbled on her lip, her eyes darting to Gia then me. "I don't like leaving her here with you."

"I don't give a shit. Get out."

Slowly, Emma got off the bed and put on her shoes. When she straightened she said, "She's a good person. She doesn't deserve whatever twisted mind games you're playing."

"Is that what she told you we're doing, playing twisted mind games?"

"No, but it's clear after watching you two together that you've got some hold over her. Are you blackmailing her? Drugging her? It doesn't make any sense."

"It doesn't need to make sense to you, Miss Mancini. And if you wish to stay alive, you will stop trying to interfere." I waved my fingers, dismissing her.

She and Vito left the room, and I stared down at Gia. She was still asleep, curled up with a pillow. Stripping out of my clothes, I pulled the covers down and stretched out next to her. I wanted to feel her bare skin next to mine, so I reached down and removed her shorts. Then I gently lifted her top over her head.

She wore no bra, so I left on her panties and clasped her tight. All her softness, the warm silky skin, pressed to my body and I could feel myself relax. As her back met my chest, she let out a soft sigh.

I kissed the top of her head. "Go back to sleep." I closed my eyes. I hadn't slept at all last night and exhaustion weighed me down. Not to mention the call with my children, which always drained me.

"You're not going to fuck me?" she asked when I didn't move.

I should. I should roll her over and fuck her into the mattress. Pin her down and make her beg for mercy. But for some reason, this was exactly what I wanted right now. "No, not when you're too tired to do it properly."

She yawned. "Fuck off."

"Disappointed, Gianna? Do you need my cock?"

She snickered. "*Cock* is such a stupid word."

I felt a smile tug at my lips. "Is *dick* any better?"

That made her laugh. "Not the way you say it, with your thick accent. *Deeeck,*" she imitated.

I dug my fingers into her ribs and tickled her. When she stopped squirming and gasping, I said in my best Canadian accent, "Would it be better if I talked like this, eh?"

"That's not what Canadians sound like, babe."

The endearment caught me by surprise. Had she even realized it? She seemed to drift off, quiet now as she lay against me. Her hands weren't touching me; instead they were tucked under her face, prayer-style. Even when asleep she remembered I didn't like to be touched.

"Sei perfetta," I whispered, hoping she didn't hear me.

———

Gia

Enzo was having a nightmare.

The whimpers and moans woke me, sounds so raw it was like they were pulled from deep inside his chest. I rolled over and found his body covered in sweat as he twitched and thrashed. His lips moved like he was speaking but no sound came out, only these pitiful cries that tore at my heart.

Was he remembering the dungeon?

Without thinking, I reached over and touched his face. He was so warm, the scratch of his whiskers rough against my palm. "Enzo, you're dreaming."

He jerked his head away from my hand, like my touch burned. "Non ti prego," he whispered, eyes screwed tight.

Okay, so no touching. I hovered near his face and increased the volume of my voice. "Wake up. You're having a bad dream."

He didn't hear me, too deep in his own personal hell. His lips twisted and he rasped a steady stream of Italian. The meaning was lost on me, but I could hear the agony behind the words.

I couldn't bear to see it. Fuck it. I splayed across him, almost hugging him. I could feel his heart racing beneath my palm, his big body shaking and trembling. "Wake up, Enzo. Please."

Was this what he went through every night? No wonder why he seemed on the edge of his sanity all the time.

He was panting as if he couldn't get enough air, sucking in great gulps. I started to move off him, to release the pressure off his chest, but he clutched me to him. "No, don't go."

"You need to breathe."

"Don't move."

"Baby, focus. You'll have a panic attack if you don't start breathing." I'd seen it happen with models when they got nervous before a show.

"I'm trying," he gasped.

I knew about breath control from yoga. "Do this with me. Inhale through your nose, then exhale slowly while saying *ha* in your throat. Sort of like you're fogging up a glass in front of your face, but with your mouth closed."

"Stupid."

"It's not stupid, I promise." Leaning up, I demonstrated twice. "Now do it."

He inhaled through his nose then exhaled, but kept his mouth open. "Keep your mouth closed," I said. "It should sound like the ocean when done correctly."

He tried again, this time with his mouth closed. I did it with him a few times. "Good. Slow down, even it out. Count if you need to. Really fill your belly with air."

We kept going, our breath in perfect sync, while our legs tangled. It was intimate, the first time I'd touched him like this, and I was dying to explore every inch of him. I knew he wouldn't like it, though, so I kept still and helped him breathe.

Finally, he seemed calmer. Big hands swept up my back and over my hip as he lifted me, angling my face toward his. "Need you," he whispered and kissed me.

I fell into the kiss eagerly, softening for him and letting him take my mouth. I could feel his urgency, his desperation, and it fed my own. His fingers grabbed a fistful of my hair to hold me in place as his tongue and lips devoured me.

The kiss went on and on, and my body responded as it always did to this man, my pussy getting wet and swollen. God, I loved the way he kissed, with such absolute force and reverence. Like he longed to destroy and cherish me at the same time. My skin crawled with need, a thousand pinpricks that made me feel alive and powerful. Bold, as if I could do anything.

I decided to take a risk.

Very deliberately, so I didn't spook him, I started moving my hand south, over his ribs and down his abs. His mouth broke off from mine and he waited, his breath coming fast. He didn't stop me, so I continued toward his crotch, and my palm skimmed his sweat-slick muscles. He was glorious, a marble statue come to life.

I found his cock, thick and hard against his belly, and I gave it a gentle brush, a tease, before continuing to his balls. He grunted when I rolled and squeezed their weight with my fingers. Most men loved to have their balls played with, and Enzo was no different. He spread his thighs to give me more room and I caressed him, exploring. When my hand swept the length of his dick, he jerked and rocked his hips, silently asking for more.

I stroked him slowly and he exhaled against my cheek, strong fingers digging into my skin, the room quiet except for our breathing. This was something unusual for us, something new, but I wasn't complaining. I liked having him at my mercy for a change.

My lower half began to throb as I worked him. I knew what it was like to have this big dick inside me and my pussy was weeping for it. I wasn't sure he'd allow me on top, but I really wanted to ride him just this once.

I shoved my panties down my thighs and slid my leg over his hips to straddle him. He held onto my waist and the feel of all his strength and power beneath me made my mouth water.

His gaze was locked on my pussy as I grabbed his cock and lined him up at my entrance. I began feeding him inside, sinking down slowly, loving the stretch and burn as he took up all the space in my body.

"Fuck, Lorenzo," I whispered, his full name falling from my lips while I paused to let myself adjust. "Jesus."

"Sì, mia bella bambina," he said softly. "Take me inside."

A rush of arousal went through my core and he slid deeper. I gasped, hovering between pleasure and pain, and his thumb found my clit, rubbing and pressing. Tingles cascaded along the backs of my thighs, through my belly, and soon he was fully seated. Goddamn, he was a lot.

I began slowly moving my hips, sliding his dick in and out of me while grinding on his pelvis. My piercing dragged between us at the end of every stroke, and it sent streaks of white-hot need along my bloodstream. Though the room was dark, I locked eyes with him, and I could see the arousal and possessiveness staring up at me. This felt so real. So intimate. Like he could see inside me, past all my deepest insecurities to my very soul.

I focused on my pleasure and churned my hips, loving the way his length tunneled in and out of my channel, the friction unbelievably good. I tossed my hair and arched my back, giving him a show as I rode him. "God, yes," I moaned. "I want to do this all night."

"Feel how hard I am?" His whisper filled my head like smoke, taking me higher. "That is all for you. Just you, *tesoro mio*."

The unguarded hunger and lust in his expression spurred me on, so I moved faster, and the bliss soon built and coiled inside me like a spring. When I placed my hands on his chest for leverage I half-expected him to shove me off, take over, and pin me to the mattress. Surprisingly he didn't, so I dug my nails into his flesh, holding on as I continued to fuck him.

"Oh, shit." My eyes slammed shut. I was so close, the orgasm right there.

"Look at me," he said sharply. "Look at me while you use my dick to get off."

I did as he commanded, so we were staring at one another when I started to come a second later. The orgasm swept through me like a tsunami, waves and waves that chased everything else away. My mind went blank, his beautiful face my only anchor as I trembled and shook. The walls of my pussy squeezed him in rhythmic pulses and his lips parted on a hiss.

Before I'd even come down, he lifted me slightly and began pounding up from below. His feet were braced on the mattress, and each powerful thrust rocked the bed and sent the headboard into the wall with a bang. Bending, I placed my face directly above his, our mouths inches apart. I was close enough to feel his breath as he grunted and huffed.

I don't know what made me say it, but I started talking. "That's it, baby. Give me all of your come. Every bit of it, deep inside. Make me your good girl."

"Cazzo!" His body went taut beneath me, and I could feel him swell just before he flooded my insides with hot lashes of his come. He held me still, his fingers clamped around my hips so hard that I knew

I'd have bruises. "You are mine," he ground out, his big body jerking beneath me.

Finally he sagged into the bed. I tried to catch my breath, my body sprawled on top of him like a rag doll. He was still inside me, and I could feel our sticky mess leaking out of me as he softened. Still, I was in no hurry to move.

Our breathing eased and his palms stroked my back. My brain grew heavy, the rise and fall of his chest lulling me toward sleep. I liked that we were still connected. It was both dirty and sweet, which seemed perfect.

Everything about this seemed perfect.

He continued to rub me, and somehow I sensed that he needed this connection every bit as much as I did. My fingers absently fondled his jaw. "I used to have nightmares after my mother died and I almost drowned. Frankie said I would wake up in the middle of the night, screaming."

"Oh?"

"They subsided after a few years, but every now and again I'll have one. My therapist said—"

"A therapist? I'm surprised your father allowed it."

"He didn't know."

Enzo huffed a small laugh. "You have never played by the rules, have you?"

"Not by any man's rules, no."

"Yet you play by mine." He squeezed one of my ass cheeks.

"Or maybe you are playing by mine."

Another laugh. "I guess we will see, no?"

I didn't like the sound of that, but I was in too deep to stop now. Besides, my heart wasn't listening. It was singing at the lingering touches and gentle words, swelling with happiness at the closeness between us. We understood each other better than anyone else ever could.

Despite how I felt, I had to get my sister home safely. If I had to deceive Enzo to do it, so be it. I didn't care what happened to me, but Emma didn't deserve to be cooped up here. She was a good person.

I had to make him understand that my twin posed no threat to him whatsoever. "You know, Emma is the one who begged Fausto to postpone killing you until we left."

"I assumed."

That caused me to pull back to stare at him. "Why? Because I'm not as nice as she is?"

He snorted and played with my hair, combing his fingers through the long strands. "Nice is boring, micina."

True. "Seriously, how did you know it wasn't me?"

"Because you understand that the world isn't all gelato and rainbows. You're tough because you have to be. Your sister has been sheltered, protected from the ugliness that surrounds us. She is a mafia don's daughter who wishes to save people, to become a doctor to alleviate her guilt. You don't have that problem. You're ruthless."

The words sent a ball of emotion into my throat, drying out my mouth. I licked my lips then pressed them to his jaw. "Sort of like you."

"Life does not reward the timid."

"But when is it enough for you?"

"When is what enough?"

"This," I said, indicating the yacht. "The money, the power. Is all of it really worth it? I mean, aren't you tired of hiding? Of not seeing your children? What are you trading away to keep all this?"

"What would you have me do?"

He started to tense, so I stroked his chest, trying to calm him. "At some point you need to set aside your pride, Enzo. If you don't, it will kill you."

"This is nothing new. Death has stalked me every day since I've been alive. If it catches me, at least I will have no regrets. My children are safe and well provided for."

"None?" Wow, if I died today, I would have a shit ton of regrets.

"One," he said after a moment. "My wife. I told you she died in a car accident, no?"

"Yes."

"She was having an affair with my guard. At the time of the accident, she was blowing him in the car, her seat belt unfastened."

I froze. "Holy shit."

Raising his head, he kissed my shoulder. "I was not a good husband and she found another. Now my children are alone."

I didn't know what to say. I just clutched him tighter. "Does anyone else know?"

"No. I have told no one, not even Vito."

"Oh, baby." I pressed my forehead to his cheek. "That's awful."

He angled toward me and began kissing me again, this time slow and sweet. I clung to him and poured everything I was feeling into the kiss. Finally, he rolled me onto my back and mumbled against my lips, "Want to fuck you again."

I nodded and slid my arms around his neck. That was the last coherent thought I had for the rest of the night.

CHAPTER TWENTY-THREE

Enzo

I awoke early and found Gianna curled around me. The sun was just starting to creep over the horizon, and my mind churned with the events of the night before. Embarrassment heated my skin. Gia had witnessed my insecurities and pain, the memories that haunted and shamed me. I nearly had a panic attack in front of her.

She'd pulled me from my personal hell with her gentle touch and soft words, which had soothed then aroused me, and I let her use my dick to get off.

Afterward I told her about Angela's death, something no one else knew. Gia responded with kind understanding, which I didn't deserve but soaked in all the same, and her sweetness filled in a few of the jagged edges surrounding my heart. A sense of peace settled inside me and I'd rolled her over to fuck her like she was precious. Like she was *mine*.

Just you, tesoro mio.

Endearments and soft words were unacceptable, especially with this woman. Was Vito right? He insisted that I was spending too much time with Gia, that I'd let her get under my skin. That she was changing me.

Last night was the proof.

I slid out of bed and went to shower. The remnants of the nightmare lingered in my sore muscles, humiliation like a stone around my neck. I pushed it aside. I pushed *everything* aside. Long ago I learned the boss must do what was necessary, no matter the cost.

So I numbed myself to thoughts of long legs and deep brown eyes. Of her sweet body and feisty spirit.

I would do what needed to be done.

When I emerged from the bathroom Gia was still asleep. Good.

I dressed, then slipped her ankle out from under the covers and fastened the cuff and chain around it, locking it in place. She would hate being restrained again, but that was too fucking bad.

I went above deck and made an espresso. After downing it quickly, I made another and carried it to the office. A very interesting email awaited me. Grinning darkly, I grabbed the satellite phone and started dialing.

I was impatient to have all this finished. It was time to see it through and get my life and children back.

A man answered after two rings. "Pronto."

"Alessio."

A long beat of silence followed. "Don D'Agostino. It has been awhile."

Alessio and I hadn't spoken directly since I'd hired him to kill Ravazzani—a job for which he'd failed to deliver results. Since then I'd let Vito handle the communication, but this couldn't wait for my brother. "This is not a friendly call," I snarled.

"I see. Still angry over wind and gelato, no?"

Alessio blamed the bungled assassination on changes in wind patterns and Ravazzani's sudden move to sample a dessert. It made no fucking sense—and I didn't give a shit. Ravazzani still breathed, so Alessio owed me. "I need you to drop everything and go to Málaga."

I couldn't hear him, not even his breathing, but I knew he was there, thinking over what I said. But he couldn't refuse. I had him by the balls.

"This is for the son, I assume. Vito warned me."

"He's using the name Javier Martín. I have images of him in the Málaga airport five days ago." Giulio had gone from Madrid to Málaga, changing his name mid-trip. Smart. But not smarter than me.

"No."

I sat up straight in my chair, my muscles tightening in anger. "Do you honestly think to refuse me?"

"You can't expect me to—"

"What I *expect*," I spat, "is for you to do anything I fucking ask. You failed in your last job for me, and with one call I can let Ravazzani know who shot him and almost killed his pregnant wife. Is this what you want?"

"If I kill his son, he will hunt me down like a dog."

"That is not my problem."

There was a long pause. We both knew he could not refuse me. If he did, I would tell Ravazzani everything I knew. Alessio would be on the run for the rest of his life.

Of course, if word got out that he killed Giulio, Alessio would also be on the run for the rest of his life. It was a lose-lose situation, but I didn't give a fuck. Not as long as I got what I wanted.

"Like I told Vito, I returned the money you paid me for Ravazzani," Alessio said, as if this excused his failure.

"That is not how it works, stronzo. And you should be grateful I am giving you a chance to redeem yourself after what happened. Imagine if word got around that you had missed."

"There are others you can hire. I can refer you to—"

"I don't want anyone else. I want the one who owes me his fucking life and will do what I need when I need it and keep his fucking mouth shut."

"Twenty million Euros," he fired back.

I would have paid more. "Done."

"Send me all the information through the usual channels," he said after a heavy sigh.

"I will. But if you fail again, I will tell Ravazzani everything. I will burn down your entire world."

"And how will Ravazzani feel about you taking a hit out on his son?"

I laughed, dry and without humor. "Honestly, he is probably surprised I haven't done so already. Feel free to tell him, Alessio. He can't find me—but he can find you."

Another beat of silence until, "I won't fail."

That was what he said last time I hired him. "See that you don't." I hung up and tossed the phone on my desk. I opened my laptop and sent the information on where to find Giulio to Alessio's contact.

I didn't think the cloak and dagger shit was necessary, but it was how Alessio worked and I wasn't trusting anyone else with this. He was the best, even though he'd missed assassinating Ravazzani by millimeters.

Vito entered an hour later, and my brother looked surprised to find me already at work. "I thought you would still be sleeping," he said, "since you were up fucking most of the night."

"Eavesdropping, fratello?"

"I think everyone on the yacht heard you, so not by choice. And I still don't think you should be fucking *her*."

I didn't need to explain myself to him, so I changed the subject. "I sent Alessio to Málaga. Giulio flew there five days ago."

Vito dropped into his chair. "You've been busy this morning."

"You say that as if I haven't been working hard lately." I scrolled through my encrypted email.

"You can't deny that you've been distracted."

"I don't need to deny anything. Now, go pour yourself an espresso and let's get to work. "

The sounds of a very angry feminine voice drifted through the open window. The yacht had dropped anchor, so the engines were quiet. That meant I could hear every word being shouted up at me.

"D'Agostino, you motherfucker! Come unlock me right now!"

Vito pursed his lips. "She does not seem happy."

Gia kept cursing and banging on what sounded like the wall. *"Unlock me, you asshole! I want to see my sister!"*

Tuning her out, I switched off the part of my brain that wanted to go see her and touch her. I was done with that.

"Can she break anything in there?" Vito asked. "Maybe I should go down and talk to her."

"Leave her alone. The staff will take her food. She's fine."

"Will you allow her to see her sister?"

"For now, no. I think it's better to keep the twins separate. Tomorrow, when they are more desperate, I will take Emma's photo and contact Ravazzani."

Vito exhaled, his body sagging in visible relief. He put his palms together, prayer-style, and shook them. "Thank fuck."

"Yes, this will all be over soon. We can get back to our rightful places in Napoli and I can bring my children home."

"I can't wait. We should celebrate."

"Tell Massimo and call some women, if you like. Have a party on the boat tonight."

"Does this mean you're done fucking Gia?"

I shrugged. "Maybe. I haven't decided." If I fucked her, it would be without sweet words and soft kisses. She was not my lover.

She was my captive, and I wouldn't forget it again.

Gia

That asshole. Rage burned over my skin like a bad sunburn. After everything that happened last night, he'd locked me up and ignored me for hours. Apparently I wasn't even allowed to see Emma. What the fuck?

Now night had fallen and I could hear loud music blaring from the back of the yacht. An hour ago, a helicopter landed on the helipad in front of Enzo's stateroom and six beautiful women emerged. Six. Women. Way more than what Massimo and Vito could handle alone. Were some of those women for Enzo? Was he fucking someone right now?

The fact that I cared absolutely infuriated me.

I paced in his suite, cracking my knuckles like a prizefighter. God, I wanted to punch him. He'd made me care about him, then chained me up again so he could screw another woman.

My heart squeezed. I was so stupid. If this were a movie, people would be shouting and throwing popcorn at me on the screen.

But I knew he cared about me. I could feel it deep in my bones. It was in the way he touched me, the soft look in his eyes when we were alone in bed. The rough growl when he fucked me, and the careful way he held me afterward.

Not to mention everything he'd shared about his wife and children. I'd seen him in the throes of a nightmare, for fuck's sake. I *knew* this man.

So what was going on out there?

I had to see. I couldn't sit here and wonder. Other women were a dealbreaker for me, so seeing him with someone else would get my stupid heart to stop romanticizing what was happening between us. It would be the dose of clarity I finally needed.

Glancing down, I studied the cuff around my ankle, the chain wrapped around the bed. *Think, Gia* . . . .

What would Emma do?

I whirled around, looking for inspiration. There was nothing to pick the locks with because I'd already searched. The bed was too heavy to lift. I had to either saw through the metal chain or the leather cuff.

Wait a minute.

I could cut through the cuff if I used something sharp enough. They hadn't given me any knives since coming on board, sadly, but there had to be a way to cut this leather. My eyes landed on the bathroom mirror.

Bingo.

And a bonus? The loud music from the party would mask any sound from this suite.

I grabbed a lamp and carried it to the bathroom. The base was heavy, perfect for smashing things. Raising it above my head, I slammed the bottom of the lamp into the mirror, which crashed into a hundred tiny pieces all around me. I held my breath, cringing at the loud noise.

I quickly picked through the shards of mirrored glass to find the perfect tool. It didn't take long. Shard in hand, I grabbed a towel and left the bathroom.

I wrapped the towel around the bottom of the shard like a handle then sawed on the leather cuff. It was slow going, but I worked the same spot again, back and forth. I kept at it, and soon the leather began to give. Red coated the towel beneath my fingers and my hand was stinging, but I didn't stop. It was working.

Holy shit, it was working!

My arm cramped and the pain in my hand became nearly unbearable as the leather weakened. I put the shard down and pulled on the leather cuff, trying to rip it apart. Taking turns between sawing and brute strength, I eventually got the thing off.

Fuck, yes! Let's go!

First stop was Emma's room.

I moved silently through Enzo's office and into the hallway. I hurried down the steps to the deck below and went to her room. Her door was locked. Damn it. "Em," I whispered through the wood. "Are you okay?"

"Gigi?" I heard her feet on the carpet. "I'm fine. Are you okay? Why won't they let me out of here?"

"I don't have any idea. Has anyone given you food and water?"

"Yes, of course," she said, like anything else was too ridiculous to even contemplate. "So you weren't locked in, too?"

"I was. I broke out." I cradled my bleeding hand against my chest, and tiny red drops fell to the carpet.

"Oh, no. I don't want you to get hurt. We should do as Enzo says until we're rescued."

Sweet, sweet Emma. There was no rescue coming, and the only thing I wanted to hear from Enzo was a goddamn apology. "I want to see what's going on up there, then I'll come back for you."

"No, Gia. Don't do that. Don't get into trouble."

Too late. "Don't worry about me. Hang tight and give me a few minutes."

Turning, I went toward the main deck. The music grew louder as I climbed, the party obviously happening in the spa area in the rear. My stomach twisted into a knot. That motherfucker was probably getting a blow job right now. I hope she used too much teeth and scraped his fucking dick off.

Still, I had to know.

I snuck toward the back of the yacht. With all the bodies and limbs, it took a minute to figure out what was happening. Massimo was kissing one woman while another rode his lap. Vito had his face buried between a woman's legs, and two more women were making out with each other off to the side. A lone woman floated happily in the pool, naked. That accounted for all the women. But one man was missing.

"Like what you see?" a deep voice said from behind me.

I started, my hand flying to my chest as I spun toward him. Enzo was there, a drink casually resting in his hand. His hair was disheveled, like he'd been running his hands through it, the lines of his face etched in grim unhappiness. Never looking away from my gaze, he took a drink from the glass, the strong column of his throat working as he swallowed.

"You locked me up so you could get your rocks off at a pussy party. What the fuck?"

"I *locked you up*," he sneered, "because you are my prisoner. And if I want to fuck a stranger, you can hardly tell me no, Gianna."

I rocked on my heels, shocked at the loathing in his voice. This was not the man who'd whispered confessions in the dark last night. This was the ruthless kidnapper who'd first put me in the cage.

Except I knew him now. After all, I'd spent almost two weeks with this man. Who was he trying to fool? "Why the sudden change, *Lorenzo*? You left me unchained for days. One little nightmare and you've got to prove I mean nothing to you?"

He grabbed my wrist. "Why are you bleeding?"

"Don't act like you care."

A muscle jumped in his jaw as he stared down at me, his dark eyes wild. He seemed to be wrestling with himself. Why the act? Why was he putting on such a show, hardening his exterior, trying to make it seem like the past several days had never happened?

Finally, he said, "I need to keep you unharmed or else you are worthless as a bargaining chip."

I ground my back teeth together. "Is that how you see me now? A *bargaining chip?*"

"That is always how I've always seen you, even when you were sitting at my feet and sucking my cock."

Before I could call bullshit, his free hand shot up to wrap around my throat. His fingers weren't tight, but they held me firm. "You are nothing to me but a means to an end. I will use you to regain my rightful place, to regain my life. That is all." There was no spark or hint of heat in his gaze like when we usually played these games.

"You're delusional," I whispered, though doubt was creeping into my mind and strangling my heart.

One dark eyebrow kicked up. "Don't believe me?" He released me and pulled out his phone. Was he calling someone?

After a few swipes, he held the phone up. "Watch."

A video started playing and my stomach dropped into my toes. I recognized the scene right away. It was the night I'd sat on his lap and he fed me dinner in front of everyone. The video had no sound, but the camera showed me curled up on him, eating food from his hand. I looked happy and eager. Totally compliant. On the screen he held a wineglass to my lips and I dutifully drank.

I hardly believed that was me. It was like watching someone else, his mistress or whatever. Not a captive and definitely not his enemy. Not a woman who definitely knew better and had sworn to bring him down. Humiliation scalded my lungs, each breath scraping like razor blades inside my chest.

The video jumped ahead to where I lifted my skirt and sat my bare ass on his dining room table. Enzo's eyes were glittering with lust as I propped my legs up, exposing myself to him. Then the screen paused, the video over.

I stared at the frozen image and wondered how I'd fallen so low. This was what he'd wanted all along, to prove that I would do whatever he wanted. That I was his play thing, his pet.

And I'd fallen right into his trap.

I knew I couldn't trust him and he proved me right. No man can be trusted.

God, I was so stupid. But there was no time to fall apart. I had to remain strong for Emma's sake.

After all, he might have a video that made me appear foolish, but I had things, as well.

My cheeks on fire, I said, "Convenient that your video cuts off right before you gave your pet a fancy *gift*. Or what about when you had a nightmare and clung to me like I was your life raft in a hurricane? We could pull that video. Or what about—"

"No one will ever see or hear of those things," he snapped. "And if you tell your brother-in-law anything I said . . . ."

"What?" I prompted, leaning in and smirking at him. "What will you do, Enzo?"

"You do not ever want to find out, troietta."

"Oh, so it's *troietta* now? What happened to *tesoro* and *bambina*?"

"I only said that to make you do what I wanted." His lip curled as he raked me from head to toe. "No one would ever believe I meant them about someone like *you*."

I knew he was full of shit, but that particular scab was old and painful. Which he was well aware of. "You're a fucking psychopath. And a liar. Go get your dick sucked, il pazzo. Maybe there's some woman out there who doesn't find you completely repulsive. All I know is it isn't me."

I couldn't stand to look at him one second longer. I would stab myself with a shard of mirror glass before I let him touch again. I pushed by him, intent on going to my sister.

He grabbed my arm, stopping me. "You haven't asked what I plan to do with the video."

Humiliate me, obviously. He'd wanted to rub my nose in his victory and put me back in my place. It wouldn't get posted online, not with his face clearly visible.

Then it hit me.

My knees actually buckled, bile rising in my throat. "You're sending it to Fausto."

"I think he will like it very much, no?"

The backs of my eyelids actually started to sting with oncoming tears, and his lips twisted in mock sympathy. "Did you fool yourself into thinking I cared for you? That I had feelings for you? Ma dai, Gia. You can't possibly be that stupid."

The words robbed me of breath and I needed to hurt him back. Before I could stop myself, my palm came up and cracked across his cheek, snapping his head to the side. "You fucking bastard. I hate you."

Very slowly, he turned to face me. Something dark and dangerous bloomed in his expression, and a sliver of fear worked its way along my spine. "You will go back in the cage for that, stronza."

"Try it and you'll lose your balls, D'Agostino."

Before he could respond, an alarm blared from a speaker in the corner. Enzo sucked in a quick breath then sprinted for a cabinet in the corner. He punched in a code and the door flew open. I asked, "What is that noise? What's happening?"

"Get down," he ordered, a gun now in his hand. He slipped something in his pocket, like a controller of some kind.

"Why? Tell me what's happening."

"The perimeter alarm is going off. Someone is approaching the boat."

What did that mean? Police? Oh, my God. Was this a rescue mission to save Emma and me? Was it Fausto?

Enzo was at my side in a flash, pushing on my shoulder. "Get down and stay safe."

I didn't move. "I won't hide until I know there's a reason to hide."

"I don't have time to fucking argue with you! Do as you are told, Gianna."

"No. This could be the cavalry coming to get me and my sister."

"You assume Ravazzani is my only enemy? Don't be foolish. Hide right the fuck now."

I started to go around him toward the open deck—and a hulking figure climbed over the side of the yacht. Bald with a scary tattoo on the side of his head, he was dressed all in black and carrying a pistol in his hand. I blinked several times, unsure what I was seeing. This was not one of Fausto's men. He looked more Russian than Italian.

Oh, shit.

Bullets suddenly exploded all around us, shattering glass and splintering wood, and we hit the floor. Enzo draped himself over my back, protecting me. "Do not move," he said in my ear.

He raised up to shoot at someone. I couldn't see anything because my face and head were covered by Enzo's chest. "Who is it?"

"It's the Russians," he said in a low voice, confirming what I thought. "Retribution for your sister."

CHAPTER TWENTY-FOUR

Gia

"Oh, my God. Emma! I need to get to her." I tried to push him off of me.

"Be still!" he hissed. "She is safe at the moment. Safer than we are."

"You have to let me go down there. I need to be with her."

"I'm not letting you out of my sight. I don't give a fuck about anyone on this boat except you."

I didn't have time to digest that statement because he was up on his elbow, firing again. I held my breath and covered my ears. When he lowered back on top of me, I said, "I need a gun."

"Cazzo, woman! Stop talking."

More shots were fired outside. Enzo's muscles tightened, his big body still pinning me down.

"What's happening?"

He shifted again, and I leaned up to see him fire at three Russians near the entrance to the salon. I covered my head again, praying he'd kill each of them.

A bullet whizzed by me and went into the floor. I yelped and tried to bury myself under Enzo's body. He fired rapidly . . . then the gun clicked, the chamber empty. "Cazzo!" he growled. "Get up, Gia. You need to run and I'll try to hold them off."

"With what? You're out of bullets."

"Just go. Don't worry about me. Crawl and hurry!"

I didn't argue. I kept low and started moving toward the back of the salon, where I could find the stairs and get to Emma. If I was going to die, I would do it with my sister by my side.

Just as I reached the corridor, a large hand grabbed me from behind and pulled me upright. It was one of the Russians. I struggled to get away, but he held tight.

I snarled, "Let me go, you sex-trafficking asshole!"

Grinning, he dragged me back into the salon, where two of his comrades were pointing guns at Enzo. Oh, God. I was going to die. Right here, on this yacht in the middle of nowhere. Because I would not let them take me alive and traffic me to some sleazy brothel. I would rather drown or be shot.

Enzo said something in Russian, but it only made the men laugh. Two of the Russians grabbed his arms and held him, but Enzo just looked at me. His eyes were flat, with no emotion whatsoever. What did that mean? Was he giving up?

I decided I had nothing to lose, so I started fighting. I didn't care if it was pointless or stupid. No way was I going down without landing a few punches and kicks along the way.

The Russian grunted when I struck his thigh with my foot. Enzo shouted, "Basta, Gianna. Do not make him angry!"

Too late.

The big man grabbed a fistful of my hair and shook me like a doll. I screamed in agony, my scalp on fire. Enzo started snarling in Russian, but I couldn't focus on anything other than trying to ease the pain. Then the man slapped me on the side of the head, right on my temple. I lost my balance and dropped to one knee, my ears ringing. Jesus, that hurt.

He probably expected me to cower or cry, but I launched myself up off the floor instead, ramming the top of my head into his chin. I heard his teeth clack before his head snapped back. When he stumbled, I kicked him in the balls and he crumpled to the floor.

Without missing a beat Enzo flew into action. He turned and bit the ear of the guy on his right—and was instantly released as the man howled in pain. Blood oozed from Enzo's mouth as he spit a chunk of flesh onto the ground and reached toward the man on his other side. Before I could blink, he grabbed the gun, twisted it upside down, and pulled the trigger. The gun went off, shooting the Russian in the chest, and he fell down, dead.

Quickly, I found my attacker's gun on the floor and pointed it at him. I felt woozy, but I was still strong enough to pull a trigger and end this piece of shit's life.

Enzo strolled over and put two bullets in the middle of Russian's forehead like it was nothing. "Bastardo," Enzo snarled. Then he tried to shoot him again, but the gun clicked, the magazine empty. So he kicked the dead man in the face instead. "That is for fucking touching her."

My heart swelled, his fucked-up romantic gesture exactly what I needed.

"Such a pity," a familiar voice said near the entry.

I spun and my lips parted on a swift breath. Fausto stood there.

Fausto.

Holy shit. My brother-in-law was here.

"D'Agostino," Fausto said casually, strolling into the salon.

"What the fuck are you doing here?" Enzo snarled, muscles tight like he was going to pounce at any moment.

"Watching. I was hoping the Russians would kill you." Then Fausto walked toward me, the lines of his face easing. He leaned in to kiss both of my cheeks. "Gianna, come stai? Are you hurt?"

"Ciao, Fausto. I'm fine. I'll have a headache, but I'm okay."

He placed a hand on my shoulder. "Va bene. I knew the Russians wouldn't hurt you. They would rather traffic you, but I never would have let that happen. How is your twin?"

"As far as I know she's safe downstairs in her stateroom."

Three men I recognized as belonging to Fausto's crew appeared in the doorway. Marco, Fausto's consigliere and cousin, said, "Russians are dead, Rav." He lifted his chin at Enzo. "Your brothers took care of them."

Enzo said nothing, just continued to pant like he'd run a race. Blood surrounded his mouth and ran down his chin. He looked like a gorgeous Italian vampire.

Fausto put a hand on the small of my back and guided me toward Marco. "Go with Marco. He will see you and Emma safely on my boat."

Confusion swirled in my brain. What was happening? *You're being rescued, dummy!* I glanced over my shoulder at Enzo, whose attention was solely on Fausto.

Was Fausto planning on killing Enzo as soon as I was out of sight? My stomach cramped painfully and I dug in my heels. "Wait."

My brother-in-law's eyebrows rose. "What is it?"

I shifted to place myself between the two men. "What are you planning on doing once I leave?" I asked Fausto.

"That isn't your concern, Gia. Go to the boat with Marco."

Absolutely not. Maybe it was the concussion talking, but I was not going to let him kill Enzo. "I'm not leaving until you tell me what you're going to do."

Fausto's mouth flattened. "I can have you carried out of here. It makes no difference to me. One way or another you and your sister will get on that boat."

"Touch her and you die," Enzo said softly, menace threading through every word.

The threat shouldn't have pleased me, considering Fausto was my brother-in-law, but Enzo's possessiveness sent a bolt of heat through me. I couldn't resist giving Enzo a smug look. *See? I knew you cared.*

Fausto's eyes darted between Enzo and me, and I could see him putting the pieces together. "Tell me you didn't," he said in a low, dangerous voice to Enzo.

Enzo stayed silent and the two men stared each other down.

I licked my lips. "You can't hurt him."

"And why not?" Fausto asked.

Because he is a tortured, misunderstood man who loves his children.

Because he is the first man to ever really get me.

Because he is the man I love.

I straightened my shoulders. "Because you've both done enough damage to the other. This has to stop."

"You know nothing of which you speak," Fausto said.

"I know everything," I said. "I probably know more than you do. You can't kill him. I won't allow it."

"You assume he can get the better of me?" Enzo said softly, lifting his gun threateningly.

"That gun is out of bullets," Fausto said. "So I think we all know who has the upper hand."

"No one is killing anyone," I snapped.

"Get on the boat." Enzo sounded like he was grinding his teeth.

"What? No." I searched his face for clues, but he stared only at Fausto. I crossed my arms over my chest. "I'm not leaving you alone with him."

Enzo dragged his eyes off Fausto briefly, and a muscle jumped in his jaw as he glared at me. "Do as you are told."

"I won't, not when it means you die."

"I don't need you to protect me."

He clearly did, if the grim mood in the room was any indication. Fausto would shoot Enzo dead the second I left. So I would do whatever it took to prevent that.

"Cugino," Fausto called. "Get Gianna on the boat."

Enzo took a step toward me, his body swelling aggressively. "Whoever touches her will permanently lose the use of both arms."

I couldn't help it. I moved closer to him, my mouth fighting a smile. Most women—sane ones—would've been horrified by a blood-soaked man making threats on her behalf . . . but I wasn't. I was a mafia princess, born in this life. Violence and danger ran in my veins, and no amount of pretending or moving or dating boring men would ever change that.

Maybe that made me fucked up, too, but I couldn't deny it any longer.

"Il pazzo," I said quietly, my palm caressing the side of his face.

"Madonna!" Fausto barked from behind me. "What have you done to her?"

Enzo swallowed hard, his expression pained. "Get on the boat, micina," he murmured. "Please."

"What the fuck? You think I'm going to leave and let him murder you? I'm not going anywhere."

"Do as you are told," he snarled, grabbing my wrist and shoving me away from him. "Vattene! Go, woman!"

I didn't want to leave him. Not like this, when I knew he would die. "No. I'm staying with you."

His eyes were flat and cold as they raked me from head to toe. "I don't want you here. You were just pussy to me, nothing more. I wanted to ruin you and I did. Look at you! Begging to stay with a man who treated you like nothing better than a whore."

I knew he didn't mean it, but it was still hard to hear. "Stop," I said weakly.

"Why? Can't handle the truth? Should I tell them how eager you were for it? Should I show them the videos I made of you on your knees, sucking—"

"Stop! Don't do this, Enzo. I know you're saying it just so I'll go."

We stared at each other. Finally, he said, "Leave, Gianna. You'll always be the enemy, the woman I used for revenge. Nothing more."

Pure revulsion filled his expression, like I was dirt beneath his shoe.

It was how Papa's guards looked at me years ago when they called me names.

And it was also how Grayson looked at me when I caught him cheating, like it was *my* fault.

It hit me then. This wasn't about Fausto or the Russians or my safety. This was about *me*. He meant those hurtful words, even after I'd opened up to him. *Trusted* him.

I couldn't breathe. My heart tore in half, crumbling right inside my chest. I willed him to take it back, to tell me he cared, but he didn't. The silence spoke volumes.

Enzo didn't want me.

I'd been a goddamn game, a piece on his chessboard. He hadn't cared about me at all. None of them ever cared about me enough for something lasting.

It was a blow but I wouldn't beg. I wouldn't remind him of everything he said and did during the two weeks I was on this yacht. If he wanted me gone, I would walk out with my head high, no matter how broken I was inside.

But I couldn't leave without securing a promise first, even if Enzo didn't deserve it.

I turned to my brother-in-law. Fausto was frowning, his eyebrows pulled low in confusion. I closed the distance between us and said quietly, "Swear that you won't hurt or kill him."

His lips pressed together. "Gianna—"

"No, Fausto. Swear it. Swear on the lives of your children that you won't do anything right now or else I'm not leaving with you. You'll have to tell my sister that you failed in getting me back."

Oh, he didn't like that one bit. His voice hardened. "You threaten me?"

I let out a trembling breath and changed my tune. "Fausto, please. You've done enough to him. Swear it."

A long moment passed where he studied my face. "I swear it. I won't hurt him or kill him right now on this boat."

I supposed that was the best I could hope for, considering. "Thank you."

I walked out onto the deck and didn't look back.

Enzo

Numb, I stared at my greatest enemy, the man who'd ruined my life. I had thought of this moment many, many times over the last four years. I imagined the hatred and violence I would feel when we finally saw one another again. Had dreamt of my retribution, my vengeance.

But now? I felt nothing.

The hurt in Gianna's eyes, her ravaged expression, was all I could see. I hadn't liked hurting her, but what choice did I have? I had to keep her safe. So I lied and told her those ugly words. It would be better in the end. She could hate me and move on with her life.

She would be grateful once she was in Siderno with her sisters and I disappeared again.

I stared at Ravazzani flatly. "Well?"

"You fucked her."

I said nothing. We both knew the answer.

"You're a real piece of shit, D'Agostino. It wasn't enough to kidnap my wife, you had to kidnap her sisters, too? Did you rape both of them?"

I didn't owe him an explanation. I wasn't a rapist and I hadn't touched Emma, but let him think the worst of me. I slipped my hands into my trouser pockets.

Ravazzani didn't like my silence. His mouth twisted as he glared at me. "You are making it very hard not to shoot you right now."

"It would be a mistake to try."

Shaking his head, he leaned against the wall and studied me. "You kept to the water. Smart."

"Not all of us have a castle."

"Mine is nicer," he said off-handedly, gesturing to the interior. "Bigger, too."

"How did you find me?"

He flicked a piece of imaginary lint off his suit jacket. "The Russians. They led us right to you."

"Cazzata. How?"

"My contacts in Milan helped us track Emma down when she went missing. Imagine our surprise when we missed you by just a few hours. At that point all we had to do was wait for the Russians to go looking for you. Apparently they put a tracker inside Emma when she was first captured. No doubt they sedated her so she wouldn't remember, but it was foolish of you not to check for one."

Yes, clearly a mistake. I didn't regret going after Emma or leading the Russians here. I'd done it for Gia, to save her twin. To make her smile at me like I was a king among men.

Though I was impatient, I waited and kept quiet. Fausto liked to make a big Hollywood production out of everything. I preferred efficiency, but I had to let this play out.

"Are your children on the boat with you?"

I wouldn't give him any information, so I said nothing.

He nodded when the silence stretched. "I think the answer is no. You've hidden them somewhere far away from you to keep them safe. You must miss them."

Pezzo di merda. He was surrounded by his wife and children, living happily on his estate, while I was alone and miserable. My hands curled into fists at my side.

"And your wife?"

Again, I gave no response. He didn't deserve to know anything about me or my family.

He pushed off from the wall and closed the distance between us. Then he lifted his gun and pointed it at me.

Calmly, I met his gaze. Did he honestly think I would make this so easy? "I wouldn't do it, if I were you."

"Fortunate that you aren't me, then. I promised I wouldn't kill you on this boat. I never said anything about another boat. Get moving."

"No, it is you who will be leaving, alone." Stepping back, I reached into my pocket and took out a small device. "Do you know what this is?"

His lips flattened, so I assumed he recognized it as a detonator.

I held it up. "I have the entire boat wired with explosives. I press this button and we end up as little pieces of skin and bone in the water."

"You would blow up yourself and your brothers just to kill me?"

"In a fucking blink. I will *never* be taken alive again. Not by you, not by anyone."

I let him see the truth of the words in my expression. Massimo and Vito knew of my feelings on this and had agreed. *Stronger together.* Even if it meant death.

Slowly, Ravazzani lowered the gun. "I have imagined this so many times, how it would play out, but you're different. You are not the same man who leered at my wife's ass and kidnapped her."

"No, I'm not," I agreed. "I'm worse."

Ravazzani cocked his head, his expression thoughtful. "That may be true, but I also think you are miserable and alone. It pleases me very much."

When is it enough for you?

Gia's words from last night rang in my head, but I pushed them aside. I didn't want pity from anyone, especially Ravazzani. "Get off my fucking yacht."

He moved toward the doorway. "You know how all of this ends, no?"

"With one of us dead, obviously. Because I will never give up half of my computer empire."

Pausing, he sneered at me over his shoulder. "No, that's what I wanted before you kidnapped my wife. Now I want half the computer fraud, half your drug business, and all of the construction contracts in Napoli for the next fifteen years."

Che palle. Acid churned in my stomach at the outrageous demands. The stronzo had no right to any of it. "You will be disappointed, then."

"We will see, D'Agostino."

He stepped out onto the deck, and I couldn't resist adding fuel to the fire. "Before you go, I have one final piece of advice for you."

"And what is that?"

"You better stay inside your castello in Siderno. Because the next time I see you, I will kill you. Even if I must also kill myself in the process."

"Fucking lunatic," he muttered before shaking his head and disappearing.

CHAPTER TWENTY-FIVE

Gia

Ravazzani Estate, Siderno

"What's wrong with Zia GiGi?"

I could hear Raffaele's voice from the other end of the pool as he asked his mother—again—what was wrong with me.

If only I could explain it.

"She's just a little sad, baby," Frankie said to the four-year-old boy.

"But she's been sad for days," he complained.

"Sometimes that happens."

"Why is she sad?"

I could feel tears threatening again as I stared out over the rolling hills of the estate. I should leave. I thought coming out to the pool and getting some fresh air would be a nice change from staying in my room, moping. I was wrong. Out here, I was ruining everyone's fun.

"That's none of our business," Frankie said. "And it's not polite to talk about other people."

A small finger tapped my shoulder. I looked over and found Noemi, my two-year-old niece. "Here, Zia." She held out a small yellow flower. "Feel better."

God, these kids.

I swallowed the lump in my throat and accepted the tiny bloom. "Thanks, Mimi," I croaked, using the nickname I'd coined for her because it was like mine. "You're so sweet."

The little girl skipped off toward the vegetable garden. I twirled the stem in my fingers and watched the petals spin. When would this heaviness leave my chest? I've been here for five days. I should feel better already.

You were just pussy to me, nothing more.

I dragged in a deep breath and tried not to think about him. He didn't deserve my time and energy, not after the hurtful things he'd said.

If only my heart was on the same page. I knew Enzo was an asshole, but I couldn't stop thinking about the way he'd made me *feel*. Like he saw me, like he cared about me. Like I mattered to him.

Lies. It had been nothing more than lies. I couldn't forget it.

Someone sat next to me and I didn't need to look over to know who it was. I could always sense when my twin was nearby.

"You're not ruining anything," Emma said. "So put that right out of your mind."

Unsurprising that she'd read my thoughts. "But—"

"They're kids, Gia. They've already forgotten about you. See?"

It was true. A laughing Raffaele was jumping off the side of the pool into Frankie's arms, and Noemi was eating peas in Zia's garden. "I'm sorry," I couldn't help but say.

"There's nothing to apologize for. We're worried, that's all."

"I'll be fine."

"That's what you keep saying."

"Because it's true." Soon I would forget all about Enzo D'Agostino.

Sighing, Emma wrapped her arm around me and dropped her head on my shoulder. We watched Raffaele—mini-Fausto—splash around in the pool. Really, what more could be said?

I'd filled my sisters in on everything when I arrived in Siderno.

Well, not everything. I told them the sex was consensual and fun, that it meant nothing. I didn't tell them about the cage. I didn't reveal how Enzo had degraded me and how much I enjoyed it. I certainly didn't tell them that I'd fallen in love with him.

They would have me committed.

The nanny came out to collect Raffaele and Noemi for their naps. Frankie got out of the pool with her son, then kissed both kids and promised to see them in a few hours. She walked over toward us, a tiny baby bump peeking out from her bikini. I thought she might get back in the pool, but she sat on my other side instead, her feet dangling in the clear water.

"I hate seeing you like this," Frankie said after she settled. "It makes me wish that Fausto had killed Enzo that day on the yacht."

I didn't regret keeping Enzo alive. Even though he'd broken my heart, Enzo didn't deserve to die. His children had lost their mother; they shouldn't lose their father, too. "I'm fine."

"You're not fine. You aren't sleeping, you aren't eating. You're not even drawing or designing. All you do is lay in bed."

Sisters were a pain in the ass sometimes. "I went through a traumatic experience, Frankie. Maybe it's PTSD."

Emma stared at her feet and I knew she didn't believe me. After all, she'd been on the yacht and saw me on Enzo's lap, eating from his hand. "You have a broken heart," my twin said. "You're in love with him."

Frankie shook her head. "God, that is really fucking hard for me to understand."

My oldest sister was starting to piss me off. "*Really*? You fell in love with Fausto, who kidnapped you and brought you to Italy to marry his son. Can you really not understand what I'm going through?"

"It's not the same. Enzo kidnapped me when I was pregnant, Gigi. He put a gun in my mouth. Che cazzo?"

She often switched between Italian and English now, so this didn't surprise me. "Fausto kidnapped Enzo's kids and held them at gunpoint. His *kids*, Frankie. Babies in their pajamas. So please get off your high horse."

Emma leaned forward, her brow wrinkled as she looked at Frankie. "Is this true?"

"Yes, it's fucking true," I snapped.

Frankie pushed to her feet and dragged a hand through her wet hair. "Okay, fine, but Fausto only did that to rescue me. Did you not hear the part about me being kidnapped and a gun forced into my mouth?"

"Think about your kids," I said, shifting to see her better. "Think about how you would feel if someone took them from their beds, kidnapped them and held them at gunpoint."

She pressed her lips together and closed her eyes. "I didn't agree with that choice at the time. I tried to apologize to them and I made sure—"

When she didn't finish I instantly knew. "You made Fausto promise not to hurt them."

"Yes," she said after a long pause. "But I don't believe the promise was actually necessary. Fausto wouldn't have hurt Enzo's family."

"Now who is being foolish?"

Frankie's neck flushed as she folded her arms across her chest. "You're being a real bitch, you know that? You need to lash out at someone? Fine. I guess it can be me. It's certainly not the first time."

I got to my feet, anger burning hot in my lungs. "I'd rather be a bitch than a naive mafia wife. You excuse whatever Fausto does because he's your husband. You sound like Mamma."

Frankie's face paled. "Take that back. I am nothing like her and Fausto is nothing like Papa."

I lifted my hands. "I'm sorry, but don't you see the hypocrisy? And what the fuck is wrong with us? We all swore to get out of this world, not to end up with mafia men, and instead we both fell in love with one. Jesus Christ. If anyone should know better, it's a Mancini daughter."

While my twin stood and put her arm around me, Frankie didn't move, just stared off across the estate at the vineyard. "I never wanted this for myself or for either of you," Frankie said. "It was why I never argued with Papa over my future, so that you two would be able to make your own choices. I wanted you to have a different life, one with freedoms I never had."

"I know, which is why I feel like a fucking failure," I said quietly. "I feel like I've let you down, like I've let Mamma down. Emma. Even myself."

Frankie's expression softened as she came over to hug me. "You aren't a failure and I'm not disappointed in you. I just want you to be happy. If a mafia don makes you happy, then who am I to judge?" She gave a dry laugh. "I'm Mrs. Ravazzani, for fuck's sake."

"But would you change it if you could?"

"I wouldn't change a damn thing. I'm beyond happy here. Every day is . . . bliss. I just wish—"

"You wish, what?" I asked.

She moved back but kept her hands on my shoulders. "I just wish you hadn't fallen for this particular mafia don."

I rolled my eyes and strode away from both my sisters. "Do you think I planned this? That I'm thrilled with that development?"

"No, but I can't see how you let it happen."

"Jesus, Frankie. How did you just *let it happen*?" I gestured to the estate. "You act like I have some kind of control over my feelings."

"I saw how he was with her," Emma said to Frankie. "I think he cares about her, too."

"Not if what Fausto heard on the yacht is to be believed. He said Enzo called you terrible names and had some kind of video of the two of you together."

"If you're trying to make me feel shittier, it's working." My voice quavered.

"Oh, Gigi," Emma said, pulling me tighter. "No one is trying to make you feel worse."

Because they couldn't. I hated myself at the moment. I'd fallen in love with the wrong man who was totally right for me—he just didn't want me. A tear slipped out of my eye. "Why am I like this?"

Frankie's hands swept down my arms. "Like what, honey?"

"So fucked up."

"You are *not* fucked up," Emma said sharply. "Do not let him make you think that."

I shook my head. He hadn't. Enzo was the one person who made me feel normal. Like I was okay.

Except it hadn't been real.

Did you fool yourself into thinking I cared for you?

Yes, I had. God, I was pathetic. No wonder Fausto could hardly stand to look at me and my sisters were gazing at me with pity in their eyes all the time.

I needed to pull myself together. This was ridiculous. Crying over a man was not my style. I needed to focus on myself, my family. My career. This had gone on long enough.

But I couldn't stay in Italy. As much as I'd loved my time in Milan, this country and that city were tainted with bad memories. "I want to go back to Toronto," I announced.

My sisters exchanged a look. Frankie said, "Just stay a little longer. There's no rush. I'd like to spend more time with you both."

"You want to keep an eye on me." I knew my sister. Even though she was two years older, she'd practically raised Emma and me, and she acted like a mama bear whenever we were upset about something.

"Yes, I do. But I also want to hang out with my sisters while I still can. When the baby arrives I'll have my hands full."

"I finished my classes remotely." Emma bumped her shoulder against mine. "So let's stay a little longer, Gigi."

"Besides, I think you should consider another internship," Frankie said. "Paris has a ton of designers. Fausto could make a call or two."

Hmm. There were some really great designers there. It wasn't Milan, but it was a close second. "I'll think about it."

"Good. See? You'll bounce back from this, Gia. I promise."

I stared at the water in the pool. I didn't think so. Enzo had changed me, shown me parts of myself that I barely understood. It was like he'd uncovered my secrets but didn't help me decode them. I was an unfinished design, a mess of fabric and pins I couldn't make sense of. And there wasn't anyone I could confide in, not even my sisters. I needed time by myself to figure it all out.

To figure myself out.

Frankie leaned back and tilted her face toward the sun. "Em, will you grab my sunscreen from the kitchen? I left it on the counter."

"Sure." Emma strode toward the castello, while Frankie and I retook our seats at the edge of the pool.

Frankie said, "Now that we have a moment alone, I want to apologize. I'm not trying to make you feel worse. This has been a lot for me to wrap my head around, and I'm all juiced up with pregnancy hormones. So please forgive me. I still love you and I'm here for you, whatever you need."

"Thanks, sis. I appreciate it."

"I have to ask. Are you pregnant?"

My eyes went huge. "No! Oh, my God. No."

"Good. And don't sound so surprised. It happens. Hello?" She waved her hand to indicate the estate.

"I know. But you're the reason I got an IUD, so thanks."

"You're welcome." She bounced her foot against mine playfully. "Did he treat you okay? Seriously, Gigi. You can tell me."

Hadn't we gone over this? "There's nothing to tell. He's into some twisted stuff, but it turns out I am, too. I liked it."

"That's what I assumed. Fausto said you two looked . . . close. Emotionally. Like you were, you know, a couple."

"God, you are so bad at this stuff." I rolled my eyes. "I hope you get better at talking about sex before Raffaele and Noemi start dating."

"Shut up," she said with a small laugh. "I just never had to worry about you with men. You're so strong and I always knew you could hold your own."

I bit my lip to stem the sadness welling inside me. "I guess I'm not so strong after all."

"Stop. Loving the wrong person doesn't make you weak. It makes you human. But staying with someone who is bad for you, someone who doesn't lift you up, is a mistake. You need an equal partner, one who supports you in all things. Enzo will never be that person for you."

"I know."

"Do you? Because if you had stayed with him, I'd never be able to see you again."

My stomach turned over. I hadn't really thought that far ahead, about what staying with Enzo might mean. "You would do that to me?"

"Honey, I wouldn't have a choice. I'm Team Ravazzani now. Whatever I do is for the good of my man and my kids. Do you honestly see Fausto welcoming Enzo to family barbecues?"

"Do you even have family barbecues?"

"That isn't the point. Enzo is the enemy. That won't ever change."

I lifted my hair and pulled it up into a messy bun. "Then I guess we're lucky he kicked me off the yacht."

"I think he did it to protect you. So you didn't see what was about to happen with Fausto."

This had occurred to me. But if that were true, then why say what he did before Fausto arrived, before the Russians attacked? Why show me that video and taunt me with it? I feared the video would be leaked online or sent to Fausto. There was nothing stopping Enzo from humiliating me, from using that video to his advantage. "That's not true. Trust me."

"Well, it's a moot point because you're here now. And you're going to stay with me until you feel more like yourself. Then you can figure out your next step."

More like myself? Sure, right. Except I no longer knew what that meant. I guess I had to figure it out soon, though. And to do that, I needed distance from my family. I wanted to go somewhere new, where no one knew I'd spent two weeks on Enzo D'Agostino's yacht.

I needed to put all of this behind me with a fresh start. No more wallowing.

"You know, I like your idea about Paris. If I give Fausto the names of a few designers, do you think he could call today?"

"Gigi, are you sure? It feels too soon."

"I've never been more sure about anything. I need to stay busy and forget any of this ever happened."

Enzo

Pully, Switzerland
One week later

"God, this sucks," Massimo muttered for the hundredth time since I'd purchased this estate. "This is worse than the yacht."

The massive house had five floors, ten bedrooms, a swimming pool, and sat on the shores of Lake Geneva. And this was worse, how?

I didn't speak. We were eating dinner—Massimo, Vito, and me—in the kitchen. Massimo had made chicken piccata and, despite his excellent cooking skills, it didn't taste as delicious as I knew it must be. The dish had too many memories now for me to enjoy it.

Cazzo, I fucking missed her. It had been almost two weeks and I could hardly function. A mafia zombie, Massimo had called me.

Is all of it really worth it?

She'd asked me that during our last night together. At the time I thought yes, the money and power were worth all my sacrifices, even the ones that pained me most.

But over the last few days the doubt had started to creep in. The nightmares made it impossible to sleep, and I couldn't stop thinking about Gia. It was like losing my fingertip all over again—I had to relearn how to do everything, because I was now missing something important, something vital to my well being. I fought with my brothers constantly and I couldn't focus on work.

I tossed down my fork, unable to finish my meal. Madre di Dio, when would this end?

Vito's brows shot up. "Don't like it?"

"It's fine. I'm not hungry."

"I'll try not to take that personally," Massimo said.

"I said, it's not the food," I repeated.

Massimo exchanged a glance with Vito. They were doing this a lot lately and I didn't like it. "What? If you two have something to say, then spit it out."

Massimo went back to his food, so I focused on my consigliere. "Well?"

Vito put down his knife and fork, then wiped his mouth with a napkin. "How long do you see us staying here?"

"A little while." The house was gated and walled, in a great location. Nearly impenetrable. We'd rented it under an assumed name, so no one knew we were here. In a few months, we'd go somewhere else, staying quiet and remaining anonymous.

What other choice did I have? Another yacht was out of the question now that Ravazzani had discovered this tactic.

Vito lifted his wine glass. "Let's use the video you have of her to force Ravazzani—"

"No." My refusal was instant.

"Why not? I thought that was the plan. You wanted to turn her into your whore and you did."

I ran my hand through my hair, feeling my irritation rise. "I said no. Drop it."

He rubbed his jaw thoughtfully. "I need to understand. We have the ability to blackmail Ravazzani with that video and you are refusing to use it. Am I wrong?"

I aimed the tip of my dinner knife at his face. "I said fucking no, fratello. Bring it up one more time and I'm going to stab you."

I knew this was ridiculous. I should send the video to Fausto to use as blackmail and get my life back. Get *all* our lives back.

But I couldn't do it. She was perfect in the video, being so sweet while doing everything I ordered that I could fucking choke. I didn't want anyone else to see those things—and I didn't owe anyone explanation about it, either.

Fuck this. Getting up, I decided to go work for the rest of the night.

"Hey, Zo," Massimo called as I was halfway across the room. "Look at this."

"Not now."

"Gia's in Paris."

I drew to a halt. Che cazzo? Why wasn't she in Siderno or back in Toronto? Why was she in Paris?

I was at Massimo's side in an instant, taking the phone from his hand. It was a photo from Gia's social media account with her posing in front of the Seine. She wasn't smiling, and there was a sad haunted look in her eyes that perfectly complemented the gloomy gray Paris weather. She looked so fucking beautiful. I ached to touch her just once more.

My chest felt like it was caught in a vise as I scrolled through her other photos, which showed the food and sights of Paris through her eyes. She didn't appear in any more, though, and I wanted to howl with frustration.

Vito was looking at his own phone. "She's working for Matthieu LaCrocq."

I went back to the Seine photo and memorized every detail. Maybe I would download these stupid social media apps just to see her.

Massimo spoke up. "LaCrocq is a piece of shit."

That got my attention. "What does that mean?"

"He's very hands-on with the female employees and models—and not in a good way."

"How do you know this?" I asked.

My youngest brother's eyebrows pulled together. "Didn't you ever talk to the French models we brought onto the yacht?"

No, I hadn't.

"Forget it," Massimo muttered. "I forgot who I was talking to."

"Get to the point, stronzo," I snapped.

Massimo exchanged another look with Vito, and I swore I was seconds away from strangling them both with my bare hands.

"There are a few creepy designers," Massimo said, "and the more experienced models avoid them. LaCrocq is one."

"Creepy or dangerous?" Vito asked.

My youngest brother gestured with his hands. "I don't know, but is there a difference? Rumors usually start for a reason."

"Get Domenico on the phone," I said to Vito.

My consigliere hesitated. "Zo, are you sure? Knowing your connection to him, Ravazzani could have Domenico's phones—"

"Get him on the phone or I will do it myself."

"Madre di Dio," Vito grumbled as he rubbed his eyes. Then he pulled out his phone, pressed a few buttons and handed it to me.

After two rings, a male voice answered. "Pronto."

"It is Enzo D'Agostino. I need a word."

Domenico paused, then ordered some people out of his office. When it was quiet, he said, "Ciao, Don D'Agostino. How may I assist you today?"

"I need information on a designer, a man in Paris. LaCrocq."

"Are you thinking of investing in him?"

"No, someone I know has just gone to work for him. A woman." I didn't tell him it was Gia.

Domenico hissed through his teeth. "LaCrocq is a pezzo di merda, capisce? I wouldn't recommend she ever be alone in a room with him."

"Tell me why."

The designer launched into a story that turned my blood cold. A few years ago a model friend of Domenico's was drugged and raped at the hands of LaCrocq. When she refused to press charges, Domenico gave her the money to move to Los Angeles and get as far away from LaCrocq as possible.

And now Gia was going to be working with this monster?

I couldn't think. A sweat broke out on my brow. I thanked Domenico and rang off, then banged the edge of Massimo's phone against my forehead several times. What the fuck had Ravazzani been thinking, letting his sister-in-law work for such a man?

I couldn't allow this. LaCrocq would try to get Gia into bed. What sane man wouldn't? He'd put his hands all over her body, whether she gave him permission or not. He'd touch her thighs, her ass. Her tits. Her pussy. *My* piercing.

"Cazzo!" I roared and slammed the phone down. My hands were shaking as I braced them on the marble countertop.

I had to stop this.

"She can hold her own, Zo," Massimo said. "Gia's a ball-buster."

"What about when he drugs her?" I snarled. "Can she hold her own then?"

Vito pointed to the phone. "We can have one of the boys find Gia's number. Then you can call her and tell her what you know."

She wouldn't answer if I rang her. She might pick up for one of my brothers, but that didn't mean she would listen. She was stubborn and hated to be told what to do. No doubt she'd continue working there if only to prove me wrong.

I had to handle this directly.

But this meant going to Paris.

My temples pounded. We were hidden here in the middle of

nowhere, safe for the time being. There was no guarantee I could retain my anonymity in Paris while dealing with Gianna. The woman never made anything easy.

But what choice did I have?

"You are planning on calling her, no?" Vito asked. "Because contemplating anything else would be crazy."

Was he reading my mind?

"Wait," Massimo said. "You mean to go to Paris? In person? Ma che cazzo! We can't go visit our own *sister* because it's too dangerous, but you can run off to Paris to warn Gia about her new boss?"

I growled and dragged my hands through my hair. Everything Massimo said was true, but I didn't care. I started pacing, my shoes slapping on the worn kitchen tile. Her absence made it impossible to think, to plan and strategize. My mind was stuck on the danger she had unwittingly put herself in.

"Calm down, Zo," Vito said. "You know it's too dangerous for us to go to Paris right now. Let's call Ravazzani and tell him what you know."

"As soon as I do he'll know she means something to me."

"But she does mean something to you," Massimo pointed out.

True, but I didn't want my enemy to know it. I didn't want anyone to know.

Is all of it really worth it?

I could still hear her voice in my head. Hardly anyone understood what it was like to have the weight of the entire 'ndrina on their shoulders. I was the boss. I made the hard decisions, took the risks, and suffered for any mistakes.

And yes, I had made mistakes—the biggest being partnering with Mommo against Fausto.

The old don of a rival 'ndrina, Mommo had approached me with the idea, saying Fausto was ripe for the picking. I'd just taken over as Don and was looking to prove myself. The chance to get the best of a big fish like Ravazzani was too tempting, especially when one of his supposed allies was helping me orchestrate it.

The plan had backfired against me and my family, as well as cost Mommo his life.

And I was still being punished every day for this. Me, Nic, Luca. Massimo and Vito. Our sister. Now Gia.

Is all of it really worth it?

Grabbing the half-empty wine bottle on the counter, I launched it against the wall. The heavy glass shattered and red droplets splashed on the tile, pooling into the grout.

I went to the cupboard and found a bottle of bourbon. Carrying it in one hand, I snatched a glass with the other. Then I walked out of the kitchen. "I need to think."

CHAPTER TWENTY-SIX

Enzo

The cameras whirred as they turned to see me.

I came on foot, knowing it was the only way to catch them by surprise and get close to the gate. The castello was impressive, I would give him that. I hadn't seen much of the estate during the last, and only, other time I'd been here. But right now the afternoon sun shone down on the old brown stone, bathing it in a burnished gold.

It made me hate him even more.

Before I could buzz at the gate, three armed men appeared, guns drawn, and I immediately showed them my hands. I knew the drill. They would want to check me for weapons and bombs.

After all, who was crazy enough to come here unarmed?

Only me.

My brothers tried to talk me out of it. But my mind was made up. I had to do this. There wasn't time for anything else.

The guards watched me carefully through the iron bars. They didn't ask for my identity; they already knew.

I raised my shirt slowly with one hand, showing them I had no weapons. "You will take me to him."

"We are not doing shit until he tells us it's okay."

"Call him, then."

More guards came around the side of the castello, an army ready to defend their king. I once had the same, before I went on the run.

Minutes later Marco Ravazzani strolled forward, his hands shoved in his trouser pockets to show he didn't consider me a threat. He approached the gate, his gaze cool and flat. "You are a long way from Napoli, Don D'Agostino."

"I want to see him."

"He told you what would happen when he found you again."

"Do you think I am so stupid as to come here with nothing?" I gestured to the guards, who had their guns pointed at me.

Marco stared at me like I was a puzzle he was trying to decipher. "I admit, I am curious."

No doubt Ravazzani was watching this unfold. I turned my gaze to the camera. "Get out here. It is time we settle this."

Marco's phone rang. He pulled it from his shirt pocket and answered. After a few seconds he hung up and pressed a button. The gate began to swing open. "Check him for weapons," he instructed.

One guard moved in and I raised my arms to the side, giving him access to pat me down. I flinched as soon as he touched me, but I knew it was going to get worse.

I was proven right when a guard handcuffed me, which triggered all kinds of horror inside me. I tried to breathe through the panic, even as I started sweating. I needed to keep calm.

As they marched me into the estate, I thought of Gia, her wide smile and sharp tongue. The way she smelled, the sound of her laughter. Those memories helped to keep the worst of the fear away.

Instead of leading me to the front door, they started around the side of the castello. "Where are we going?" I asked.

"Dai, you didn't think I was taking you inside, did you? Where his wife and children live?" Marco shook his head. "You could have a bomb shoved up your ass. Besides, what better place for a reunion than this?"

Cazzo madre di Dio. I knew where we were going and I wasn't certain I could do it. My stomach roiled as bile raced up my throat. I should have known Ravazzani would not make this easy.

I have no choice. I need to get to her. I need her back.

Marco pulled on the heavy metal door to the dungeon and the smell hit me first. I sucked in a breath, the musty scent of death bringing me back to when I was broken and beaten. I swallowed and focused on getting one foot in front of the other. I would not let them see me weak.

Darkness shrouded us as we went down the stone steps. It was like going back in time, literally and figuratively. Nothing had changed down here. No doubt my blood, sweat and piss still coated the floor of the rear cell.

If I'd hoped Ravazzani would have me placed in a different cell, those hopes were dashed as we continued toward the back. Sadistic son of a bitch. I could hear my heart beating inside my ears, the rising panic like a cacophony in my head.

As they pushed me inside the familiar cell and unlocked the handcuffs, the edges of my vision waivered. They locked me in and left, and I stood there, alone, drowning in memories. I paced, reminding myself it wasn't the same. I wasn't restrained or bleeding. I could move and breathe without pure agony shooting through me.

It wasn't working. The rising blackness threatened to swallow me, to bring me back to the pit of Hell.

I had to remain calm. Leaning against the stone, I shut everything out. My thoughts, my surroundings. I started doing the breathing technique Gia taught me during our last night together. I dragged air in through my nose, then exhaled while making the soft shushing sound in my throat. I counted and kept going, glad no one else could see or hear me. I wasn't much for mystical practices and beliefs, but this had worked once. Maybe it would work again.

Minutes dragged by. Ravazzani would keep me stewing down here as long as he liked, no doubt hoping it would send me into a spiral of memories. To thwart him, I focused on my breath and didn't think about anything else.

When the metal door finally cracked open I was no longer sweating and my heart pumped at a normal rate. I was ready to face him.

Then he was in front of the cell, his jacket off and sleeves rolled up on his forearms. It was how I remembered him down here; not as a businessman, but as someone ready to torture and kill.

"You must have a fucking death wish," Ravazzani snapped. Marco stood off to the side, arms folded, expression unreadable.

"As I said, it's time we settle this."

"So you are willing to agree to all of my conditions?"

"What you suggested is ludicrous."

He smirked at me. "Then I am not certain why you are here, other than to end your life. Perhaps you missed my dungeon?"

"I am prepared to tell you who is trying to kill your oldest son."

Ravazzani went absolutely still. I wasn't certain if he was even breathing. It was clear he hadn't expected this. The information was my only card to play, but I was willing to play it for Gia.

"Cazzata," he snarled. "You are wasting my time and pissing me off."

"If you kill me, you learn nothing."

One of his dark brows lifted arrogantly. "I could torture you for it."

"You tried your best once and I still live. I will never tell you unless I get what I want."

"Perhaps I was only getting warmed up."

"Don't be a fool. You know it won't work."

His eyes flashed pure loathing. Jaw tight, he glanced over his shoulder at Marco. Ravazzani's cousin said, "Why would we believe you?"

I lifted one eyebrow. "I know that Giulio Ravazzani has changed his identity four times. There have been three attempts on his life, the most recent in Amsterdam. He's now in Málaga under the name Javier Martín."

Ravazzani stepped closer to the bars, his voice low with fury. "Perhaps you know this information because you are the one trying to kill him."

"It wasn't me." The attempts had been sloppy, carried out by amateurs. My plans would be carried out by a professional, but I wasn't about to tell Ravazzani this.

"But you are watching him, even after I explicitly instructed everyone not to."

"I have a lot of free time," I said with a shrug.

He growled in his throat, and I knew if I wasn't behind these bars he would lunge at me. "What do you want in exchange?"

"I want your word that this is done. I want to resume my life and come out of hiding. I want my children to be safe."

"You kidnapped my pregnant *wife*," he snarled. "Put her in a trunk and shoved a gun in her mouth. I should shoot you right here and now."

I held up the hand with a missing fingertip. "I have paid for that transgression many times over."

"And yet it still is not enough."

I slipped my hands into my pockets and kept my shoulders relaxed. "You should know that my brothers are in Málaga. If they don't hear from me within the hour, your first born will die." Let Ravazzani believe I had Vito and Massimo waiting in Spain instead of Alessandro Ricci. I'd keep the information about the sniper to myself for now.

"You dare to threaten my son?" He practically roared it.

"Do you think I came here to bend over and let you fuck me?" I shouted back. "I have waited four years to do this!"

"Tell me who."

"Do you agree? The past is forgotten and we will move on?"

Ravazzani dragged a hand through his hair, a rare show of frustration. But his family was his one weakness. It was my only chance.

"I agree," he barked. "It's forgotten. Now tell me."

"And I am taking Gia."

"Figlio un cane! You don't know when to quit, D'Agostino."

"I am not asking for your approval. I am telling you." I didn't give a shit whether he agreed or not. "Gia is mine."

One side of his mouth curled. "Last I heard she was longing to cut your balls off and feed them to my pigs. Sure, you can try to take her. But I wouldn't bet on it."

I would win her over. There was no other choice. I couldn't bear to lose her for good.

Gesturing to the lock, I said, "Let me out of here."

"Tell me who is trying to kill my son first."

I shook my head. "Do you take me for a fool? You could keep me locked in here after you get what you want from me. I will tell you when I am on the other side of your gate, from inside my bulletproof vehicle."

"You doubt my word?"

"I don't trust anyone—and neither do you. I won't tell you until I am safely on the road, outside your gate."

His gaze bored into mine and I knew he didn't like any of this. But he had little choice if he wanted the information from me.

Spinning, he strode to his cousin so they could confer. I waited, knowing he would let me out. He needed to protect his son.

Because we were alike in that respect. We would do anything for our families.

Finally Ravazzani took out a key and approached the cell. "This had better be good."

He unlocked the door and I could breathe a tiny bit easier as I stepped out of it. I followed Ravazzani to the steps, Marco at my back, and in a few minutes they were leading me toward the front gate. Soldiers watched our progress, vigilant with guns held high, but Ravazzani told them to lower their weapons.

The iron gate swung open. As arranged, one of my men quickly arrived in an SUV, the engine idling. I stepped off the estate and onto the road. They closed the gate behind me with Ravazzani watching carefully. I watched him, as well. We would never fully trust the other, no matter the deals we struck.

I got into the back seat and lowered the window halfway. "The Sicilians. They were working with Mommo against you, which is how some of your shipments were seized."

"And I'm supposed to take your word for it?"

"Didn't you wonder why they dragged their feet on helping you rescue your wife at my beach house in Napoli?"

I could see by the way his jaw tightened that he had.

I continued. "Mommo held the Sicilians off until we had a plan ready, in case I was captured."

"The plan being my security expert, Vic? The one who helped you escape?"

"Sì. They are pissed you edged them out of the drug trade. Also, they didn't like how Mommo was killed. They are taking Giulio out in retaliation."

Ravazzani didn't move, seeming to absorb this information. I started to raise the window, ready to get to Paris and to Gia.

He called out, "If you hurt my sister-in-law, our truce is finished. I will come after you, D'Agostino."

"I have no plans to hurt her. But someone else might try to hurt her, which is why I need to get to her quickly."

"What the fuck does that mean?"

"That designer you let her work for is a testa di cazzo. He drugged and raped a woman a few years ago."

Ravazzani glanced at Marco, who shook his head. "We never heard a word about that sort of behavior."

"LaCrocq kept it quiet and forced her to sign an NDA."

"I will call and warn her," Ravazzani said.

"Go ahead. Even if she believes you, she's going to think she can handle it herself."

"So you are planning to go to Paris?"

"My jet is at the Siderno airport, fueled and ready to go."

Fausto's face cleared as realization dawned. "You love her."

I didn't bother answering. Instead, I raised the window, anxious to leave.

Ravazzani's voice carried through the late afternoon sunshine. "She will never give up her family for you."

Cristo, I hope he was wrong about that. I couldn't live without her. She reminded me that I was human, that I wasn't fully broken. She calmed the storm that raged inside my mind on the best of days, the panic that filled me on the worst. If she couldn't forgive me, I was truly lost.

Lowering the window slightly, I stared at him one last time. "I think she will. So you had better prepare your wife to lose a sister."

CHAPTER TWENTY-SEVEN

Gia

Paris, France

The club's bass rattled in my chest as I sipped my drink and tried to look interested. My new coworkers partied *a lot*, and they weren't keen on taking no for an answer from the sad Canadian intern who'd rather go home and drink wine alone.

I loved Paris. The city pulsed with energy and excitement, every corner alive with music and merriment. I think I would like living here. Eventually.

My new job was tough but great. They gave me more responsibility than delivering packages and getting coffee. LaCrocq, my boss, even allowed me to sit in on some of his meetings. I planned to soak it all in, focus on the job instead of my fucked-up personal life, and quickly learn the ins and outs of the fashion business. Then I would start my own clothing label.

And I would never think of Enzo D'Agostino again.

Two weeks had passed since I left his yacht. No doubt he was anchored off some coast, getting blow jobs from beautiful women again. I hope he contracted a venereal disease that rotted his dick off.

You were just pussy to me, nothing more. I wanted to ruin you and I did.

I gulped my drink, the vodka and soda burning my throat. That asshole.

A young man appeared beside me at the railing. He spoke a string of French I didn't understand, but his silky tone made it clear he was coming onto me. "I don't speak French," I said.

"He said it is a shame to see one so beautiful look so sad," a deep French-accented voice said behind me. It was LaCrocq, my boss.

Frankie called a few hours ago to warn me about him. She said there were rumors about LaCrocq acting inappropriately with a former model. After I hung up I asked a few co-workers if they'd heard or seen any indication of our boss's bad behavior, but they all said no.

Still, I was now wary around all men, thanks to Enzo. I probably always would be.

LaCrocq exchanged a few words with the younger man, who quickly disappeared. My boss was handsome, in his late-thirties, and very talented. He was more hands-on than Domenico, almost to the control-freak level. No decision was made without LaCrocq's input. The designer clearly didn't believe in delegation.

He leaned onto the railing next to me, cradling his drink. We were up in the VIP area, while the rest of the staff were below on the dance floor. "Don't like to dance?"

"No, I do," I said. "Just not feeling it tonight."

"You seem blue. Like there is a cloud hanging over you." He gave an effortless chuckle in the way the French were so good at. "I hope it isn't your job that puts such an unhappy look on your face."

"No, of course not," I rushed to say. "I'm enjoying the job very much."

"Good, good." We stood in silence for a moment, and I sensed he was working up to something. Finally, he said, "Your brother-in-law phoned me."

I straightened and blinked at my boss. "Fausto called you?"

"Yes, today."

I was working here under my real name, which had caused a stir at first. The world was surprised to learn that the Canadian mafia princess hadn't died in the tragic Milan bombing. For a few days the French and Italian press hounded me, trying to get answers, but I kept quiet and wore sunglasses, and eventually they found me too boring to follow. "What did he say?"

"That you should be treated with respect." He waved his hand. "Typical brother-in-law things. I assume it's because he is so far away from you."

"My sister is very protective of me," I offered up as an explanation.

"I can understand why. You're very beautiful, Gianna." His gaze tripped down the length of my body, lingering on my legs. Now I kind of wished I hadn't worn this tiny black dress tonight.

"Thank you," I mumbled into my drink before finishing it.

"I sense that you like to let loose. Get wild. Maybe that is why they are so protective of you?"

I hardly felt like letting loose these days. "Maybe."

His smile was a shade too wide for my liking. "Is it boyfriend troubles?"

"I don't have a boyfriend."

"A girlfriend, then?"

"No. There's no one."

"That is a shame." He bumped his shoulder against mine. Ever so carefully, I edged away to keep distance between us.

"I'm focused on my career right now," I said evasively.

"Your designs were very impressive. You have talent, especially menswear."

After retrieving my portfolio from Milan, I added new pieces I'd conceived while on the yacht and then submitted everything to LaCrocq. Never mind that the menswear ideas were inspired by Enzo. Fuck him. "Thank you," I said.

"You are obviously familiar with men's bodies. Maybe I can show you what I'm working on and we can discuss?"

Familiar with men's bodies? I wasn't sure if that was a compliment or a dig. "I'd like that." As long as other people were around.

"What about right now?"

This was becoming increasingly uncomfortable. "Monsieur—"

"Call me Matthieu."

"Matthieu, I'm really not in a good headspace right now. Maybe tomorrow. At work."

His eyebrows pulled together as if he was confused. "This would still be work, mademoiselle. But can we not be comfortable while we do it?"

"Another night. I'm sorry."

"No need to apologize. Please, allow me to get you a drink."

God, he was pushy. To move things along, I said, "Sure. Vodka and soda, please."

Matthieu slid his hand across my back before moving toward the upper level bar. Now alone, I breathed a sigh of relief. Maybe I should go. Something told me the situation was only going to get worse.

Don't go anywhere alone with him, Frankie had said. *And don't drink anything he gives you.*

At the time I thought her warning was ludicrous. Now I wasn't so sure. I mean, he wouldn't, would he? Here, with our coworkers?

I had to find out if he was actually capable of something so heinous.

Pulling out my phone, I faked like I was scrolling my social media apps, but I really was zooming in on Matthieu at the bar. The image was grainy and dark, but I saw as he accepted my drink. His hand came out of his pocket and waved over the top of the glass. It happened too fast and now he was coming toward me. Was there something in my drink?

I had to find out.

When he returned I smiled and put my phone away. "Thank you," I said and accepted the glass from his hand. "What did you get?"

"A glass of Bordeaux."

"Can I try it? Here, hold this." I gave him my glass and took the wine out of his hand. After I took a sip I said, "Oh, this is much better than vodka and soda. I'm going to keep it. You can have my drink instead."

He held my glass but didn't drink from it. "Never steal a Frenchman's wine, chérie."

"Too late!" I laughed like it was a big joke. "I should've asked for this."

Suddenly, the air in the club shifted and the hairs on the back of my neck stood up. Glancing over, I saw three men striding across the mostly empty VIP area. My attention was stuck on the man in the middle.

Enzo.

My stomach swooped. Holy shit, Enzo was here. And he looked ready to commit murder.

His eyes were scary intense, the lines of his face stark with fury. Every muscle in his body was tense, like he was about to step into the ring for ten rounds. Vito and Massimo flanked him, the three brothers forming a wall of mafioso intimidation as they descended on us.

"What are you doing here?" I blurted, but they all ignored me.

Enzo grabbed LaCrocq's shirt and leaned in. "You drugged her drink."

Fuck, I knew it! "You asshole!" I spat at my boss.

"I don't know what you're talking about," LaCrocq said.

"You put powder in that glass." Enzo pointed at the vodka and soda.

"I did no such thing. How dare you accuse me of something like—"

Enzo pulled something out of his pocket and flicked it. A long switchblade appeared, and he put the tip to LaCrocq's throat. "Then drink it."

LaCrocq appeared affronted. "I do not need to drink it. There's nothing in there."

"Drink it or lose your life."

LaCrocq paled. He must've realized Enzo was serious. "You can't kill me here."

"You must not know who I am. If you did, you wouldn't ask such a ridiculous question."

"Who are you?" My boss glanced at all three D'Agostino men. "Italian thugs? Do you work for Ravazzani?"

Enzo snarled, "I am a thousand times worse than Fausto Ravazzani. I am the man who is going to rip off your tiny dick and shove it in your mouth for daring to fuck with what is mine."

I blinked. Did he mean me? Or was this some business dispute I didn't know about? Just how many European designers was Enzo involved with?

Enzo stuck the point of the knife into the other man's skin, causing LaCrocq to flinch. Blood slowly trickled toward the Frenchman's collar as Enzo calmly said, "Drink or die."

The moment stretched with stunned silence. I couldn't believe any of this was happening. What was Enzo doing here? How did he know that LaCrocq drugged my drink? Was it safe for Enzo to be off the yacht without a disguise?

With a shaking hand, LaCrocq brought the glass to his lips. He took a small sip.

"All of it, stronzo!" Enzo barked.

The designer closed his eyes and downed the rest of the liquid. "There. Satisfied?"

"Very." Enzo turned to Vito. "Take him. You know what to do."

"Sì, Don D'Agostino." Vito grabbed one of LaCrocq's arms, while Massimo took the other. "It will be my pleasure."

Enzo moved in and whispered a string of French that caused my boss to start sweating. Though I hated Enzo, I had to admit that he was a scary motherfucker when he wanted to be.

Then Vito and Massimo took my former boss away, dragging him toward the stairs, and I was alone with Enzo. Confused and wary, I set the wine glass carefully on a table. He said nothing, merely stared at me, the gold flecks dancing in his deep brown eyes.

Questions bounced in my head, too many to even verbalize. So I blurted, "What the fuck, Enzo?"

He grabbed my wrist and began towing me behind him. I dug in my heels. "Wait. I'm not going anywhere with you."

Spinning, he jerked me toward him and I bounced off his big frame. He cupped the back of my neck, pinning me in place. "Would you rather have this conversation in public, micina? I am very angry with you for putting yourself in danger."

"Angry with me?" I rose up on my toes so I was level with his face. "You have some fucking nerve! I'm angry at *you*!"

In one motion he bent down, put his shoulder in my stomach, and lifted me off the ground. I nearly choked on my outrage. "Put me down, you dick!"

Ignoring me, he began walking through the VIP section, then down the steps, not concerned in the least that I was yelling and pounding on his back.

Once again Enzo D'Agostino was kidnapping me and there wasn't a damn thing I could do about it.

Enzo

I knew I owed Gia answers, but I was too fucking furious at the moment. What was she doing at this club? Hadn't she been warned that LaCrocq was a piece of shit? What if I hadn't arrived in time?

I ground my molars together as I placed Gia in the back seat of the sedan waiting out front. Her tiny black dress rode up and exposed long legs and gorgeous skin. I wanted to touch every bit of her, bite her and lick her. Tie her down and edge her until she promised never to leave my side. Fuck, I missed her.

I settled next to her and closed the door, then Rico pulled out into traffic. Gia immediately turned on me. "Are you seriously kidnapping me *again*? My brother-in-law is going to wear your skin like a suit, D'Agostino."

My lip curled. "Ravazzani knows I am here."

She hadn't expected that. Her jaw fell open. "What? You and Fausto made up?"

"We have a truce." I still wanted to kill him, but it was worth a truce if it meant getting my life back.

"I don't understand any of this. Start explaining, Enzo."

"When we get to the hotel." I didn't want to have this conversation in the car in front of my men.

"Oh, you aren't dragging me off to your yacht this time?"

"Eager to return to your cage, bella?"

She glared at me, but didn't argue any more. We rode in silence through the dark streets of Paris, with her typing and scrolling on her phone. No doubt she was telling someone I'd taken her from the club, or maybe letting her co-workers know that she'd gone home. I didn't try to stop her. I was just happy to sit here in relative silence with her, allowing her presence to soothe the chaos in my head. I'd missed her so fucking much.

When we reached the hotel, I got out and went around to her door. "Let's go up to my suite."

Gia didn't move, other than to lift her chin. "I'm not going into a hotel room with you."

I propped my arm on the roof of the car and bent down. "Do you think I won't carry you over my shoulder through the hotel, too? Dai, you should know me better than that."

With a huff, she scooted toward the door and slapped my hands away as she got out. "It's a waste of your time. I don't want to hear anything you have to say."

I put my hand on the small of her back and guided her into the hotel. She wore a tiny black dress that left her back exposed, and her skin was soft and silky, just like I remembered. I never wanted to stop touching her.

Then we were in the elevator. She tried to move away, but I wouldn't allow it. Instead, I pulled her closer. She let out a heavy sigh. "You're such a dick."

When we reached the top floor I nodded to the men guarding my suite. One of them pulled open the door and I led Gia inside. "Would you like a drink?"

She went over to the bar. "If you don't mind, I'll get my own."

That was fair, after what happened with LaCrocq. I poured a scotch for myself and she settled on a bottle of beer from the fridge. "I would never drug you," I said.

"Oh, so kidnapping me and keeping me in a cage are okay, but drugging me is a step too far. Good to know."

With a fingertip, I swept a long strand of hair out of her face and tucked it behind her ear. The swift inhale of her breath felt like a caress to my balls. I suppressed the greedy urges telling me to hurry and take. I had to go slow with her. "I don't want you incapacitated. I like when you fight me."

She snorted and moved away to the far end of the sofa. "I bet you do. Say whatever it is you need to say. I'm tired and I have to look for a new job in the morning."

"No, you don't."

"Uh, yes, I do. I can't keep working for LaCrocq."

I settled on the opposite end of the sofa and sipped my drink, studying her over the rim of the glass. "There won't be much of LaCrocq left by the time I get done with him."

She rubbed her forehead like she was exhausted. "Jesus, Enzo."

I didn't want to waste time talking about that pezzo di merda. There was no way to do this other than to beg for her forgiveness. "I am sorry for what I said on the yacht."

Her eyes narrowed. "Which part? You said a lot of terrible things to me."

"All of it. What I said to get you to leave with Fausto."

"Oh, you mean when you said I was just pussy to you and how you ruined me?"

"Yes, and the rest. The video, kidnapping you. Everything. I'm sorry."

She started to speak, then closed her mouth. I could see her thinking, trying to decipher what I was saying, looking for angles. She would find none. What I said was the truth.

After a few seconds, she said, "Thank you. Are we done?"

"No, we aren't fucking done," I snapped. "We are never going to be *done*."

"There's the Enzo I know. What is this really about? Be honest with me for once."

Leaning forward, I put my glass on the table. Then I rested my elbows on my knees, debating on how to put it. "I miss you."

"Cazzata," she said instantly. "You couldn't wait to get rid of me."

"I wanted to keep you safe. In case I had to blow up the yacht."

Her jaw fell open. "Blow up the yacht? You have explosives on there?"

I frowned. This surprised her? "Of course I do."

"Oh, for fuck's sake." She shook her head and drank some of her beer. "Well, what about before the Russians arrived on the yacht?

When you showed me that video and told me you were sending it to Fausto."

Her voice cracked at the end and the sound was like a punch to my gut. "I would never let anyone see that video. I was upset by what happened after my nightmare. I was . . . ."

"What?"

"Embarrassed. I don't like anyone to see me weak."

"You've seen me at my worst. What difference does it make?"

I gave her a look. "It is not the same."

"Because you're Don D'Agostino? Please. I don't care about that."

A gruff laugh escaped my lips. "I am aware. It's part of why I'm crazy about you."

"You're crazy about me?"

"Yes. Haven't I made that clear?"

"No, actually. I don't understand any of this." She stood up and began pacing. "I mean, why the sudden appearance in Paris? You could've texted or called in the last two weeks."

"I heard you came to work for LaCrocq. I couldn't allow it, knowing what he did to another woman."

"What exactly did he do?"

"He drugged and raped her, Gia."

"I've been working there for a *week*. Why didn't you call me and tell me?"

"I only just found out. And I assumed your brother-in-law warned you."

"You talked to Fausto?"

"I left his home in Siderno about three hours ago."

"You went to the castello? I can't believe he didn't kill you."

I didn't want to get into all that yet. "Did Ravazzani call and warn you about your boss?"

"My sister did."

My voice lowered into a snarl. "And yet you still went out to a club with him and let him get you a drink? Che cazzo?"

"I never had any intention of drinking it. I knew he spiked it."

"You did?"

"I'm not stupid, Enzo. After Frankie's warning, I watched him the entire time. I saw him reach into his pocket and pull something out at the bar."

"And what if he'd forced you to drink it anyway?"

She shook her head and blew out a long breath. "What are we doing here, D'Agostino?"

"I'm apologizing and telling you that I'm not letting you go."

"God, you are the worst. You threw me away, Enzo. Treated me like garbage. You can't change your mind all of a sudden and get me back."

I studied the carpet, my mind swirling. This was going badly. If she had missed me these past two weeks, I could not tell. But then, what had I expected? For her to fall at my feet?

This woman bowed to no one, which was why she was perfect for me. We were alike in that respect.

I wasn't used to talking about my feelings. I had been hurt to ensure I remained strong and never showed any weakness. I was born to be a leader, the boss. To have no remorse, to feel no empathy.

But I was nothing without her. And I had to tell her.

"Gianna, I can't function without you. There's too much up here." I gestured to my head. "I need you back with me."

"You, you, you. Have you even thought about me at all? How I might feel after you treated me like total shit?"

"I am sorry and I will keep saying it until you believe me. Perdonami. I didn't like hurting you."

"Yet you did. Now you expect me to go into hiding with you? To give up everything for you? My God, you are an egomaniac."

"I am not hiding any longer." I watched her digest this news, then continued. "As I said, I went to the castello and struck a truce with your brother-in-law."

"After four years? Just like that?"

"You weren't safe. I had to come to Paris and make sure this man didn't hurt you."

"This is totally nuts," she said. "What if I hadn't started working for LaCrocq? You would still be in hiding, ignoring me?"

"I would have come for you eventually. Perhaps this pushed me into acting sooner, but I knew I had to get you back."

"You never *had* me. You kidnapped me. I wasn't there willingly."

I couldn't stand it—I needed to touch her. I closed the distance between us and cradled her face in my hands. My heart pounded as I stared into her beautiful eyes, eyes that saw me so clearly. "This is why I am here, to give you the choice. Come to Napoli with me. Let me make you a queen. Stay at my side for the rest of my life."

Her chest rose and fell quickly, and she licked her lips. "No. This is happening too fast."

Wrong. Each second without her felt like an eternity.

Bending, I pressed our foreheads together. "I can't breathe without you. I can't think. Ti prego, amore mio. Come back with me. Let me prove to you that I love you."

CHAPTER TWENTY-EIGHT

Gia

Was he serious? "You love me?"
"I love you, Gianna."
He said it so clearly, with no hint of deception or irony. No games or machinations. Still, this seemed fast. "All of a sudden?"

He let me go and moved away, pacing like he was . . . nervous? "No, not all of a sudden. My brothers and I spent four years as ghosts, no family, no home. Living on a ship away from everything we knew. Our sister, my children. It was fucking awful, Gia."

I said nothing, and he exhaled slowly and continued. "Vito and Massimo begged me to make a deal. Make peace. Let us go back to our lives. But I refused. I would have vengeance at the cost of everything else." He slid a glance over at me. "Until you came along."

"And I made everything worse."

"You made everything *better*. You calm me, understand me. I can't function without you. Which was why I went to Siderno and into his dungeon once more. To arrive at a truce, one that would allow me to have you as you deserved."

"Are you serious? You met in the dungeon?"

"Sì."

"Jesus Christ." My brother-in-law was a sadistic son of a bitch. God, Enzo must've been a mess. "How did you manage not to lose your shit in there?"

"You."

"Me?"

"The breathing technique you taught me."

From the night of his nightmare. Oh, my poor il pazzo. My stomach twisted with the hurt he'd endured, the pain. Yet he'd gone into that dungeon for me. Had survived it to get to Paris, to make sure I wasn't harmed.

Let me prove to you that I love you.

I was beginning to understand.

He had proven it, from the way he touched me, like I was precious to him, and the way he pushed me away to spare my life. How he'd saved my sister when I asked. How he trusted me with things no one else knew.

God, he'd gone into that dungeon for me.

I stared at him, this mafioso who understood me better than anyone else. And I definitely now understood him. "You love me."

Swallowing, he dragged a hand down his face. "I have never experienced it before, but this can't possibly be anything else. What I feel for you is so twisted and mangled, like I don't know where I end and you begin. I am rotten inside, amore, full of violence and destruction. You are the only one who makes me feel human, like what happened in that dungeon did not kill what was left of my soul."

My heart squeezing, I drew in a shaky breath. "Enzo . . . ."

"You chase my demons away, amore. I need you, more than money and power. More than anything in the entire world, save my children."

My heart swelled in my chest, inflating as I let all of this sink in. He wanted me, not just as a quick fuck or his prisoner. He loved me and wanted me to stay. Forever.

But what did I want?

My vagina was suddenly in favor of shedding clothes and getting reacquainted with his dick. But sex wasn't the answer. There were too many questions to be sorted, even if I decided to forgive him for hurting me.

What of my career? My family? My sisters? None of this was simple for me. I wasn't ready.

"If I come with you, I'm giving up my entire life. My dreams of having my own clothing line. My sisters. My *twin*."

"Why must you give up these things?"

Wasn't that how it worked? Frankie gave up her life to stay with Fausto. My mother had sacrificed her career to marry my father. Mafia wives weren't exactly independent. "Isn't that what your world expects of women?"

He folded his arms across his chest, his t-shirt pulling tight over his impressive shoulders. "I had a wife once and did things the traditional way. It gave me two wonderful children, but Angela and I were both unhappy in our marriage. I don't want that again." His lips curled into a devious smile. "Besides, I have seen what happens when you aren't given your freedom."

"You would let me work and travel? See my family?"

"If it is what you want, then yes. But there is no need to work for anyone else. I will give you all the money you need to start your own label."

"That feels a lot like charity."

"I have seen your designs. It is not charity, micina. You're very talented. And I'd rather invest in you than the other designers who haven't a fraction of your skill."

I bit my lip, a rush of giddiness bubbling inside me at the compliment. Enzo was not a bullshitter. I knew he wouldn't say it if he didn't believe it. "Thank you."

"I am not saying I won't worry about your safety—I will probably have guards on you around the clock—but I don't want to cage you again. I want you at my side, my equal. Building a legacy for the next generation of D'Agostinos."

Oh, right. Kids. Was he expecting more? "I don't want children, not anytime soon. Maybe ever."

He held up his palms. "I have a son and a daughter. I will schedule a vasectomy tomorrow if you say so."

"Really?"

"Of course."

"Marriage?"

He lifted a shoulder. "I would like to call you my wife, but I understand if you aren't ready."

I liked these answers, but I had to wonder if he meant them. "You're being very accommodating for a man who takes what he wants and to hell with the consequences."

"Whatever you need to stay with me, you'll receive."

I walked toward him slowly, feeling his dark gaze track every move I made. My body tingled under his heavy stare. "So if I want to get married and wear the biggest diamond ring money can buy, you'll do it?"

"Sì, certo."

He said it so easily, with no hesitation. If he was really going to give me whatever I asked for, I had to think this through. This might be the only chance I had to negotiate with him. "I want a long engagement and a big ring."

His lips twitched and he immediately said, "Va bene."

Was I amusing him? "I want to be able to go to Siderno and Toronto whenever I want."

Any trace of amusement disappeared from his expression. "Whenever it is *safe*, Gianna. I will not risk your safety when Fausto goes to war with the Sicilians or your father is in the midst of some turf battle."

"Fine, but otherwise I want the freedom to come and go as I please."

"Fine."

Jeez, he must really want me badly.

Were we really going to do this? I searched my brain for any hesitation, but found none. It might not be the life my thirteen-year-old self —or even my nineteen-year-old self—had pictured, but I couldn't imagine anything else more perfect. I wasn't afraid of the danger or the violence. I wasn't afraid of him, either. I just didn't want to live in a gilded cage. I needed my sisters and a career—and he was willing to give me both.

Was I ready to run my own design house? My internships had been short, and I didn't feel like I was capable of starting a business like that yet. Even if Enzo was footing the bill.

I lifted my chin. "I want to work for another designer so I can study the business before striking out on my own."

"*A Napoli*, sì."

"In Milan."

"Absolutely not. I don't want you living far away from me."

"It's only an hour by plane. I'll come back every weekend. And I'll only do it for a year."

We stared at each other, the room crackling with his unhappiness. But I wouldn't bend on this. He was lucky I wasn't demanding to stay in Paris.

He nodded once. "You will work Tuesday through Friday. I get you in Napoli every Saturday, Sunday and Monday."

"Fine."

"You will use my jet," he said with a very Italian wave of his hand. "This will save you time at the airports."

Skip the security line and get treated like a celebrity? I wouldn't argue that. Happiness fluttered inside my chest, and I felt light and giddy, as if I might float away. "If that's what you need to do, baby."

His nostrils flared. "What else, tesoro mio? Hurry up so we can settle this and I can fuck you again."

God yes, I needed that. But there was something else first. "I don't want your kids to know about us."

He blinked, his expression wiped clean, like he was hiding his reaction from me. Or maybe he didn't know what to think.

I rushed to explain. "Yet. I mean I don't want them to know about me yet. I want to be like a fun aunt instead of their new mother. If they meet me right away, they'll think I'm trying to take her place."

"You don't want to be a mother to them?"

He asked it like I'd offended him. "Enzo, I know what it's like to lose a mother. There's no replacing her and I would've resented anyone who tried. Let me meet them eventually, as your friend, someone they don't see as a threat. We'll get to know each other slowly, but don't push them. It's a lot of change."

He was already shaking his head. "I don't want to hide you. And they will know when you come to visit every weekend."

"This needs to be handled gently."

"Gently means I have to fuck you in secret. No, Gianna. I want you by my side as much as possible. My children will understand. I won't coddle them."

"You'll only upset them and give them plenty to talk about in therapy for the rest of their lives."

He came toward me but I didn't move. I held my breath, aching with the need to touch him, to kiss him. To explore every inch of his body. We had to finish this first, though.

When he reached me he cupped the nape of my neck with one hand and put the other on my hip, pulling me close. "There is no hiding, no secrets. You are coming with me tomorrow to England to get them. They will see that we are together from the beginning. Give them the opportunity to understand that I love you and you are important to me."

"You really love me?" I whispered, unable to believe it.

"Of course I do. Ti amo, micina."

He bent and placed a soft kiss to my lips, and a jolt of electricity raced through my veins. My fingers wound through his hair and I held on as we paused to breathe each other in. "Ti amo, il pazzo."

"Fuck. I am so relieved." His eyelids swept shut. "Are we done talking now?"

"I suppose, though I hadn't expected you to give in to most of my demands so easily."

"I would have given up more to be able to keep you."

"Oh? Then I should think of some more."

"Too late." His mouth moved to my throat and he kissed me under my jaw. "Fuck, Gianna. I love you."

I smiled up at him. "Ti amo, Lorenzo."

Growling, he lifted me to my feet and crushed his mouth against mine. He thrust his tongue past my lips, kissing me like his life depended on it. I wrapped my legs around his waist and held on as he walked us toward the bedroom.

Toward our future.

CHAPTER TWENTY-NINE

Enzo

Stately and imposing, the boarding school stretched out across the English countryside. The gray stone matched the sky, and I couldn't imagine a more depressing place. I hated that my children had lived here for four years.

But it was their home no more.

Gia and I flew to England after spending the night together in Paris. I wanted her here from the start, so that my children would know what she meant to me.

She was my everything, just as much as they were.

I held her hand in the back of the car, my leg bouncing in agitation. She scrolled on her phone with her free hand, reading what my men had done to LaCrocq the night before, a small smile on her lips.

"Should I have killed him, micina?" I asked.

"No, this is much, much better. I mean, you humiliated him."

The video went viral overnight. My computer guys uploaded it from an anonymous account, then shared the video enough times to get it started. It soon exploded. The world loved when a powerful celebrity was taken down.

LaCrocq would never recover.

The video showed him fully naked, passed out on a couch from his own date rape drugs, a sign hanging around his neck:

I tried to drug and rape a girl tonight, but she switched our drinks.

The words, *I'm a rapist*, had been carved into his belly with a scalpel. LaCrocq would wear those scars for the rest of his life.

We pulled to a stop and I bolted from the car. I was taking my children out of this godforsaken country and back to Napoli where they belonged.

I walked around to help Gia out of the car. Vito emerged from the front seat, saying, "Good luck." He clapped me on the back.

I introduced myself as Mr. Peretti at the front entry, and we were quickly shown to the headmaster's office. Mr. Payne came out immediately, the lines of his brow deep with concern. He shook my hand as I introduced Gia, then led us into his office. "Mr. Peretti, this is quite unexpected. We were not notified of an impending visit."

Like I cared. Calmly, I said, "I am here to withdraw my children from your school and take them home."

"But . . . ." The headmaster looked between Gia and me, his head swiveling. "Things are done differently here. There are procedures and rules. You must wait until the end of the term—"

"Now, Payne. Get my children right now or there will be hell to pay."

Mr. Payne gaped at Gia, probably thinking my woman would intervene or be a softer touch than me. "Miss," he started helplessly.

She held up her palms. "Oh, don't look at me. I'm just the woman he fucks. You know, a *lot*."

Payne's face twisted like he'd swallowed a lemon. "This is utterly outrageous. We are a very prestigious institution. You cannot walk in here and make threats and lewd remarks."

Gia cocked her head at me, a smirk playing on her lips. "I don't think he likes us very much, amore."

I leaned closer and caressed her cheek. "Do you feel insulted, micina? I don't like when you feel insulted. Should I make him apologize to you?"

Payne quickly jumped up from his seat and started for the door.

"Now, there's no need for that. Let me just see if we are able to locate your children, Mr. Peretti, and we'll send all of you on your way."

He closed the door behind him, leaving Gia and I alone. She bit her lip, her eyes dancing. I already fucked her on the plane ride here, but I could feel the need for her rising, clawing inside me. "Have you ever wanted to fuck on a headmaster's desk?"

"I did. Junior year of high school."

Jealousy slashed through my chest and turned my mouth sour. "Who was this boy?"

"Who said it was a boy?"

I threw my head back and laughed. "La mia troia! Was it the headmaster?"

"One of the teachers. He was twenty-five and Swedish. I seduced the poor thing."

"I bet he never stood a chance against you." I kissed her hard, using my teeth and tongue until she whimpered.

When we broke apart she said, "He was a terrible lay, more worried about getting caught than getting me off."

I cupped her breast over her blouse and pinched her nipple. She rewarded me with a gasp. I said, "That would not be a problem with me."

"Yes, but your kids are on the way. We don't want them walking in on that."

"I will lock the door."

She glanced at the desk like she was considering it, and my heart pumped hard. Madre di Dio, this woman.

"That asshole deserves to come back and find jizz all over his desk," she said. "How quickly can you—?"

The door opened to reveal Mr. Payne. "If you will both come with me. The children have been located and are packing their belongings."

"Is there anything to sign?" I waved my hand at his desk.

"I will see that the release forms are emailed to you. It will take a bit of time to draw them up and there's no reason to make you wait."

In other words, he wanted us gone. That suited me perfectly.

He walked us back through the halls toward the entryway. At the doors he offered his hand, which I shook. "My very best to you and your children, Mr. Peretti. They are bright students. It has been an honor to have them here these past few years."

After a nod in Gia's direction, the headmaster hurried away, like he couldn't escape fast enough. Gia chuckled as we descended the steps. "I don't think he'll be readmitting your children any time soon."

"Good, because I'm keeping them with me. But I will be thinking about fucking you over a desk all the way home."

"I could have Emma send my old school uniform, if you like."

I pictured her in a small plaid skirt, bent over my desk with her hair in pigtails. I grabbed her and growled into her ear, "Tell her to overnight it."

Vito straightened from where he was leaning against the side of the car. "What happened? Where are Luca and Nicola?"

"Coming," I said. "They preferred we wait out here."

My brother studied my face and then Gia's. "What did you two do in there?"

Gia laughed and wrapped her arms around my neck. "He thinks we caused a scene, il pazzo."

I kissed her, happier than I'd ever imagined. Once I had my children back, life would be perfect. The doors flew open and there was my son. No longer a little boy, but not yet a man. While I saw him on video calls and during our summer breaks, nothing could have prepared me for seeing my son right in front of me for good. I blinked, my throat suddenly tight. "Luca."

I reached him in four steps and pulled him close. He nearly reached my chin and his arms were strong as they hugged me back. "Papà. I can't believe you're here."

"Figlio mio." I dragged in a ragged breath and whispered, "I'm never letting you go again."

"You're crushing me."

With a laugh, I released him. "Come. Say hello to your Uncle Vito. Then there's someone I want you—"

The door opened slowly and a young girl rolled her suitcase onto the landing. It was my principessa. "Nicola."

She tucked a piece of hair behind her ears. It was longer than I remember, pulled up into a ponytail. Mamma mia, she was gorgeous. I immediately wrapped my arms around her and lifted her off the ground. "Oh, how I've missed you."

She hugged me back. "Ciao, Papà. I thought you said you weren't coming for us."

"Things changed. It's safe for you both to come home now."

"Oh."

I drew back to see her face. "Are you disappointed?"

"No, but what will we do there? Will we go to an Italian school?"

"Let's worry about that when we get home. Come say hello to your uncle and to Gia." I led Nic closer to the car. Vito was slapping Luca on the back while Gia hung back, her expression unsure.

Nic dropped my hand and went over to Gia. "I'm Nicola."

Gia's eyes widened a fraction, but then she put out her hand. "Hi. I'm your dad's girlfriend, Gia."

"Girlfriend?" Luca turned to me. "*Hai una ragazza?*"

I gave him a flat smile full of warning. "Say hello to Gia. She's going to be living with us."

My son shook Gia's hand. "Hello, I'm Luca."

"Hi, Luca," Gia said.

Luca kept hold of her hand as he said to me, "Lei è uno schianto, Papà." *She is a knockout.*

I rolled my eyes as Vito barked a laugh. "Get in the fucking car, figlio." I kissed my daughter's head. "You too, principessa."

When I got into the SUV I found Nic sitting next to Gia. Luca waited for me in the back seat. I sat and the wheels started moving, taking us to the airport. My throat closed when I heard Nic asking Gia about her hair. I couldn't listen more, though, because Luca started talking.

"Can I still play rugby in Italy, Papà?"

"If you like. But football is better, no?"

"It's boring."

I didn't wish to discuss rugby. "I have something to tell you," I said quietly. "About the night I was taken, when you were brought to the beach house."

Luca's face shuttered and he drew himself up. "What is it?"

Nic didn't remember much from the night Ravazzani took them

from their beds, but Luca did. They were not pleasant memories for him, so he needed to be prepared. "The woman that night, the one who told you everything was going to be okay?"

"I remember her."

"My girlfriend is that woman's sister."

"Isn't that woman married to Ravazzani?"

"Yes. Gia is Ravazzani's sister-in-law."

His eyebrows shot up. "Che cazzo?"

"He and I have made a peace of sorts, and she was part of that process. But I wanted you to know."

He looked through the window for a long moment, the sharp angles of his face so much like mine. I gave him time to digest it, and he finally turned back to me. "Does she make you happy?"

"Very."

"Okay. Should I start researching rugby teams in Napoli? I assume you're sending us to an Italian school, so I'll probably have to join a local club."

Was that it? Had Luca just accepted this about Gia and moved on to rugby again?

I pointed to his phone. "Why don't you start researching schools?"

"Luca shouldn't be the only one to pick our school." Nic angled to see me from her seat. "I want to have a say, too."

"I'm older," my son said, his attention now on his phone. "I should get to choose."

"No, you don't. And girls' brains develop faster than boys' do, so technically I'm as old as you."

Luca snorted. "In your dreams."

"Papà, tell him he's wrong. Tell him I get a vote."

As they continued to argue, I looked at Gia and found her watching me. "*Congratulations*," she mouthed, and all of the worry and anxiety I'd carried for the last four years melted away. After what felt like an eternity, I had my children back for good. I had my empire and I had Gia. It was more than I'd ever hoped for.

Sometimes the villain ended up on top after all.

EPILOGUE

Gia

Off the coast of Greece
One year later

We were celebrating.

Except my mafioso and I never did things like other people. So where some couples might go to dinner or a hotel to celebrate a milestone, we were back where it all began.

On the yacht. With me in the cage.

I was naked, of course, relaxing against the metal bars. The room was dim thanks to a sliver of daylight coming through the curtains. This had been my idea. Enzo liked when I was his needy micina and I loved when he dominated me. We were fucked up—but we were each other's type of fucked up. It was why we worked so well together.

I had no idea how long he would leave me in here. It had been probably about twenty or thirty minutes since he locked me in and told me to be good.

I had no intention of doing that.

No doubt he was watching me on the cameras as he tried to work. I decided it was time to torture him a little.

Standing, I began performing my yoga poses, making sure to keep my ass to the camera. I went through my routine slowly, feeling the stretch in my sore muscles. I returned from Milan last night and Enzo had wasted no time in bringing me to the yacht, then fucking me for hours.

Hard to believe we'd been together a year. I finished my internship yesterday and was now permanently living in Naples, ready to take the next step in my life. I couldn't wait.

Bossy and controlling, Enzo was not an easy man and we fought often. Like when Frankie's baby was born and I went to the Ravazzani estate for an extended visit. Enzo tried to forbid it, saying Fausto wouldn't let me leave or some such nonsense.

But I won that battle, as I had every other argument when my sisters were involved. He would learn. Nothing would come between the Mancini sisters, not even if their last names changed.

Besides, making up with him led to amazing sex.

I finished my yoga several minutes later, but still no Enzo. This was starting to piss me off. For real, how long was he planning on dragging this out? I was thirsty and would eventually need a bathroom.

It was time to level this bitch up.

I sat on the floor of the cage and faced the camera, letting my legs fall open to expose myself. My mafioso loved to watch me get myself off. We had regular video sex while I was living in Milan, so I had a good idea of what would drive him wild.

I bit my lip and began playing with my nipples, pinching and pulling on them. They were sensitive from Enzo's mouth last night and the pleasure echoed in my core. I moaned and closed my eyes. Then I let my hand travel south, along my stomach and mound, until I reached my pussy.

With one finger I found my piercing and moved it around, not stroking but enjoying the feel of the metal on my sensitive skin. My piercing was one of Enzo's very favorite things. He liked sucking on it and dragging it across his teeth.

What he didn't know was that I'd traded out the jewelry this morning before our little role play session.

This jewelry had a tiny bell at the bottom of the bar. With each roll of my fingers, the bell made a soft tinkling noise. Oh, shit. That was sexy, like something a pet would wear. Exactly as I'd hoped.

I moved faster, loving the idea of it, especially inside the cage, and I could feel myself growing wetter, my clit swelling behind the jewelry. The backs of my thighs sizzled and my toes curled. Fuck, that felt good.

Heavy footsteps thumped in the hall, drawing closer. He could be silent when he wished, so I knew he wanted me to hear him. Anticipate him. My skin tingled as I kept playing with myself.

The door cracked but I didn't bother opening my eyes. I kept going, allowing him to watch in person after seeing it so often through a computer screen. I could feel him though, his lust and hunger unmistakable, like the very air had changed. Became electrified. I breathed it in and let it fill me.

"What have you done, micina?" he rasped. "Is this a gift for me?"

"Maybe it's for me." I flicked the bell and lifted my eyelids. The wild light in his gaze sent a thrill down my spine. "Do you like it, padrone?"

He grabbed onto the bars, watching me intently. "Keep going, my good girl. Show me what needy sluts do in their cage when they've been left alone for too long."

I sucked in a breath and kept circling my fingers. The bell didn't make a lot of noise, just enough to let you know something was down there. I stared at him as he watched my pussy, his chest heaving with excitement. The bulge in his jeans made my mouth water, and all I could think about was having that big cock ram inside me.

He waved me over. "Come here."

I dropped my hand, got onto all fours and crawled to him. He licked his lips, liking my position very much. Though I wanted to lunge at him and take what I wanted, I knew that wasn't happening today. I was at his mercy in here, which I both loved and hated.

When I reached the side of the cage I sat on my haunches, thighs spread wide, and waited. He reached through the bars and stroked my head. "*Sei obbediente.* Sei perfetta. Take out my cock and lick it as your reward."

Rising up onto my knees, I reached through the bars to the button of his jeans. My fingers shook as I worked the button free then unzipped him. He did nothing to help me, merely waited with his hand on my head, as I took his heavy erection out of his clothing. He was already so hard, the head flushed, and a drop of moisture was waiting for me at the tip.

With my hand wrapped around the base I started to drag him closer to my mouth, but he snapped, "No hands."

I immediately put my arms behind my back. His hips were pressed against the bars, his cock pointed straight at me, so I angled forward and stuck my tongue out, ready to devour my favorite treat.

He was smooth and warm, and I caught the leaking liquid on my tongue. "Yum."

"You love my dick, don't you? Show me how much, micina."

I licked all around the head, then along the side, nuzzling the base near the bar of the cage. I loved the way he smelled, the way he kept his pubic hair trimmed just for me. His dick was a work of art, and I was happy to worship it whenever he'd let me.

My lips and tongue traveled the length of him, then I used the flat of my tongue on the underside. He was much more sensitive than a lot of the guys I'd been with, probably because he was uncut. It made handjobs a lot easier, that was for sure.

Grunting, Enzo cupped the back of my head. "Suck."

Yes, please.

He pressed me forward and I opened wide, eager to please him. The thick shaft stretched my lips and slid across my tongue, the heavy weight a reminder of his dominance. His deep groan filled the room. "Sì, sporca puttana! You make me want to fuck your face until you cry."

I scooted closer and stared up at him, ready to let him use me for his pleasure.

"Ah, that is what you want, too, no? Dio cane, you get me so hard."

Pulling free, he reached into his back pocket and dug out a key. Within seconds, he had the cage door open and was inside.

"Va bene," he crooned, palming the back of my head once again. "Deep breath because it will be your last."

I obeyed and he was thrusting past my lips. He shoved his cock to the back of my throat and I gagged, so he paused and let me adjust. But after a second, he kept at it, fucking my mouth, angling my head to allow him into my throat. Spit flooded my mouth and ran down my chin as he worked and I listened to him grunt and gasp. I lost count of the number of tears that leaked from my eyes. It was glorious.

"You're so good at taking my cock," he said. "That's it, baby. I can feel your throat squeezing around my head. Fuck, yes. Such a perfect, perfect girl for me."

A rush went through my entire body and settled between my legs, a Pavlovian response to his praise that I couldn't control. Suddenly, he withdrew. "Get on your back. I want to see what you've bought me." Chest heaving, he shoved his briefs and jeans down his legs, stepping out of them before stripping off his shirt.

I reclined and spread my legs, letting him see the new piercing. "Do you like it?"

He flicked the bell with the tip of his finger and I shivered. "I like it very much."

Bending his head, he used his tongue on the bell, moving it all around. "Mmm. I want to hear this bell ring as I pound your pussy."

His fingers dipped to my entrance and he gave me a knowing smirk. "So wet. You were made for me."

My head was spinning, my body on fire. I could hardly breathe with how much I wanted him to fuck me. When he removed his hand I exhaled in frustration. "Please."

"I know, I know. You need me so badly. I'm going to reward you, baby. Get up on your hands and knees."

When he folded his jeans and put them under my knees, I knew he meant business. "Should I be worried?" I asked with a soft chuckle as he lined up behind me.

"Yes. I'm going to fuck you so hard that we might sink this yacht from all the rocking." His crown nudged my entrance. "Let me inside." He pushed in slightly and I gasped, squeezing my inner muscles reflexively. He grunted. "Sì, sì. *È così che lo voglio.* Just like that."

I did it again, and he thrust all the way inside, his fingers holding my hips tightly. "Porca puttana! So hot, so tight."

He felt enormous, my tissues still sensitive from last night. "Fuck, Enzo."

Bending, he dropped kisses along my spine, his lips warm and smooth. He whispered into my skin, "You are gorgeous. Just looking at you makes my dick ache to be inside you."

I started to rub my clit and my body quickly adjusted. A light sheen of sweat coated my skin and my legs trembled. "Oh, God. Yes."

He dragged out then pushed back in slowly, widening me once again. "Look at you, stretched tight around my cock." He rocked his hips. "Are you ready, troietta? Are you ready to let me have my pussy?"

As long as I could come, I would give him anything. The words fell out of my mouth naturally. "Sì, padrone."

He started fucking me then, jerking my body back onto his cock roughly, and I had to put both hands back on the floor to brace myself. The tiny bell on my piercing tinkled softly over the sound of our hips slapping together. I never wanted this to end. He was inside me, over me, all around me.

"Listen to that sound. A bell on my pet's pussy. You are mine to use, no?" He slapped my ass cheek. "Who do you belong to?"

"You." I moaned, my eyes closed tight as the pleasure coiled low in my belly.

His fingers grabbed my heavy length of hair, wrapped it around his fist, then pulled. My body bowed, but he didn't let up. He kept riding me, maintaining the perfect pace while his cock absolutely destroyed me, hitting just the right spot. I was so close, right on the edge. "More," I gasped.

He growled deep in his throat. "I love fucking you. I need you all the time. I want to tie you to my bed, naked and helpless, and fill you with my come. Never let you leave my side."

The words were so wrong, but they tipped me right over the edge. My orgasm rushed up from my feet and detonated inside me like a bomb, more forceful than I could ever remember. I convulsed and cried out, my walls clenching in rhythmic pulses around him.

"No, no, no." he said. "It's too soon. Minchia! You are pulling it out of me!"

With a roar, he began shooting inside me, his cock swelling as his hips grew uncoordinated. It went on and on, and I reveled in the helpless noises he let out. I did that. I made this powerful man lose his ever-loving mind.

He gave one last grunt and pressed deep, fingers digging into my flesh. "Yes, take it," he rasped. "Take all of it."

We hung there after, both struggling to breathe. Finally, he pulled out and collapsed onto the floor. "Fuck, woman. You wear me out."

I rolled my eyes. "My sore throat means that I did some of the work."

He shifted to his side, his mouth curving into a smirk. "You like being my caged little pet."

"It's called a fantasy for a reason, D'Agostino."

"Cazzata." He scooted closer and cupped my face in his large palm. Then he was pressing soft kisses to my eyelids and forehead. "I want to keep you locked up here forever."

He was delusional, but telling him *no* would only make him more determined. "And how would you explain this cage to your kids, mafioso?" Luca, Nic and I had become friends over the last year. I loved playing the part of fun stepmother, taking their side against Enzo every chance I got.

He pushed me onto my back and lowered his head to kiss me. Just before our lips touched, he whispered, "I will tell them this is where their Papà fell in love with you."

Thank you so much for reading
MAFIA MADMAN!

Want a sneak peek at the next book in The Kings of Italy series, MAFIA TARGET, featuring Giulio Ravazzani and Alessio Ricci? Keep scrolling!

feel it through some mafioso sixth sense or something. I was getting harder by the second, just imagining grabbing that long thick hair while I fucked his mouth.

I hadn't fucked or been fucked in a long time, not since I left Belgium. Instead, I stuck to hand jobs and blow jobs, which were fast and impersonal. I got what I needed without leaving anyone at risk. I learned the hard way that my father's enemies were all around, and anyone close to me was in danger.

The darkness enveloped me as I reached the back of the club. I could hear grunts and groans, see the shape of straining figures, but I didn't stop. I liked this feeling, the buzz building in my blood right before we finally got our hands on each other.

A palm landed on my shoulder, spinning me just before I was slammed against the wall. *Che cazzo?* Once I recovered from my surprise I shifted, quickly reversing our positions until he was the one pinned. We held there for a moment, assessing each other close up, breathing hard. It was the man from across the bar. He'd followed me, tracked me to this dark corner, and now I could feel his erection pressed against my hip through his jeans. I was dying to taste him.

But that wasn't how this worked.

I forced them to their knees, they sucked me off, and I disappeared. No promises, no hard feelings. No reciprocation.

This man, though. I could see myself on my knees for him.

His muscles tightened beneath my fingertips and he readied to move. To leave? To kiss me? "*Quédate*," I growled, telling him to stay as I wrapped my fingers around his throat. His pulse was slow and steady, despite his hard cock, and I wondered if he was truly excited.

It didn't matter. Not to me.

My dick was stiff and throbbing, eager. I needed this fast and rough, then I had to leave.

With a little pressure I pushed him toward the ground. He resisted for a half second until he sank to the floor, his face in front of my crotch. I unfastened my belt and unzipped, but that was as far as I went. I liked for them to do the rest, to reach inside my clothing and pull out my cock. To prove they were needy little sluts, gagging for it.

He didn't disappoint. Thick fingers dug into my jeans and briefs, finding my length and exposing it. My skin was hot as he gripped me tight, and I shoved my clothing lower on my hips to make it easier. His dark gaze met mine as he parted his lips and without warning sucked me deep inside his mouth.

Wet heat surrounded me and my eyes nearly rolled back in my head. It had been too long. "*Joder*," I gasped, using the Spanish equivalent of *cazzo*.

He bobbed, his mouth creating ideal suction while one hand remained on the base of my shaft, pulling. There was no teasing, no uncertainty. Just a fast blow job intended to get me off. *Perfetto*.

I let myself sink into the sensation, drifting, turning off my brain. He was good, taking my cock to the back of his throat as I thrust my hips. I wished we had time for me to slip inside that tight passage so I could fuck his throat until he couldn't breathe, but that was too intimate for this. There was no time for training. I didn't do those things anymore.

He relaxed and let me use him. I threaded my fingers through his thick hair and speared his mouth with my cock, the pleasure inside me coiling as I rocked. His tongue slid forward, gliding over my skin, and he gave me the tiniest scrape of his teeth.

Madonna, I never wanted it to end.

All too soon my balls were tingling, my muscles clenching, and my cock swelled against his tongue. With a groan, I began coming, thick jets shooting into his mouth, my hips jerking. He kept sucking, draining me, and it prolonged my orgasm. If I weren't pretending to be someone else, someone Spanish, I would praise him in Italian with all the words I knew. But my Spanish was limited, so I just stroked his hair, petting him, as I tried to catch my breath.

He eased off my cock and looked up at me with an unreadable expression. Then he swallowed, the muscles in his throat working as he drank my load down.

Madre di Dio, that was hot.

I inwardly sighed, wishing I'd met him in another life. One where I could sink to my knees and pleasure him in return. One where I wasn't Fausto Ravazzani's son, a former 'Ndrangheta soldier.

One where I wasn't always on the run from the life I'd left behind.

I stepped back, tucked myself away, and zipped up. With a nod at the beautiful man still on his knees I turned and went in the opposite direction, intent on getting outside as quickly as possible.

No one stopped me. No one followed me. I was just another young man in a sea of them, grinding and moving to the beat. I could see the faded light of an exit door, so I headed toward it. A minute later I was standing in an alley, the cool Spanish night washing over me.

Walking toward the street, I pulled out my phone and dialed. He answered on the first ring.

"Why the fuck didn't you pick up?" Fausto snarled into my ear.

"Perdonami, Papà."

"Would I call you five times if it wasn't a fucking emergency?"

He had before. My father didn't like to be ignored. "Is it Frankie or one of the kids?"

He gave a long exhale and I knew the sound well. He was trying to rein in his temper. "It's you, figlio mio."

Relief filled me. This was nothing new. I was in constant danger. I started in the direction of my apartment, which was four blocks away. As always, I checked my surroundings. This had been ingrained in me since birth. "Yes?"

"Someone has taken out a hit on you."

I wanted to roll my eyes, but that was disrespectful to my father, even if he couldn't see me. He had no idea of the number of assassination attempts I'd survived over the years. If he did, he would surely order me back to Siderno, back to the castello, under his thumb. I would never let that happen. I would never go back.

I was a gay man, the former heir to an empire, one the 'Ndrangheta would clearly prefer to make disappear. My very existence embarrassed them, and I would never bring that kind of danger near my half-siblings and stepmother. I was better off living far away from them.

"Oh?" I said to my father.

"You sound unsurprised at this news."

Nothing got by Fausto. "What do you know?"

"Have you heard of Alessandro Ricci?"

"I remember the name." Ricci was a sniper, trained by the Italian military. He was rumored to be the best, used by countries to take out heads of state and other politicians. Very high level wet work, not the kind of person normally used by the 'Ndrangheta, who preferred to handle their own murders quietly. An assassin like Ricci was too high-profile.

"Good, then I won't have to explain how dangerous this is for you. I want you to come—"

"No." I shut down that thought before he even verbalized it. "I won't, so don't ask it."

I heard a thud and imagined him pounding his palm on his desk. After a few beats, he said, "Dai, Giulio. This is not like the others."

My heart thudded in my chest, but I had to play dumb. "Others?"

"Did you think I didn't know? Do you think I am not having your every move watched?"

Figlio d'un cane!

Goddamn controlling asshole. I lowered my phone and disconnected. There. He could stew for a few days.

I continued on to my apartment. I didn't want Fausto tracking me. I wasn't his responsibility any longer. He should be focusing on his other children, his wife. His empire. He didn't need to worry about me, a grown man.

I visited Siderno a few days every year, but only when I knew it was safe. Not once during those trips had he mentioned anything about the attempts on my life or where I was living. He asked if I needed money and then we talked about superficial things.

I unlocked the door to the old building where I was renting a room under my new identity, Javier Martín. As I climbed the stairs, I decided I needed information. But I couldn't ask Marco or Fausto. I had to do this quietly.

The piece of hair I placed between the door and the jamb was still in place. I did this every time I left to let me know if someone had been in my room. Tonight I was safe, so I entered and shut the door behind me, engaging all four locks.

Pulling out my phone, I spent a few minutes searching the internet, but failed to uncover a photo of Ricci. So I rang someone I knew would help me and keep their mouth shut.

Benito answered instantly. "Pronto."

"I need a favor."

Movement sounded in the background before he said, "Whatever you need, you know that." Benito had been my closest friend and ally in my father's 'ndrina. We practically grew up together, rising through the ranks as young men. He was there the night I was inducted, when I made my first kill. He was loyal to my father, but he was also loyal to me. I knew I could trust him.

"Are you alone?" I asked.

"I am now. I was in the guard house but stepped outside. What is it?"

"I need you to send me a photo of someone. Alessandro Ricci."

"The sniper? Why?"

"Fausto thinks someone hired Ricci to take me out."

"Cristo santo! But why bother after all this time?"

"I don't know, but I'd like to keep an eye out all the same. Will you send me a photo of him?"

"I'm on it. Stay safe, amico."

We disconnected and I began undressing, more tired than I expected. My limbs were loose, the kind of peace only a great orgasm could provide. I missed having them regularly with someone I cared about, but I couldn't risk it. I couldn't go through that pain again.

Paolo had died because of me. Blown up in a car bomb meant for me in Belgium. I'd never forgive myself. I still ached for him, still thought of him every day. *La mia splendida bestia.* My gorgeous beast.

My phone chimed with a text. It was from Benito.

I opened the message—and all the air left my lungs in a rush.

Dropping onto my bed, I stared at the image, unable to believe it. This . . . couldn't be right. There had to be some mistake. My ears started ringing as I tried to make sense of it.

The man from the club? The one who had sucked my dick and given me the best blow job in years?

It was Alessandro Ricci.

Preorder MAFIA TARGET on Amazon!

ACKNOWLEDGMENTS

Wow, what a ride!

Thank you to Jennifer Prokop (jenreadsromance.com) for her amazing editing and help with this book. (You can listen to her every week on the Fated Mates podcast, along with co-host Sarah MacLean!) I am so grateful for her guidance and suggestions.

All my love to my amazing writer pals who beta read at the very (very!) last minute for me: Diana Quincy, Nicola Davidson, Sierra Simone, and Kenya Goree-Bell. All of their feedback was so smart and thoughtful.

A huge thank you to Letitia Hasser at RBA Designs, who rocks every single one of these covers.

Thank you, thank you, thank you to all the romance readers who have supported this series. I'm eternally grateful! You make this the BEST job in the world.

I would be nothing without my very own Paparino, Mr. Finelli, who helps me with these books and dinner and laundry and a thousand other things that make it possible for me to write. Ti amo, baby.

ABOUT THE AUTHOR

Though she is a *USA Today* bestselling author in another genre, Mila finally decided to write the filthy mafia kings she's been dreaming about for years. She's addicted to coffee, travel and Roy Kent.

For signed books, news & more, visit Mila's website at milafinelli.com.

Join Mila's Famiglia on Facebook!

Want to get updates about the next book? Sign up for Mila's newsletter here.

ALSO BY MILA FINELLI

Start at the beginning with Mafia Mistress, Part 1 of the Kings of Italy duet!

MAFIA MISTRESS

Part One of the Kings of Italy Duet

FAUSTO

I am the darkness, the man whose illicit empire stretches around the globe. Not many have the courage for what needs to be done to maintain power . . . but I do.

And I always get what I want.

Including my son's fiancée.

She's mine now, and I'll use Francesca any way I see fit. She's the perfect match to my twisted desires, and I'll keep her close, ready and waiting at my disposal.

Even if she fights me at every turn.

FRANCESCA

I was stolen away and held prisoner in Italy, a bride for a mafia king's only heir.

Except I'm no innocent, and it's the king himself—the man called il Diavolo—who appeals to me in sinful ways I never dreamed. Fausto's wickedness draws me in, his power like a drug. And when the devil decides he wants me, I'm helpless to resist him—even if it means giving myself to him, body and soul.

He may think he can control me, but this king is about to find out who's really the boss.

MAFIA MISTRESS is available in eBook, Print and Audio.